A STAR IS DEAD

ALDHILL MYSTERIES

KJ LYTTLETON

MIRAMUS BOOKS

For my teachers Karen Malin and David Allott

A NOTE FOR AMERICAN READERS

A Star Is Dead is written in UK English. For you, that will mean an awful lot of extra vowels, for which I apologise. You might also notice some different past participles as well as some stray Ls scattered about the place. In many cases, there will be an S where you would prefer a Z. I hope you can forgive all this.

If in doubt, please assume it's a UK spelling and not a typo. (That's my story and I'm sticking to it.)

ONE

The journey was a disaster.

The man in the beige anorak found himself stuck next to a young lad who kept rising to thwack his little brother in the seat in front, or to beg crisps and other unpleasant snacks from his frazzled mother. The boy ate for the entire journey, pausing only to visit the lavatory – yet another ordeal. Having somehow trampled on the man's sandwich (still enshrouded in its Boots bag), the boy discovered the lavatory was out of order. With a great hubbub, the boy's mother marched to the front of the coach and began berating the driver. The driver instructed her to sit down or, he told her, he would stop the bus and make her and her little vermin get out.

The man in the beige jumper (having used the opportunity to place his anorak in the overhead locker), watched this scene unfold with growing dread. Was it too much to ask to have just one day where humans didn't have to spoil things? Wasn't being on the bus crammed together bad enough – everyone's hot breath slowly sucking the oxygen from the air, the smell of flatulence and anti-social crisp flavours mingling with the three pine air fresheners hanging from the coach's giant rear-view mirror? Wasn't all that enough suffering without this woman and her offspring and the bus driver making it worse? Why couldn't everyone just be polite? Why must people go through life causing strife where none had been before?

All it took was for one grumpy person to spoil the day for everyone. The sort of grumpy person who shuffled into the kitchen, made a beeline for the teapot and said: 'I'm not a morning person, me,' as though that made it acceptable to behave like a truculent teenager. They were the ones who would huff and jostle past on the morning commute as though their job in sales at a part-baked bread company was more important than whatever it is you do. One grouchy little shove from them would set off a chain reaction of irritation and, before the morning was out, everyone within a three-mile radius would feel cross and impatient. How else could you explain this contagion of seething rage that seemed to ripple through a space?

It had ground him down.

The man in beige wondered if, in fact, he was the grumpy man who started off these angry chain reactions. Certainly, he hadn't been friendly when he'd climbed onto the bus. He hadn't wanted to sit next to the boy and had been unyielding when the mother had asked him to swap seats so the lad could be near a window.

'He pukes otherwise,' she had explained matter-of-factly.

The boy had looked at him with round, soulful eyes, but the man still declined to swap. He had booked the window seat for a reason; had arrived early in order to request it specifically. The mother had arrived late – harassed, blonde hair in disarray, breathing ragged – dragging her kids along to reach the coach before it left. The seats in front of the man and the one next to him had been the last ones left. Despite the harried start to her day, as she made her way down the aisle, the mother's eyes were bright with adventure. Until he had refused to swap places, that is, at which point the metaphorical skies darkened and the woman had harrumphed down into her seat, arms and legs folded, short-tempered with her littlest one who was already bored. She had the last laugh, of course. The older boy had puked twenty minutes after she prophesied it, lurching forward without warning to leave a puddle of breakfast cereal on the floor by the man's Boots bag.

He'd swapped seats after that.

After the lavatory kerfuffle and the vomiting, the soulful-eyed boy appeared to tap out so his younger brother could take over the mayhem. Despite being fully aware that the lavatory was broken, the younger child had begun requesting a 'wee wee' shortly before the end of the journey. His mother told him to shut it, and this was when the theatrics had begun. The child spent the last half-hour squawking and squealing and insisting an accident was imminent. It was utterly infuriating! The coach had stopped for a pit stop back in London and everyone – including the man – had dutifully emptied their bladders then. Why had the child ended up so desperate? Did he not avail himself of the facilities?

The man despaired for humanity.

Perhaps if the mother hadn't allowed the boy to drink an entire can of pop to himself, a coach full of innocent people would not have had to suffer. (Besides which, to his mind, all that sugar and acid was not good for the boy's teeth, not to mention the detrimental effects of the caffeine.)

When they arrived at their destination, it felt as though they had all aged ten years. The man clutching the beige anorak sighed as he waited his turn to shuffle down the bus aisle. He was glad he would no longer be an unwilling part of the woman's family. She had disembarked and headed off in the opposite direction. He watched as she struggled with the luggage while trying to wrangle her wretched kids. Thank god he'd never had to do any of that nonsense with anyone.

It was only afterwards, carrying his black rucksack towards The Marchmont Hotel, that he wondered if he should have offered to help her with her bag. Perhaps he could have seen her on her way.

But no.

She would have rejected the offer.

He was quite aware that he looked like a creep – at best. His thin legs (in needle cord trousers), large weepy eyes (magnified by his corrective lenses for extreme long-sightedness) and down-turned mouth (inherited from his mother), gave him the appearance of a disappointed frog. He knew that, on the whole, his demeanour did not endear him to people. Had he always looked like this? Even when he had been an optimistic youth, braced and ready to face life's challenges? Or had his expression transformed as his optimism waned? Perhaps he had once had a countenance of warmth and vitality to match his mood. But those days were long gone and now he was the sort of man who frowned at children on buses.

He shifted his rucksack to the other shoulder and carried on walking.

At the hotel desk he waited for the woman to give him his key card.

'Room 302,' she said.

He thanked her and headed for the stairs.

The man struggled to remember a happy time in his life. His mother had loved him; at least he assumed she had. Was he happy then? He didn't remember. She had always been so anxious about life, always filled with dread that she would tumble and break her neck or slip from a high place and split her head into a thousand pieces. When her son was born, she became as obsessed with his mortality as she was with her own. She lived in horror of his inevitable demise, forever foreseeing a million ways for him to perish, either by his own hand (a trip on the pavement) or by another's (dangerous driver, mugger, sexual predator).

Her capacity to imagine gruesome deaths for him would have been impressive were it not so inhibiting. She could barely stand to see him leave the house. On cold days, she wrapped him up in so many clothes he could hardly move. He was more in danger of being hit by a passing car as he crossed the road with all those layers on (blinded by his own anorak hood, unable to breathe), but her fears paid no heed to statistics. It didn't matter that he was more likely to fall down the stairs, the play park was her enemy. She was convinced he would encounter a knife attack around every corner, but she hadn't got round to putting new batteries in the smoke alarms for years.

Inconsistency was her most reliable trait.

She went through a phase of insisting they stand up every twenty minutes to avoid blood clots, but stopped worrying about it once she was too old to leap from her seat. Once, she spent a summer cutting all his grapes in half but let him scoff cherry tomatoes straight from the greenhouse.

But he must have been happy once, mustn't he? That cheerful fellow who had moved to this seaside town all those years ago, without a friend in the world, but with optimism in his heart and a passion for his chosen profession. He had been happy – surely he had? Or was it just a lie he told himself?

He plonked his rucksack down on his crisp hotel bed linen and looked around. It was a beautiful room.

The perfect place to end his days.

TWO

The young woman passed the doorman of The Marchmont Hotel and paced confidently across the tasteful Persian rug. She reached the front desk and smiled a big, broad (usually extremely winning) smile at the hotel clerk.

'Oh, hello! I don't suppose you could help me,' she began. 'My name's Kirsty Mathieson and I'm meant to be interviewing Oli Cromwell, but – god, so embarrassing – I've completely forgotten his room number.'

The older woman – Judith Jones, according to her name plate – eyed the young woman with a sour expression that suggested she too had used a winning smile to her advantage in days gone by and wasn't about to be fooled by someone else's attempts. The young woman knew she had a challenge on her hands. Boy, she would have given anything for an easily flustered young man. They were so much easier to deal with. The Judiths of this world did not suffer fools – gladly or otherwise. Judiths made excellent company on a night out – they had all the best stories – but behind the desk of a hotel reception, a Judith made a fearsome nemesis. Nevertheless, with nothing else at her disposal, the young woman turned her smile up a few megawatts.

She was the epitome of wasted charm.

She nodded towards Judith's computer. 'I'm from *The Observer*. I should be on the guest list.'

She stood on tiptoes and leaned over to see the screen – as though expecting to spot her name on this mythical list. Judith grasped the monitor protectively, and the younger woman dropped back from the desk.

'Perhaps you can just check?'

Judith raised one arched, pencil-drawn eyebrow. 'What was your name again, Miss...?'

'Mathieson... Ms Kirsty Mathieson.'

Judith's expression soured further. It was as if someone had passed her a lemon to suck and she was grimly determined to eat it all.

'Just one moment, Miss Mathieson.'

Judith turned to her screen and began typing, her nails clacking on the keyboard. The lobby hummed with a soporific buzz. Well-heeled visitors murmured in soft tones as they passed, soothing piano muzak piped out from the bar lounge area beyond the glass doors. The woman claiming to be Kirsty Mathieson inhaled the hotel's soft perfume – a combination of the fresh-cut flowers displayed on every surface, and the sumptuous, soapy concoctions provided in the hotel toilets. The Marchmont punched above its weight for a hotel in Aldhill-on-Sea, a slightly careworn south-coast seaside town.

Judith was still tippity-tapping away. She'd been at it so long, the young woman began to suspect Judith was no longer dealing with her enquiry, but was actually using this time to catch up on some emails. No one types for that long without using the mouse unless they're writing a newsletter, she thought. She was just about to deploy a polite cough when Judith stopped typing and looked up. Her tone was a masterclass in poorly concealed contempt masquerading as politeness.

'I'm afraid we've got no one down on the guest list with your name, Miss...'

'Mathieson.'

She sensed Judith was hoping to catch her in the lie, but the young woman was an old pro at fibbing: she had once spent a week pretending to be an intern called Scarlett Stevens. Still, she acknowledged with an inward sigh, the jig was probably up. Nevertheless, she decided to keep going. In for a penny, in for a pound and all that. 'You don't get to sit on the best seats if you only use half an arse,' as her mum Angela would say – one of Angela's many saws that sounded like wisdom but didn't hold up under scrutiny. Still, the woman claiming to be Kirsty Mathieson was going to take her mother's advice. She was going to give it her whole arse. She smiled again.

'No matter, I can just let myself up. Mr Cromwell's publicist Marilla Hunter Davy organised it for me. I was supposed to be there ten minutes ago, and I'd hate to keep him waiting. You know what these celebs can be like.'

'Yes,' said Judith, 'I do.'

Judith's citrus levels had surpassed lemons and were fast moving on to pickled gooseberry proportions. Soon her lips would be so puckered she wouldn't be able to prise her mouth open to speak.

'Oh! I sense a great story in that reply! You're clearly a dark horse.'

Trying to flirt with a woman nearly as old as her granny;

she'd like to say it was a new low, but really it didn't get a look in. She had done a lot worse for a lot less.

'I know what celebrities are like because they always choose to stay at The Marchmont,' said Judith. 'And do you know why?'

The woman claiming to be Kirsty Mathieson picked at the pleather edge of her camera strap. She recognised a verbal landmine had been laid, but the trick was trying to avoid it.

'I expect most people would say it's because this is the best hotel in town?'

She tried to scrutinise Judith's face for clues, but it was too late.

'Then most people would be wrong,' said Judith. 'It *is* the best hotel in town. We all know that. But celebrities stay here because we're discreet and we don't give their room numbers out to any old Tom, Dick or Kirsty off the street. Now, if you wouldn't mind stepping aside... What was it again? Ms Mathieson? It's funny, you know, you don't look like a Kirsty.'

The young woman was about to say 'Oh really?' in her most innocent voice, when Judith, the wind now fully in her sails, continued.

'No, you look much more like a Philippa McGinty, who works at the local newspaper and keeps trying to wheedle her way into rooms at The Marchmont whenever a celebrity deigns to visit.'

'Never heard of her... She sounds dreadful.'

'She is. She's so dreadful that reception has a picture of her to remind us not to let the rabid little pap past the front desk.'

Judith spun her computer monitor round to reveal a giant

police custody mugshot (a misunderstanding with the local rozzers, soon cleared up amicably after she had spent a day in the cells.)

'Oh no. That is a terrible shot. I'd be happy to supply a more accurate one.'

'The only reason you've been able to continue in your pitiful charade is because Duncan here was on his break and I needed to keep you occupied until he'd seen my message.'

The woman claiming to be Kirsty Mathieson (but looking increasingly likely to be Philippa McGinty) turned to see Duncan the security guard shuffle reluctantly forward. A rather sheepish-looking man in his early seventies. Another of Angela's saws popped into her mind.

'We all have to get on our knees sometimes, whether it's to pray, beg or do the unspeakable.'

Perhaps that advice wasn't the best to give a (then) nine-year-old, but it made more sense to her now. Kirsty-Philippa was willing to try the begging and the praying, but she drew the line at the third option. She reached across the counter and put her palms together.

'Just a teeny little glimpse of him. I won't cause any trouble. I just need to get a photo and a quote. You know what a big deal this is! "Local legend returns to hometown for the first time in fifteen years." It's a big story. What do you say, Judith?'

'Duncan, my love, would you be so good as to escort this piece of work off the premises?'

'I'll make it worth your while.'

The young woman knew she was debasing herself for nothing now. Women like Judith could not be bribed – at least, not with the things she could offer.

'I suggest you take her through the fire exit, Duncan,' said

Judith. 'We wouldn't want the guests thinking we let her sort in here.'

The young woman deflated in defeat and drew her arms back from the counter.

'Come on then, Duncan, lead me away,' she said, offering her hands like he was going to cuff her.

Duncan took her by the arm.

'You don't remember me, do you, Duncan?' she said. 'We've met before.'

'I think you've had more than enough adventure for one day,' he said as he pushed down on the metal bar to open the fire door. The heavy wood swung out and Duncan, shoving it open further with one hand, firmly ushered the woman out into the courtyard beyond. 'And, yes, I do remember you. More's the pity.'

She didn't resist, stepping out into the cooling afternoon air with weary resignation.

'It's a fair cop, Duncan.'

She turned to wave, but Duncan was already closing the door behind her so he didn't see her lunge forward at the last moment to stick her plastic library card between the door and the lock.

He didn't notice the sound of plastic snapping as he pulled hard on the security bar and broke the library card in half.

He didn't hear the young woman cursing as the door locked behind her.

Phil McGinty, junior reporter for *The Aldhill Observer*, stared at her broken library card.

'Shit it,' she said.

THREE

Phil hadn't always been this sneaky. Standing out there in a muddy pothole in the staff car park, near the rank-smelling kitchen refuse bins, Phil had a chance to consider the choices that had led her to this moment.

When she started in journalism, she had been one of those bright young things who imagined themselves cracking conspiracies wide open or dealing with nervy whistleblowers in desolate multi-storey car parks. Instead, like so many others before her, she discovered the life of a lowly junior reporter on a local newspaper mainly involved copying the names of funeral wreaths (for god's sake, don't get the spelling wrong), and interviewing indignant locals about the shocking state of the dog-shitted pavements in their post-war cul-de-sac.

At least all that involved dealing with members of the public. She could kid herself that it counted as journalism. But, thanks to the internet, she was now also expected to churn out at least six listicles a day. It didn't matter how banal, so long as there was a list.

'14 places in Sussex you should visit before you die.'

'23 celebrities who lost weight this year.'

All with the sole aim (as far as she could tell) of getting the paper's Facebook subscribers irate at the parlous state of today's journalism.

'Is this the kind of dross people call writing these days?' they'd fume.

Phil imagined them, red-faced and personally insulted. They still clicked on the link to read the articles, though, didn't they? How else did you explain the page views? They couldn't contain their curiosity.

That was the other type of article she wrote: 'curiosity gap' pieces.

'You'll never guess what rubbish people read on the internet.'

Or articles that seem to be caught midway through a conversation.

'She thought she'd found a stray dog. What happened next left her speechless.'

It didn't matter how disappointing the actual story was, so long as the headline got people clicking.

Phil sometimes wondered if her job was just one big exercise in disappointing those who hoped for better. Imagine if the stray dog turned out to be something astonishing. A thylacine back from extinction... But no, it was just a dog, after all. Pointless.

And now she had AI coming for her job. The large language models could churn out internet slop at an alarming rate, so why bother hiring a human being with all their pesky employment rights and holiday requirements? The social media commenters were right: journalism was doomed. (The commenters weren't right about everything, however. For example, she wasn't convinced she deserved to 'die in a fire' just because Nathan from Sedlescombe thought the 'He rescued a baby rabbit, then something amazing happened...' piece was a let down.)

'If you're disappointed,' she wanted to say to them, 'imagine how I feel.'

Sometimes she did actually feel like dying in a fire.

That's why she had been coming to The Marchmont in search of celebrities, no matter how minor (a weather reporter from the eighties was a recent mark). That's why she was chasing this story. She was convinced an interview with Oli Cromwell was her ticket into the big league. She had already begun proving herself at *The Aldhill Observer*, but it still wasn't enough.

'It's good, but don't get cocky. It's not going to get you a Paul Foot award,' said Adam Jenkins, editor, when she did an exposé on Benji Maddox, the man who kept hanging dog poo bags on a rowan tree in an estate behind the big *Tesco*. For that story, she had been rewarded with the nickname Poodicca by her fellow hacks.

Phil's piece may have just been a story about dog poo, but it was inspired. It was the sort of thing locals were passionate about and her instinct to spend time uncovering the man's identity had been spot on. The front page headline, 'Phantom Poo Fiend unmasked' was bound to sell copies and set tongues wagging. The paper hadn't named the suspect to begin with; Phil made a big drama about how '*The Aldhill Observer* has handed over a dossier of evidence to the local police,' and Adam Jenkins's editorial preached a dramatic sermon about how the police must prosecute to 'the full extent of the law'. He'd even suggested locals contact the police if they suspected anyone else in the local area was guilty of turd-based crimes. The police had not been impressed to find their phone lines jammed with nosy neighbours trying to shop every unsavoury-looking dog owner within a hundred metres of their property.

With such a huge public outcry, the council had no choice but to prosecute the Phantom Poo Fiend under the Clean Neighbourhoods and Environment Act 2005 section 65. They'd have preferred to simply issue the usual Fixed Penalty Notice fine and get on with the more important work of painting white circles around the crater-sized potholes and neglecting to meet their recycling targets, but there was no getting away from popular opinion, especially not in an election year. The Poo Fiend was fined £1000, his mugshot printed in the local paper.

'It's not really my finest hour, is it? Getting Benji Maddox to hand over his pension money for not walking the three metres to the nearest bin.' Phil had commandeered Angela one Sunday afternoon during an existential crisis. 'I'm hardly changing the world.'

Her mother wasn't in the mood to listen to her grousing. 'I expect the people on the Acorn estate are pretty pleased now that they don't have a tree filled with poo outside their windows,' she said. 'And, no, you haven't exactly fed the homeless or done anything particularly worthwhile with that big brain of yours, but we can't all be as wonderful as me.'

She was joking, but Phil knew she sort of meant it too. Angela had been proud of her when Phil went undercover to investigate her dad's death, but she didn't want that to be Phil's whole world.

'Your dad would have wanted you to get out there and live your own life,' she told her.

Phil had been instrumental in reopening her father's case

and had even helped solve another murder along the way, but the final reporting had been handed to Barry Brooker, their senior reporter, and Phil's piece about Virtua Services, the company at the heart of the deaths, had been nixed for being too much hearsay and not enough evidence.

'You'll get your turn,' said Adam Jenkins, who never shied away from a hackneyed expression.

She needed something to get her noticed outside of the town, and a candid interview with an increasingly global movie star like Oli Cromwell was just the ticket. Shame she'd fallen at the first hurdle. She stared at the bins gloomily just as the fire exit door swung open on her and out walked a member of the kitchen staff.

Phil managed to get half an eyeball on him from her accidental hiding place behind the door. The chef, or perhaps sous chef (Phil wasn't clear on kitchen staff ranks), was a young man; about the same age as Phil, but with the portly, ruddy complexion of a gouty colonel from days gone by. He was all shiny, round and hot from the kitchens. He looked familiar, but she couldn't quite place him. Living in Aldhill-on-Sea all her life and being naturally chatty meant that Phil recognised most people in the local area, but sometimes it was hard to work out if she recognised them from the bus stop she walked past every day, or if she once snogged them at a house party.

He was leaning on the heavy door, preventing it from swinging back into its rightful place. He'll be breaking some staff rule, thought Phil. This was HR 101: don't block the fire doors. She had briefly worked in HR when she had spent a week pretending to be Scarlett Stevens and, despite her best efforts, had absorbed a lot of boring information about health and safety rules.

The chef, frowning into the afternoon sky, took out an elaborate-looking vape with one hand and his phone with the other and, inhaling deeply on the vape, began texting. He was agitated, responding to his messages with his large, prodding thumb. Soon the air was thick with vapour. A sickly sweet scent that Phil, not being an aficionado of vape flavours, couldn't quite place.

Vanilla and caramel maybe?

After a particularly large pull on his vape, he held his breath and tucked the contraption under his arm so he could go at his phone keyboard with both thumbs.

Alongside her notorious dog poo exposé, Phil had garnered a reputation at the paper for always knowing what was happening on the roughest estates. It helped that she had grown up in Roosevelt Court, one of four identical council tower blocks at the northern end of the town, and knew nearly every teenager, mum, homeless person and elderly resident in the local area. They were her eyes and ears on the ground, trusting her despite her chosen career.

The fancy camera helped, too.

People often turned their nose up at telling their story to a tape recorder, but ask if you could take their picture and they soon perked up, especially if you promised to send over a few for a new profile picture for whatever dating app they were on. The promise of a high-resolution image seemed to work wonders for loosening people's tongues – helped by Phil's natural gifts. She sometimes considered if she had missed out on a lucrative career in crime as a confidence trickster. But she still couldn't escape *The Aldhill Observer* and get her foot in the door at a bigger paper.

'Trust you to try for a career in a dead medium,' Angela said.

And it was true. But she had tried getting a job with a YouTube politics channel, and her forays into TikTok had so far been excruciating. What kind of young person was she? Answer: the kind who is never quite in sync with her generation's trends. She wanted to be an old school newspaper reporter; she had been born in the wrong decade.

She was dragged back into the here and now by a voice.

'Hello,' the chef said to his phone.

If the Silicon Valley tech bros could build a sentiment translator (maybe they already had), it would translate that, 'Hello' as 'Why don't you just sod off and leave me alone?'

Whatever the caller said had made the chef agitated. 'I told you, I'm doing it. Why are you calling me? We said not to ca–'

Phil could just about make out a small voice on the other end interrupting him. Whoever it was sounded angry (or was it scared?) The sentiment translator would be having a field day.

'Look, I said I'd do what you asked... Yes, I've got the stuff and I know what room he's in, but I'm not exactly going to go barging in now, am I? I'll do it tonight when my shift is over... They'll notice I'm missing... No. Later is better.'

Phil heard the buzzing sound of the – probably male – voice from the earpiece and the chef pinched the bridge of his nose and looked up to the sky. 'I said I'd handle it and now I want you to LEAVE ME ALONE.'

No need for a sentiment translator now: he had said exactly what he meant.

'Now please – *please* – just leave me alone.'

The chef hung up, jabbing the phone with his finger. He leaned down, hands to his knees and burst into tears. He looked like a drunk outside a nightclub, retching forwards, body racked with ripples of anguish. If Phil wanted to cry like that, she would have to lock herself in a bathroom with very loud music playing and a huge pillow to muffle the sound, along with a cast-iron guarantee that no one would find her. Only then might she have at it. Yet, she wasn't sure she'd be able to employ as much gusto as this bloke. She was torn between fascination and admiration, with no room for any real sympathy.

A small inner voice sometimes told her she was becoming one of those scumbag journalists they always slag off in crime dramas. The sort the police officers sneer at and describe in less than complimentary terms when they peer out through the plastic shutters of the local nick. Of course, they were the same officers who wanted the press to make as much noise as possible when they were on the hunt for a killer or in search of a missing child. But only on their say so. Whatever you might think about journalists, having them under police control was not a good idea – unless you were a fan of police states. Nevertheless, she had to concede she *was* currently one of those rodent hacks in an alleyway, spying on a man in the midst of some kind of personal crisis. '*You'll be amazed at how low this once-optimistic journalist has sunk.*'

But even if she did want to comfort him with a pat or a '*There, there,*' she wasn't quite sure where she would insert herself. What would she do? Jump out from behind the door and start offering him a cuddle? No, better to stay where she was and wait for him to cry it all out without being inter-rupted by a weird peeping Tom. He couldn't be expected to cathart with a random stranger trying to give him a back rub next to some bins.

She definitely recognised him. She wanted to take a photo, but he would hear the shutter. It was digital, so instead of making a pleasing click and whirr, it beeped and then emitted a kind of chomping noise like it had just eaten the daylight for photo processing purposes. Her phone was more useful when it came to taking illicit snaps. She raised it now and took a shot just as a dribble of an unidentified liquid dripped onto the cobbles at the chef's feet. Snot, tears, spit or a combination of all three? It was impossible to know.

'Argh,' said the man to himself. It was a statement of intent as much as anything, full of anger and sadness and annoyance and self-reproach. With that one cry, he recovered his composure, and, just as he had begun, he abruptly stopped weeping, wiped his red raw eyes, took a few breaths, lifted his vape to his mouth with a wobbling hand, and chugged out another plume of smoke before striding back into the building.

Phil froze, stunned by the suddenness of his recovery, before swiftly and silently jumping through the fire door after him.

FOUR

Marilla Hunter Davy's day wasn't going to plan. Come to think of it, her life hadn't really gone to plan either. As the third daughter of the Hunter Davys of Sussex, Marilla had been born with all the privileges that money, beauty and breeding could bestow. Like something out of an Austen novel, she thought. Not that she had read any, but watching the TV adaptation gave her the gist: she was a lucky young woman. Or she should have been.

Things had started to go wrong early on, when, as a teen, she had begun developing the wrong sort of nose. It was a nose intent on continuing its outward trajectory indefinitely, presenting a serious challenge to family expectations. The bony, ridged protuberance bore no resemblance to her father's own snub-like appendage. In fact, it looked rather more like the family lawyer's (something her father chose not to notice, given that Perry knew where all the bodies were buried).

But the Hunter Davys were made of stern stuff and they could not be thwarted by the wrong nose. The problem was soon rectified with a visit to Brazil, where Marilla was sadly involved in a 'car accident' that required reconstructive surgery.

'Happily only on her nose,' her mother announced. 'The rest of her was unscathed. A small miracle!'

Soon Marilla was back safe in the Hunter Davy bosom, complete with the family's trademark snub, and all the Hunter Davy equanimity fully restored.

The next setback came when her small boarding school – the sort attended by ruddy-cheeked daughters of local gentleman farmers and posh girls who didn't pass the common entrance – failed to steer her through her A-Levels with the right sort of grades. But again, the setback didn't last long. After a year spent abroad doing the sorts of jobs girls like Marilla do – nanny, chalet maids, good company for old men – she had returned to the family seat to the news that her mother had arranged an internship at her friend Della's PR agency. 'Unpaid to begin with, Rilla, but I'm sure you can work your way up if you don't make too much of a nuisance of yourself.'

Rilla would rather have been a veterinary nurse or a zookeeper, but she had never learned the art of disobeying her mother. So she started on Monday, and somehow, despite being just one of a bevy of blonde girls with disappointing A-levels and well-connected parents, she managed to get herself noticed.

'Gosh, another promotion, Marilla. However do you do it?' her mother asked in a tone that suggested there must be some mistake.

Marilla didn't have the self-confidence to imagine she might have had anything to do with it, so she simply shrugged.

'Right place at the right time, I guess, Mummy.'

Whatever the reason, Marilla's latest role had given her some much-needed kudos in the family.

'Rilla's the publicist for that Oli Cromwell fellow now,' her mother would inform friends and acquaintances. You know, the Hollywood star? I hadn't heard of him, but apparently he's quite the thing.'

A lie. Of course she had heard of him; she just didn't want to risk making the brag sound too vulgar. Better to affect ignorance whilst also being sure to mention it at the slightest opportunity.

'Rilla, tell them what this Oli fellow is like.'

'He's awful,' Marilla would reply dutifully, while her mother let out a great peal of delighted laughter.

To begin with, Marilla found small comforts in her unchosen career – after she had learned to avoid the icy stares of the receptionists who had actual degrees in marketing, but sadly no parents who'd been on skiing holidays with the company founder. Instead, Marilla had made some friends with the other rich disappointments in the troupe. The posh girls travelled in packs, their insecurities mingling with their entitlement to create a group of monsters each only one espresso martini away from a mental breakdown. They were fun on a night out, so long as you left before their smiles started to crack.

But things changed for Marilla when she began working with the film star Oli Cromwell. She still went out with her friends on the occasional Friday night, but she no longer felt like part of the inner circle. She suspected some of them resented her success. In time, she wondered if maybe they hadn't been very good friends to begin with.

So Marilla Hunter Davy's life had not gone to plan

(although, truth be told, she wasn't sure she'd actually made a plan), and yet somehow she had ended up in a career she was good at. That she hated it hardly seemed to matter at all. And now, her day was turning out to be the sort that makes you question every decision that brought you here. Because she was in Aldhill-on-Sea, a backwater town unnervingly close to her family home, with a truculent film star and no friends to complain to.

Coming had been Oli's idea. *The Times* were doing a big cover story on him, and Oli thought it would be good to have them follow him round his old stomping ground.

'It'll be fun. Go back to my old schools, see some of the numpties I used to hang out with, get all the adoration from my hometown. They'll be fucking thrilled to see me. Probably throw a massive ticker tape parade or some shit.'

He planned to tell *The Times* all about his rough upbringing and his shady past. He wouldn't elaborate much to Marilla.

'I want to see your face when you hear it for the first time,' he said.

Not ideal; the agency liked to control the messaging, but then again, being shocking was part of his brand. Marilla's boss, Della, gave it the reluctant sign off.

'Just keep an eye on him, and if you have to stop him speaking, just smash the fire alarm or something.'

But then he arrived and, as soon as he got into the hotel, he refused to honour any of his engagements. He made her cancel the interview with *The Times*. She was also the one who had to ring his old schools to pass on the bad news that he wouldn't be visiting them after all. Telling the head teacher at the primary school had been the most difficult.

'Oh, the children were so looking forward to it,' she told

Marilla. 'They've been decorating their classrooms for him all week long. We ran a portrait competition we were going to ask him to judge.'

Some of the older years had designed their own movie posters for their favourite Oli Cromwell films. One child had written him a poem she was going to perform. It was too much. Marilla could picture the little girl tramping out the school gate with slumped shoulders to tell her parents about her terrible day. She went back to Oli and begged him just to pop by. She gave him the full sob story, told him the children had spent all week drawing his face (appealing to his vanity was always the best way), and all he had to do was pick a favourite.

He refused.

She pressed him again, told him a lot of little kids would be crying all because of him. He had the decency to look ashamed, shuffling on his feet and scratching the back of his head, but he wouldn't be moved.

'I'm sorry for the little buggers, I really am, but trust me, their day is nowhere near as bad as mine,' he said. 'I think it was a mistake coming here.'

What the hell was he talking about? He hadn't had a bad day. He spent all morning being driven around by a chauffeur and – as always – had been offered everything his heart might desire.

I think it was a mistake coming here.

What a spoilt horror show this man had turned out to be. Marilla shook her head in wonder at his vanity and childishness, but she knew she was complicit in creating this beast. This is what happens when you build an industry where the stars are constantly being asked if they need anything. It just encouraged a kind of helpless entitlement.

On a righteous crusade now, she rang her office and instructed an intern (another failed rich girl), to put together a goodie bag for every student, along with extra prizes that the teachers could hand out to the portrait artists and the poet.

'Get them couriered over to the schools before the end of the day,' she said.

Then she rang both headteachers again and, after some conversation, agreed that Oli would pay for the following: a stack of new iPads; some colourful stepping stone mushrooms for the primary play park; and a substantial contribution to the secondary school theatre fund. She also sent flowers for the heads of department and the staff common room.

It was the least she could do.

'Bloody hell, do you think I'm made of money, or summink?' he complained when she told him. He liked to keep an eye on his cash. He would buy ridiculous cars and expensive watches then bemoan the cost of parking or the price of a battery.

Thankfully, he didn't quibble over the cost of the iPads and the theatre fund for long; even he knew he owed it to the kids. Nevertheless, she organised the bank transfers straight away before he could change his mind. She couldn't bear letting the schools down twice. If he complained later she would offer to let him take it from her pay. He wouldn't agree to that; she knew too many of his secrets. The last thing he wanted was her going off and ringing the papers. And in a week or so he would have forgotten all about it, helped by the enormous pay cheque his agent was currently negotiating for the next movie.

After she had spoiled the children's day and attempted to

buy back their goodwill, Oli made Marilla ring his parents and cancel on them too.

'I'm sorry? You want me to cancel on your parents?'

His parents were heading over from Eastbourne to take Oli out for a meal that evening.

'Yeah, tell 'em I'm poorly or... I dunno, think of something. I just can't see 'em. I need a kip. I'm wiped out.'

He got up from the sofa he had been slumped on and went to the bedroom.

Marilla waited for a few beats as though expecting him to leap out laughing, 'Ha! Got you!' while she pretended to find the joke amusing. But Oli didn't appear and so she returned to her room to make the dreaded call to his parents. Then she made a call to her boss to break the bad news about her recalcitrant client.

'Oh for god's sake, Marilla. You do realise this is literally your job?' Della hissed.

Once that ordeal was over, Marilla took out Oli's credit card once more and ordered a huge bunch of flowers for his parents and a big bottle of Bollinger for Della. She didn't tell him about that expense. She couldn't bear anymore of his *Cor blimey, guvnor*ing over the bill she was racking up.

Oli was not quite the working class gangster he made himself out to be. In fact, he had been raised by a nice lower-middle-class family in a bungalow in the suburbs. His dad worked his way up from the factory floor to manager. His mother worked part-time as a nursery receptionist, spending her days off humming to herself while she attended to the flowerbeds, and taking short naps on the sofa after lunch.

'They probably call it a settee,' Marilla's mother said with a shudder. 'Or a couch.'

Marilla liked Oli's parents. They loved attending Oli's

premieres, and she made a point of inviting them. They may not be particularly interesting company, but they clearly cared about their son and took shy delight in his success. For Marilla, that was all you could ask for in a parent.

'They're alright, I guess,' Oli said. 'The old man's a bit of a ball ache, but he means well.'

'They sound dreadful,' said her mother. 'I expect they've never done so much as an interesting fart their entire dull little lives.'

Oli had been charming and fun when Marilla first started, but it didn't last; he soon turned into a sulky pain in her arse. Now, she could barely remember a time when she wasn't dealing with one of his little tantrums. This latest one shouldn't have surprised her. Perhaps he really had expected a ticker tape parade. Maybe he thought the entire town would come out to wave as he passed. Was it not enough that half of the staff at the hotel had been lined up in the foyer to greet him like he was the lord of the manor returning to the big house for the summer?

Apparently not.

Marilla had marvelled at the sight of it. No wonder the power went to rich people's heads: someone passed him flowers; another gave him a gift basket; one woman actually curtseyed. And yet, despite his desperate need for attention, Oli had gone quiet and scurried off to his suite, pale as a sheet and needing to take to his bed.

I think it was a mistake coming here.

He wasn't the only one.

That's why Marilla had been glad to bump into the journalist. Sure, she'd been loitering in a stairwell when Marilla came down, ('Always take the stairs, darling,' her mother told her, 'your buttocks need the workout.'). And, sure, the journalist was just some junior on the crummy little local rag, but she was still *The Press*, damn it, and when Marilla offered to buy the girl a drink, it was only partly because she wanted to butter her up for a positive article. Truth was, she was lonely and this Phil McGinty person seemed like she might be good enough company. Someone fun to sit with while Marilla sank a couple of gins. She was well into her second double when she began ranting about her paymaster.

'Thing is,' she told Phil (strictly off the record, she wasn't a complete idiot, despite what those A-level results suggested). 'I even told him I'd administer the blow job he'd been pestering me for if he just agreed to do the bloody *Times* interview. But even then, blow job very much on the table, he wouldn't do it,' she hiccuped. 'Little shit.'

'That's sexual harassment! You should sue.' Phil looked down at her Old Fashioned as if it had insulted her, swirling the ice round and slugging down the last mouthful like she was in a saloon bar in Deadwood. 'Men like that make me sick, they really do.'

Marilla was surprisingly drunk. Perhaps she should have had something to eat first, but it was still too early for dinner. Strictly speaking, it was still too early for the gins. Even her parents, who were old hands at functional alcoholism, waited until after six for their first cocktail – perhaps because they were still sobering up from the bottle of wine at lunch. But breaking four hundred primary school children's hearts had made her brittle, and speaking to Oli's parents had finally snapped her in two.

'You can't sue,' she explained, raising her finger at the bartender to get a couple more drinks. 'If you sue you never work in the industry again, or – worse – you're stuck working for the company you sued for the rest of your life.'

'What's that?' said Phil, who also looked a trifle worse for wear. 'I don't understand.'

'They want to keep you close by, you see. You sue them, they want to make sure you never speak a word of it. They tell all their competitors not to hire you – give you crummy references, put the word out you're bad news. Then, when you're really desperate, they offer you a nice job, preferably abroad – in the Japan office, maybe. You'll accept anything by that point. So now you've signed a non-disclosure and you've got a cushy new job tucked away somewhere out of sight.' She smiled bitterly 'And they've got you, lock, stock and barrel; your soul in their hands.'

'Well, shit.'

'Sorry, that was all thoroughly depressing, wasn't it? What fun company I am.'

'I'm a bit bummed out, I'm not going to lie. You certainly know how to keep the mood light.'

Marilla laughed at that. For a journalist, Phil was alright.

'So, do you still want to meet him after all that?' she asked.

'If anything, I want to meet him even *more*,' said Phil. 'Before, I just wanted to meet him professionally, for the sake of work, but now I want to see him for myself. He sounds like a monster, and who can resist having a look at a monster? Narcissists are like our generation's freak show.'

Marilla laughed again. 'Oh, I'm probably being unfair. He can be really good company at times.' She gave her ice cubes another prod. 'Just not recently.'

'Any particular reason, do you think? What could have triggered it all?'

'Nice try, journo, I know what you're doing,' Marilla

leaned in a little drunkenly, her warm juniper breath on Phil's arm. 'Digging for dirt, poking around for a story.'

The journalist held up her hands in surrender.

'It's a fair cop. Although, in my defence, it's second nature to me – I hadn't even realised I was doing it.' Now it was her turn to lean in. 'Although, if you do want to give me an exclusive, I'm all yours.'

Marilla looked at her for a moment, an alien thought occurring to her.

'Do you fancy a drink in my room?' She hadn't intended to say that. She had intended to say: 'Well, anyway, nice to meet you, good night,' but the Dutch courage was now doing the talking for her.

'Sure,' said Phil with a grin. 'Sounds like fun.'

Maybe, thought Marilla, life might start getting a little better after tonight.

FIVE

The man in the beige trousers had long ago eschewed a book.

A book may be the usual companion of a person dining solo, but the pages flapped around and he didn't enjoy the wrestling that had to go on in order to read and eat at the same time. There was always a risk of spilling gravy on the precious paper. He preferred to give one thing his full attention. At meal times, it was eating. Later, he would sit and read one of his history books with the pure focus of someone who had not been infected by the world's short attention span.

He had never owned a smartphone, didn't know what it was to pause every five minutes to check social media or attend to whatever beep or ping the phone emitted to catch his attention. He had never stopped to google something, didn't know what it was to go down a rabbit hole of information he'd never remember: he had only ever owned a basic Nokia that made and received calls.

No one ever rang him, anyway. His mother had died a year ago. Knocked down by a car, would you credit it? She hadn't even been crossing a road – her old Nissan had simply rolled off the driveway into her. Dodgy handbrake. His mother hadn't known enough about cars to add faulty brakes to her list of horrors and she had died blissfully unaware of the murderer sitting on her own driveway.

He missed her, for the most part.

Anyway, he had only ever taken a book to restaurants for the sake of the other diners. It pained them to see a person alone unoccupied. It made them feel guilty. Worse, it moved some to pity and – horror of horrors – solicitude. They'd often invite him to join their table, scooching up to make space and inducing him to drag his chair over to join them in a threesome. He would rather boil his own head than sit with the sort of gregarious people who invited strangers to dine. He couldn't imagine anything more exhausting than having to make small talk with someone you didn't know all evening long. What a tax on the spirit! He would end his meal feeling exhausted and wan, which made eating fuel a fruitless exercise.

These days he was good at spotting the gregarious folk trying to make eye contact. He usually managed to engineer a table far away, but you could hear them a mile off, noisy, chatty and bold. No, no, no, it wouldn't do at all; they were insufferable. He'd much rather sit alone, staring into space than spend an evening politely enquiring if their daughter was enjoying her new role at the currency exchange kiosk, or hearing how their mother was coping after her hernia op (amazing what these people felt comfortable sharing). Now he wouldn't suffer them; he would reject the slightest outreach before it could go anywhere. Any hint of a friendly nod or a joke (shouted out into the room for his benefit so they could force him into a polite smile) and he would either

glance away hastily, or he would stare long enough to make
them wonder if he was a little unhinged, perhaps a serial
killer (one of those 'he seemed so bland and average' types,
not one of the charismatic ones), or a tax accountant:
someone you wouldn't want to get caught sitting next to all
evening.

It didn't always work. He wasn't brave enough to stare
for more than a few seconds. He didn't have the serial killer
look off pat, really. He wasn't threatening enough. It was easy
to tell he didn't have a dark heart: he had a pedant's heart. He
looked more like a failed librarian or a third-rate history
lecturer than a killer. Someone who wouldn't say boo to a
goose.

If the stare didn't work and he found himself wearily
dragging a chair over to the couple's table, he would excuse
himself for the lavatory and flee the scene. He'd climbed out
of a window once; left a whole plate of spaghetti uneaten;
went home and ate some instant noodles. The noodles were
still crunchy when he started forking them in. It didn't
matter; it was just fuel.

Luckily, no one tried to befriend him as he sat eating at
The Marchmont. Some fidgeted in their seats at the spec-
tacle of a man alone, but they wouldn't dream of inviting him
over (thank god). This was an aspirational crowd, and the
man in the beige sweater didn't look like he could give them
any boost in society. That said, they might consider striking
up conversation in the lounge during coffee and petit fours in
the hope of extracting some tax avoidance tips. In the meantime, they avoided eye contact whenever they felt his gaze
pass over their table.

The man munched on, masticating his food with scant
enjoyment. He had never been much of a gourmet. He had

ordered the simplest dish (chicken salad and chips). Anything more exciting tended to mess with his innards. He had his mother to thank for that inherited affliction. He certainly wouldn't consider the fish (his mother had a dread of the fish bones choking him to death – was that even possible? He wasn't sure), or the shellfish (food poisoning). Steak was bad for the heart (and created skid marks, which was revolting and unacceptable in a hotel where a poorly paid cleaner would have to scrub them away). Pork and lamb were too fatty (not to mention the most endearing of the plated animals). He had toyed with being a vegetarian, but his palate was already limited enough. If he had his way, he would eat boiled potatoes and a chicken fillet every night. Or maybe a bowl of porridge. Hearty and easy to microwave.

In fact, he did have his way now mother had passed. Yet, somehow her opinions lingered, controlling him from beyond the grave. That was why he still avoided taking the lift. She'd read an article once about a group of people who had plummeted to their death in an elevator, their final journey captured on CCTV and shared onto the internet by the sorts of revolting people who put up grisly photos of train suicides or mafia decapitations.

He could never kill himself with a train. He wasn't worried about putting the passengers out (as far as he was concerned, most of them were far too in thrall to the daily rat race and could use a little time sitting on a platform contemplating life's great questions). He didn't care that news of his final moments would be greeted with a collective eye roll and disapproving tut from a group of middle managers. He wasn't even that bothered that he might traumatise an innocent train driver – after all, surely they got counselling and some extremely satisfactory payment for the distress caused?

No, he just didn't want photos of his brain matter being cackled over by internet numbskulls who took delight in the gruesome.

It was unconscionable. Giving those people even a moment of joy in their pathetic little lives was too much to bear. No, when he ended his days, he would do it in the least gruesome way possible, just to spite them. He had a plan. He would spend a week by the sea, revisiting old haunts, taking in the various attractions – perhaps a show at the local theatre, or a meal at one of the cosy, well-reviewed eateries that had popped up after he'd moved away – and he would destroy all his final possessions, anything that might identify him. He had been careful so far, giving a false name, insisting on paying in cash, so that, when the week was out, he would not only end his life, he would obliterate his entire existence.

SIX

'Hello Judy,' said a voice.

Judith Jones turned slowly. She knew who it was, and she was in no hurry to see him. And yet, despite her reluctance, she felt her stomach flip. Must be pheromones or something, she thought, some sort of animal response to this man she detested. And of course he still looked amazing. How? It was decades since she'd last looked into those cool grey eyes and yet if anything he seemed to have become more distinguished. The flecks of grey hair at his temples brought out the flashes of green in his eyes, the creases on his brow adding a rugged...

She stopped herself.

Her thoughts sounded like a bad romance, swooning over his rough good looks as though he were a dishy hero from a novel. How *embarrassing*. And she didn't even enjoy those kinds of books; she preferred a gritty crime thriller or something funny to make her howl with laughter in the bath. She wouldn't get lost in those eyes again, like some fainting girl.

She was not some hapless heroine who had just bumped into the air pilot or surgeon of her dreams. She was *not*.

Yet here she was, on an empty, dark street, in very great danger once again. Annoying, really.

She'd only just got off work.

Her shift had been surprisingly lively. Usually, her time was spent standing at her reception desk, doing the occasional check-in or -out, answering a few phone calls, glancing up at the clock every few minutes and looking forward to the time when she'd be back at home, watching a true crime documentary in the bath with a martini and a giant spliff: her Friday night ritual. But today's celebrity guest had set everyone into a flutter, with Ruby the manager marching about in her polyester blazer overseeing the floral arrangements and the reorganisation of the leaflet display on the table by the door (presumably in case Oli Cromwell wanted to take a trip to the local goat rescue centre, or visit a castle ruin), and generally just getting in everyone's way. Even Judith had not escaped Ruby's micromanagement, which only added to the atmosphere of tension that pervaded the usually tranquil space.

And then he had arrived, and they lined up to doff their metaphorical caps, tug their metaphorical forelocks and, in one case, much to Judith's disbelief, curtsey. Judith found she couldn't look at him, averting her eyes and smiling nervously. But when she did finally look up, she saw his handsome young face suffused in what she could only describe as terror. He was smiling, making jokes to Ruby and a few of the cleaning staff, charming the pants off anyone within a hundred yards, but to Judith's eyes he looked like a lost little boy woken by a bad dream, scared of what might lunge from a cupboard or slither from a cellar door. She wanted to rush over and gather him in her arms.

Then, of course, the journalist had shown up and Judith was annoyed that Duncan hadn't been there where he was supposed to be. It really wasn't a hard job – or not usually, anyway. All he needed to do was stay on his post, but he kept wandering off. And they already had a few fans outside by the time the journalist appeared, the rumours that Oli was in town and staying at The Marchmont spreading around social media.

By the evening things had calmed down a little, and Judith had returned to her customary clock staring. It was only 8pm but she was already looking forward to her night. Her nephew had got her the weed off The Dark Web. It reminded her of the happy times she'd spent with her friends in that squat in Brixton. One night, a beautiful Jamaican man named Colin had taken her proffered joint, given her a blow-back and then taught her how to knit. She already knew how to knit, but that didn't matter. She liked having Colin show her, holding her slender wrists in his strong hands as he helped her to cast on. They had enjoyed a very nice night together. A smile formed on her lips until a disgruntled voice had intruded on her thoughts.

'Excuse me, there's no trouser press in room 302.'

Colin evaporated, refocusing into a fretful little frog-faced white man standing before her. Was he Welsh? She peered at him. He seemed genuinely concerned about the trouser press. Honestly, the things people get their knickers in a twist about, she thought. She wondered how they coped with actual trauma.

She bared her teeth in a simulacrum of a smile and

wished for a lightning bolt to strike him down. 'I'll have one sent up right away, sir.'

'And a chocolate on the pillow would have been nice.'

Was he really wringing his hands? Judith had thought that was just something they say in books. He was like a yappy dog: terrified and yet still making a noise. He wanted you to know he suffered, but he was scared you might thwack him round the head for it. He shifted his weight onto his back foot, ready to run. A bullied child with an indulgent parent, Judith thought. She was good at assessing people – apart from when it came to men she liked, that is – and she was willing to wager that Mr Fretful had seen the bottom of a few toilet pans in his time. She expected he spent many school days being pressed down into the brown water by a brutish bully with a low IQ.

She hoped so, anyway.

'I'm afraid we don't do the chocolates anymore,' she said. 'We had too many complaints about them.'

She could have continued, but that's what he wanted. She could see it in his eyes. He was desperate to know why people complained about the chocolates. Of course, he'd be too timid to ask now – especially as he'd come out fighting (or yapping, really). He couldn't very well try to strike up a conversation about the many and varied chocolate complaints Judith had listened to through the years – she could fill a book – not now that he'd used such a combative tone. And this, she knew from experience, was a brilliant way to disarm disgruntled guests. Give their brains a little puzzle and watch all the steam evaporate from their anger. The mystery would keep this man up in the night, wondering. That made her happy.

'You're welcome to take a sweet from here on the counter, sir.'

She gestured to the bowl of boiled mints on the desk in front of her. Individually wrapped, since they'd had complaints about the unwrapped ones. (Germs, naturally. Lucky they never saw what the kitchen staff did with their hands before cooking, Judith thought.) But the man in 302 was already fleeing; his weight shifting further onto his back foot and momentum taking him towards the foyer.

'I'll get the press sent up now, sir.' She picked up the phone, ready to do his bidding. 'Was there anything else I can help you with? Will you need an iron or an ironing board as well?'

'No, just the press,' he stuttered from the doorway.

She was overwhelming him with offers now. What was it men liked to blame their mothers for? Engulfment or something. Her own son had pinned that on her a while back. Apparently, by loving him too much, she had made him the disappointment he was today. She couldn't remember the ins and outs of it. She'd stopped listening after a while. There comes a time in every man's life when he has to stop blaming his bloody mother for bloody everything.

After her son had made his laundry list of complaints (the only laundry he'd ever done), he'd kissed her and said goodbye. That was years ago now. In some ways, it had felt like a strange relief. The wonderful baby he had been had vanished a long time ago. This disappointing man-child pecking her on the cheek for the last time was not the boy she had loved. A part of her was glad to see the back of him. He wanted her to beg him to stay. He wanted her to apologise. For what? Loving him? She'd rather let him go than say sorry for the love she had given him – that he had returned so fiercely. It would be a betrayal to the memory of it.

She would never be sorry.

She had smiled and looked down at the phone, pretending to ring for the trouser press, making it clear that she was done talking to him. He scurried for the door as though she was threatening to throw the phone at his head. He vanished and she dropped her smile and put the phone back on the receiver. Let him wait.

She stole another glance at the clock. Only 8.05pm. Damn it.

Laughter. Judith glanced over at the Lounge Bar. The young woman who accompanied Oli Cromwell into the hotel was laughing. Judith assumed she was Oli's PA or his manager or something, although she looked like a child to her eyes. Everyone did these days. The girl was talking to another young woman to her right. Judith couldn't see who. The girl (was it something old-fashioned – Lucilla or Matilda?) glanced over and gave Judith a tight, polite smile. The sort you give someone when you catch their eye by mistake. Judith responded in kind.

Later, she noticed the girl at the bar getting up to leave (Marilla! That was her name). She squinted at the woman she was with. Even from behind she looked familiar. But Judith didn't have time to consider for long because her manager came in asking if she knew where Callum the sous-chef had got to. How on earth should she know? Not that she said that to the manager, of course.

The manager was called Ruby ('a servant's name', her mother would say). Ruby was half Judith's age – much more than half – but she had the right kind of corporate-speak and a degree in French and Hospitality Management. Judith couldn't compete. Luckily, she didn't want to.

'Would you like me to see if I can find him?' she said to Ruby.

It would be something to do. Anything to escape the front desk. Ruby, being bone idle, would welcome the opportunity to let Judith go on the hunt instead of her. And of course, she wouldn't want to be seen wasting her precious time looking for one of her own staff.

'That would be wonderful, Judith. Thank you. I'm absolutely shattered. I could do with a few minutes of doing nothing.'

Judith blinked, unable to believe her own ears. All that management training and Ruby still didn't know how to talk to her staff. What happened to making your employees feel good about the work they do? She herself, as a lowly underling, was expected to work with 'purpose and passion' – they'd had a workshop (off-site!) on the subject – but her own boss thought she did nothing. Good to know.

'Right you are,' she said.

She avoided saying Ruby's name because Ruby liked to be called Ms Davies, and Judith objected to giving her that much respect. She could just about cope with being bossed around by the children that ran The Marchmont – it wasn't like she had thwarted ambitions to be a great leader in some hotel chain – but she drew the line at tugging her forelock. Oli Cromwell line-up notwithstanding.

Callum the sous-chef had been undiscoverable.

She'd gone to the kitchen first, of course – the obvious place to look for a cook. It was a scene of crisis and disarray, thanks to Callum. Chef was huffing and puffing around the place looking like he was one high cholesterol meal away from a fatal collapse. She offered to help and found herself delivering a couple of room service orders whilst checking a few obvious hiding places. Better than standing at the front desk with a rictus smile and sore feet, she decided.

'What has happened to him, then?' said Ruby when Judith returned with bad news. Ruby was browsing holidays on the internet, Judith noticed. It was a toss up between Portugal and Goa.

'You know what these youngsters are like,' said Judith, as though she'd been any different in her youth. She was always bunking off with her pals whenever she could get the chance, especially when she worked in the nightclubs. Any excuse to chat up one of the fellas in the VIP area. She lived in the hope of finding a sugar daddy to keep her in the manner to which she'd like to become accustomed. Sometimes Judith missed those days, but on the whole she preferred a quieter life. Still, it would be nice if you could open a magic door to the past and go back just for a night or two every once in a while – and then get home in time to slip on your PJs and catch your favourite show on the box.

'Lazy, that's what they're like,' said Ruby, sagely. She could only have been a couple of years older than Callum.

'I'll look for him again if you want?' said Judith, sensing another opportunity to escape.

So that was her evening, a night spent gallivanting about the building like a headless chicken, and she had been looking forward to her bath when that voice broke into thoughts from

'Hello Judy.'

Calm as you like. What do you say to that, after so many years?

'Hello Charles.'

He winced a little. She'd always called him Charlie, or Charlie-darling ('Charlie-darling, buy me another drink'). Charles was what the judge called him during his sentencing: 'Charles Nicholas Walsh, I sentence you to twenty years.' And here he was: her past staring straight at her, danger incarnate. She was disappointed at how weak-kneed she felt. Was it fear or excitement? What a letdown. All those years of believing she had freed herself from his power only to find herself, heart a-flutter and knees a-knocking all over again. She gave herself a little mental kick.

Pull yourself together, woman.

'You're looking beautiful as ever, Judy,' he said.

'Even a consummate liar like you can't make that believable. What do you want?'

It irritated her the way men seemed to age into their faces while women were constantly chasing what was fading before their eyes.

'You'll always be eighteen to me, sweetheart,' he said, giving her one of his cheeky grins. She resisted the urge to smile back and almost succeeded.

'What do you want, Charles?' she said again, her body half-turned away, ready to flee. It wasn't just that he scared her (although he did), it was that she was scared of herself when she was with him.

'Who me?' Another grin. His eyes crinkled into handsome crow's feet. Typical. 'I don't want anything, Judy. I was just in your neck of the woods and I thought I'd look you up. See how the old girl is getting on, you know?'

He was so good at this – at pretending to be harmless.

'Do you want to go for a drink?' he said, 'for old time's sake.'

For old time's sake? He's a giant walking, talking cliché, she thought. She would have liked to roll her eyes, but even now, all these years down the line, she knew it wasn't a good idea to make him angry.

'Yes, OK,' she heard herself say.

He took her to a little place he said he knew.

'I've just bought it, actually,' he said.

She insisted on paying for her own drink and they found a table together by the window. And just like that, she felt trapped all over again.

It was only much later, after she'd got home, she remembered she hadn't sent up the trouser press for the man in room 302.

SEVEN

Marilla – Marilla Hunter Davy, no less – didn't let Phil accompany her to check on Oli Cromwell, preferring to take the temperature of his current mood before exposing him to a local hack. Instead, Phil nosed around Marilla's room, opening drawers to see what the hotel had provided, pocketing the notepad, resisting the urge to pull Marilla's expensive clothes out of her suitcase and admire them. And eventually, Marilla returned with the news that her charge was fine.

'He managed to order room service all by himself and I made him a Jack Daniels, so for now we can do whatever we want.'

Phil wasn't sure this was a good thing. She was pretty confident Marilla had never slept with a woman before, and the fact was, Phil wasn't keen on being her first. She hadn't intended to catch the young woman's eye in quite that way. She just wanted to be chummy enough to get what she wanted. But now here she was, sitting in the publicist's room, drinking miniature whiskies, ordering chips from room service, and trying to work out if she was expected to provide chaste good company or a mind-blowing first time.

She hoped it was the former.

Not that she didn't find the publicist extremely attractive, she just wasn't up for the rigmarole of introducing her to the process, bearing the burden of ensuring it was memorable and perfectly managed. She may have only been in her twenties, but just thinking about it made her feel tired. A casual shag was one thing, but a first time was sacred. She couldn't be the one to disappoint.

'What shall we drink to?' said Marilla, rising awkwardly from the carpet where they were lounging to stand to attention and raise a glass.

'The King!' Phil energetically raised her glass while remaining sprawled out on her stomach on the floor. His majesty seemed fitting, given Marilla's decision to stand. Phil's dad Clive always stood to toast the Queen every year at Christmas. It was never entirely clear if he was doing it in jest, posing with such exaggerated pride, puffing out his chest, looking into the middle distance. But there was always a twinkle of naughtiness in his eye. To this day, Phil couldn't tell you if he was a fervent patriot or a mocking satirist.

'Not the King,' giggled Marilla. 'You can't toast the monarch when Oliver Cromwell is in the building. Whatever will he say if he hears us? We'll be locked up for sedition.'

'Wasn't Cromwell the one doing the sedition?' Phil's grasp of history was growing hazier with every sip of whisky. 'Yeah, I'm pretty sure Cromwell was the one doing all the seditioning.'

'Haven't the faintest clue,' said Marilla. It soon became clear she wasn't sure who Oliver Cromwell was in the scheme of things. 'Was he something to do with *Wolf Hall*, or was that his brother?'

'His great-great-something-or-other, I think,' said Phil.

She was only slightly exaggerating the slur on her words. It was a good option for getting out of a tricky situation. If the worst came to the worst, she would just pretend to have passed out. Marilla raised a glass again.

'Let's raise a glass to mothers. To the women who gave birth to us and then crushed our souls.'

'Our souls? Arseholes,' giggled Phil. But then she sat up. 'Hang on, that's a terrible toast. My mother is a supreme being who has not crushed my soul, but does occasionally bust my balls. But only when it's absolutely necessary. She always says, "Sometimes you've got to bust some balls to make an omelette."'

Marilla blinked.

'No, I've got no idea what that means either,' said Phil.

'To Phil's mother,' said Marilla, 'the wisest woman who ever lived.'

'To Angela,' toasted Phil, 'Queen of Roosevelt Court.'

'Sedition!' screeched Marilla.

'Is your mother really that brilliant?' Marilla asked Phil later. It was during one of the less raucous points of the evening, one of those moments when secrets are shared. But Phil had no intention of sharing anything at all.

They had moved from lying on the floor to lying on the bed, both of them standing to discover they had developed a dead body part. Phil made Marilla snort gin out of her nostrils by hopping about and crying, 'I've got pins and needles in my fanny.'

'Don't be ridiculous, that has never happened to a human EVER!' Marilla had insisted, laughing uncontrollably.

'Well, write to Guinness because this girl has just become the first.'

After a brief discussion about whether Guinness wanted to hear about firsts or if they only had eyes for longest, tallest, biggest, smallest and so on, Marilla's interest in Angela came out.

'Yes, my mother really is that brilliant,' said Phil, rolling over into the centre of the bed to meet Marilla, who was lying up the other way, her head dangling off the bottom edge. Marilla sat up to look at her more seriously.

'I mean *obviously* she can be a total pain in the arse, and she annoys the hell out of me,' said Phil. 'But she's also a brilliant laugh and full of cracking sayings that I think she must have got from an alternative reality, because I have never heard them anywhere else.'

'What about your dad?'

'No, it's my turn to ask a question now,' said Phil, smiling adorably so Marilla wouldn't notice the change of subject. Phil didn't want to talk about her dad with someone she had only just met. She could only talk about Clive with people who had known him and loved him as much as she had. There were plenty of dark stories in Phil's childhood. It hadn't been a peachy bed of roses in Roosevelt Court, but her parents had never featured in any of her unhappy memories, and thinking about Clive was still fraught with grief and regret.

'Tell me about your family – no wait! Let me guess,' Phil said. 'Your dad is aloof and distant, and your mother is passive aggressive and deeply critical. Your dad never attended a single school nativity and your mother tells herself she's not an alcoholic because she doesn't start drinking until after five o'clock.'

Phil stopped abruptly because Marilla was staring at her in shock. Had she gone too far?

She was about to launch into a stuttering apology in the vain hope of salvaging the evening, but then Marilla smiled. If it had hurt her feelings, she was doing a sterling effort of masking it – like any good upper middle-class girl.

'Don't be ridiculous. They don't start drinking until six. They're not savages, you know.'

Later, in a quiet moment, Marilla said: 'How did you know about my mother?'

Phil shrugged. 'I was probably just making huge assumptions about your class, upbringing and job – and that will tell you just as much about me and my prejudices as anything else.'

Then Marilla told Phil a story about how her family had gone to see the play of *Wolf Hall*. Marilla had enjoyed it until the interval when her mother gave her a slip of paper with a phone number on.

'She told me, "Dr Findlater will give you a prescription to help with those little love handles, darling." I was fifteen. I didn't pay much attention to the play after that.'

Somewhere along the line, Phil had given in to the inevitable.

When they first went to Marilla's room, she had told herself sleeping with the girl would be a Bad Idea. Later, when they were lying together on the bed, woozy with booze, she was no longer able to remember why it was a Bad Idea. In fact, she started to wonder if it was, in truth, a Very Good Idea. She hadn't slept with anyone in a while. The temptation was too great.

Marilla surprised her by being unexpectedly well-versed,

which made Phil wonder if perhaps she was more knowl-edgeable about female pleasure than Phil imagined.

But afterwards, Marilla said, 'That was my first time. With a girl, I mean.'

Phil smiled. 'Glad to be of service. I hope I lived up to expectations.'

'Well, now I actually know what an orgasm feels like, so I'd say you did,' said Marilla.

Phil wasn't surprised. She had written an article about it once: '22 Surprising Facts About Sex, Number 6 Will Blow Your Mind'. According to a survey, eighty-six percent of lesbians 'usually or always orgasm' during sex, versus sixty-five percent of straight women. That piece had attracted a number of furious comments about the gutter state of modern journalism and was by far their most clicked on arti-cle. Job done.

She gently brushed aside a lock of Marilla's hair and planted an affectionate kiss on her warm lips. Marilla smiled.

'You know you didn't have to sleep with me just to get an exclusive? I would have given it to you, anyway.'

Phil said: 'Marilla, you do know that not every sexual encounter needs to be transactional, right? I'm not Oli Cromwell. I don't expect you to offer blow jobs for kickbacks, and I wouldn't dream of offering you sex for a reward.'

'But I would, right?' An expression flashed across Maril-la's face. Hurt? Irritation? Embarrassment? It was unclear. For a moment Phil thought Marilla was going to lose her temper and throw her out, but she simply rolled away and looked glumly down at the floor. 'You're right. I guess it just never occurred to me I was worth any more than that.'

'Listen, sweet cheeks, for lips like yours, I'd be asking for the moon on a stick. Oli Cromwell got you far too cheap,'

Phil used a silly voice and a cheeky grin and made Marilla smile again.

'And by the way, I'm not judging you,' she continued. 'I don't blame a woman for hustling to get by. I just meant that the thought had never occurred to *me* to offer myself up that way... I wonder if Adam would give me a better beat if I offered to lick his balls.'

Marilla laughed, appalled, 'One: who is Adam? And two: please don't ever say "lick his balls" again. Just the thought of it makes me sick.'

Phil looked at her. 'But since you offered, I would actually really like that exclusive.'

Phil and Marilla giggled down the corridor. Phil was still a little drunk. Possibly a lot drunk. Oli's suite was on the floor above, something that had proved to be both a blessing and a curse. Marilla was far away, which meant he couldn't be bothered to keep turning up at her door, but it didn't stop him ringing every five minutes to ask for some small service (*how do I change the TV channel?*) or large service (blow job).

'At least the walk gives me plenty of time to calm down,' she told Phil.

Phil had spruced herself up for the meeting, tidying up the worst of her bedragglement and leaving just enough of it to make her acceptably casual-cool for her celebrity encounter. There wasn't much she could do about her mental bedragglement, however, aside from gulping down a glass of water and borrowing Marilla's toothbrush. Unfortunately, despite what the movies suggest, slapping her face a few times and shouting, 'Sober up, woman,' into the bathroom mirror hadn't helped at all.

'I think you might need to knock a bit louder than that,' whispered Phil. She had adopted the whisper in honour of the smallness of the hour and the quietness of the knock. It would have felt rude to speak any louder. But by the third quiet rap, she got impatient and banged loudly on the door.

'Mr Cromwell, are you in there? It's Marilla,' said Phil, putting on a posh voice as Marilla laughed and shushed her. Then, quietly, she whispered: 'She's come to turn down your penis.'

Marilla slapped Phil's arm in scandalised laughter. Phil grinned. 'If penis talk doesn't wake him, nothing will.'

A few minutes later, with Oli still not responding, Marilla remembered she had his key card. She ran back along the corridors to collect it and returned brandishing it like a winning raffle ticket. Before breaking in, they tried one more knock.

'Please god, I don't need to see him naked *again*,' said Marilla.

'Oh, I don't know, it would certainly make a good headline for *The Observer*,' said Phil. 'On second thoughts, I'd rather not see it, it might not live up to expectations.'

But when no answer came, they had to risk the nudity. Marilla was growing slightly worried. He was an insomniac: late to bed and early to rise, usually hitting the gym at five thirty at the latest.

'Maybe he went to the gym early,' she said.

'Perhaps he dozed off in front of his latest movie,' said Phil. 'I know I did.'

Then, with the guilty air of drunken teenagers trying to

creep up to bed without their parents catching them, they snuck inside.

The TV was talking quietly to itself, playing an old film from the '80s that Phil didn't recognise. They tip-toed through the sitting room before exchanging a glance and making the unspoken decision to enter the bedroom. Phil wondered, given that he was so averse to the press at the moment, if Marilla hadn't better go in on her own first. In fact, maybe she shouldn't even be in the suite at all.

'It's fine, he won't mind,' Marilla assured her in a loud whisper. 'He'll forgive a good-looking girl anything – even if she is a lowdown dirty journalist.'

Phil gave her the stink-eye and Marilla grinned. But despite her assurances, Phil held back when Marilla opened Oli's bedroom door. She didn't want to be caught peering at him as he slept. In fact, the sober thought came: perhaps it was better to wait outside in the corridor until she was invited in. She had begun creeping for the exit when she heard Marilla cry out.

'Shit! Call an ambulance!'

Phil raced into the room and tried to register what was happening.

'Oh my god, oh my god,' Marilla cried.

There, on the bed, lay Oli Cromwell, face down, sprawled out naked, completely dead.

EIGHT

Marilla's mind is a chaos of thoughts all piled on top of each other in random order, like a drunk making a sandwich. She tries to settle into one thought at a time, but it's like trying to grab water: she can't get a grasp on any. The children at Oli's school; the iPad order; her night with Phil; her mother talking about 'dykes at the BBC'; the body on the bed; the food tipping from the plate as Phil leans over to check Oli's pulse; the coolness of his soft skin. Then Oli turns to her and says, 'I think it was a mistake coming here,' and she gasps as if she's just remembered how to breathe.

Marilla isn't entirely sure what happened after they find Oli. She can't think about him as 'the body,' it is just Oli spreadeagled on the bed. Naked. Diagonal, arms outstretched. The way he always sleeps. It is a strangely confident pose, not like Marilla, who curls into a foetal ball. It is the sleeping position of a man who knows he deserves his place in the world. But now he is dead. She tries to collect her memories, to lay them out in order, snapshots in an old-fashioned album, but they jumble into chaos.

'We've got to get out of the room.'

She remembers Phil saying that at some point. Then: 'This might be a crime scene.'

But that was later, after they had first tried shaking him, then splashing some water on him from the glass on his bedside table, and then, eventually – with growing dread – after they had checked his pulse and listened for his breath.

Marilla had wanted to perform CPR, but Phil shook her head. 'It's too late. His body is cold.' And all she could think was, *let's give him a blanket, then.* That is when, she realises, her brain stopped firing correctly.

A strangely sweet smell hangs in the air. She doesn't recognise the scent as one of Oli's. Vanilla and caramel. Suddenly, the hotel seems too alien and strange. He shouldn't have died somewhere that smelled wrong.

'We should dress him,' she remembers saying, 'before the ambulance arrives.'

She felt protective. She didn't want the ambulance crew to see him naked and vulnerable. For all he had driven her nuts, he was a nice bloke in many ways. It wasn't really his fault that Hollywood had got to him. She was sure he had been a sweet child once.

'Yes, I suppose,' Marilla remembers saying when Phil had pointed out it might be a crime scene, even then aware that her grip on the moment was loosening. She could feel little bubbles of panic rising in her throat, like silent cries wanting to break free. She would have liked to scream or shout or freak out, but she knew it wouldn't be appropriate. Her mother wouldn't approve of her becoming emotional.

'For god's sake, don't have hysterics, Marilla.' She can almost hear her saying it. When she was a child, her mother would rebuke her whenever she fell over or got into a fight with her sisters. 'I can't bear the histrionics, Marilla, I really can't.'

Bit rich coming from a woman who requested pills from Dr Findlater for every minor emotional setback, thinks Marilla.

Oli Cromwell turns to her and says, 'I think it was a mistake coming here.'

One of the police officers, a handsome young guy called Dean – DC Dean something-or-other – has brought up a couple of muffins for them from the hotel breakfast buffet. Marilla had been looking forward to breakfast. It is one of her favourite things about nice hotels (the other being the amazing smelly stuff). She had planned to order eggs Benedict – with the sauce on the side because they always put too much hollandaise on. Then she was going to pocket a couple of croissants off the buffet for later. As it is, she must make do with the muffin.

Somewhere in the recesses of her conscious mind, it dawns on her that Dean knows Phil already. In fact, judging by their slightly strained greeting, she is sure they know each other very well. Marilla feels a pang of jealousy. She doesn't have any claim on Phil, but she would have preferred not to bump into an ex, especially not in this state. It doesn't matter, she supposes. She can't imagine seeing Phil again after all this is over. It's not exactly a great way to meet someone, is it? What would she tell her family?

'Mummy, meet my new girlfriend. We shared a moment over the corpse of my employer and I knew we'd never part.'

Too weird.

Her mother likes stories that make neat anecdotes at

supper parties; she doesn't want something that makes everyone squirm. It is vital that every anecdote ends with the opportunity for roaring laughter, but Marilla can't think of a punchline for this tale. Not unless Oli jumped up and shot them with finger guns and said, 'Ha ha, just joking, you should have seen your faces. Priceless.'

It could have happened – he has pranked her before, after all. But she remembers the body, cold and still. No neat ending for this story.

DC Dean something-or-other takes them to an alcove near the lift with an empty seating area – the sort of unused little pockets you get in hotels. Marilla wonders how many other people have sat on her chair and what they might have been doing here. Why choose to sit here when there is an executive office space upstairs or a selection of far comfier lounge spaces downstairs? Who would choose to sit in a thoroughfare in the gloom of a corridor? It reminds her of those people you see sitting in a country lay-by eating sandwiches when just around the corner is a breathtaking view point with parking and picnic tables.

She is glad they are sitting here, though. Now the table and chairs won't look so sad and lonely – at least for a little while.

'I think Marilla might be in shock,' says Phil.

Marilla glances up. Is she? That might explain it. She doesn't normally feel sorry for tables and chairs, and she has never before been handed a muffin she hasn't wanted to consume. She has been picking the blueberries out and slowly eating them one by one, but she has yet to take a proper bite. Perhaps if she is in shock, she should try eating it. Does food cure shock, or is it just tea?

'Marilla, can you tell me when you last saw Mr

Cromwell alive?' Dean is staring at her kindly, holding his notepad out in a hopeful manner as though she is going to come back to her senses and offer him a sensible account of the evening. She hopes she can reward his optimism.

'I need to ring his parents,' she says.

She thinks suddenly about the giant bouquet she sent them. A funeral condolence sent a day early. She supposes her flowers will soon be swamped by all the other well-wishers' displays, and she hopes her very obvious, 'Sorry your son is crap' apology bouquet doesn't add to their distress. People can focus on the wrong things in their grief, she knows. When great-aunt Dodie died, her mother had fixated on the scaffolding on the front of the house.

'It's defacing the building!' she screeched, clinging to a handkerchief with a shaking hand. 'Aunt Dorothea would be horrified – horrified – to know people were seeing it like this.'

'For god's sake, don't have hysterics, mother,' Marilla had wanted to say.

And, this being her mother, Marilla soon realised she wasn't really bothered about appearances or the insult to Dodie's memory. She was simply terrified of someone breaking in and stealing the family jewellery, which, to her mother's mind, was her birthright.

And great-aunt Dodie got her own back from beyond the grave by leaving all the jewels to Marilla and her other grand-nieces. Not a single pearl for greedy, grasping mummy. She was left the contents of the greenhouse. The house went to a favourite nephew. When you're rich, you get to have fun beyond the grave too, thinks Marilla. She wonders if Oli has similar plans, but she doubts it. He believed he would live forever.

'Maybe we can do this later, Dean?' says Phil. 'She's not quite with it.'

'It's better if we do it now, while the memory is fresh,' says Dean kindly. 'If you could just tell me as much as you remember and then we can do a proper follow up later, when you're feeling a bit less stressed, ok?'

He puts a hand on Phil's shoulder and Marilla frowns. It is too intimate.

'It must have been about nine or maybe ten,' Marilla says.

Dean's hand drops from Phil's shoulder, as she hoped it would. He makes notes in his little pad as she speaks.

'I went in to ask him one last time if he'd speak to *The Times* tomorrow and to check what he was doing for dinner. He said no, he wouldn't do the interview and that he had ordered room service. I made him a drink... JD and Diet Coke as usual... and then left him to it.'

She has been staring off into the middle distance as she speaks – Dean hastily jotting everything down – when she stops suddenly and looks at Phil.

'You should ring your paper, Phil. This is a huge story.'

Phil looks surprised. Perhaps she doesn't have the killer instinct it takes to be a really good reporter, thinks Marilla. Screw the parents and the police, get on the phone to the editor. That's what Marilla would be doing in her shoes... Isn't it? She can't make her brain work how it usually does. Maybe if it was working better it would be telling her to flee for the hills, take a flight to Monte Carlo. *Run for your life.* But here she is in a hotel alcove, feeling sorry for a chair and trying to make sense of her day. Her mother would have shrugged off the police like a pashmina and been drinking a cocktail at a hotel in Morocco by now.

Phil laughs suddenly, 'Yeah, I guess I should... I think I'd forgotten I was a journalist there for a moment.'

Marilla doesn't know whether to believe her. She gets the sense that Philippa McGinty is very good at telling people what they want to hear, and perhaps she even convinces herself. She wonders if Phil could even say for sure when she was lying.

'Not till you've given us your statement, Phil,' says Dean, putting a hand out, as though she is going to make a run for the door. 'And for god's sake, let us inform the next of kin first.'

'Of course, Dean, I wouldn't dream of doing any different,' says Phil.

She has such an easy manner about her. Marilla is sure she is a brilliant journalist: knows everyone, can make easy small talk with anyone, isn't afraid to bullshit her way into a hotel. Marilla had laughed until she cried when Phil reenacted her attempt to get past Judith, the evil dragon on the front desk. She is a con artist. Marilla has met plenty in her life – so many faux rich folk with massive overdrafts living the life of Riley and praying the bailiffs don't show up to take away the Jag during the main course.

With a jolt, Marilla wonders if Phil telling her about the front desk woman was just another bit of trickery: giving Marilla a bit of power, telling her a secret, putting her safety in Marilla's hands; it is a great way to get someone to trust you. It had worked too; she doesn't know Phil at all, yet she has entrusted her with so many of her own secrets already.

'Are you warm enough? Do you want me to get you a blanket?' says Phil.

It is true, Marilla is shivering. Probably the shock, she thinks. Brandy, that's another thing they give you, isn't it? Or smelling salts. Or is that for something else? Marilla once found a little pot of smelling salts in her grandmother's jewellery box. She'd fished out the cotton fluff inside and given the bottle a good hard sniff and then clutched her nose in agony as the smell seemed to travel up her sinuses and pierce her brain. What became of granny's smelling salts, she wonders? Her mother probably binned them (after checking if the pot was worth anything, naturally). If Marilla, her sisters and her cousins hadn't commandeered granny's ashes to scatter in the woodland beyond the garden, her mother probably would have binned those too. Like she did with the contents of great-aunt Dodie's greenhouse.

Marilla wonders if her head is spinning from the lack of sleep or the alcohol or the shock. Maybe it is all three. Eggs Benedict would have fixed the problem. Of course, she'll have to ring his parents. Someone should do it sooner rather than later. Or do the police do that? Yes, that's what Dean told Phil, didn't he? So she could cross that one off her to do list. What a relief.

Dean is still talking. She isn't sure what about. The sound provides a comfortable hum for her thoughts to wander over.

He has slept with Phil, Marilla is sure. Phil strikes her as the sort who would cheerfully sleep with whomever is nearest. Marilla wonders if that makes her cool and desirable or cheap and broken. She has inherited her mother's opinion of 'tarts.' That's what happens, isn't it, she thinks? Children just inherit the parents' opinions wholesale until they take the time to look at them under the light. She makes a mental effort to remove 'cheap' from the list of options. 'Broken' can stay for the time being; she isn't done with broken, yet.

Perhaps Phil is trying to make up for something missing

in her life. Perhaps her father didn't love her as a child? Phil has only mentioned a mother, come to think of it. She wonders if she will get the chance to ask Phil about the dad. She expects not. This business with Oli means she will probably be expected back in London to do whatever damage limitation is required.

Marilla thinks: what is Phil's policy when it comes to one-night stands? Is she now cast aside? Is she cheap and broken now, too? She can't imagine Phil ghosting her; she imagines the journalist is probably keen to stay on the right side of people wherever possible in case she needs them for a quote or insider intel in the future. In her swift, unprofessional psychoanalysis, she imagines Phil likes to collect friends and is good at shifting her conquests into the *Friend Zone.*

While she is contemplating her journey to the Friend Zone, another officer appears and Dean heads off to talk to him. When Dean returns Marilla can see he is saying something. With a force of will, she manages to tune back into reality just in time to catch him saying, 'Can you tell me what these were doing in Mr Cromwell's kitchen?'

He is holding up a packet of pills inside a plastic evidence bag.

'They're my sleeping tablets,' Marilla says. 'I don't know why those are in there.'

'How many were in the packet, do you know?' says Dean.

'I can't remember,' says Marilla. She can feel herself panicking slightly, yet still she can't lift the detached feeling in her brain that is making her feel like she is two steps behind reality, living in the minutes after you awake from a Sunday lie-in. 'I only got them a week or so ago, so...'

'And how many do you usually take a day?'

'I don't, really. I only take them if I'm struggling to sleep.'

Dr Findlater, her mother's magical physician, had given her a prescription for the sleeping tablets when she'd seen him about those *Wolf Hall* love handles. He'd given her the diet pills, and some super-strength painkillers for migraines. She knew she didn't really need the diet pills – despite her mother's constant disparagement and endless salads, she had miraculously avoided body dysmorphia – but she was ever-dutiful, and, when her mother's doctor gave her the pills, she had accepted them. This was years ago. She hadn't taken them at the time and there were newer, better diet drugs now, but Dr Findlater still hands these out for those who have grown to enjoy the side effects.

Taking them is like taking speed. On busy days, she is glad of the boost of energy. They help her get her work done, even if they leave her head pounding the day after. The days when the diet pills keep her up are the days she takes a sleeping tablet.

A thought floats by: are diet pills even legal? She isn't sure, suddenly. In fact, it has never been clear to her how legit Dr Findlater is. As she considers this, the other officer reappears. He is holding another plastic evidence bag containing a box of tablets. Marilla's diet pills, taken from his suitcase.

She has no idea how they got into Oli's room.

'Well, they didn't walk there on their own, did they?' says the officer. He is older than Dean, and more sarcastic. She doesn't like him. Her mother would call him an 'oaf'. She explains about her mother and Dr Findlater.

'They're diet pills,' she says. 'They help you lose weight.'

'What weight?' scoffs the oaf, looking her up and down. 'A mouse could blow you over.'

Phil steps in. 'What's your name?'

She seems to be protecting Marilla and Marilla likes the feeling, but she isn't sure why it is happening. Does she need protecting?

'DC Grant Pitman,' says the detective. 'I did introduce myself.' And then he stares at Phil, 'But you know who I am, Ms McGinty.'

'Can't you see she's in shock,' says Phil. 'She needs a doctor or something.'

'She's clearly seen plenty of doctors,' the oaf scoffs, again. Does he have any other settings, wonders Marilla. So far she has seen 'scoff' and 'sarcasm.'

'Miss Hunter-David,' he says, incorrectly. 'I'd like you to come down to the station to answer some questions.'

He is about to take her arm, but stops short and instead points her towards the door.

'But I haven't had any breakfast,' she says. 'Phil and I are going for eggs Benedict.'

'She's in shock. She doesn't understand what you're saying,' says Phil. Marilla wants to protest. She understands just fine, doesn't she? She tries to track down her own thoughts. Somewhere in her brain a little bell has started going off.

The oaf gives Phil a pointed look and sighs. 'Why is it that everywhere there's trouble, there's Philippa bloody McGinty?' he asks.

'Phil, we know how to deal with people in shock,' says Dean. He is trying to reassure her, but it seems to annoy Phil even more.

'How's that? By extracting a false confession and

convincing them their pills killed someone?' Phil seems really furious. She is vibrating with a righteous energy. This must be what it feels like to have a knight in shining armour, Marilla realises.

'You're being ridiculous – as always. You shouldn't believe what you read in the papers,' says the oaf. Grant! That is his name. Marilla is pleased to have remembered.

'You need a solicitor, Marilla,' says Phil.

It sounds like a good idea, but Marilla isn't sure what that involves. Probably she should speak to the family lawyer, Perry. He always likes to talk to Marilla. He is a nice man.

Grant puts up his hands as if trying to herd Phil back away from them. He seems to be making a concerted effort to calm the situation.

'Now why would Marilla need a solicitor? No one's accusing her of anything. She's not under arrest. I'm going to ask you to step aside and let us speak to Miss Hunter-David without you interfering. This is a very tragic, very sad event. I understand that you're both incredibly distressed, but this is an unexplained death and we do need to ask some questions.'

Another detective approaches. She is attractive, in her late thirties – at a guess. She looks tired. Marilla assumes she is of mixed heritage, but equally she might just be Mediterranean. It is hard to be sure because she has olive skin but pale eyes – although Marilla had been to enough south Asian countries to know that pale eyes weren't that uncommon. As the detective approaches, she can see Phil deflating a little, the fire going out of her righteous indignation. She knows this woman too.

'Hello Philippa,' says the woman.

Not another love interest, Marilla realises gratefully. But she's important.

'Hi Jen,' says Phil.

'Grant,' says the woman, 'why don't you take Philippa for a coffee and find a quiet spot to take her statement. Dean and I can finish up here with Marilla before we take her down to the station for a more formal interview.'

Marilla can tell the detective is speaking for her and Phil's benefit, and she appreciates her control of the situation.

'Yes sarge,' says the oaf.

He gives a polite, closed mouth smile to Marilla and heads off. Maybe he isn't such an oaf after all. Perhaps she only thought he was because he is scruffy and his tie is a terrible colour for his shirt and it looks like someone has suffered a stroke in the middle of cutting his hair.

Dear god, she thinks, I really am turning into my mother.

If only there was some kind of conversion therapy you could go on. A kind of anti-conversion therapy, where instead of attempting to fill you with other people's beliefs, they could drive other people's prejudices out like an exorcism. She would pay good money for that. She knows a few people who would. She could probably fill a couple of coaches with young women who would like to undo the lessons their parents taught them. Lessons that were all very well in the clubs around Sloane Square, or on the cracked leather sofas in Wiltshire pubs, but out in the real world, with normal people, make her feel bigoted and a step out of time.

'Shall we head down to the station?' says Jen, although Marilla can tell it isn't really a question.

Phil is going to protest again, but Marilla smiles at her.

'I'll be fine, Phil,' she says. 'I'll see you later.'

Look at the bright side, she thinks. The morning may not

have gone to plan, but at least she now has a punchline for her anecdote.

'And then they carted me off to the station!'

She can see her parents roaring with laughter at the dinner table, her mother covering her mouth with a napkin as she weeps with laughter.

'Oh darling, do tell the story about the time your celebrity friend was found dead surrounded by your tablets.'

Marilla feels herself go cold all over.

NINE

Once Phil finished giving a statement to DC Grant Pitman, Dean Martin tried to get her to leave and Phil implied she absolutely would. When Dean bumped into her half an hour later he gave her a look and she threw up her hands and claimed she was just on her way out. He tried asking the manager to invite Phil to leave, but Ruby Davies apparently had bigger fish to fry. Phil, having already made herself scarce, lingered just around the turn in the corridor and heard Ruby rebuffing Dean's efforts. She was agitated about the body, keen to get Oli Cromwell out of her hotel so the guests weren't distressed.

'I don't want to have an exodus on my hands,' she told Dean. 'I've already had the chairman on the phone twice this morning.'

Clearly, the owners of The Marchmont had employed a woman willing to consider the bottom line in any situation.

'Now, you'll have to excuse me,' Ruby continued. 'I'm sure you can appreciate how busy I am. And, of course, we're always delighted to help here at The Marchmont, so please do ask for anything you need.'

With that, she pounded down the corridor on her court heels, phone already glued to her ear. Clearly there were fans blighting the front entrance already and Ruby couldn't have The Marchmont's illustrious guests picking their way through a bundle of caterwauling teens and tear-tracked middle-aged women. She swept past Phil, discussing the need to organise some floral displays round the side of the building.

'Let's get them away from the entrance. They're an eyesore,' she told the person on the call. 'Encourage them to gather somewhere out of the way.'

Ruby vanished into the lift. And so, somehow, Phil evaded capture. For now, at least.

The first thing she did was make a call.

'Get interviews with everyone.' said Adam Jenkins, editor of *The Aldhill Observer.*

Phil could see him in her mind's eye, pacing, barking orders, barely concealing his delight in the loss of another human life. For him, it was thrilling to have a proper news story happening on his home turf. He dispatched two of his senior reporters to The Marchmont before they even finished talking. Phil tried to convince him to let her write the story, but he wasn't having it.

'No way, José,' he said, pronouncing the J on purpose. 'Barry's coming to save you from yourself. I'm not leaving this to some young pup reporter who doesn't always copy the names correctly off the funeral wreaths.'

'What are you even talking about?' she said.

Still, she dutifully went off gathering quotes from guests

until the bigger boys arrived to take her work. Poodicca rides again.

Most of the quotes she gathered were of the, 'Isn't it terrible, he was so young and handsome,' variety, with a couple of, 'Couldn't care less, thought he was dreadful,' types thrown in, and a surprising number of, 'No idea who he is, dear, don't you have better things to do with your time?' judgments from disapproving retirees.

Many hadn't known Oli was staying here. Presumably the people who could afford a stay at The Marchmont weren't necessarily up to date on the latest film in the *Speed Demon* franchise (*Speed Demon 6: Demon Spawn,* in which Oli Cromwell's character discovers he has a grumpy tween son who steals his car, with hilarious consequences). And even those who had heard of him hadn't seen him in the hotel, which was no surprise, since he hadn't emerged from his suite.

Finally, she spoke to one particularly jittery man who looked like he was searching for his wallet, nervously touching himself all over. He was in the room next to Oli's but had heard nothing. That was odd because the woman in the room below said Oli had been pumping out loud music and action movies late into the night.

'Yes, now you mention it, I did hear his music,' conceded the jittery man, who had reluctantly obliged her by spelling out his name – Llewellyn – but then refused to say if it was his first or his last.

'I heard two women go in as well.'

He remembered that vital detail just as she was wrapping up the interview. He said it with reluctance, as though the inconvenience of getting involved irked him.

'Two women?' Phil had prompted him when he failed to elaborate.

He shuffled in frustration. 'One young woman just after eight and one older woman not long after. There were raised voices, but I couldn't make out what they were saying.'

'Did you tell the police this?'

'I only just remembered,' he insisted, but his eyes darted to the ground.

'You need to ring the police now,' Phil said, feeling a rising anger that surprised her. 'My friend is with them right now answering questions. They think she had something to do with it. You can prove he was still alive after she'd left his room.'

She was being dramatic, she knew. They hadn't even established the cause of death; they were only asking Marilla a few questions. But she couldn't help herself. And anyway, why was he so reluctant to go to the police?

'Authority figures make me nervous,' he said, as though that was a reasonable excuse from a grown man. 'They're bound to think I had something to do with it.'

'And did you?'

He looked at her like she'd just broken wind directly into his face.

'I am here for a quiet holiday.'

She laughed at that, suddenly disarmed.

'Not going too well then, is it? Noisy neighbour who turns up dead and brings journalists and police to your door?'

'I suppose not,' he agreed. 'But I'm quite happy, thank you. Now if you don't mind, I need to pack my things.'

'After you've rung the police, of course, Mr Llewellyn.'

He looked at her peevishly, but eventually nodded. 'Oh, all right, I'll do it now.'

As he headed back into his room, she gave him one of her brilliant broad grins. He didn't seem to notice. Apparently, this hotel did a good line in people who were immune to her charms.

'Oh, before you go,' she said. 'What do you do for a living, Mr Llewellyn?'

He hesitated before replying, as though trying to decide whether to tell her the truth or not. Eventually, he pursed his lips.

'Teacher,' he said.

Phil laughed out loud.

'What's so funny?' he said.

Here was a man who'd spent his life being laughed at by children, Phil thought.

'Sorry, nothing,' she replied.

An authority figure who was afraid of authority figures. What would the world show her next?

Hunger caught up with her and she headed to the breakfast room where a cheerful woman in a blazer stood behind a wooden lectern as though preparing to give a keynote. Phil gave her Marilla's room number and the cheerful woman, whose name badge said 'Anya', led Phil to a table laid with heavy cutlery and crisp white table linen. She was a long way from Roosevelt Court now, Phil thought. She loved where she lived, was proud of it, but boy did this place smell good.

'Can I get you anything from the menu?' said Anya.

Phil had planned to simply raid the buffet and run, but Anya stood there, head cocked, smiling, and Phil found herself ordering eggs Benedict. After all, Marilla had been going on about it, and now she felt duty-bound to honour her plans.

'Wonderful,' said Anya, as though Phil had made the best decision in the world.

Phil filled the time before her eggs arrived by getting herself a tiny glass of orange juice with bits in.

'Isn't it dreadful?' said the woman next to her.

She looked like a Margery or a Miriam; something soft and buttery to go with her cheerful plumpness and the expression of naughty delight in her eyes. If it were nearly anyone else, Phil would say the woman was standing too close to her, but like all good fun gossips, the closeness felt like a cosy connection of intrigue and conspiracy. Phil could imagine her with her feet up in the living room with the cat on her lap and a giant box of chocolates enjoying the latest *Vera*. She liked the comforting warmth of this woman's soft arm pressing into hers.

'He was so young, too,' Margery or Miriam continued. 'Apparently, it was an overdose, but they're not saying if it was suicide or foul play. I think someone poisoned him. Why would a handsome young chap like that want to do that to himself?'

'Awful,' said Phil, mirroring Margery or Miriam's tone.

'I mean, the poor lad. Can you imagine? It doesn't bear thinking about.'

Could Phil imagine Oli Cromwell being dead? Good question. Yes, she could. Currently, when she closed her eyes, it was all she could see. Would Adam Jenkins, editor, make her write up her firsthand account as a clickbait piece for *The Aldhill Observer* website? 'You'll never guess what this journalist found in Oli Cromwell's hotel room.' Or a listicle. '13 things that run through your mind when you find a dead body.' She hoped not, but she wouldn't put it past him. She could imagine Margery or Miriam's delight if she told her she'd been a witness. But Margery or Miriam could buy the paper like everyone else.

'Terrible,' was all she said.

Thankfully, Phil was saved by any further buffet-based gossip by the arrival of her eggs Benedict.

She eyed the hollandaise with suspicion and said a private thanks Marilla wasn't here to witness her prodding at the yellow gunk flowing over her eggs. She had a child's taste in food, something she was trying to evolve out of, but every new taste was a challenge, and being watched while she sampled something made it even harder. Eventually, she tried a small bit off the edge of her knife and decided it was close enough to mayonnaise to risk eating. She took the precaution of scraping the bulk of it off her eggs first, however, leaving her with just a thin glaze to contend with.

After the events of the morning, this felt like more than enough bravery for one day.

Adam Jenkins, editor, might be sending his seasoned reporters to cover the story, but it was hers! She had eyewitnesses and a timeline; she had details from the hotel room; she had quotes from the hotel's various Miriams and Llewellyns to flesh out the tale. But still, Barry Brooker was probably right now pressing his rumpled trousers into the seat of his battered Honda Jazz. Phil had to move fast.

Already the rumours were beginning to ripple around the hotel: he'd had a girl in his room; he had been making so much noise there had been complaints from people in neighbouring rooms; he had been killed by a fan who wanted notoriety for murdering a legend. Phil heard plenty of theories and nearly every one contained a seed of truth. On her way to the second floor, she spoke to a blabbermouth hotel worker called Jay Hamble, who said he wanted to speak off the record and then requested an exorbitant fee for an interview. There had been a few complaints about noise.

'He was having a one-man rave,' said Jay. But it had stopped abruptly late in the evening. 'Maybe that's when he topped himself.'

Phil thanked him, handed him a tenner and suggested he try the national press if he wanted to sell his story. He scurried off, clutching his money, cheeks pink with the thrill of betrayal.

'He probably thought he was like a Russian spy, bless him,' said her mum Angela when Phil rang to update her. 'You made his day.'

Phil left out the details of what happened with Marilla (she was close to her mum, but she wasn't that close), skipping straight from the drinks in the room to the discovery of the dead body and onto the moment where Marilla got taken to the station.

'You did the right thing there,' insisted Angela when Phil questioned if she'd made matters worse by getting angry. 'It sounds like she was in shock. She needed an ally, and you were there for her. Imagine if she says something to incriminate herself and ends up locked up for a crime she did not commit, like the A-Team.'

'Are they like the Central Park Five?' Phil asked.

Her mother launched into a two-minute ramble about the history of the A-Team before Phil established they were fictional characters from the old days of TV.

'I guess I shouldn't stay on the phone too long in case Marilla tries to call,' said Phil. It was impossible to have a truly short conversation with anyone in her family, so it was important to have an emergency exit button ready to press. In this case, an imminent call from the local police station.

'Do you think she did it?' said Angela, ignoring Phil's attempt to extricate herself.

'No, of course she didn't do it,' said Phil. 'She was with me all evening. When would she have had the chance?'

'Phil, you could sleep through anything,' said her mother reasonably.

She wasn't wrong. Phil had been trying not to think about the possibility that Marilla had committed a heinous crime while she slept. She seemed like such a nice person. Considering her life of privilege and gifts, she was surprisingly down-to-earth and Phil had been drawn to her for her open, honest expression as much as her good looks. Plus she laughed at Phil's jokes, which always helped.

'I really hope she didn't do anything, mum,' said Phil. 'But I'd like to know why her pills were in the room with him.'

'Did you see Dean?' Angela asked her out of the blue. 'He's a detective now, isn't he? I did like Dean. I can't believe he became a rozzer.' Angela liked to speak about the police as though she was a seventies criminal instead of a civil servant. She still saw herself as the council estate rebel who had tied herself to railings and marched against everything, rather than the woman who rang social workers to enquire if they'd been disrespectful to the sex offender in their care.

'He was the one questioning Marilla,' Phil admitted. She had conveniently left that bit out of the story. Her mother let out an abrupt laugh.

'You're telling me your ex-boyfriend interviewed your new girlfriend over the corpse of your failed interview subject?'

Her mother had always had a way of distilling a story down to its bare bones, often with a neglectful attitude to the absolute truth – or at least the nuance of a situation. And, of course she had read between the lines and figured out that Phil and Marilla had hooked up.

'We weren't standing over his corpse, mum, that's grim. And I have never heard the word girlfriend used so inaccurately. I know you still think we're all nine years old, but it's not like school. You don't become someone's girlfriend by getting your friend to pass a note to them in class. We literally spent one evening together.'

'Ah, those were simpler times, weren't they?' sighed her mother. She had recently got back into acting, a passion from her youth, and her love of melodrama was being put to good use. 'You'll always be a little baby to me Philbo. Only seems like yesterday I was holding your little hand on the way to school.'

'And on that note, I've got to go.'

She hung up and, just like that, it popped into her brain: she realised who the crying chef was.

TEN

Judith had had a relaxing morning at home. These days she made sure to give herself plenty of little luxuries – a silk robe, cashmere socks, posh tea leaves. The sorts of things Charles used to buy her back when her life belonged to him. For years after she left him, she had been too poor to afford treats, and now they felt vital. On Maslow's Hierarchy of Needs they came above 'Belongingness and Love'. She needed the treats to remind her that she didn't need Charles, nor anyone else for that matter.

Perhaps that's where she had gone wrong.

Her need not to need anyone had made her harder, less loving. But she had adored her son, and had made space for him inside the armour she presented to the rest of the world. It had opened up and wrapped itself around him the moment she laid eyes on his little red body – hands flexing, feet kicking, furious at the indignity and violence of birth. Apparently, that hadn't been enough. Or was it too much? *Engulfment.* That's what he called it. How can you love a child too much?

Ungrateful little shit.

She had left early so she could catch the mid-morning sunshine and pay a visit to the sea. She liked her swimming club pals. They reminded her of friends from her nights working in the clubs, full of laughter and easy chatter. But today she wasn't in the mood for their cheerful camaraderie. Instead, she walked to a different beach further along the promenade where there were beach huts and wildflowers and patches of scrubland; the type of secret, empty beach only locals know about. Stripping off her outer layers with deft efficiency, she tiptoed over the stones and into the cold water, waiting for the shock to shake her out of whatever insanity had taken hold yesterday.

What could have compelled her to go with Charles to a bar last night? She had come to her senses shortly afterwards, excusing herself for the ladies' room and fleeing out the door when he turned his back. She wondered how long he'd sat there before he realised she wasn't returning. And what could he possibly want with her? He wouldn't be interested in her romantically, that was for sure. She had been barely out of her teens when he went to prison, but he had already begun casting about for a younger model. He liked them innocent and unworldly – just as she had been when she met him at fifteen. But a few years later, she had already seen too much and done too much. She had developed a vinegar wit and a sarcastic tone and he didn't like it, and he made sure she knew.

Perhaps he had tracked her down because he had finally found out about the boy. She hadn't told him she was pregnant. She had wanted to start a new life. She didn't want to be surrounded by petty criminals and posturing kingpins, and their tedious obsession with honour and violence and revenge. Even now she couldn't watch TV shows about men in suits shouting and waving their guns – had no interest in their macho world. Organised crime? They were children playing grown-ups.

'Why don't you all just pull down your trousers and I'll let you know whose is the biggest?' she said one day when a group of them were together, jostling for supremacy. Later, Charles made her pay for it.

And yet, when her son grew up to be a drippy and complaining teenager, she couldn't help comparing him to those tough men she had known. Kenneth had been such a cheerful, happy baby, and a lovely, sensitive child, but as a young man, he was just Charles without the charm. Yes, his father had been whiny and immature, easily hurt and offended, quick to bear a grudge, but he also had a silken tongue that could talk himself back into her good graces. Not to mention his uncanny ability to attract money.

Maybe it was her fault – her DNA causing the lack of wit or the clumsy lucklessness. Or perhaps she had raised him badly. People didn't read parenting books back then, no one *she* knew anyway. She thought Dr Spock was Kirk's friend on the Enterprise. Parents didn't spend their time fretting about whether they were doing a good job, and God knows, there were things she did then that no parent would do now.

You see them all the time, she thought. Grandparents ushering their precious grandchildren around parks, watching over them with so much troubled care. *Don't fall.* Tracking their every movement like worried hens. Tutting and clucking. This was the same generation that sent their kids off into the morning air with a jam sandwich, an apple and instructions not to return until the street lights came on.

The attention they now lavished on their grandchildren seemed like some kind of penance, and she knew she would have been the same with her own grandchild. If only she'd had the chance.

She let the cool water freeze her limbs a moment longer, sweeping her hands around her, already looking forward to the endorphin rush that would follow. But she wouldn't stay in too long. A memory came to her, as it always did when she was swimming, of a young woman she had found, disorientated and shivering on the promenade, unable to see properly, unsure who she was and what she was doing there. Judith stayed with her until she had warmed up, wrapping her with a coat and filling her with tea until she recovered her identity and eyesight. The memory made her shudder at the thought of something like that happening to her. When you're a young woman, being saved by kindly strangers is acceptable, but over a certain age, people just assume you are a confused old lady escaped from your care home.

That said, she wouldn't have wanted to be saved as a young woman either. She had spent too many years feeling helpless when she was with Charles.

'Keep me warm,' she used to say, curling into him and staring up through her big false eyelashes. She looked like Jane Fonda in *Barbarella*. She only realised how beautiful she had been when she was older, looking back at photographs.

'Come here, you wally,' he would say, giving her a squeeze. 'You know I'll always take care of you, don't you, Judy?'

He was soon gone, and she was left to take care of herself – and the new life that was growing inside her. And it was a surprise to discover she was capable. Yes, she had done things then she wouldn't do now, but what choice did she have? She used to put Kenneth to bed and then go out to work in the nightclubs, getting home just as he was waking for breakfast, shuffling in bleary-eyed in his flannel pyjamas in search of cornflakes. Or sometimes she would get in and he'd woken early and was already tucking into a bowl, seemingly oblivious to her absence.

'Morning darling,' she would say, sweeping him into a fierce hug and lavishing him with kisses. 'How's my beautiful boy?'

He would pat her on the face and then wriggle away, the bowl of cornflakes calling him back. It seemed amazing to her now – that she had left him on his own like that. The very idea! Back then, houses were always burning down – forgotten fag butts, flammable furniture, dodgy wiring, faulty cookers. The entire flat must have been one huge fire risk. The thought of leaving a small boy locked inside to fend for himself gave her the heebie-jeebies. Carol next door had always kept an ear out for him, of course, and she did the same for Carol when it was her night out on the razzle, but even so. It was the sort of parenting that would get your child taken away from you now.

Mind you, she saw much worse along the promenade.

She may have been physically absent, but she was never physically violent – a couple of clips round the ear notwithstanding, and that time she'd slapped him for calling her a slag when he was twelve (apparently it was what his friends called girls and he didn't know what it meant). But aside from that, she'd been the picture of patience and good humour.

That's how she liked to remember it, anyway.

Immersed in her reverie, she had stayed in the water longer

than she intended. With a start, she stepped out of the cold waters and headed straight for her towel. It was all there ready in her waterproof bag: towel, hot drink, warm clothes, two pairs of socks. She was battle-hardened, but she always brought her supplies just in case, always remembering the bewildered young woman on the promenade. She could feel the shivering starting, and with the shivering came the euphoria. She'd read it kept dementia at bay, which was a nice side effect, but really she was just in it for the high. She dressed quickly and sat for a moment, sipping a little of her hot tea before packing her stuff away. It was better to get on the move as quickly as possible, and now she collected her things, slung away the dregs of the tea and stepped off the pebbles onto the lower promenade.

Last Christmas, Kenneth sent a card out of the blue. He hadn't sent her one for her birthday two months before, perhaps that would have felt too personal. But a Christmas card – given alongside client gifts and notes to the bin men – apparently felt anonymous enough. A perfect tentative outreach to your estranged mother. When she spotted the handwriting she started quivering, afraid it would contain more reproachful parenting critique. Nothing so thoughtful, sadly. Despite her fear of further tin-pot analysis and peevish judgments on her fitness as a mother, it was something of a disappointment when it turned out to be so much less personal than that.

'Dear mother... Love Ken.'

She had stared at it a good long while, trying to parse it. What did it mean? Dear was a good start, but mother was less promising. To her mind, mother was what you called someone to whom you reluctantly issued a faint peck on the cheek at Sunday lunch once a month. Love seemed fairly straightforward, but then again, why not 'lots of love' or 'all my love'? Was that really the most he was prepared to give? An indeterminate amount of love? It was a start, she supposed. At least it wasn't 'regards' or 'best,' which people seemed to write on emails nowadays instead of something more formal like 'sincerely' or 'faithfully'.

But then she came to the final sign off. Ken was an odd choice. She had scrutinised that bit the longest, trying to work out what he could have meant by it. No one ever called him Ken when he was a boy. He was Kenny or Kenneth, or – most likely – Kenny-darling ('Kenny-darling, get mummy another drink'). Ken was someone else, someone she had never met. Is that what his wife called him? Did his work colleagues invite a man called Ken out for after-work drinks? Kenneth had been her grandfather's name. She knew it was old-fashioned when she picked it, but she had loved her grandfather and to her the name felt sacred. Ken seemed like a totally different person.

She would need to hurry up if she wanted a shower before her shift started. And she definitely needed a shower. Whatever horrors lay in the water – toxic waste, bird shit, effluence – she'd lived long enough without troubling too much about those, but she didn't want to get after-drop and start wandering the hotel lobby like a confused granny. And really, given the option, she'd rather wash any effluent off than not.

After the 'Ken,' the thing about the card that troubled her the most was the full stop. So final, so formal. And no kiss. She didn't know what to do with the card. And nearly a year had passed, and it was still perched on her mantelpiece, tucked behind a plant pot. She'd heard nothing from him since, not even on her birthday, but perhaps this year he would send another card?

She stopped. Something wasn't right at the hotel. First glimpse suggested it was just Oli Cromwell fans, camping out in the hope of seeing their hero, and assembled members of the press waiting for his promised junket, although he hadn't left his room since he arrived as far as Judith could tell. But a closer look told a different story. Yes, there were the fans, but many seemed to be holding candles or flowers or teddy bears. And, yes, there were members of the press – buzzing around like grubby little flies eyeballing a squatting dog – but there was a third group too. Police. What were they doing here? And was that an ambulance?

She felt her pulse quicken.

'Ah, there you are, Judith,' said Ruby, the child-manager, heading her way. She looked like Margaret Thatcher heading into Number 10: head lunging forward like a chicken racing towards a juicy worm, one arm out stiff, as though a handbag was hooked over it. Ruby the manager was accompanied by a young man who smiled cheerfully. Despite their different skin tone, he reminded her of Colin, the beautiful man who'd taught her to knit in that Brixton squat.

'Judith, this is DC Grant Pitman.'

Ruby had reached her now and was standing too close, the buzz from her skin making Judith's hackles raise.

'He wants to have a word with you about last night,' Ruby was saying.

'What do you mean?' Judith said. 'I have no idea what you're talking about.'

Her heart was pounding.

'About last night's tragedy,' said Ruby, puzzled.

'I don't...' Judith began, then tailed off. She was feeling a little disorientated. She thought of the woman on the promenade.

'Have you not heard?' said Ruby, failing to mask her delight at being the one to share the news. 'Oli Cromwell was found dead last night. Suspected murder.'

'Are you alright, miss?' said the constable, looking at Judith with concern.

But Judith just stood there, her whole body quivering, teeth chattering, her mind a fog of confusion. She couldn't see. She couldn't breathe. She gasped for air, and felt a hand grasp her by the elbow as she stumbled towards the floor.

ELEVEN

Marilla thought DC Dean Martin was one of the most beautiful boys she had ever seen. He had kind dark eyes – framed with ridiculously curly eyelashes – dark skin and the mouth of an Adonis. Or maybe she was just tired and emotional, and his clear complexion was the only thing keeping her together right now. There was a good chance she was still wearing yesterday's beer goggles and that, at some point, she'd look up from the interview desk and he'd just be an average twenty-something with a kind face. There was a chance, too, that she was just comparing herself to Phil's ex and finding herself wanting.

She was confident he was the ex. She had asked him outright in the car on the way to the station and he had mumbled and looked down at the floor.

'Bit awkward, this, isn't it?' Marilla had said eventually, the silence of the journey beginning to get to her. 'Not every day you get to arrest your ex-girlfriend's... you know...'

Oh god. She wished she hadn't said that. It wasn't exactly good chit chat, was it? Trying to have a laugh with a copper over a girl you'd both had sex with. Especially not when you're heading to be interviewed about the death of your boss. Marilla would rather be checking out Phil's ex-lovers the old-fashioned way – by stalking them on social media. Doing it from the back seat of a police car left her at a very uncomfortable disadvantage. DC Dean Martin was visibly squirming.

'You two think it's awkward,' said Detective Sergeant Jen Collet. 'Imagine what it's like for me.'

The detective stared ahead and Marilla took the hint, shifting in her seat to look out her own window. Outside, it was shaping up to be a lovely day. Over on the green near the seafront, a fair was setting up, the colourful lorries glinting in the morning sunshine. Excited children gaped at the caravan and began tugging at their parent's sleeves, hoping for an evening of wonder. Marilla's parents thought the fairground vulgar, of *course*. It wasn't until she was at boarding school that she had the chance to sample the delights of the dodgems, her lips covered in spun sugar as she tramped through the muddying field arm in arm with her friends. It had been a fun day until she found herself round the back of the waltzers vomiting cider and toffee apples onto the damp lawn.

Not the best daydream to have right now: her stomach was feeling volatile enough without memories of past excesses. She would give anything to be back at the hotel with Phil, eating eggs Benedict, nursing her hangover, laughing about their evening, groaning about the day ahead. Wondering what to do with a peevish and truculent Holly-wood star. But now the star was dead and Marilla's hangover was the least of her worries.

Marilla thought about the time she had walked in on him

– a few months ago now. He was crying his eyes out. He'd been living in a hotel while his house was extended and refurbished. The house, already massive, only recently refurbished, was apparently, 'too small and looking tired.' Marilla suspected he preferred living in the hotel. Attention on tap. He would ring down to the front desk for the slightest thing – to ask the time, to get weather updates, to flirt with the clerk on the front desk. And food was available day or night. He may be loaded, but he still didn't feel quite rich enough to employ live-in staff. He'd have to move to the US for that, anyway. Then he could employ a load of immigrants and take away their passports for safe keeping.

'That's what I've been told anyway,' he whined when he noticed Marilla's eyes boggle. She came from money, but even her family drew the line at slavery – in modern times, that is. She hadn't yet looked into the true source of the Hunter Davy fortune, but she suspected she wouldn't like what she found.

'I know, I know,' he said. 'It didn't seem right to me either, but that's just the way they do things over there. Can't argue with that, can you?'

What could he do? He really wanted those live-in staff and he was willing to 'pay a heavy price' to get them. She was impressed how he cast himself as the true victim in all this. She imagined the slave owners of yore managed their consciences in much the same way: 'It's just the nature of the economy, what's to be done? It's really out of our hands.'

She had rushed over when she saw him crying. He looked so pathetic, perched on the edge of his giant white hotel sofa, chewing on his fingernail, tears trickling down his beautiful face, shoulders shaking with misery. She thought someone must have died.

But no.

'I think I might have sexually assaulted someone,' he said.

It had taken her a while to calm him down enough to speak. He kept looking at her, shaking his head, biting his nail down so far the bed was getting raw. He was in his grey tracksuit bottoms. He cupped a hand over his privates, like a child with a comforter.

'I think I might have sexually assaulted someone.'

He'd been reading an article about some male celebrities who had been cancelled for inappropriate contact with women.

'It made me wonder if maybe I'd done something similar,' he said.

'Right,' Marilla had managed to reply eventually. She wasn't sure how to proceed. What did he want her to say? 'Never mind, I'm sure you didn't mean it. There, there. Promise not to do it again?'

Her mind started racing. I should ring Della and tell her our client is a sex pest; I suppose I'll have to find a new job; he thinks he's sexually assaulted someone? How is that possible? I need to cancel tonight's awards. Should I call the police? That poor girl; I bet there were others.

She wasn't proud of the litany of thoughts, especially the self-serving ones. But she could cope with her treacherous brain so long as her actions were right.

'Who have you told?' she said.

Failed at the first hurdle.

'No one.'

She remembered walking over to the window. Outside, the city lights were glowing. People rushing home or to bars, blissfully unaware that right above them a Hollywood A-lister was confessing to rape.

'She was asleep. I didn't think she'd mind,' he said. 'Only, then she woke up and... turned out she did mind.'

'Right,' said Marilla.

What she wanted to say was, 'Of course she minded. What the hell were you thinking?' She tried to imagine what it would be like to have a man looming over you when you woke up, pumping away. What a grim thought.

'She started shouting and crying and saying I'd violated her. I told her I hadn't meant anything by it. It was just a laugh. But then she started threatening to ring the police. So I said I was truly sorry, and I'd do anything to change it. I told her she was beautiful, and I just felt so overwhelmed at seeing her there. She was lovely, you know? She cheered up after that. I took her out for lunch, bought her some flowers, told her how great she was.'

What was he after? Benediction? Did he think the flowers made up for the assault? Was she supposed to pat him on the head and tell him he'd done the right thing? Did he think it wasn't his fault because the girl had been so beautiful? A thought soured in Marilla's mind and began to curdle: if he was so sorry about the rape, why did he pester Marilla constantly for sexual favours? He wasn't sorry at all. Marilla had forgiven him so many transgressions, brushed them off as just a bit of laddishness, or just a typical guy doing what guys do. But she was part of the problem. Girls would continue to get raped, would continue to let it slide in the face of a handsome man's self-pitying apologies, would continue finding ways to convince themselves it hadn't been that bad, because the alternative was so much worse. And people like Marilla would fail to make it stop.

Probably this girl knew there was nothing to be gained from telling the police or the papers. The police would be reluctant to prosecute a star for fear of unwanted attention; the press would blame the girl for being naïve enough to go to his room in the first place. What did she expect was going to happen? Did she not know that when a man offers you a massage and a glass of champagne, you should run like the wind? No, easier for the girl to just shrug it off and remind yourself how lucky you are to catch the eye of someone like Oli Cromwell.

Thinking about it now in the back of this police car made Marilla's stomach churn. She had sat there that day, unsure what to say, running through all the worst-case scenarios, coming up with possible solutions, composing mealy-mouthed non-apologies in her mind.

What she wanted to say was, 'You're a disgusting pig. You made a young woman feel like your behaviour was her fault. You reminded her she was mortal and made her feel afraid.'

But she didn't. And when it came down to it, she suffered similar treatment herself and kept her mouth shut.

She looked at the bright palm trees and the wide prome-nade and all the people heading off to the sea or to buy donuts or to lie in the sunshine and she wished she could take back the last twenty-four hours of her life. Or maybe even more than that. Maybe if she could go back to the day she found Oli Cromwell crying on a hotel sofa she could do everything differently. But if she had, she would never have come to the hotel, never have met Phil, and Oli Cromwell would still be at large, leaving a trail of sad-eyed young women in his wake.

The female officer – Jen – escorted her from the car.

Marilla was willing to bet the detective, with her olive skin, got asked where she was from by people who were desperate to get her origin story. This was a micro-aggression, Marilla had learned. They told them that at her company's unconscious bias training. Marilla had initially found that hard to understand and had felt a little prickly and defensive. She had asked people about their heritage, but only out of a genuine sense of curiosity and interest – the same way you might ask about what a person did for a living or enquire after their siblings. There was no judgment and no racial bias. At least, she hoped not.

It was only when she was eating lunch later, after the unconscious bias training had been ticked off HR's list, that she thought about her own background. She would find it exhausting to have to explain her heritage any time someone enquired. What would she say?

'I come from a long line of privilege and unearned wealth.'

She would certainly feel defensive. Not only was there the dubious source of her family fortune to consider, she couldn't entirely vouch for all of their loyalties during World War II either. If the boot were on the other foot, she would rather not have to explain that her origin story began with a clutch of Norman and Anglo-Saxon high flyers and ended with weak chins and off-shore trusts. After that realisation she resolved never to ask. Let people exist on their own merits, for better or worse.

'Just through there,' said Jen.

Currently, Marilla thought, her own merits seemed to be falling more on the worse side than the better. She took a breath and walked into the interview room.

TWELVE

DS Jen Collet had opted to drive the witness back to the station. That was a mistake. It hadn't been long into the journey before she had begun wishing she'd left the new DC to drive and made her own way there. Perhaps on the bus. She shouldn't be expected to sit in the car with these two – one of them trying to sound the other out, the other (the copper, no less), trying to melt into the footwell in embarrassment. But of course it had to happen to her. It pretty much summed up her luck in life. They had all sat in silence after the posh girl's attempt at small talk had backfired (thank god). Now Jen just needed to get through the rest of the day.

She had left Grant back at the crime scene to finish up the interviews. He was a good copper in general, but she could do without some of his more loutish tendencies. He'd probably be annoying the SOCOs and patronising the female witnesses. For him that would count as a good day.

She looked in her rearview mirror at Marilla. The girl was shook up, there was no doubt about it. But that didn't mean anything. In days of yore (not so long ago, really), police had been taught to follow their gut, to eyeball anyone acting shifty. But these days, their training was keen to stress that people don't always act the way you might imagine. The girl seemed jumpy and stressed, but she had just seen a dead body. There was no playbook telling humans how to react when they find a corpse. Especially not the corpse of an erstwhile boss. Too many mistakes had been made by people jumping to conclusions. So Jen kept an open mind. But she still pinned 'suspect was jumpy and stressed' to her mental Crazy Wall along with the prescription tablets. She could always mentally bin it all later.

The young woman was bound to be a problem. Jen smelled money on her. Even with the police making the most innocent enquiries, she was likely to start calling in the legal teams. People like Marilla wanted a solicitor present when they passed wind in case anyone accused them of stinking up the joint. God forbid they answer a straight question with a straight answer. She assumed it was because the truly wealthy so often lived close to the line of the law, skirting near to breaking tax rules or bending import regulations, winning hefty government contracts with a newly minted limited company. They imagined everyone else was up to no good because they usually were themselves.

Jen was expecting to have the mayor on the phone in the next half hour. She would be keen to make sure the police were seen to be doing all they could. And the DI would appear at some point to throw his weight around. DI Lee Hudson, king of the smug git tribe. A man who snorted contempt through his nostrils so many times a day it was a miracle he hadn't blown his septum. He'd come barrelling in any second demanding updates and wanting to know why nothing was being done. Jen half suspected he waited out in the hallway for the right moment so he could make yet another big entrance. She still looked back fondly on the day he had tripped as he entered and ended up stumbling into the edge of a desk, catching his groin. He had walked funny for the rest of the afternoon. It had made her week.

Jen listened carefully as Marilla ran through the day's events: the arrival at the hotel, Oli's reluctance to honour any of his engagements (including one with his parents) and Marilla's decision to drink her cares away in the hotel bar with a stranger. A stranger who turned out to be a journalist from the local paper hoping for an exclusive. Had she slightly misjudged Marilla, Jen wondered? Maybe she wasn't one of those suspicious rich women after all. She had invited a journalist up to her room, which seemed to Jen the actions of someone without guile. Or maybe there had been something in it for Marilla. She was a publicist, getting publicity was her job. Still, it seemed a risky choice. Better to just take the journalist straight to Oli's room if she wanted him to do an interview.

'We were slightly worse for wear by that point,' said Marilla by way of explanation. She flushed slightly. There was another reason.

'And you were having fun just the two of you?' said Jen. Marilla flushed again. Jen had gathered from the awkward car ride that Marilla and the journalist had hooked up, and now she knew for sure. It wasn't a case of quid pro quo (a press interview), it was just an old fashioned one-night stand.

'Ok, so you two had some drinks, had some laughs, and... whatever else,' Jen waved the detail away. 'And then you decided to go and see Oli after all.'

'Yes, well, once we'd had more to drink, it started to feel like a good idea,' said Marilla sheepishly.

We've all been there, thought Jen.

'And to be honest,' Marilla continued, 'I didn't think Oli would mind.'

'Why's that?' said Jen.

'Well, he is a party guy,' Marilla replied. Her face dropped. 'Was. Was a party guy. He tended to stay up very late and he hated being alone.'

This news didn't surprise Jen, but she pinned it to her mental Crazy Wall nevertheless. *Suspect hated being alone.* It wasn't a reason to kill yourself, but perhaps his isolation had triggered something in him.

'So, asking you to leave him alone was out of character, you'd say?' said Jen.

'No,' said Marilla. 'Because he often had a nap in the afternoon. He was a party guy like I say, so he tended to lie in or sleep whenever he could. That way, he could stay up till late every night and still look good the next day. But it was weird that he didn't summon me back later on. That was definitely out of character.'

'So, why didn't you go and check on him at that point?'

'Because I'm not his mother? And because I was having a well-earned evening with a new friend?' Marilla was irritated. Rightly so, in Jen's view. Why should she have checked on a grown man? But she still felt the young publicist had something she wasn't quite saying. Something she might have wanted to get off her chest.

'And maybe you were a little annoyed with him?' said Jen. 'I know I'd have been annoyed with him.'

'Yeah, I was a little annoyed,' Marilla conceded. 'If he was feeling a bit lonely... Well, that was probably what he deserved after ruining those kids' day.' She looked up suddenly, alarm registering on her face.

'But I didn't know he was going to kill himself,' said Marilla. 'I would have absolutely gone to check on him if I'd known he was feeling suicidal.'

'I'm sure you would,' said Jen. And she meant it. She looked at the young woman for a while, deciding what to say next. 'You think he killed himself, then?'

'Well, yes,' said Marilla, pink rising in her cheeks. 'It seems the likeliest explanation, doesn't it?' She looked at Jen, waiting for an answer.

'Yes,' agreed Jen. 'It does.'

Marilla's eyes welled with tears at that.

'Poor Oli. I should have checked on him.'

'Like you say, you weren't to know.'

Marilla chewed on a nail, her other arm hugging her stomach, her leg jiggling.

'It's easy to say that, but really I'm going to wonder for the rest of my life if I couldn't have done something more.'

Jen nodded and stared at Marilla in mute sympathy. She would be the same – surely there must have been signs? Time to ask. She began gently.

'And... thinking back over the past week – I know this is hard to do, Marilla, but just do your best – can you think of anything out of the ordinary, anything unusual?'

A pause while she thought. 'Nothing springs to mind,' she said and Jen studied her face, trying to decide if she was telling the truth. She knew better than to imagine she could really spot when someone was lying – had read enough about human failings when it came to identifying falsehoods. Nevertheless, they all did it, all secretly believed they could buck the trend. But all of a sudden, Marilla wasn't giving anything away. No more nail chewing or self-soothing. In fact, she was frowning, giving the question serious thought and coming up with something.

'The cancelling plans,' said Marilla. 'That was out of the ordinary.'

'Because he was a party guy?'

Marilla nodded. 'He loved attention, buzzed off it. He couldn't get enough of hearing fans screaming his name.' She smiled. 'I honestly believe that if he didn't have a publicist to prevent him, he'd have turned up at anything he was invited to – supermarket openings, second-hand car dealership promotions – he'd have no discernment whatsoever. We always joke about what a tart he is...'

Marilla trailed off, looking guilty. Jen cocked her head and smiled.

'It's easy to forget, isn't it? That someone you cared for has died.' Marilla nodded and squeezed her eyes shut.

'Did you care for him?'

'Not in the way you're implying, no,' said Marilla, a hardness entering her tone. Jen was pleased to hear it. So she had some steel about her, after all, she thought – the sort of person who would suffer fools, but only up to a point.

'How did he seem to you?' said Jen, changing the subject. 'You know – in the days leading up to his death.'

'The same as always,' said Marilla. 'Sometimes a bit glum, but that was normal for him – his moods tended to flip-flop somewhat. You know, cheerful one minute, towering gloom the next. But it was always short-lived and always about something trivial – some awards snub or a part he didn't get or whatever – and he was usually bouncing around again a few hours later.'

'Bouncing?' said Jen. 'How so?'

Marilla looked at her. 'Are you asking if it was natural bounciness or drug-induced?'

'It's certainly a consideration,' replied Jen. 'After all, he did have your drugs in his room.'

'As far as I knew, it was just his natural state, but you're right I suppose, it could have been drugs.'

'Let's talk about your prescriptions,' said Jen. 'What were they doing in Mr Cromwell's kitchenette?' She hadn't noticed how ridiculous the word kitchenette sounded until she said it out loud. Thirty-five years on this planet and she couldn't remember ever using that word.

'I have no idea,' said Marilla, throwing up her hands.

Jen thought she had the slightly hunted look that interview subjects often get when they feel suspicion falling on them.

'Care to hazard a guess?'

'Not really, no,' said Marilla, eyes beginning to fill with tears again.

'And how did you have so many? It's more than a GP would prescribe at a time.'

Jen had been given sleeping tablets after Nate died. The doctor had given her a measly four in a blister packet and told her to come back if she needed more. Which she did – more than once.

'Where did you get them from?' she asked, but she was willing to guess the answer. The pills almost certainly came from someone less conscientious – the sort of medical professional used to catering to the needs of a rich clientele. She was entering dangerous territory. One wrong move and the family's favoured law firm would descend.

'He did sometimes steal my prescriptions,' said Marilla,

apparently ignoring all the other questions and returning to why Oli Cromwell had the pills.

'Steal?' said Jen, frowning slightly.

'Not steal, exactly.' Marilla looked flustered. 'I knew he was taking them. He would ask for them sometimes.'

'And what did you tell him?' Jen said.

'I told him he couldn't have them.' Marilla picked at the stitching on her sleeve. It was something pricey and she was ruining the cuffs. Jen resisted the urge to tell her to stop.

'So you never let him take your pills?' said Jen. And she could almost hear the sound of solicitors from some venerable firm in London pressing the ignition buttons on their Mercedes and speeding along the potholes towards Aldhill-on-Sea. Marilla swallowed.

'I don't think I should answer any more questions until I have my lawyer with me,' she said.

THIRTEEN

'Oi oi!' said Phil.

Phil was poking her head around the swinging fire doors, grinning at Callum Geering, a boy she'd been at school with and The Marchmont's sous chef.

'Fuck off, Phil,' said Callum, blowing out a cloud of sweet vanilla vapour.

She snapped a photo of him without warning on her posh camera.

'What are you doing?' Callum said.

'Just getting some candid snaps – it's good practice,' she said.

'Bollocks,' he replied. 'Everyone knows you work for the paper, Phil. That had better not end up in print or I'll sue.'

'Sure you will, Callum,' she replied, grinning blithely.

'Well, it's lovely to see you and all that, but I'm working, so...' He leaned forward and made a little scooting motion with his hands. 'Bugger off.'

'Looks like you're on your break,' said Phil.

Phil and Callum were back at the fire exit, but this time

Phil wasn't hiding behind the door. She also wasn't standing outside: she wasn't about to risk the door closing on her again, and she didn't want to be kicked out. She assessed him. He was bulkier and less cheerful than he had been at school. She hadn't known him that well, but he'd seemed a nice enough boy – albeit one into the usual vices favoured by teenagers. Namely, sex and drugs and petty shoplifting.

She would love to just ask him outright what he was doing, bawling his eyes out next to the hotel bins yesterday afternoon, just before a man was found dead. She had always been a plain speaker, her family not really the type that skirted round an issue, but she'd discovered in her years spent talking to members of the public that not everyone appreciated being asked a straight question. And they didn't like talking about death, either. *Passed, fell asleep, moved on* – all euphemisms for dying that a lot of the mourners she spoke to seemed to prefer. But she had never found a use for euphemisms.

'My dad died.' Even that was no good. It sounded too past tense, when in fact it was still truly present – and future: 'My dad is dead. My dad will be dead. ' Always and every day. It was so clear to her that her father had not *moved on* – was not simply *in a better place.*

If Clive had moved on, she was sure she'd still be able to hear him wherever he was, and she'd certainly have heard him leaving; he was larger than life and loud, too. He could never make an exit without coming back to chat a little bit longer, he was the king of the fifteen goodbyes. Clive never left quietly like he did when he died, vanishing suddenly, missing for hours, found silent and entombed in the cavity wall at a school building renovation.

He was dead.

HE IS DEAD!

Just like the film star in room 301.

'So come on then,' said Phil. 'What's the goss? Who does everyone think did it?'

Callum took a suck on his vape and smiled up to the heavens. The face of a man who was getting exactly what he'd expected. 'Phil, you're a nosy little shit aren't you?'

He shook his head ruefully and smiled at the floor. Everywhere but at her, she noted.

'Yep,' she agreed. 'It's literally my job. I'm paid to be a nosy little shit. Come on, though, there must be some theories going around. He's a film star! They don't just turn up dead on the floor of a second-rate hotel in the Arse End of Nowhere-on-Sea.'

'Oi!' said Callum, 'We're not second-rate. We got mentioned in the Michelin guide five years ago.'

'That before you started here was it, Callum?'

'Ooh, cutting. I have not missed the Phil McGinty banter.'

What he didn't know was that Phil simply had a gift for speaking other people's languages. With the popular girls she could gossip and chat about hair, with the brainy crew she could formulate opinions on the state of modern society, with the sporty lot she could criticise the back six. But what no one really noticed was that she mostly just asked them all questions. She was a born reporter. Or, nosy little shit, depending on how you liked to frame things.

'I'll have you know I'm the sous chef here now,' he continued. 'I'll be in charge in a year or two.'

'Oh really?'

'Chef's heading for a heart attack any day now. He can't get through a service without stopping to lean on the worktop and do some heavy breathing. We're all just standing there, waiting to see if he's going to collapse on this shift or the next.' He winked at her, 'I'm thinking of starting a sweepstake. You want in?'

'What a charming working environment. Doesn't sound at all toxic,' said Phil. She was ready to push her luck, but first she wanted to disarm him with a few more insults. She wasn't sure why so many men loved being ribbed, it must be how they knew they were loved, while for a lot of women, it was how they broke each other into a thousand little pieces. 'You must be really talented if your path to leadership relies on your boss dying.'

'How's your career doing, Phil? I saw your dog poo exposé. Was that the moment you peaked?'

'No, I reckon I've got a few more high-profile pieces like that in me, Callum. For example, I heard there's a celebrity dead in the hotel I just happened to have been staying in last night. Rumour has it, he died from eating your food. Care to comment?'

She held out her phone like a mic and Callum turned extremely pale. Not what Phil was expecting at all.

'What's the matter, Callum?' she said. 'Is there something you want to tell me?'

'What? No, you daft cow,' Callum recovered his bluster, but it felt forced. Normally she'd have made a thing about the 'cow', but she wanted him to keep talking. Another skill with being a good interviewer was knowing when to shut your mouth and let someone dig themselves a hole.

'I didn't do the dinner shift. I wasn't on until a lot later. So if anyone killed him, it wasn't me.'

'He didn't use the restaurant last night,' said Phil. 'He did order room service, though. Chicken salad and a side of fries.'

She didn't tell him how she knew that, didn't mention that she had found him lying next to the remnants of his meal on a tray, the mayonnaise congealing on his plate, cold chips brushing his bare leg.

'Nothing to do with me,' said Callum. 'But I like the idea that you think I poisoned Oli Cromwell.'

His smile was fixed. Perhaps he was just high – flying and trying to keep his shit together. She would have asked him normally, but she had the feeling she had just one or two questions left before he told her to shove it. He had that look about him – a man ready to bolt. Her next question needed to be carefully considered.

'So come on, then. Who took up his room service?'

FOURTEEN

Callum Gearing stuffed the chef's whites into the staff laundry basket, grabbed his bag from his locker and headed out.

The events of the day had rattled him. Police everywhere, chaos out in the front of the building, teenagers lurking round the back where he took his vaping breaks. They'd closed the gates at the rear eventually, with extra security keeping the place effectively on lockdown, no one in or out without checking with the doorman first. And of course Phil McGinty had been there, somehow. She'd always had a gift for sniffing out trouble (was that what he was now – trouble?) At the start of school it meant she was going to uncover your transgressions and then dob you in to the teacher, but after her father died, she was more likely to be seeking out trouble so she could join in. Not that she went off the rails in any real sense. To Callum, it seemed more that she wanted to be where the action was.

Perhaps it took her mind off her dad. It can't have been easy. Callum's dad had died a year ago and that had been tough enough. God knows what it would be like for a teenager. Phil's dad Clive was a great laugh. Popular in the area, larger than life, always ready with a joke. He'd been Father Christmas in the shopping arcade, the leaf-covered 'Jack in the Green' in the May Day parade, and a booming pirate leading the treasure hunt at the Pirate Day festivities. When Clive died, it felt like the whole town had come out to watch the funeral cortège pass, many of them dressed in costumes, others wearing their most extravagant finery knowing how much Clive loved an opportunity for a party.

You could barely move in the funeral service. So he'd heard, anyway. Callum hadn't been there – he'd been one of the mourners on the roadside. He hadn't known Phil and her father well enough to get a seat in the service. Instead, he dressed up in his own dad's old wedding suit from the early nineties. Grunge hadn't reached their little seaside town when his dad married; they were still in the dying remnants of the previous decade. Callum stood waving and clapping like an eighties throwback, all shiny grey suit and shoulder pads. He wouldn't get into it now. He'd always been a big bloke, but years of working as a cook had broadened him in every way possible. He knew how to make crème pât, but he also knew how to eat it. He was younger than his dad had been on his wedding day and already too broad to fit in the suit he'd worn.

The police hadn't spoken to him, partly because he kept making himself scarce any time he saw a uniform, and partly they were still treating Cromwell's death like a suicide. Perhaps if he was lucky they wouldn't seek him out at all. God knows, he could do without their attention: the last thing he needed was the cops breathing down his neck when he had a baby on the way. Liane's announcement had coincided with his own promise to give up his life of petty crime and focus on his cooking. No more deals on the side, now he had an incentive to turn into the sort of upstanding citizen who gets to watch their kids grow up.

Turns out, it's not that easy to break away from the drugs trade. Callum's boss apparently viewed it as a job for life. Liane might have recently discovered she wasn't, after all, a 'valued member of the team' now that she was pregnant, but he apparently was. They had offered him all kinds of perks when they found out about the pregnancy. They were this close to offering six months paid paternity leave and private healthcare. He hadn't told them about the baby, of course – it's just that word gets around.

'Yo, Callum, what's this I hear about your missus being knocked up?' said Dan Mehta.

He'd walked up behind Callum on his way to work one afternoon and then proceeded to accompany him the whole way along the promenade.

'Who told you that?' said Callum.

He stopped and turned towards Dan, feeling the cortisol and adrenaline sending his heart into overdrive. He would have happily thumped Dan right there and then, but Dan threw up his hands in surrender.

'Woah, woah, woah chief! No need for all that big man stuff. We're friends, you and me, innit? I know when a man's telling me to back off. Didn't mean nothing by it, I swear. Ain't got nothing but respect for you and your fam.'

Dan was a slippery little shit. He had been a nice middle class Hindu boy at school, but slowly he'd transformed into a bag man for the big boss. He hadn't quite nailed the patter though, continuing to sound like a good boy doing a bad impression of a tough gangster, complete with the pimp roll. But on Dan it was more 'spiv with a limp' than 'playa'.

Callum had once seen Dan out with two Indian women, talking like he'd just arrived on the last flight from Kolaphur, natty in his smart clothes and slick hair, giving it all the 'Yes mummy, yes aunty.' If only they knew.

Dan leaned in and put his hand on Callum's arm. Callum wanted to grab it and fling the little arsehole into the sea.

'Yo, it's nice, man! It's *nice* you're having a baby. I'm happy for you,' said Dan. 'We're all happy for you, bruv.'

Callum set his jaw and continued walking.

'We thought we'd have a whip round, yeah?' said Dan, tripping along next to Callum, skinny legs taking double-quick steps to keep up with the chef's big stride. 'We could get you something nice for the baby. A present.'

'We don't want a present,' Callum said. 'We don't want anything from you.' He was keeping his voice down, trying not to draw attention, realising how his anger might look: like a white man was about to commit a hate crime. A few people glanced their way, and Callum made a conscious effort to open his fists and take a step back. Dan's face broke into a slow smile.

'Alright chief, don't have a coronary. You had your blood pressure checked recently, yeah? You look like my uncle just before he had the bypass. You need a sip of water, bro?'

'It's very kind of you, Danny,' Callum said, speaking precisely – like a man with a new set of teeth. 'But we're good. There's no need to get us *anything*.'

In the silence that followed, Callum felt the temperature drop.

'Are you saying,' said Dan, eventually, 'that you're too

good to take a present from your old friends, is that it, bruv? Because let me assure you, we find that a little bit hurtful. Nah, nah,' Danny brushed off Callum's conciliatory gesture. 'No need to apologise. We feel you chief, we hear you loud and clear. Our money's no good to you – we hear you, bro.'

'Danny,' began Callum.

'You don't want to run with us no more, innit? You've got your job, your girlfriend and your baby – whole new life.'

At the mention of his family, Callum's anger returned. He got very close to Danny, his rugby player physique intimidating even for someone as cocksure as Dan.

'Don't talk about my family.'

'Woah, woah there big man, you're back on the heart attack again. You're gonna wear yourself out if you keep this up, chief. You don't look like you've got the form for all this stress, man. You want to watch yourself. Watch what you're saying. You feel me?'

All Callum wanted was to have that day to do over again. He'd take a different route to work, avoid seeing Dan altogether. Or he'd talk his way out of trouble, be cheerful, keep things light, somehow extricate himself before he got into the mess he was in now.

'I tell you what,' said Dan, deadly serious all of a sudden. 'You accept our generous gift for your little family, and I won't tell the boss man about your insult.' The smaller man leaned in and all the blood left Callum's face. 'And in return, we've got a tiny little favour for you to do for us.'

The sun was shining as Callum walked back to Liane and the bump. He'd seen some video recently that claimed the average number of human skeletons in a person was more than two because there were always pregnant women on the planet. He thought of them now, all those little skeletons swimming around in their warm amniotic goo, safe in the darkness.

No worries, no guilt, just a tiny life, perfect and full of potential.

He trudged onwards, his feet scuffing the pavement, vape trails swirling in the mid-morning light.

FIFTEEN

Marilla had given Phil her room key card before she was carted off. She wasn't really carted, more politely escorted, but Phil preferred to keep her descriptions tabloid-y wherever possible. Life was more exciting when you lived it in hyperbole.

'A life without hyperbole is the world's worst tragedy,' Angela would say.

It felt weird being back in their peaceful little nest. It still contained plentiful evidence of last night's fun – little miniatures of booze, a chaos of bed linen, strewn clothes – all the usual suspects. Phil resented the tableau. She hadn't slept with anyone in over six months, and now she'd lived a cliché of excess and frivolity. Usually, she preferred the more damaging route to self-destruction. The one where you get together with someone you really like and then you dump them as soon as you feel like they might be getting too close. Another cliché: the girl who wouldn't let anyone in after her father died. Maybe the tabloid-y descriptions were starting to affect her behaviour.

Phil had managed to keep under the radar all morning. Even better, so far *Aldhill Observer* journalists Barry Brooker and Mike Hungerford hadn't been able to gain access to the building. The police and security presence on the front doors was tight; the staff entrance and rear fire door secured against incoming paps and hacks, and Phil had been swerving Adam Jenkins's calls and texts requesting that she open the fire door to let them in. There was no way she was handing this scoop over to one of the elder statesmen of the paper, especially not Barry Brooker.

Barry had been the one to dub her 'Poodicca' after her dog poo piece got a front page,

'Watch out lads, Poodicca's arrived on her winged chariot to request your heads on a platter,' he had cried the day her story came out. For a man who made his living out of words, he was surprisingly ill-read. Phil had refrained from beginning a lecture on the difference between Salomé and Boudicca, reaching instead for some witty banter.

'Barry's just jealous because all his stories are full of shit and yet he still can't get a front page.'

She had said it in the obligatory joshing tone, but she saw immediately she'd misjudged it. The riposte had cut a little too deep. Barry had been having a bad run with his stories and his dry spell with front page news had not gone unnoticed. His most recent front page had been found for him by Phil herself, something that would certainly have added to the insult. There was an audible intake of breath as everyone turned to see what Barry would say in response. He melodramatically mimed being shot through the heart with an arrow.

'Oof, she got me. Poodicca shot me straight through the heart.' A ripple of laughter and Phil felt cheated. Not clever or witty – just the same insult repeated. She watched Barry elaborately writhing around, milking his moment for every laugh he could get, realising with a gloomy resignation that she would be called Poodicca for some time. She lifted her hands in surrender.

'Ok, Ok, I give in,' she said. 'Looks like I've been hoist by my own pootard.' She had been hoping for a groan at the very least and she wasn't disappointed. Nina Dinmore, picture researcher and general dogsbody gave her a sarcastic look of disapproval and began a slow hand clap. Mike Hungerford chuckled into his sandwich. High on success, she hazarded another.

'What can I say? It's not every day you get to solve your very own "poodunnit".'

It was too much. Adam Jenkins, editor, poked his head out of the glass doors of his office, a stern look on his face.

'Both of you should be ashamed of yourselves.'

He pointed to a jar in the corner marked "Bad Puns". He continued pointing at it until the pair of them dutifully went over and chucked in a handful of coins.

'I expect better from both of you, you have brought shame onto the sacred art of pun creation, and for that you must be PUN-ished.'

'I mean, arguably your one is the worst of the bunch,' said Phil.

'Shut your face, Poodicca,' said Adam poking a finger at her. But he took out a coin and tossed it into the jar before ducking back into his office. The staff topped up the Christmas party budget with the money from their Pun Jar. This year was going to be a bumper one if the past few minutes were any indication.

Phil had rolled her eyes and laughed along with every-one, taking the ribbing. Secretly she would have liked to stab

Barry through the eyeball with his own Bic. On second thoughts, that was going too far. She'd settle for seeing his trousers fall down at an editorial meeting. It wasn't that she minded being ribbed – she could give as good as she got in normal circumstances – but this felt personal. Barry wasn't just having a laugh, he wanted to keep her in her place. She was a young journalist – an upstart in his eyes – and she had just played a major role in solving two local murders. But Adam hadn't given her the scoop. Meanwhile, Barry was a man who hadn't had much success of late, keen to regain his position at the top of the pecking order.

But Phil was coming for him. She just needed to get a few more quotes and she'd have a great story. Callum had insisted he didn't know who had taken up Oli Cromwell's room service.

'I'd left for the day by then,' he said.

It was a shame. It would have made a nice addition: last person to see Cromwell alive. But she thought she had another angle.

'Ok, so tell me something else,' she had said. 'You went to school with him, didn't you? What was he like?'

'I went to school with him for, like, five minutes back when I was in year 7 and he was in year 11,' he said. 'But I never spoke to him. He left not long after. He had some alter-cation with a teacher, I think.'

Phil was aware that Oli had been a naughty kid – it was all part of his image. British bad boy turned Hollywood heart throb had a certain ring to it. He had moved schools a few times, but really that wasn't unusual in this town. Certain kids were playing an endless game of musical schools, moving around the county education establishments like a marauding band of pubescent mercenaries.

'So you never sold him any drugs or anything?' she asked.

He gave her a sarcastic smile. 'He was four or five years older than me. I think if anyone was selling drugs to anyone, it would have been him to me.'

'Why?' said Phil, 'Was he into drugs?'

Callum's face clouded. 'Stop it,' he said. 'Stop trying to get dirt out of me. He's dead, for god's sake. Show some respect.'

He walked off leaving Phil wondering if she was really cut out for this journalism lark. It seemed like she had spent the past year questioning if there was any honour in this profession at all. She had only become a journalist so she could investigate her father's death on a building site, and now she was digging for dirt on a dead man. She decided to wash away her sins, making the most of the facilities by taking a nice hot shower and pocketing all the smellies.

Phil had stowed her laptop in Marilla's safe and, before she went to retrieve it, she scanned the room for treasures that Marilla might want her to stow. She found a set of earrings and a small gold necklace with a couple of tiny gold horseshoe pendants. Perhaps that's why Marilla had been taken in for questioning – she didn't have her lucky charm. It worked for Phil, however, since somewhere in the recesses of her brain she managed to dredge up the four-digit PIN. Not that she believed in lucky charms.

'Luck is just opportunity with better PR,' as her mother would say.

Still, a whim took her and she clipped the necklace around her neck.

She opened the safe and somehow found herself reaching for Marilla's computer. Would it hurt to have a quick look? She felt the cool metal of the MacBook in her hand and weighed up her options. She could just take a quick look at the laptop; Marilla would be none the wiser. And with thoughts of Barry Brooker outside somewhere, pressing his nose to the glass, trying to get in, Phil felt the pressure of finding out everything she could about Cromwell – and the publicist who may have supplied the pills for his overdose.

Taking a breath, resigned to yet another failure of her moral compass, she opened the lid. The giraffe on the desktop screen was frozen in motion, forever taking a giant bite out of some foliage, its lips and blue tongue curling out in a comical expression. Phil hit the mouse pad and the password box appeared. Marilla was a conscientious employee who had locked her computer – safe from the prying eyes of (increasingly) scummy journalists.

Phil tried the obvious ones – '123456', '123456789' and 'password' being, she knew, three of the most used passwords in the world – but once she'd failed several times, she was met with a glorious sight: the password hint.

'Ideal job.'

Ideal job! She could have hugged Marilla. She could see her own happy face reflecting back at her in the glass of the laptop's retina display. She knew what the password was.

She'd read a book about early hackers once. It was like reading a book about the talkies or steam trains. Phone Phreaking and toll fraud seemed so quaint to her – a relic from a bygone age. She hadn't even been born when the first hackers were in the ascendant, but in this historical document, she had learned a lot about extracting information from unwitting subjects. 'Social engineering,' the script kiddies of yore called it. They'd all be old men by now, easing into their fifties, dealing with their own delinquent teenagers.

And Phil hadn't been able to resist giving it a try, using her easy charm to ferret out mothers' maiden names and first schools ever attended. What had started as a fun pastime had soon turned into a habit. Now she data-mined everyone she met without really thinking about it. And, sure enough, it had been her game last night: asking Marilla as many personal questions as she could in the space of one minute. It was amazing what information people were prepared to give up. They never questioned her motives – they assumed she found them as fascinating as they found themselves. Or maybe, unlike politicians, they were simply too polite not to answer a bald question when it was put to them.

Even other journalists weren't immune. She could probably hack the accounts of most people in her office. Apart from Barry Brooker and Adam, of course. They were suspicious of everyone.

'Stop asking questions about my mother,' Barry instructed her one night down the pub. 'It's weird.'

But it had worked on Marilla.

'If you could wave a magic wand, what job would you do tomorrow?'

Everyone loved answering questions involving the waving of magic wands.

'I'd be a zookeeper,' Marilla had told her. No hesitation.

'Wow, that was fast,' said Phil. 'You must have given this some thought.

'It's literally all I've ever wanted to do,' Marilla told her. 'Well, maybe I thought about being a vet or a show jumper first, but I wasn't clever enough to be a vet and I wasn't good enough to be a show jumper. Plus, I fell off too many times and lost my nerve.'

'Sounds like you literally need to get back in the saddle,'

said Phil, amazed that anyone could live a life where they considered show jumping a career option. She couldn't imagine Miss Gilly, the school careers advisor suggesting that as one of her options, alongside 'Tesco till worker' and 'dental assistant'.

Marilla shrugged. 'Maybe you're right. But I'd still rather be a zookeeper.'

Phill took a breath and typed 'zookeeper'. It didn't work. Damn it! She tried some variations thereof (Zookeeper, Zookeeper, Zook33p3r etc) but got nowhere. She was close to quitting when it struck her: the answer was staring her in the face. She typed "giraffekeeper" and the laptop whirred into life and began opening up apps. Phil couldn't quite believe her luck. The necklace's magic had worked again; she was rapidly becoming more superstitious as the morning wore on.

She didn't have time to sit and go through Marilla's entire computer. She wanted to get more interviews before the unwanted backup arrived; before Barry Brooker came barrelling in to steal her exclusive. It was the only way she could demand a byline. Her fervent hope was that police and staff would prevent other journalists from getting in the building, but she didn't want to get complacent. So she took a deep breath, took a memory stick from her backpack and copied Marilla's hard drive.

She wondered if Marilla would say the orgasm was worth it in exchange for this massive betrayal. She wondered if she herself would say losing her integrity was worth it in exchange for this data.

Best not to think about it.

She packed Marilla's laptop into the safe, texted Marilla the new passcode along with a cheerful note telling her to call when she could, pausing for a moment before adding the kiss at the end of the message. And then took out her own laptop.

'Well,' she said out loud, 'time to face up to it, Philippa McGinty.'

Time to admit to herself what she'd done. She took out her camera's memory card and plugged it into her machine. Seeing the photos line up before her on screen, the reality of what she had done seemed to stop her heart for a few seconds. She felt it restarting at twice the speed, thumping in her chest and throbbing in her ears as she went through the photos one by one. There he was, lying on the bed. Oli Cromwell, Hollywood heartthrob. His plate of food next to him, his bed clothes half-covering his naked body, two glassed next to him on the bedside table. He looked so young. Younger than he looked in his films.

Abruptly, Phil closed the lid on her machine. What kind of person does this, she wondered? She had seen a dead body – been present at a crime scene – and she had chosen, in that moment, while she waited for Marilla to summon the emergency services, to take out her camera and record the scene. What for? Titillation? Evidence? Could she claim it was for the sake of good journalism? She had always believed she was above the members of the gutter press; now she wasn't so sure. If she was looking for evidence, there wasn't much to be found.

She rang her mother again, seeking something that would take her mind off her own failings. She would reckon with those at a later date.

Maybe on her deathbed.

'I didn't tell you about my encounter with the dragon Judith on the front desk,' she said.

She soon had Angela in fits of laughter. She put all her weight into the story, painting a picture of Judith's epic war paint and the wonderful 'gotcha' moment when she turned the computer screen to Phil to reveal her own face staring back at her.

'You know what I always say,' said Angela. 'I always say: you meet an arsehole every day. Judith was your arsehole yesterday. Who knows who today's arsehole will be.'

That saying always cheered Phil up. The idea that she might just be collecting a daily arsehole – like figurines or pin badges or Wordle scores – appealed to her natural optimism. *It's ok, it's just my daily arsehole count meeting its quota.* Shame she couldn't track it on her smart watch. So it seemed to go against Phil's sense of fairness, and the whole spirit of the one a day rule, that she walked out of Marilla's room and bumped straight into yesterday's arsehole.

SIXTEEN

Judith let the warm water from the shower wash over her, quivering as her body began the slow process of regaining warmth, her blood getting to work restoring heat to her extremities.

She hadn't known the boy at all. She was only recently aware of him, this big movie star who seemed to her to have sprung from nowhere in her life. She had been to see a handful of his films – two on nights out with the swimming girls and one on her own when she was at a loose end on a rainy Sunday morning. He was talented – she thought so anyway – one of those proper movie actors who could make a naff line sound plausible, make a preposterous film watch-able and fun. He was a boy with a lot of charm, and those eyes! Judith imagined plenty of young women (and a few older ones, if her swimming pals' reactions were anything to go by), would like to go on an exploration of those sparkling eyes.

The boy was obviously fit and healthy. She liked to see a man who took care of himself, but you could take these things too far. Some of these movie stars started exercising at 3am! She had read an article. Men didn't go to all that trouble in her day. It was enough if they kept their beer bellies at bay and bought a nice car. They might do a couple of press ups or lift the odd weight here or there, but six packs were in short supply in the seventies – even on movie stars. Women were more easily pleased back then. She remembered seeing the new *James Bond* actor (she still thought of him as new, anyway). She watched in amazement as he emerged from the sea like Ursula Andress had done so many years before. Eye candy for the men replaced by eye candy for the women. Roger Moore wouldn't have had quite the same effect if he'd risen from the waters in his swimmers, she thought.

It wasn't necessarily a good thing – all that exercise, all those perfect torsos. The way she saw it, it was a sign of failure. Instead of freeing women from all those surface-level expectations of beauty society had somehow trapped men too. Now the boys were all plucking their eyebrows, whitening their teeth and watching their carbs. And all the botox! Even the men were at it, everyone leering out of the screen with their UV teeth on a Saturday night, having to show their happiness by clapping mindlessly or telling you how amazed they were ('Kelly, you have such a lovely singing voice, I'm amazed') since it wasn't possible to tell from their immobile expression. She wondered if Oli Cromwell plucked his eyebrows. All the better to see those sparkling eyes, she supposed. The thought trickled through: they won't be sparkling any more.

Stepping from the shower, she began the process of becoming Judith from the front desk, applying her war paint, putting on her armour, spritzing perfume. Everything she needed to feel like she could get through another day.

Who was she kidding? She would almost certainly have partaken in a bit of Botox if it was available when she was younger. And Charles certainly would have been tempted. He was a vain man – even more so than Judith, who had spent her youth earning money off the back of her looks. Perhaps men back then weren't so different after all. She lined her lips with a pencil and filled in the colour, catching her own eye in the mirror, seeing the self-reproach.

She would have to tell the police who she was at some point, she supposed. Would they work it out otherwise? Maybe she could keep quiet, pretend she was just an innocent member of staff. She was the last of the generations that kept their secrets bottled up, kept them close to their chests. It was second nature not to speak about private matters. These days everyone was always sharing and oversharing, emoting left right and centre, unloading the burden of their anxieties onto the world, filming themselves crying and posting it on social media, snapping photos of bad news at the doctor's, taking sad selfies at holocaust memorials, wanting to discuss their mental health struggles like it was an episode of last night's telly. In her day people just kept their mouths shut.

Her mother had kept all kinds of secrets in her closet – lost babies and mental breakdowns, an ongoing day-drinking habit, a husband who got mean on match day, an uncle all the children knew to avoid – sometimes Judith would catch little hints of them, especially towards the end when her mother's mind was failing and she began to spend so much of her time living in the past, in her memories. People say it's a sad way to go, watching an elderly loved one slowly slipping away from you, forgetting who you are, but Judith found it strangely comforting, knowing her mother was spending time with her sisters and brothers, imagining she was seeing her own mother again, losing herself in the memories of times when she was a little girl, safe and happy.

What kinds of memories would Judith get lost in when bits of her mind started to break off and tumble into dust? Perhaps she would be with her beautiful Kenneth again. When she thought back to all those happy days – just her and him, the two of them thick as thieves, eating ice creams and visiting the seaside town she ran away from at eighteen – she couldn't square it with what had happened to their relationship in later years. It didn't make any sense. Where was he now, that smiling boy, so happy, and full of sunshine? Lost somewhere in the bloated, bearded fellow in the chunky knit jumpers and the grouchy churlishness.

Now *there* was a person who liked to talk about his feelings.

Unfortunately, all his feelings appeared to be about how terrible his mother was, how stifling, how limiting, how uncaring towards his needs. She was glad her own mother wasn't around any more to see what a whining human being he had become. But still, her body ached for him. She longed to see him, to touch his hand, to hold him close and tell him she would die for him. What a terrible hash she had made of the whole thing.

In the ambulance, after her "funny turn" (since she was too old now to simply faint), the paramedic had wrapped her in a blanket and patronised her loudly, and Judith sat there, sipping weak tea, her thoughts meandering like a boat come loose from its mooring, knocking into other boats and bashing gently into the soft shore.

'How are we feeling, Mrs Jones?' said the paramedic, her voice slow and loud, her fingers searching out Judith's pulse on her blue veins.

'I'm fine,' Judith had said through gritted, chattering teeth. 'It's just from the swimming. I'll be alright again in a minute.'

'Absolute nutters the lot of you,' said the paramedic. 'You wouldn't catch me out there in my cossie in this weather. Far too cold.'

Judith didn't reply. She wasn't about to start preaching on the many wonderful benefits of cold water swimming; she didn't feel the need to convert anyone to the cause. If this woman thought she was crazy that was her own look out. Plus, she was hardly in a position to talk someone into giving it a try, sitting there wrapped in a blanket apparently suffering from the early stages of hypothermia. She watched the paramedic completing her checks.

'You'll live,' the woman pronounced.

So much for bedside manner. But maybe Judith was an idiot, getting herself in such a state, sitting here like she was in the final scene of a disaster movie. Except rather than recovering, soot-faced, from saving someone from a burning building, or breathing hard on some oxygen after surviving a terrorist bomb, she'd just been for a dip in the sea and got a bit cold. For shame.

Deep down she knew the truth, of course. And now, pulling on her tights and smoothing down the bow on her neckerchief, she began slowly edging her mind towards acceptance. It wasn't the cold that had made her quiver like a chihuahua in spring. Sure, it didn't help, but the cold hadn't sent her reeling. Her embarrassing display of dizziness wasn't something she could shrug off as a bad reaction to the water temperature. With glum resignation she forced her mind to think the thought: it wasn't the swim, it was the shock.

Oli Cromwell was dead – his body lying cold and inert, she imagined, his sparkling eyes unstaring, his muscles turning from rigor mortis and back to soft flesh as they prepared to lift his body from the scene to transport him to a steel table in the hospital's underbelly.

He was dead. Here, in her hotel.

She opened the door and made her way towards reception. Except she didn't. That was what she had intended, yet somehow she found her feet carrying her up the stairs and onto the third floor where Oli Cromwell's body was still lying waiting for the forensics team to give the coroner the all clear to remove the body. She hadn't meant to visit the scene of the crime – never wanted to go near it again – but here she was. Noises from the room brought her to her senses and she turned back, regretting her decision immediately, and that's when she walked straight into Philippa McGinty, the scummy little journalist she'd evicted yesterday.

SEVENTEEN

The man in the brown pyjamas felt like he was wading through soup. He had never slept in so late in his life. His head pounded as he made himself a cup of tea from the hotel kettle, tipping the complimentary biscuits out of the little cup in order to brew himself a restorative black tea. He had been reckless, he realised, and he had allowed his thoughts to become muddied. He needed to get back to his plan.

He had already packed up his bag and now he needed to leave. After seeing the kerfuffle caused by one man's death, he had no desire to emulate it. He wanted leave as slight an impact on his passing as he did while he was living. If he could plunge into the cold sea water without causing a single ripple, he would. As it was, he would settle for making the smallest wave possible. It was a shame there were no simple ways to dispose of your body: a giant incinerator you could lower yourself into like the *Terminator*; a vat of acid at the local tip; a giant blender that could whizz you up into a smoothie to be fed to dogs.

He had never asked the universe for much, hadn't even

expected love, really. He had learned long ago that none was coming unless you counted his mother, and the jury was still out on how she felt about him. His parents had pottered their way through life, barely troubling to glance up when he entered the room. They weren't cruel or even unkind. They just weren't very interested. They kept him fed and watered, but they didn't need to hear about his day. If he wanted to tell it, they would listen politely (so long as the TV was off) and then return to the paper or the carrots or the compost with a brief, 'that's nice, son' or a 'well done, love'.

His mother, so obsessed with his inevitable, horrible death, and yet she seemed utterly indifferent to his life. He sometimes suspected her fears of him dying were more to do with concern he might cause a scene than fears for his safety. Certainly, when she was wrapping him up in cotton wool, she never took the time to kiss him before he left the house, or let him know she loved him.

He used to come home armed with anything at all that might provoke more than a line: art from school, pretty leaves, cookies from home economics class. He once picked up a dead bird and brought that back. 'Go and chuck it outside, son,' his father said after staring at it a moment over his paper. 'Don't want your mother to see that near her carpets.'

But while he hadn't asked for much, and hadn't expected anything either, eventually, he had to concede that the quiet limbo of his life was unbearable. A shock or a surprise – or anything really at all – would have been welcome. Anything more than the dreary greyness of his life, the constant tick-tock of nothing eventful happening. It seemed to him now that barely a day stood out from another. Every meal had been adequate. If it surpassed his low expectations, that was enough to make it worth mentioning in his diary. Every night had been silent, apart from the TV talking, the electrical hum of the three-bar fire on cold nights and the sound of his mother's slow, heaving breath.

The man in beige hadn't expected to make a connection, yet here he was, standing next to a woman who seemed genuinely delighted to be talking to him. She was a florist. The hotel had employed her to create a floral tribute at the side of the building and he watched as she used wire and sphagnum moss and flowers to fashion a huge 'O'; a wreath, an initial, and an exclamation of surprise. How apt.

He hadn't intended to stop and speak to her. He never stopped and spoke to anyone. But when he walked out of The Marchmont carrying his backpack, and glanced over at the car park in the distance, he was struck immediately by the beauty of the creation and the care of the woman attending to her flowers. And so without really thinking, he found himself approaching. There he stood, admiring her deftness and precision, watching as she considered each stem before finding it the perfect home. And eventually, she had noticed him, had glanced up towards him with a smile. Usually, he would take such open friendliness as a sign to move on – after all, such warmth could only be disappointed. But something about her expression, the slight quizzical tilt of her head as she squinted up at him through the sunlight, gave him confidence, and for once he stayed.

'It's beautiful,' he told her.

'Thank you,' she said. 'I try my best.'

'I've never seen anything like it.' In all his years, he

wasn't sure he had seen such an intricate and beautiful display. 'A wonderful tribute.'

She smiled. 'I don't know. It's what the hotel asked for, but I'm not sure it's what he would have wanted.'

That surprised him. 'What would he have preferred?'

'Oh, I'm not sure. Somehow this feels a little bit too sedate. Tasteful. He was still so young. I think he would have liked something with a little bit more danger. Something more masculine.'

She was probably right. The hotel had chosen something that suited their brand, but he preferred it. It had class, unlike the deceased.

'Well, I'm glad you're here,' he said and felt his cheeks go pink with embarrassment. He had not meant to say that out loud. Or at least he hadn't realised quite how it might sound.

'I'm glad I'm here too,' she said simply. He stood for a moment longer and was about to go, feeling that he had run out of things to say and had no possible excuse for hovering as he was. He was acutely aware that by now most people would be feeling uncomfortable in his presence. He half expected her to start losing her cheerfulness if he lingered any longer and he couldn't bear the pain of witnessing the inevitable coldness appear in her grey eyes. But then, just as he was about to turn to go she glanced up again.

'Would you mind passing me those flowers?' She nodded towards the open rear doors of her small transit van parked nearby. 'Only if you want to, of course. Usually I would have my assistant with me. She hasn't turned up for some reason. I think perhaps she's too devastated about his death.'

'Certainly,' he said.

She smiled. She wasn't beautiful; she wasn't even particularly attractive, he thought, aside from her hair, which was thick and long. But something in the way her long fingers weaved in the flowers, placing each stem with such a light dexterity, made her seem more beautiful than anyone he had ever met, and her broad, cheerful face with pale freckles made him sure he could share any secret with her, even the worst ones.

So he went to the car and fetched the stems, helping the florist and finding things to say in reply to her cheerful comments, doing his very best not to come across as weird or creepy or annoying or boring.

And somehow, as if by some strange miracle, he succeeded.

EIGHTEEN

Phil had survived. She had met with her nemesis and emerged unscathed. She was still in the building. Even better, she had just booked a date with said nemesis. It was unclear how that had happened, but she wasn't about to look a gift horse in the mouth. She had expected to be evicted on the spot, taken by the ear, frog-marched through the building, chucked out onto the street, legs and arms flying before she landed in a sprawled heap on the cobbles below, Judith dusting off her hands with satisfaction of a job well done. Instead, Judith had been the one who looked guilty at being caught out.

'Hello!' Phil had said breezily. 'What are you doing up here?'

'What are *you* doing up here?' said Judith, eyeballing her. 'I thought we'd made it very clear that you are not welcome in The Marchmont.'

'I met a friend,' said Phil. 'Well, technically she wasn't my friend when I met her, but she most definitely is now – if you catch my drift.'

What had she been thinking? What had possessed her to try being cute? She already knew Judith did not appreciate cuteness. She probably wasn't too keen on the strangely nudge-nudge-wink-wink tone, either. Phil started to sweat.

'I just needed to get something from my friend's room and then you won't see me again.' It was technically true: she needed to get her laptop and then she intended to hide from Judith for the rest of the day.

'Well,' said Judith, 'just be sure you don't go snooping around the crime scene. The police aren't letting anyone close to the room where... you know... he *died*.'

So that was what Judith was after: she was being a nosey parker, she'd come to rubber-neck. An opportunity for Phil to ingratiate herself with her nemesis presented itself.

'Oh, I've already been to the crime scene,' Phil said. 'I was the one who found the body.'

Judith had tried to act like she just wanted to start over. 'Let's have a coffee and make peace,' she had suggested.

Phil waited for the punchline, still expecting to be turfed out, but the receptionist had a strangely plaintive look on her face and Phil agreed before she turned cold again.

'I love peace,' she said. 'And I love coffee. Let's do this!'

She winced at the slight flash of annoyance on Judith's face. Why was she so compulsively irritating when she was with this person?

'Great,' said Judith. Then she vanished – her neckerchief wafting as she strode away.

So Judith wanted to ask her about Oli. Why? Or maybe she had a story, in which case why choose her? A woman she clearly hated. Phil's stomach rumbled. She wasn't able to speculate further until she'd eaten something. She headed for the dining room where her intention was to eat as much of the free food as she could possibly stomach so she wouldn't have to cook an evening meal (assuming she'd left the hotel by then). Lunch wasn't technically free, she supposed, but it wasn't on her tab and that was what counted. She was pretty confident Marilla's company credit card would cover the additional cost of lunch. If not, she would offer to pay her back, and the girl with all the gifts would surely shrug it off and tell her not to worry about it.

Phil had met two types of rich people so far in her life: the ones who considered money to be a trifling matter that didn't concern them, and the ones who counted every penny like it could make or break them. From what she'd witnessed, Marilla was in the first group. Speculating on Marilla's wealth had become a new pastime for Phil. It was hard not to think about money when you lived in a council house with your mum and brother, your gran just a few doors up, when you had been raised by a single mother – until Clive came along, that is – and had days where the free school meal was what got you through. But she wasn't ashamed of taking the free lunch.

She imagined Marilla had never asked for a handout, but had never refused one either. If she had to guess (and she fully intended to), she'd say Marilla's parents took subsidies for the farmland they owned. They let the government subsidise their minimum wage staff's living expenses with tax credits. Marilla probably had a nice additional income from a trust fund and a few policies in her name that would mature soon. She'd most likely been put on the payroll of one of her father's limited companies in her teens. That limited company was, Phil knew, almost certainly owned by a shell company held off-shore – reducing the family tax liability and paying Marilla a nice monthly allowance at the same time. It was pure speculation, but Phil expected it probably barely scratched the surface. She had been trying to get to the bottom of the byzantine architecture behind the Virtua Services business interests. The company that, in her view, had been responsible for the death of Clive McGinty. Not just because they had unsafe buildings, which they had known about and covered up, but also because, she was convinced, someone within the organisation had ordered her father's execution. She just needed to find out who.

She had first learned about the myriad ways rich people organised their finances at university. Her posh friend Rufus had failed to get the grades for his chosen universities and was now slumming it at a second tier establishment with the hoi polloi. He was more than willing to divulge his family's secrets. Phil had learned a lot from Rufus, much of it shocking to her at the time. Now she realised it was just rich people doing what rich people do. She couldn't entirely blame them for taking advantage of a world built for them.

But, no, she didn't feel ashamed of taking a free lunch – at school or here at the hotel.

She turned her attention to her plate, which was rapidly running out of salad space. Most of it would be sampled and rejected. Phil's limited palate made her suspicious of anything too strong, but she felt it was important to take a selection from each bowl so she didn't miss out on the salad jackpot. She already knew the coleslaw wouldn't pass muster, however. She should have avoided it altogether and left more space for other salad options. And anyway, it was no use trying to interview people with that many alliums in your system – trying to stifle digestive processes while requesting soundbites – it wasn't appropriate.

'Goodness, these onions have strong opinions,' her gran

(Angela's mother and another fan of the pithy saying) liked to mutter while belching. 'And they keep repeating themselves.'

Phil shunted the coleslaw to the side of her plate and piled on a tomato and mozzarella combo. The salad was only the beginning, however – the first course in a hearty lunch. Once she finished that course, she moved on to the mains. The last vestiges of her hangover were still present when she began the odyssey into the hot options, but thanks to a veggie sausage casserole, she was beginning to feel more alive.

She used the meal to read back over her notes, trying to put together as much of the evening as she possibly could. From conversations with Marilla the previous evening and interviews with hotel guests today, Phil knew Oli had arrived at the hotel at around midday. At that point, he headed straight to his room, refusing to see anyone. Marilla had been forced to cancel all his press interviews with the national media and he failed to honour the planned visits to his old schools that afternoon. Phil wrote a note in her book, 'Ask Marilla why?'

She underlined why. The night before, Marilla had happily told her about the cancellations, but had pushed back when Phil tried to get her to spill the beans on Oli Cromwell's reason. What had she said?

'Nice try, journo.'

Phil smiled at the memory. She'd chanced her arm, asking her again after a couple more drinks and Marilla had simply said, 'I dunno, because he's a prick?' and then continued talking about how distraught the children prob-ably were and how all she could see when she closed her eyes were hundreds of disappointed little faces peering back at her, tears welling in their sad little eyes.

'All because Oli Cromwell wanted a nap.'

Perhaps now he was dead, Marilla might be willing to think harder about what prompted the cancellations. Perhaps he had seen someone he knew, or had a phone call off someone with bad news that he wasn't ready to share. Maybe he'd split up with someone – Phil remembered he'd recently been linked to some Hollywood star. If she got the chance, she would ask Marilla to formulate a couple of theories.

What else? Phil flicked through the pages in her notes. She should follow up with that Llewellyn bloke to see if he'd called the police as he said he would. He had heard two voices last night. Marilla was the first. Who was the second? Callum said room service had been taken up later into the evening, but he insisted he didn't know who delivered it – no matter how many times she pressed him. If Llewellyn was right, it had to have been a woman.

What time does the whole turn down service thing happen, she wondered? Did he have a Do Not Disturb sign up? If so, does room service simply knock and leave the food outside on the floor? Phil's inexperience with posh hotels was hampering her. She could do with a friendly hotel worker to talk her through The Marchmont's systems. Maybe the porter would help if she gave him another tenner. Or perhaps she could ask Judith now that she had extended the hand of friendship.

Phil glanced about and surreptitiously undid the top button on her jeans. She had eaten her fill and was now regretting some of her decisions, but she liked to think Marilla wouldn't begrudge her the food. 'Can I get you anything else?'

Phil looked up into the smiling face of Anya and hoped the maître d' hadn't noticed her undone top button. She sat up straight and tried to pull the napkin over her lap.

'Coffee, tea? Dessert menu?' said Anya.

'Do you know, I'd love a coffee,' said Phil. Anya agreed this was a wonderful idea and went off to make it so. 'And maybe I'll look at the dessert menu,' Phil called out after her as she walked off, much to the maître d's delight.

That was how she found herself eating a baked cheesecake and unbuttoning another fly on her jeans.

'Anya?' said Phil, when Anya next walked by 'Can I ask you a strange question?'

Anya's expression suggested she couldn't think of anything better. Here was a woman born to work in the service industry. If Miss Gilly the careers advisor had met Anya, even she couldn't have suggested a more suitable role than a maître d'. It was either that or magician's assistant.

'I don't suppose you know who took up Oli Cromwell's evening room service do you? I mean, you probably don't, but I just thought I'd ask.'

Phil was in her cocksure charmer mode, but inside she was squirming. It was one thing to sneak around like a grubby little hack, but it was quite another to have Anya the maître d' thinking badly of her. But Anya leaned in conspiratorially and said:

'I do, actually. Everyone's talking about it because it was just so out of the ordinary. Between you, me and the gatepost, it was Judith from the front desk.'

NINETEEN

Once, Jen had mentioned to her mother that she liked bees. It was just a throwaway observation. She couldn't even remember what had prompted it now. Perhaps she had seen one happily buzzing down the funnels of some foxgloves in her mother's garden one sunny afternoon and been struck by how industrious and benevolent they seemed. But thanks to that one observation she spent the next six Christmases being overwhelmed with bee-themed presents. She had almost been at breaking point, ready to tell her mother that she couldn't face another year spent opening lotions from Burt's Bees and T-shirts with 'Buzz off, I'm Bizzy,' and other nonsensical bee-based puns on them, when her mother went ahead and spoiled Christmas a different way by dropping dead of a heart attack while she was attempting to cram the turkey into the oven.

Jen had missed the bee presents after that.

She hadn't been close to her mother, but the bees had been a sign that, deep down, the woman did care, even if she didn't know her daughter all that well. And of course, while her mother was alive, there had always been the hope that maybe they could still fix their relationship, have the kind of mother-daughter relationship other people seem to have. The sort of relationship where you thank your parents first and foremost in any acceptance speech, or where you can pick any Mother's Day card that says 'Best Mum Ever' without wondering if there's a blander option available. 'Thank you for birthing me,' for example, or 'You provided adequate warmth and shelter and I appreciate that.' Perhaps if she's been able to find a way to fix their relationship, Jen might even have found a way to tell her mother about the bee mix-up. Perhaps they'd have laughed together about it.

She was only thinking about her mother because of something Marilla had said: I only got the tablets to keep my mother happy. Bee-themed gifts were something you got in order to keep your mother happy, not potentially life-altering drugs. She might as well have said, 'I only got the eating disorder to keep my mother happy,' or 'I only risked kidney disease and other serious side effects to keep my mother happy.' It was another world to Jen. For all her mother's faults, she never expected Jen to take weight-loss supplements for the sake of her happiness. What a messed up world these people inhabited.

From what she had told Jen, Marilla apparently did a lot of things for the sake of other people, including giving drugs to a Hollywood actor because he asked for them, and attempting to organise exclusives for journalists of crummy local papers. Marilla's inclination for people-pleasing didn't exactly scream 'murderer' to Jen.

'What do you think then, sarge?' said Dean.

The detective constable had brought them both a coffee from over the road after Jen had sent him off to run the gauntlet between the gaggle of foreign students hunting caffeine and the yawning hipsters who'd come to use the free electricity and wifi. It was a welcome change from the terrible instant stuff in the staff kitchen ('kitchenette,' Jen supposed).

It was unusually quiet in the Incident Room. Grant was still finishing up at the hotel and DI Lee Hudson was yet to make his grand entrance. The DCI – hollow cheeked Petra Gull – was off in Eastbourne overseeing something or other. Smart-mouthed DC Nandini Roy was working with Petra, something Nandini treated as a kind of sackcloth and ashes penance. She was much missed by Jen.

Jen frowned and thought about her answer to Dean's question, blowing through the plastic spout on her scalding hot flat white.

'Hard to say without any definite cause of death,' she said. 'What's your take?'

'Well... Seems a bit odd that her tablets were in his room. But, then again, maybe what she said about him asking for them is true. Who's to say he's not taking advantage of his assistant by making her get prescription drugs for him?'

Jen was relieved. The younger lads coming up the ranks were a lot less likely to cast women as mad harridans out for revenge. The age of the Yorkshire Ripper old boys and their talk of 'respectable women' and 'innocent victims' had passed. It wasn't exactly a Golden Age of right-on coppers – god knows they still had a way to go on that front – but she was glad to see there were at least some younger men on the force willing to consider things with a slightly more enlightened mind.

'Still,' said Jen, playing devil's advocate. 'She was very defensive right away.'

When Marilla had asked for a lawyer, it had taken a while for Jen to calm her down and convince her she didn't need one.

'You're not under arrest; you're free to go whenever you like. You're welcome to one, of course, but I'm not sure why you think you'd need a solicitor?'

Marilla had hesitated. Jen's tone made it clear that asking for a solicitor at this stage would most definitely be pinned front and centre to Jen's metaphorical 'crazy wall', the mental evidence board where she housed all her favourite suspicions.

'Our main concern is just establishing what happened that evening,' Jen continued. 'We're not going to start accusing you of being his dealer for the odd sleeping tablet here and there.'

'He used to ask me for them and I found it hard to say no,' said Marilla, 'because he was my boss.'

Then:

'And because I'd never hear the end of it if I didn't give him what he wanted.'

That statement had stuck with Jen and she mulled it over now. What else did Marilla do for her boss for the sake of a quiet life? Jen hadn't decided how she felt about Marilla yet. She had googled the Hunter Davy name and swiftly concluded this was not a family to be messed with. There were lots of fingers in lots of pies. Never mind the mayor of Aldhill, if they started making too much of a fuss about Marilla Hunter Davy's involvement, they'd have the Prime Minister on the phone.

Dean was still looking at her expectantly. She'd lost her train of thought.

'I think you could be right,' she ventured.

Of course they'd saddled her with the newbie again. It was always the way. She had terrible luck. She sometimes wondered if a family member had wronged a witch somewhere down the line and she was the one who now carried the curse. Despite having no nurturing instincts her bosses seemed to be labouring under the illusion that she loved taking the kids under her wing. She did not.

'It's weird, though, don't you think?' she continued. 'Sleeping tablets and diet pills are not obvious bedfellows. What was he trying to do? Get an amphetamine rush or a good night's sleep? It doesn't make sense.'

'I guess it will all be cleared up with the toxicology report?' ventured Dean.

'Let's hope so,' said Jen. 'And what did you think about the scene? Any initial theories?'

This was why she always ended up with the newbies, she realised: she couldn't help walking them through things. She blamed her father, a lifelong autodidact with a compulsion to share his knowledge, often with lengthy speeches. Luckily, unlike him, she resisted the urge to give a daily TED Talk, but she couldn't help teaching. Maybe she did have a nurturing instinct after all. It was a reluctant confession – she would much rather be the hard arse cop she had in her mind's eye.

'I think it was probably an accidental overdose.' Dean looked up at her hopefully.

'And what makes you say that?' said Jen, trying to coax more from the lad (so much for the hard arse).

'The way he was lying. He didn't look like someone who

had been drugged. He hadn't collapsed on the floor. He was in bed with no clothes on. Like he'd got himself ready for bed and then taken too many pills by mistake.'

'You know what I've noticed?' said Jen, taking the lid off her coffee to speed up the cooling. 'People don't like to think about their favourite celebrities topping themselves. There are so many conspiracy theories around celebrity suicides – that they were killed by the mob, or the FBI or whatever, or that they did it by mistake. Oops, I accidentally took a lethal dose of my medicine, silly me. It's like, people aren't willing to admit celebrities might have sad lives. They'd rather believe they were incapable of counting their tablets or had been murdered by spies than believe they might have chosen to end a glittering career by gobbling down a fistful of pills.'

Dean was already protesting before she'd finished this speech.

'No, no, it's not that. I just think it's strange, isn't it? To come all this way to your hometown where you're meant to meet all those kids at your old school, only to top yourself instead.'

'But he cancelled the school visits. Don't you think that's the actions of someone tidying up before they end their lives?' said Jen. 'And anyway, suicide is much more likely to be an impulsive act rather than a grand plan. Five minutes of sadness and–' she clicked her fingers. 'Gone.'

'So, you think it was intentional suicide?' said Dean.

'I didn't say that. I'm keeping an open mind until the coroner gives a verdict,' she said. 'Can you check in with Grant and find out why the hotel hasn't provided the CCTV footage yet?'

Whorls of steam rose from her coffee but she risked a sip anyway. She had stuff to be getting on with. She spluttered as the scalding coffee hit her mouth and dribbled down her hand and onto some paperwork.

'Shit,' she said, hunting for tissues.

'Bad luck,' said Dean.

Yep, she thought, definitely a witch's curse.

Later, Jen was working on a different case. A mother had been stabbed by her own son, and they had just had the news that the poor woman hadn't made it. The whole case was a massive bummer. The woman's sister said the boy had been terrorising his mother for months, giving her a black eye on a couple of occasions and waking her one night with a knife to her throat. But of course, the mother had protected her son and refused to ring the police. And the boy had pursued a path that, to Jen, seemed sadly inevitable.

Another woman dead.

A week ago, the start of the stabbing case had coincided with an email from the fertility clinic asking her to book an appointment:

Dear Jen,

We're delighted to say that your samples have been located and are ready for you at your earliest convenience. Please book an initial consultation with us so we can get the ball rolling!

Warm regards,

Deborah Ellis.

· · ·

Jen was taken aback by how chatty the email was. She had expected something more professional-sounding ('get the ball rolling' felt like an unfortunate turn of phrase given the circumstances), but Deborah was unconcerned with formalities. She had offered her 'warm regards,' as though she was getting back in touch with an old school friend rather than inviting a stranger to come over and collect her dead husband's sperm. When Jen called to make the appointment, Deborah had answered the phone.

'Oh yes, Ms Collet, I remember this one! It took us a while to track your samples down. Just as well, we wouldn't want to give you the wrong stuff, would we?' Deborah said this with such good cheer that it was almost possible to forget she was joking about impregnating Jen with the wrong man's semen. Except that when it came to this particular subject, Jen was unlikely to forget for even a second.

It was typical of course – getting the mother-son stabbing case just as she was considering bringing her own child into the world. And yet it hadn't put her off motherhood. Neither had Marilla's toxic relationship with her mother. Or the bees, come to think of it. Surely the bar, set that low, would be easy to vault: don't make them take diet pills, don't buy them gifts they hate, raise them not to stab you. The last one might be tricky. Who knows what monsters lurked within her ovaries? But she was hoping the addition of lovely, kind Nate's gamete would cancel out any congenital psychopathy on her side. And so, in spite of her insistence, she didn't have a nurturing instinct, and in spite of her ambivalence about children in general, and the bees and the stabbing and the pills, she was finally convinced this was the right thing to do. She knew that if she didn't do it now she would regret it forever.

She had booked the next available appointment.

Dean brought her back from her daydream. She had been imagining herself raising Nate's curly-haired, multi-racial bundle of love when he said, 'Sarge.'

She brushed away a tear and hoped Dean hadn't spotted it.

'What's up?' she said.

'Grant says the CCTV from Oli Cromwell's floor is missing.'

TWENTY

Liane Benbow's morning had gone from bad to worse.

'What do you mean it's all gone?' said Stephen Murray, Liane's manager.

'They're saying that the CCTV files were erased or something,' she said.

This wasn't usually Liane's job. Usually she worked on a housing association account as a customer experience advisor. But Telligence Industries, the company who so generously administered her zero-hours contract, had recently given her extra shifts on the account for a new IT helpdesk service for a company called Inference Technology Solutions – or, IT Solutions for short (clever, she thought sarcastically). And she needed all the shifts she could get. She hadn't been at Telligence Industries long enough for maternity pay, and once she had the baby, it would all be down to Callum and his work at The Marchmont.

Customer experience advisor was a pretty lofty title for someone who usually spent her days listening to people complaining about the mould in their bedroom. She didn't blame them for yelling at her; the housing association loved talking about how customer-focused it was and how every call mattered to them. Telligence Industries itself made similar bold claims. 'We care for your needs,' was the slogan pasted below the company logo on every van and brochure. But every day she spoke to people who had been living with leaking roofs and broken toilets and no heating for months on end.

She had thought the IT helpdesk might be different. This time she would really be making a difference. But it turned out this new contract involved cold calling people and offering them a free virus check. On the rare occasion she succeeded, she connected them to the IT team, who seemed to mostly be based abroad, who would take over the person's computer (it was nearly always an older person), claim to have found and removed a virus or Trojan horse, and then request money for an enhanced clean along with a monthly maintenance fee. A scam if ever she saw one. Callum told her just to put her fingers in her ears and go 'la-la-la' and grab the money and run. She wouldn't be able to do it in a few months anyway, so she carried on, and tried to think of it as the older generation funding the next one.

Now, somehow, she was in trouble, because The March-mont Hotel had just called to ask where the CCTV footage had gone from the previous night, and it had been Liane's job to inform them it had been lost – vanished in a puff of zeros and ones presumably – and now she was the one copping all the flack for it.

Stephen Murray was not impressed. It was his job to ensure that enquiries were handled with the minimum of fuss.

'There was something wrong with their server and the backup server failed too,' said Liane.

It sounded like a poor excuse to her ears, even as she said it. IT Solutions? More like IT Problems.

'You'll need to stress that this absolutely isn't Telligence Industries' fault.'

'It is our fault, apparently,' said Liane.

Because, as she learned, Telligence Industries actually owned Inference Technologies.

'So TI owns IT?' Callum said when Liane called to tell him.

'Yep,' said Liane. 'I saw someone mention it on an email chain.'

'Sounds dodgy to me.'

Me too, thought Liane.

The news that this was after all an internal problem was the final straw for Stephen Murray and confirmed what Liane always suspected: that her manager was a chump who would struggle to locate his backside with both hands. He stood over her and tapped a finger as he held his hips. She knew he would now get an earful from *his* line-manager – something to do with customer satisfaction targets – and she imagined there would be some internal debate over who to pin the blame on. Clearly, he had decided the only option was to punch down.

'I think we're done here, Liane,' he said. 'I think it's probably time for you to head home and get ready for that baby of yours to arrive.'

'But–'

Stephen lifted his hand and Liane suddenly felt all the power and energy leave her body. It was amazing, the change in her. She was usually mouthy and bold, but pregnancy had turned her weepy and feeble. She thought with despair of her lost ballsy attitude and hoped it hadn't left her forever. Was she doomed to spend her life acting like a giant doormat just because her hormones had taken over? *I just answered the call*, she wanted to say. *That's all I did. You can't let me go.* But she couldn't.

'We'll send through the final payment in our next pay run,' he said. 'You can leave your ID and everything on the front desk.'

Now he was glancing about, caught in the headlights of Liane's lost expression and the reproachful eyes of the other customer service workers. Liane looked at his guilty face and wished she was her old self. The sort of person who would tell him where he could shove his regret. She rose from her seat, her bump preventing her making any kind of dignified exit. In the last few days she had developed a definite waddle. At times, it felt like the baby was head-butting her in the privates. Like her line-manager, it seemed her child was adept at punching down.

She just wanted to get home, eat a big family-sized bag of crisps, and have a good cry. She knew Callum would be lovely – wouldn't make a single reproach, would tell her they were a bunch of arseholes and she wasn't to worry. But somehow that made her feel worse, because all the time he was saying the right thing, holding her head to his chest and kissing her hair, he would be working out how much money they would be short now she didn't have a job. He would be thinking about how many more shifts at the hotel he could squeeze in without collapsing from exhaustion.

She took her bag from her desk (the line manager suddenly unable to meet her gaze), said goodbye to Faith in the adjacent booth – who shot her a sad smile – and headed wearily out of the door towards the lifts.

Perhaps her body was more defiant than she was right now; perhaps the baby inside of her was ready to make a stand even if Liane wasn't; perhaps it was just dumb luck. But, for whatever reason, as Liane waddled along the carpet tiles, bereft and ready to blub, her baby punched down, the muscles in her uterus squeezed tight, and, with a bubbling surge, her waters broke all over the floor.

TWENTY-ONE

Phil blew at the weedy froth on her coffee – the bubbles clinging on pitifully under the force of her breath – and tried not to let her mind boggle. She couldn't quite believe what was happening. Judith Jones, her nemesis from the front desk, had agreed to speak to her, and now they were in Marilla's hotel room – Phil perched on the edge of the bed, Judith on the neat parlour chair by the window.

Phil wanted to know why Judith had taken up Oli Cromwell's room service when she worked in reception.

More than that, she wanted to know what they had talked about. Llewellyn in room 302 had heard Cromwell talking to two women. The first had to be Marilla, and the second? Surely it was Judith. And if it had been Judith, why had Phil bumped into her as she made a beeline for the crime scene the day after Oli's death?

'This is why no one trusts the media,' said Judith, sipping her coffee and grimacing. 'You lot just make up any old rubbish. This is all off the record, by the way, and no you may not record me.'

The dreaded words. Phil couldn't help but admire Judith's common sense. For whatever reason, the receptionist had agreed to talk, but Phil got the impression that Judith wanted something from Phil as much as she wanted something from her. And that made her curious: what could Judith possibly want?

'Listen, help me out here,' Phil said with one of her expansive grins. The more Judith resisted her, the more she felt compelled to try winning her over. It was faintly pathetic. 'Are you saying it's perfectly normal for a front of house employee to take up room service?'

'No,' said Judith in exasperation. She was acting as though Phil was a small child who'd asked her the same question for the umpteenth time that day. 'It's not perfectly normal. But I told you, Callum had gone AWOL and it meant the kitchens were short-staffed.'

'Actually,' Judith corrected herself, 'they're always short-staffed, but with Callum on the gadabout god only knows where, they were struggling to get their covers out. So, when the room service orders came in, I said I'd take them up. His nibs was the last one I did before I headed home at the end of my shift. Callum had reappeared at that point and so they didn't need my help any longer.'

'Right,' said Phil, jotting down as much as she could. 'Can I check this again?' she said, risking Judith's wrath. 'It's just that Callum insisted he hadn't started his shift when the room service order went up.

'He bloody well had,' said Judith. 'That's what all the fuss was about. Ruby the manager sent me off looking for him. When I got to the kitchens it was total chaos. They were still serving guests for dinner and trying to get the room service out. Callum had prepared Oli Cromwell's order and one other and they were sitting on the side, going cold. Anya couldn't take them up because she had front-of-house to organise, and all her staff were going nineteen to the dozen, so I offered to take them.'

'What did he order?' asked Phil. She already knew, of course. She had seen the cold chips and the chicken salad tipping off the plate towards Oli's naked leg.

Judith rolled her eyes, 'Oh, I don't know. Chicken and chips I think.'

'And did you speak to him?'

'He answered the door and I handed the food over. He said, "thanks" and then tipped me – I think it was a twenty – and I left.'

'Sounds like it was all over pretty quickly?'

Judith pulled a face that said, '*obviously*' and didn't dignify the question with a response. Phil tried to formulate a new question fast.

'You must have impressed him,' she said.

She could see the magic of the curiosity gap doing its thing; Judith gave in.

'What do you mean?' she said.

'From what I've heard he's notoriously tight,' Phil replied. 'Twenty is a big tip for one tray of food.'

'It might have been a fiver,' said Judith with casual nonchalance.

'Surely you'd have remembered?' said Phil. 'I assume you kept it?'

Judith's look this time said, are you mad?

'You didn't keep it?' said Phil. 'Isn't it a collector's item now?'

'If it is, it's under new ownership,' Judith said, sardonically. 'It's now in the hands of the new wine bar in town.'

'Judy's?' said Phil.

Judith turned pale. 'Is that what it's called?' she said, faintly. 'I did wonder.'

Was she going to be sick, Phil wondered? She glanced around for a dustbin, but then Judith shook herself and shifted her weight in a way that suggested she was about to wrap things up. Phil panicked and threw out another question, hoping to keep her a little longer.

'What was it like – Judy's? Did you go after work?'

'Only briefly,' sniffed Judith. 'Bit tacky if you ask me.'

'And what was it like, meeting Oli?' she said. 'Were you a fan?'

It was a poor choice of question. Judith had already made it perfectly clear she found Phil both inane and idiotic, but it seemed to do the trick.

'Not particularly,' she said. 'I'd only seen one or two of his films. I hadn't even heard of him until a few months ago.'

'Oh really?' Phil smiled impishly. 'You hadn't heard of Aldhill's most famous son?'

Had Judith flinched a little when she said that?

'What happened a few months ago?' Phil asked.

Judith looked at her for a moment until she realised what Phil meant.

'My friends invited me to the cinema,' she said. 'One of those car films with all the loud explosions and the girls with no clothes on.'

'I think you just described every film Oli Cromwell made.'

'Not that I mind girls with no clothes on,' Judith continued. 'I just don't think it's practical to fix a car in hot pants and a bikini top.'

Phil laughed. She was referring to the *Speed Demon*

franchise's young mechanic, who seemed to run her garage wearing beach wear and heels.

'Yeah, that sort of get-up's probably more of a hindrance than a help when you're trying to do an oil change.'

'It was quite fun, though,' said Judith, seemingly still determined not to bond with Phil. 'I do enjoy a good action movie. I've seen a few of his others since then – tracked them down on TV – mindless entertainment's sometimes all you're fit for after a day at the hotel.'

'But you weren't starstruck to meet him?' said Phil.

Judith shrugged. 'Oh not really.'

Her tone was so light, so full of studied indifference, that Phil instinctively didn't believe her.

'We've had celebrities at the hotel before,' Judith continued. 'I'll be honest with you. I was more excited when Mendy Millar came in a few years back.' Phil's blank expression prompted further explanation. 'She was a famous weather girl, back in the '80s,' she explained. 'God, I expect you weren't even born then.'

'I'll ask my gran later,' said Phil cheekily, and Judith threw her another sour expression.

'Anyway, I liked Mendy when she was on. Course, she probably got too old and they gave her the heave-ho. You know what TV's like. Any woman hits the menopause and she's out on her ear. The men just keep turning into withered old testicles before your very eyes.'

'You're not wrong,' agreed Phil, laughing at the image.

'People don't like seeing an older woman on screen; reminds them of their mothers, doesn't it? They just see old nags when a woman stops being fertile. A crone only fit for public flogging.'

'Oh, I don't know,' said Phil. She didn't really believe the public all hated their mothers that much. 'I like to think things are getting better in that regard.'

It was a risky move – disagreeing with the woman she was trying to butter up. But it seemed to pay off.

'Do you think so? I hope you're right,' she said. 'I'm not ready to be put out to pasture just yet.'

'So when they asked you to take up the room service, you didn't request specifically to take up Oli's?'

'Why would I?' said Judith. 'He was just another guest as far as I was concerned.'

'Weren't there any other staff members keen to meet him?' asked Phil. She got the distinct impression that Anya would have jumped at the opportunity.

'As I said, everyone was rushed off their feet, running around like blue-arsed flies, not able to catch their breath. I had the time to help, so I did.' She looked at Phil, irritated again. 'I know what you're trying to do, you know.'

'What?' said Phil.

'You're trying to make a story out of this so you have something to send to the nationals. I've seen plenty of ambitious people in my time and you're the worst I've come across.'

Phil was surprised by how much that stung. She blinked as the insult landed and burrowed deep into her, twisting her insides.

'Wow,' was all she could say.

'What do you hope to gain from all this? Do you imagine you'll get some marvellous promotion? An invite to the big table?'

Phil shifted in her seat. Judith's words seemed to come at her like a physical attack and she felt herself shifting backwards.

'And then what?' continued Judith. 'You'll finally be a big success? You'll have made it as a journalist? Is that really the sum total of your ambition? To write a big exclusive about some dead local lad and his sad, sorry end?'

Phil wasn't sure where to go from here. Judith hadn't said anything that wasn't true. She was ambitious, perhaps distastefully so, and yet somehow it didn't seem to stop her impulse to keep on asking the questions. For all Judith's brutal home truths, Phil still wanted to know why she had taken up the room service. She still wanted to hear what they had talked about in the room that night. She looked down at the floor, her arms folded around her, and took a few slow breaths while she tried to collect herself. She hoped Judith would be doing the same. But when she looked up, the receptionist was looking out of the window, her coffee cup at her lips, tears streaming down her face, her lips shaking at the cup edge as she silently wept.

'What...' said Phil. She couldn't form the rest of the question: what are you doing; what are you crying about; what aren't you telling me?

'I can't believe he's gone,' said Judith. 'I'd only just met him.'

TWENTY-TWO

Liane hadn't gone straight to hospital. She knew the rush to the labour ward was a myth the film industry liked to peddle. And she knew, despite what TV suggested, it wasn't the norm for her waters to break before labour began. The contractions were mild and erratic, and she had no plans go anywhere only to be sent home again.

After she had created an almighty headache for the cleaning staff – and she had a brief moment to hope that the liquid wouldn't stain before remembering that she shouldn't care less about ruining the carpets – she had been ushered to an office chair where Stephen Murray, in a state of pure panic, had offered to ring 999 or summon any number of medical professionals, including Sue from HR who had done her basic first aid training.

'No, it's fine,' said Liane, busy trying to count contractions. So far they were barely worth mentioning, coming a good distance apart and not staying for long when they did. 'I'll just sit for a minute.'

There was no way in hell she was going to hang around

here any longer than she had to. She didn't want to get a cab, though. She didn't want to have a cleaning bill to pay if her waters decided to go for a second act. No, she would be fine to walk so long as she took it slowly. For now, it was enough just to get as far away from Stephen Murray and Telligence as she could. Having him flapping about her face like a panicked bird trapped in a building was irritating in the extreme, and so she waited for a contraction to pass before hefting herself up out of her seat and heading for the lift.

'Good luck, babes!' called Faith, who had muted her call in order to shout across the room.

'Yeah, break a leg, hon,' called Dashae, another friend and colleague. 'Keep us updated.'

'Take care!' squawked Stephen as Liane lumbered through the sliding doors.

Somewhere, from the depths of her being, some of Liane's old spirit surfaced.

'Go fuck yourself, weasel,' she said as the lift doors closed.

The walk home was slow. Her waters breaking had made everything feel heavier. She had never been more pregnant in her life; she was the living embodiment of 'cumbersome'. She rang her mother Diane, who squealed and told her she would finish her shift early and head over as soon as she could.

'Don't worry, mum, I'm ages away ye–' the rest of the sentence ended abruptly so Liane could grasp a wall and have a contraction, the wave of pain sending her up onto her tiptoes. She dialled the hospital after that. The midwife on triage told her to pop in to check if her water had actually broken before they made any decisions.

'What else could it be?' said Liane before the penny

dropped. She was offended at the idea. 'I think I can tell the difference between my waters breaking and me pissing myself,' she said.

'You'd be surprised,' said the midwife. 'It's ok, you can go home afterwards.'

Liane knew she was on a countdown now. The call to the midwife had started the clock. She had twenty-four hours to hit established labour or they would insist on inducing her. She really didn't want that. She had been the birthing partner for her cousin, had witnessed the horror show of that labour, which seemed to involve endless pain and blood; scenes from a mediaeval torture chamber. She remembered watching the grisly mess unfold and thinking, *why haven't they found a better way to do all this by now?* All those great leaps in medical science and women still ended up on all fours mooing in front of a roomful of strangers.

She didn't head for the hospital. The midwife might suspect her of being an idiot, but to Liane's mind, wetting yourself and your waters breaking were very separate events. The latter felt like passing a water balloon, the former like an embarrassing end to a night out. If she went to the hospital, she'd be stuck there for hours waiting to be seen. She knew midwives and nurses were rushed off their feet – she had friends and family in the NHS and she was well aware of how busy they were – but on every hospital visit she was struck by how sleepy and slow everything was. Perhaps her year as an Aldi checkout worker had rewired her brain. Now, everything could benefit from a bit more urgency. She couldn't face watching them all shuffling round, stopping to borrow a pen from a co-worker, discussing another patient, joking with a colleague. Better to wait at home until her labour was established. If she arrived at triage ready to go, she'd be ushered straight through like a guest of honour. Fast checkout service.

She didn't ring Callum, either, she wanted to focus on getting home now. The walking was good for the contractions. She had prepared for her cousin's birthing partner duties by watching a doula's YouTube channel. Now she knew all about the 'miracle of movement' (as the doula breathlessly called it). In fact, Liane knew more than she'd like to about the mysteries of childbirth. There was a reason women only shared all the gory details of their birthing story with other mothers. It was nature's way of making sure more babies were born. Her experience with her cousin had shattered her innocence and there had been sights she couldn't unsee.

No, she wouldn't ring Callum just yet; let her keep her secret a little while longer. Let him sleep off his morning shift while he had the chance. She stopped as another wave of pain gripped her around her middle, the muscles in her stomach and back compressing the breath from her body.

She shut her eyes and took a breath.

By the time she got home, Callum had headed off to his next shift at the hotel. He left her a little note on the pillow, reminding her that he loved her and telling her that he left her a bowl of pasta in the fridge that she could eat for dinner.

Her cousin spent an entire day and night pacing back and forth, trying and failing to get her contractions moving faster, leaving her tired and exhausted when it finally came time to push. Liane didn't want to make the same mistake and so she decided to take a nap; she was sure she could get a little sleep in snatches between the contractions. She popped a couple of paracetamol, strapped on a TENS machine, set it to a gentle thrum, and climbed into bed.

And that's where things started to go wrong.

It seemed to her that as soon as she nestled into bed, her body decided to up its game. Suddenly, she was having strong contractions every every six minutes. She realised she was in more danger than she had imagined, but her mother was finally on her way, so there was no need to panic.

She took herself off to the kitchen and heated up the pasta. Might as well eat it now; she was already starving. Callum would be starting his shift, which meant his phone would be in his locker. He'd asked Chef if he could keep it on him in case his wife went into labour and had been instructed that if he was caught using it during work he'd be out on his ear. Better to ring the hotel itself and asked to be put through to the kitchens. Callum would be allowed to take that call. Chef was from that generation that venerated the landline.

On her tenth attempt to get through, she gave up. The reception number was constantly engaged. So was the accounts department. She wasn't even getting placed on hold. The Oli Cromwell effect, presumably. The death of a celebrity was quite the marketing coup. Eventually, the contractions began getting longer and closer and she gave up trying to reach Callum, opting to leave a breathless voicemail and a brisk text: 'The baby's coming.'

Her mother Diane arrived, all bluster and plastic bags. She took one look at her daughter and said, 'Right let's get you to the hospital'. Liane checked the gap between her contractions – four minutes – and agreed. 'Heading to the hospital,' she texted Callum.

She sent him a few more after that.

'Where the hell are you probably need to get here now.'

'Get here soon!'

'Callum, where the duck are you for ducks sake?'

Then, finally:

'They're taking me to the labour ward. Pls come find me.'

She didn't write what she really wanted to which was: I'm scared.

TWENTY-THREE

Judith stared at the wall behind Ruby. The staff had been summoned for a meeting to discuss the 'Oli Cromwell situation' as Ruby called it. (She said the same when there was an accident in the hotel toilets: 'We have a situation in the lavatory, Judith, request a clean-up.') Judith found that by staring at the wall behind Ruby's head she could appear to be paying attention while also thinking about anything else at all, thus stemming her desire to run out of the room and fling herself in the sea.

'What we really want you to do,' Ruby said in her most corporate voice, 'is keep smiling, business as usual, best foot forward.'

The woman was speaking gibberish as far as Judith was concerned – like some third-rate poster in a corporate well-being retreat.

'And if you're feeling a little down – maybe it's starting to get to you and you want a bit of a time out – you can come and speak to us whenever you like, because I don't bite, do I David?' She threw a toothy smile in David the deputy manager's direction. He was lounging on the edge of the desk, arms hugging each other, dark suited legs stretched out with a louche little ankle cross revealing some playful socks. Judith wanted to slap his face too. A man had died and this insufferable pair were using it as an excuse to give a corporate pep talk. She despised them.

'You don't bite, Ruby no,' said David.

He was like a smug estate agent trying – and failing – to present a children's TV programme without appearing wolfish. They were the worst double act in history.

'See?!' said Ruby. 'Please do remember my door is always open, ok?'

Having announced her door was always open, Ruby and David promptly walked into the office and shut the door firmly behind them, presumably satisfied they had done their bit to boost staff morale. Judith could see them in her mind's eye, patting each other on the back for that rousing little performance, ringing the board to update them on how well they were handling the unfortunate snafu with the dead celebrity.

'They'll say anything to keep our noses to the grindstone, won't they?' smiled Anya, leaning in towards Judith in a cheerfully conspiratorial manner as they headed back to the hotel lobby. She was a lovely woman, Anya. Judith couldn't fault her at all, except to say she was a tad too cheerful at times. Judith smiled and rolled her eyes.

'I thought they'd never stop yapping. That poor man's still lying dead up there and they're telling us to act like nothing's happened. Makes you wonder if they've got a shred of feeling in their bodies.'

She knew she'd gone too far for Anya, who was willing to voice gentle mockery when it came to the management, but wouldn't indulge in a full-throated character assassination. Worst luck. Anya's unwillingness to get stuck into a good moan was, Judith reflected, perhaps her only other flaw alongside her unrelenting good humour.

'Have the police spoken to you yet?' said Anya.

'No,' said Judith, trying to sound relaxed.

'Really?' said Anya, 'I'm surprised to hear that, I thought you'd be top of their list.'

'Why's that?' said Judith vaguely. She could feel her heart beating in her throat.

'Well, because you took up the room service.'

'Oh. That.'

Of course everyone had noticed. Of course they all knew she had delivered the food to the film star. She should never have offered to take it up.

'You must have been the last person to see him alive. Isn't that awful to think of?'

'I expect they'll get round to me eventually.' Judith's smile was strained as she peeled away and headed towards her post at the front desk. 'Anyway, must be getting back to work. Don't want her ladyship accusing me of bunking off.'

'Back to the hamster wheel,' smiled Anya as she headed to the dining room.

Judith reached the front desk and tried to suppress the panic welling up inside. After the incident in the ambulance, Dean Martin the handsome young detective had taken off with a female detective and Oli Cromwell's PA (or whatever she was). And, now they were removing the body, Judith had assumed they had asked all the questions they wanted to ask, but apparently not. What would she say to the police when they asked what had happened that night? Would she tell the truth? She thought about the conversation she'd had with Phil McGinty. Why had she spoken to that girl? She was mystified by her own behaviour. But the truth was, she wanted to talk to someone who had seen him. She wanted to know how he had looked. Did he seem serene, or was he in pain? As though somehow the truth of his death would be written there in his lifeless face.

'Just got a few questions for you, Judith, if you don't mind.'

DC Grant Pitman had found her. Judith composed herself. She would brook no nonsense, especially not from this scruff who stood before her, his shirt half untucked, his grotty shoes in need of a good polish. She marvelled at the state of his hair, which looked like a bad wig made entirely from the soft down on a dog's tummy. It wafted and waved in the air like seaweed underwater.

'Ms Jones,' she corrected. She had no intention of hearing her name on that man's spittled-lips.

'Apologies Ms Jones, quite right.' Grant gave her a wide smile and put his hands out in apology. 'You get so used to everyone wanting to be called by their first names these days. I admit, I prefer last names – keeps everything as respectful as it should be, doesn't it?'

Judith had been around the block enough to know when someone was blowing smoke up her jacksey, but she thought it better not to get on the wrong side of the copper – not any further on the wrong side, at any rate.

'Can I suggest we go and find somewhere a little bit more comfortable?' said Grant. 'Ruby – Ms Davies – has given us a room to use.'

Judith was about to protest that she couldn't leave her post, when Anya appeared, smiling.

'Here I come to save the day!' she said cheerfully. 'I'll cover the front desk.'

'Are you sure?' said Judith, in the faint hope the woman would have a change of heart.

'Of course I am!' Anya beamed sunshine down upon them. 'Take as long as you need.'

'Thank you,' said Judith weakly.

'Much obliged Miss...?' said Grant.

'Call me Anya,' said Anya.

'Follow me, Ms Jones,' said Grant.

A few months after the Christmas card from Kenneth, Judith had gone for a girl's night out with her swimming pals. When she moved back to the area recently, knowing that Charles had long gone and aware via the grapevine that Kenneth was nearby, the Blue Tits swimming group had welcomed her with goosebumped arms.

They usually did dinner and dancing (or, more realistically, dinner followed by cocktails in a bar and some drunken booty shaking just before closing time), but this time they had ended up at the cinema. They'd been a little bit worse for wear from the bottles of house white at the chain pizza restaurant, and as they edged clumsily into their seats in the dark theatre, they were already making enemies among the other cinema goers.

They quietened down a little when the movie started, interrupting proceedings only occasionally with unwanted commentary.

'Ooh, that's a bad idea,' said Tina as Oli Cromwell decided to enter the disused factory.

'God, I can't look,' declared Kath noisily as she hid behind her popcorn, pieces flying into the laps of her neighbours.

'Watch out!' cackled Denise, sweeping up the fallen popcorn from her lap and stuffing it cheerfully into her mouth.

'Shh,' said the man behind them and Denise and Kath turned to apologise noisily. The swimming pals were too caught up in their own drunken antics to notice that one of them didn't seem to be joining in the silliness. At the end of the row, staring silently up, Judith sat, bleached by the light from the screen.

'You alright Jude,' said Denise as the credits began to roll and they stood to go. Judith, still sitting in her chair, was was blocking their exit. 'You look like you've seen a ghost. Film wasn't that bad, was it?'

'He's the spitting image of my Charlie,' said Judith, still staring up at the screen as the credits whizzed by accompanied by a thumping soundtrack.

'Charlie who?' said Denise. But Judith wasn't listening. Oli Cromwell was the spitting image of Charles in every respect, apart from one thing: he had Kenneth's eyes.

TWENTY-FOUR

DS Jen Collet sat at her desk and tried to quash the sudden rage that was bubbling up in her chest. It wasn't because of the CCTV, although god knew, that was galling enough – causing unnecessary complications to an otherwise open and shut case. It was because she was having to make a life-changing decision all on her own. Weeks ago, when she had booked the first available appointment at the clinic, she had been utterly sure it was what she wanted – what she ached for. At the time, the appointment had seemed an age away, but now, with the reminder pinging on her phone's notifications for this afternoon, it was all happening far too fast. In fact, she was beginning to regret the whole thing. And the regret made her angry.

This was something that needed a lot more thought, wasn't it? She shouldn't have to make this decision without someone else. How could she possibly know how she would feel in the next nine months, or in the next two years, or in the next ten years? It was a stupid decision to make with no one else to talk it all through with, with no one else to blame or to console with if it all went wrong.

What happened if the magical baby that she longed for turned out to be a complete little bastard? Or a psychopath? Or even just a really irritating person? The sort of person who pulled out in front of you at a junction at the last minute and then drove really slowly. Or someone who liked to talk in granular detail about what route they took on the motorways to get to you. Or, what if they were someone who thought nothing of tossing litter into the street? How could she be sure she wouldn't raise some little arsehole who would spoil the day for anyone they encountered? And what happened if she awoke one day, like the mother in the stabbing case, to discover her son in a towering temper, ready to take his anger out on her?

People liked to claim they had an awful lot of influence over their children, but Jen was dubious. She had met so many little shits through the years. She believed that parents taught the basics, the pleases and thank yous. They ensured you understood that murder was socially unacceptable, and that it was important to keep your trousers on wherever possible, but outside of those basic human societal obligations, people were pretty much born as they were. The worst parents could do was mess them up, leave them with a shattered psyche or damaged ego or broken head. But the rest of it, the passions, the fantasies, the things they loved, the things they hated, the way they responded to a joke – their whole view of the world, really – that was inside of them from the day they were born. It was the only way to explain why she was so very different to her sister.

Then again, some of the kids she came across in her job didn't stand a chance. She'd watched some truly wonderful children slowly slink inexorably to a life of petty theft and drug abuse. It was handed down to them by their abusive parents and society's indifference. She knew kids at the top of Aldhill who had never even been down the road to the beach, because they had no one to take them. When you met kids like that, you knew it was just the law of averages that at least a couple of those good eggs would turn bad. Even if they were born with the best personalities in the world, at least some of them would still end up having their collars felt by the Jen Collets of this world. But *how* she rooted for them in the meantime; how she hoped they would make their escape, and that one day she'd spot them out and about, wearing their childhood lightly thanks to years of happiness (and, no doubt, an awful lot of therapy). It didn't happen often.

The CCTV footage they did have didn't tell them much.

'That's handy, isn't it?' said Jen to Dean. 'Got the footage they need by law.'

Dean looked confused.

'They'd get their licence revoked without CCTV from the bar,' explained Jen. 'And here it is, miraculously surviving the big data wipe.'

'Right,' said Dean catching up. 'That is handy.'

The two of them watched what scraps the hotel had managed to send though, which consisted of a view over the bar next to the lobby. Together, they suffered the sight of Marilla and the journalist Phil McGinty flirting over cocktails before getting up and leave after a good few drinks. But apart from that touching moment, there was nothing else to write home about.

That's when Detective Inspector Lee Hudson turned up. Lee arrived at the same time as DC Grant Pitman, which felt apt. In Jen's mind, Grant was one of Lee's loyal spear carriers in the smug git tribe. Lee made his usual grand entrance, his knock-kneed, flat-footed gait not preventing him from swaggering in like the last gunslinger in town, the open jacket of his biscuit-stained Burton suit sending the pile of paper on Dean's desk flying. It was surprising to see the detective inspector turn up so late. On days like this, with an exciting, high-profile case, Lee usually made his grand entrance early, barking orders and then retiring to his desk at the far end of the room to hold court with the pompous air of a sea lion at a podium.

'Been with the boss and the mayor,' he growled, as though Jen should be impressed that he'd been with the DCI and a woman who ran the hospital radio station in her spare time. The mayor was a nice enough woman, but she was hardly the Queen. 'It's a PR disaster for the town. The fella comes here for the first time in umpteen years, causes a great hullabaloo about it and then promptly holes up in his hotel room and tops himself. Hardly the grand return of our favourite son the mayor was hoping for, is it? She says they're planning some kind of parade to escort his body out, so the riff-raff can stand on the street bellyaching about what a sad loss it was. Selfish bastard if you ask me. I was looking forward to the *Fast & Loose* sequel. Anyway, what's the update?'

'We let the publicist go for now,' said Jen. 'She couldn't confirm if Cromwell was suicidal, but she said he often stole her tablets, and he had been in a strange mood since they got to the hotel. Refusing to come out of his room, cancelling media appearances.'

'Sounds like a diva,' said Lee. 'What have you got, Grant?'

'Ruby the manager mentioned the chef—' Grant checked

his notes, 'Callum Geering had gone missing for quite a large chunk of the evening,' he said. 'According to her, Judith the receptionist had gone to look for him.'

Jen resisted the urge to tell him he sounded like something out of a children's book. What next? Roger the roofer and Bob the builder?

'But then,' said Grant, 'Judith buggered off, too – says Ruby. She claims she was stuck at the desk waiting for Judith to come back for most of the shift.'

'That's the person who took up Oli's room service, right Dean?' said Jen.

'Yes, although she was in shock when I tried to speak to her,' Dean said. 'Something to do with the cold water swimming, I think.'

'They're all nutters,' said Jen. 'Some of them do it on Christmas day.'

'Well, I did speak to her. That's why I'm giving you the update,' said Grant sarcastically. Clearly, he didn't appreciate Jen's attempt to bring Dean into the conversation.

'Sorry,' Dean said and Grant gave him a pointed look before continuing.

'So, yes, according to the kitchen staff, Judith came by the kitchen offering to deliver the meal. I spoke to her – didn't have much to say for herself,' he said. 'She took up the food, handed it over without a word beyond a few pleasantries and then she left. Didn't even get an autograph – what a waste! Ruby, the manager, didn't see anything and no one else went anywhere near the third floor that night.'

Grant looked disgusted, but Jen didn't bother pointing out that a man had died and probably wasn't the time to mourn the loss of an autograph.

'And what about this missing chef?' she said.

'His shift finished before I had the chance to catch him,' admitted Grant. 'I did ask them to tell him to stick around, but I was too busy trying to track down the CCTV footage at that point.'

'What's this?' said Lee, paying attention suddenly.

'There's no CCTV footage,' said Jen. 'They're claiming they've lost it.'

'What do you mean?' said Lee. 'There must be a backup. What about the cloud storage?'

'Nope, all gone,' said Grant. 'The hotel doesn't have any footage at all apart from the bar and the lift. From what I can make out,' said Grant, 'the security firm is owned by the *Chuckle Brothers* and they don't understand how backup servers work.'

'Which makes two of us,' said Jen.

'That can't be right,' said Dean.

'I don't suppose it could tell us much, anyway,' said Grant. 'He didn't leave his room once he arrived and the only people who went in were his publicist Marilla Hunter-posh-bird and the person who took up his room service.'

'Unless it turns out the chef poisoned the food,' said Grant with a grunt of laughter.

'We're not testing the food' said Lee. 'It was suicide.'

'What about the glasses?' said Jen.

'If you must,' said Lee. 'Try not to waste resources on this one, though. Let's keep things nice and tidy, shall we?'

He gave Jen a pointed look.

'I was going to look into the CCTV company,' she said.

Lee stopped her.

'Don't bother until we get the labs back. If you ask me, the fella ended it, no question – probably saw the reviews for

Death and Justice. No point making a stink unless we have to, Jen.'

'Quite agree,' said Grant.

Kiss-arse, thought Jen.

'No, sir,' she said.

'Speaking of making a stink, I'm off to the bogs. The mayor drinks coffee like it's laced with crack. I tell you what, my bowels feel like the site of an ongoing massacre. Carry on without me,' he instructed as he waddled off to the toilets. 'And no one follow unless you're in full HAZMAT.'

Grant guffawed in delight at this.

'What?' he said, turning back to the stoney faces of his colleagues. 'You two have no sense of humour.'

'You two have no sense of decency,' said Jen in a tone that could have been serious, could have been joking, so that Lee couldn't be sure whether she was being insubordinate or joining in the fun. Dean smirked down at his paperwork.

After Lee left to commit crimes against the lavatory basin, the three of them continued discussing the case. But there wasn't much to talk about. DC Nandini Roy appeared not long after, wanting a full update, by which she really meant 'all the gossip.' Gobby, blunt and a fine connoisseur of potato-based snacks, Nandini was Jen's favoured co-worker when it came to solving crime. But with no indication of any foul play in the death of Oli Cromwell, Lee had decreed that Nandini's time could be better spent elsewhere: namely, in Eastbourne working on a case with DCI Petra Gull. The torture of not being at the heart of the action was too much for her.

'I snuck away as soon as I could,' she said. 'So, come on then, give me the goss.'

They filled her in and she looked a bit disappointed.

'What, no three-in-a-bed sex romp gone wrong?' she said.

'I'm sorry the tragic death of a young man wasn't spicy enough for you,' said Jen.

She had meant it to sound funnier than it came out. Jen had occasionally found it harder to take the dark humour of her colleagues since Nate died, and these days her sarcasm turned sour more often than she'd like. Nandini looked taken aback for a split second before she returned to her usual relaxed state.

'Yeah, fair point, that was a bit harsh,' she said. 'Still, can't blame me for expecting a bit more drama. I've been stuck with the DCI all week. It's like being trapped in a PowerPoint.'

'The biggest drama so far is that the CCTV has magically vanished,' said Jen. 'And Lee has gone to take a dump.'

'In that case, I'll see myself out,' said Nandini. 'East-bourne, with the queen of corporate-speak, suddenly doesn't seem so bad.'

Jen caught up with her in the corridor. 'What do you make of the missing footage?'

'Jen, don't start seeing crimes where there are none. Not everything has to be some grand conspiracy,' said Nandini.

She was referring to Jen's work on the Virtua Services case. Not content with solving one murder, Jen had unearthed another, forcing her superiors to reopen the file on Clive McGinty's death and creating an almighty headache for East Sussex police.

'But,' continued the DC. 'If you think there's something going on, then I'm the last person to tell you not to follow your instincts. I've seen what happens when you have a funny feeling, you weirdo.'

· · ·

From what Jen could tell the CCTV had been lost by a security company called Inference Technology Solutions or IT Solutions for short (clever, thought Jen drily). Searching for them online was unusually difficult. Their website was vague, more like a holding page, populated with stock photos of smiling, white-toothed blonde women in headsets answering phone calls. If Jen had to sum up what the website was trying to convey, it would be, 'Try not to look at our website too closely. Nothing to see here.'

Inference offered a range of vague services, although CCTV didn't get much of a mention on the website. Really they seemed to be more like an IT help desk. To Jen's mind that made The Marchmont's decision to use them as their security firm an odd choice. She typed the name 'Inference Technology Solutions' into Companies house and was left none the wiser. If she had to guess, she would say it was some kind of shell company.

The person of significant control (PSC) was called Mrs Cat Starling. The signature had a long tail at the end of the final 'S' that swept across the bottom of the letters like a cat's tail. Mrs Cat Starling lived at '9 Mewling Street, Whisker-ton, PRRRRR'. Her date of birth made her three years old. Whoever had filled this in hadn't even been trying. They couldn't even be bothered to concoct a believable lie. That was how much contempt they held this process in; how sure they were that the UK was a wonderful place to hide a dodgy business.

She looked up the director's names but they seemed to be incredibly generic. Lots of Sarah Smith and John Clark-types. The kinds of people you couldn't google.

'Dean, how do you fancy a bit of nerd-work?' said Jen.

'As long as there's no cosplay,' said Dean, looking up from his paperwork.

'Perfect. See, you're already more nerdy than me,' said Jen. 'I have no idea what you're talking about.'

Dean opened his mouth to explain but Jen cut him off, 'And I'd like to keep it that way.'

Dean shut his mouth again.

'I need you to find out everything you can about this company,' said Jen. She handed him a piece of paper with some scrawled notes. 'You can see I've managed to get some way into it.'

'Looks like my first bit of detective work will be trying to decipher your handwriting, sarge,' said Dean.

Jen gave him a look that said, 'Alright smart Alec' and swatted him with the sheet of A4. The paper took on air and flapped into his face harmlessly.

'I'll get on it now, sarge,' said Dean.

'Thanks,' said Jen. 'Maybe don't mention it to Lee though, ok? I don't need a lecture on stretched resources.'

'Got it,' said Dean.

'And don't spend too long on it either. If you're not getting anywhere in the next half hour, set it aside. If you can't find out anything I'll see if I can get the digital media investigator on the case, but I don't want to use up her time until I know it's something worth looking into.

'Will do, sarge,' said Dean.

Half an hour later, Dean turned in his chair and answered Jen's expectant look by handing her his notebook.

'I couldn't find out much about the company, I'm afraid,' said Dean. 'But, I checked the "WHOIS" on the domain name.'

'Why do I feel like you're just making up words,' said Jen and Dean smiled but didn't stop his flow:

'And their company website is registered to a Stephen Murray at Inference Technology Solutions.'

'Right,' said Jen, still waiting to see where this was leading.

'There's no one called Stephen Murray on the Inference website. But I looked up his work profile and he works for Telligence Industries. It's a local call centre and serviced office business.'

'They act as virtual receptionists for other companies, right?' said Jen.

'Yeah and they provide office space and marketing calls, lead generation, stuff like that,' said Dean. 'That's what Stephen Murray's profile says. They've got some council contracts too.'

'Right. But presumably, if they work for this IT Solutions company, they just took the call?'

'Maybe yes – if they've got the contract. But why is Stephen Murray's name listed on on the website?'

'Could that be a service Telligence offers? Web hosting and design?' said Jen, pulling words out of the air.

'Maybe,' said Dean again, although he didn't seem convinced. He carried on, however. 'Usually companies pay a fee to avoid having their details listed on the WHOIS database, but these guys didn't. So I thought I'd check who built their website and it was a small local firm called Virtua Creatives.'

'Virtua?' said Jen, surprised. 'As in Virtua Services?'

A name that needed no introduction in this office. Virtua Services was a large outsourced services firm that ran outsource contracts all over the region. Their signs hung from many local council buildings and schools, often for months on end as the work – whatever they were doing – dragged interminably on. Their dodgy building work was currently the subject of an ongoing enquiry thanks to a couple of school buildings that had fallen down with, it turned out, human remains inside.

'I checked on Companies House, but it seems like Virtua Creatives and Virtua Building Services are separate companies,' said Dean. 'No directors in common. So maybe, I thought, it's just a fluke, right? They just happened to have the same name? But then I looked closer. Virtua Creatives is run by Dan Mehta. I went to school with Dan.'

Jen could see he was excited with his detective work and felt a moment of reluctant pride in his efforts. This was why they gave her the newbies, she realised. He continued his tale.

'Dan went off the rails towards the end of year 10, started dealing in drugs and acting like a big man. But he was clever, too, you know? I thought maybe he turned things around and started a design agency. So, I looked him up on Facebook. Most of his posts are private, but a couple of public ones are posters for events down at The Red Room.'

The nightclub in town. Jen felt like they were creeping towards some kind of explosive denouement and she hoped for Dean's sake the big reveal was as impressive as he clearly thought it was.

'Go on,' was all she said.

'It's not weird in itself, is it, sharing club nights for a nightclub? Pretty normal behaviour, on the whole. But the way the posts are worded... Here's one, for example,' Jen peered at Dean's screen as he brought up a post that read, 'Feeling so hyped about this line up I've put together. So, so pumped that I've tempted these legends down to our club along with my bro Jo-Jo aka Dr Funkbruvva. Too hot damn! Come down, shake a leg and bust shapes, people!'

'Wow,' was all Jen could say initially – amazed at the language – but then she started to catch up. 'Kind of reads like it's his club.'

'Exactly,' said Dean. 'Or maybe just his club night – it could just be a hobby, right?'

'True,' said Jen, but she could tell Dean wasn't finished.

'So then I checked who owns the club...'

Dean paused for dramatic effect, savouring his moment. Jen stared at him and Dean, sensing he was losing the goodwill of his audience, brought up Companies House on his browser. 'And one name appeared as the club's director that rang a bell. So I googled him and sure enough...' Now Dan switched tabs and a face appeared on screen.

'Well, I'll be...'

Jen was looking at a photograph in *The Aldhill Observer* of the mayor and DCI Petra Gull at a local fundraiser. Next to them both was a photo of crime boss turned respectable businessman, Charles Getgood.

TWENTY-FIVE

Charles Getgood woke slowly. He inhaled a deep, sniffing breath – as if trying to suck energy from the room and into his body. Outside, the day was in full swing, but Charles lived on a different timeline. He stared at the ceiling, eyelids still heavy, before lurching up out of bed and towards the bathroom. He emptied his bladder noisily, leaning heavily on the wall behind the toilet, the striped winceyette of his pyjamas quivering.

At the sink, he looked in the mirror and saw his father staring back. When did that happen? He had become his father seemingly overnight, or maybe in such quiet increments he hadn't noticed until today. He leaned forward and washed his face as though hoping to rinse away all evidence of his old man.

Sometimes he wished he could start his life again. Have a do-over. Would he make a better go of it? He couldn't be sure, but he'd like the chance. He was in his seventies now, still tall and lean, still strong and powerful – like Clint Eastwood, he chose to think. But the truth was, he felt stiff and jaded. He'd barely woken up and he already felt like having a lie down. He was tired of all the late nights and late mornings. A few days ago, he'd spotted one of his old classmates riding a mobility scooter down the promenade, ice cream in one hand. The bloke was taking no prisoners, veering haphazardly into the paths of pedestrians and cyclists alike, barely in control of his vehicle as he tried to steer one-handed while licking at his raspberry ripple.

Boy, Charles had envied him.

He was not about to change, though, was he? He was hardly the sort to go hunting gelato. And if he was going to terrorise pedestrians, he'd rather do it from behind the wheel of his Bentley. No, it was better to accept reality: Charles would always be Charles. If I got the chance for a do-over, he thought, I would still turn out the same. He stared at the disappointed face of his father looking back and wished that wasn't true.

His dad was always ashamed of his crooked son, and Charles no longer resented him for it. He was right: Charles could have been anything he wanted. He could have actually been Clint Eastwood, probably. Instead, when it came down to it, he didn't want to be anything other than a criminal. So, no settling down for Charles, no ice creams on the beach, no mobility scooter, and no long afternoons in the armchair listening to the clock tick and waiting for 'his programme' to come on. He had a criminal empire to run. He reached over for his toothbrush and took another long breath.

If only he didn't feel so knackered.

Showered and shaved, Charles returned to his bedroom and opened the door to his large walk-in closet. The lights switched on as he entered, hundreds of glinting LEDs bathing his clothes in a tasteful glow. He selected a three-piece from his rail of Saville Row and Italian suits, picked out a shirt and tie, and began dressing. He wore moisturiser these days, though he would never admit it. Fifty years as a tough businessman and the last ten had been spent with a skincare regime. Retinoids and vitamin C masks and fruit acids. What would the boys who worked for him say? Mind you, it wasn't unusual for young men to care about their skin these days. If he told them, they'd probably share their favourite products.

Once he was toned, moisturised, and dressed, he headed to the kitchen and made a strong coffee with his little Italian stovetop espresso maker. He didn't eat breakfast any more. His appetite seemed to be non-existent these days. On the plus side, he had retained the cheekbones that had kept him in girlfriends all his life. On the downside, he was starting to get a little cadaverous. Oh well.

His classmate on the mobility scooter had seemed well fed – cake and biscuits, no doubt. Charles had seen them take the waistlines of many of his peers. It was easier to stay thin in the old days. Portion sizes weren't so ridiculous, and walking was a necessity, not an occasional pastime. These days, people had to wear special watches just to remind them to move their legs. And it wasn't just the leg movements and the portion sizes. According his girlfriend, Nancy, food used to be healthier. Apples in the old days had more nutrients. At least, that's what he thought she said. People in the 1980s could eat the same as people today and still stay thinner. She was a Pilates instructor studying part time for a degree in nutrition, all jobs that didn't exist when he was a youngster – not that he knew of, anyway. Still, it wouldn't have made a difference if they did. He still would have chosen to be a criminal.

Charles finished his coffee, grabbed his keys, and headed

for the Bentley in the garage. He had back-to-back meetings all afternoon, so he would have to forgo his usual walk and get straight to the office. It wasn't only gut biomes that were better in the eighties; Charles had preferred being a crook back then, as well. It had all been so much more straightforward. These days it was all shell companies and tax evasion and bloody PowerPoints. Back then, they'd laundered a bit of money and kept the coppers sweet with a few free lap dances on a Saturday night. Now, his staff seemed to want him to stare at spreadsheets and talk about EBITDA and staff retention and other corporate guff that bored him to tears. Since when had being a criminal become so respectable? It was almost impossible to tell his dodgy business dealings from his legitimate ones.

He started out a working-class boy and had accidentally acquired the sheen of respectability thanks to his business associates. What he discovered was that their activities were only legal in the very broadest sense. Legal, yes. Moral? Not particularly. Really, what separated the white-collar criminals from the blue collar criminals was better suits and better lawyers – and often the ear of the government. If working-class people hid their money overseas and created Byzantine business set-ups, the government would have made it illegal immediately. But since those were gentleman's pursuits, and much of the cabinet seemed to indulge in the same activities, no one batted an eyelid. So Charles had become a respectable local business owner with partnerships and properties all over the town. He'd been buying into them long before he came back to the area, funnelling his County Lines cash into his legitimate enterprises to launder the money and create local jobs for his hometown. Win-win as far as Charles was concerned.

He had intended to stop selling drugs in the area – for the town's sake, and so he could look his mother in the eye – but when he returned to his hometown, he realised it would be impossible. The area had a terrible drug problem, with addicts shambling down the high street in a sorry state. He couldn't run the risk of letting another outfit take over his patch. What if they brought in low-grade drugs and poisoned his people? No. Better he supplied them with the good stuff and made sure that they were safe from any of the poisons his competitors might bring into the area. Instead, he used his legitimate businesses to fund drug rehabilitation programmes and gave money to any politician lobbying to legalise drugs. It was the only responsible option available: get these people the help they needed, stop criminalising them, and then we can start to make the world better. Win-win.

But then this Cromwell boy had come along and started making trouble. Charles's business associate had tipped him off. Cromwell was planning a story in the papers about his criminal past. Charles had laughed when he heard initially. What criminal past? Cromwell had worked for Charles many years ago as one of his runners, delivering drugs and selling them in the local schools. ('Hardly a kingpin, was he?' Charles observed to Dan.) Charles had never even met him, not that he recalled anyway. Honestly, these pampered celebrities who liked to make themselves sound hard. Charles sighed. Just when it was all going so well, the snot-nosed little luvvie had to come along to drag Charles back into the gutter. He did not like getting his hands dirty any more; it wasn't his scene. Not that he could say what his scene was, truth be told. He didn't particularly enjoy spending time with his posh business associates either. He lived in a kind of no-man's-land between worlds.

His phone rang and he ignored it. He knew who it was. Dan Mehta with an update on his desperate attempt to clear up the mess he'd made. He had asked the boy to do one job and the boy had presided over an almighty cock up. His phone rang again.

'Dan,' he said. 'This had better be good news.'

But it wasn't.

TWENTY-SIX

Phil was surprised by how happy she was to see Marilla.

'You're back!' she said, when the publicist knocked on the hotel room door.

'You're still here!' replied Marilla with delight.

'I was interviewing people. And eating food on your tab.'

Marilla laughed. 'I'm glad someone got to enjoy it.'

'How did it go?'

Judith's words had cut Phil earlier – '*Is that really the sum total of your ambition?*' She wondered if her eagerness for news was caused by a concern for Marilla or a journalist's desire for a story. But, why not both? If she was going to make a living as a decent investigative journalist, why couldn't she juggle genuine human feelings with her own mercenary ambition?

'How are you?' she added.

'Well, spending all morning in a police station isn't exactly my idea of a good time, but my mother will be glad I've got something to talk about at her next supper party,' Marilla threw herself onto the bed and gazed up at the ceiling. 'Sorry, that sounded dreadful. I shouldn't have made a joke about it. Oli's parents will be frantic. Everyone will be frantic. I should ring them. I need to ring the office too. I hope someone's put out a statement? I sent them a draft of something on my phone earlier, but it was probably just mad nonsense. I was in such a state.'

'Yes they did,' began Phil, about to tell her about their reassuringly banal announcement.

'Oh god,' interrupted Marilla, her hand flying to her head. 'Did you see the fans out the front of the hotel? They've corralled them into a pen by the carpark so they don't get in the way. Like a load of sheep or something. I should go and talk to them. It's just too awful.'

Phil watched Marilla's eyes welling with tears at the thought of the fans. This is a good person, Phil told herself. Or at least, if this is not a good person then Phil wasn't sure she knew how to spot one. In that moment, she decided that Marilla couldn't possibly have had anything to do with Oli Cromwell's death.

'It's OK,' said Phil.

'No, it really isn't,' said Marilla, tears welling up in her eyes. 'I think I might have killed him.'

She went to the window, and hesitantly, Phil joined her.

'What do you mean?' she said.

'I don't know,' Marilla said.

So Phil did what she always did in tricky interviews: she tried to take the long way round, hoping to catch the real answer on the other side.

'Can you tell me about the evening?' she said. 'From your perspective.'

She had expected Marilla to resist. She wasn't an idiot; she knew she was talking to a journalist, and an ambitious one at that. But for whatever reason, Marilla didn't even say, 'this is off the record.' She simply began to speak.

'He'd been such a dick that day. I mean SUCH a dick. He'd made such a song and dance about coming here and doing the big *Times* interview. But then he cancelled on all those kids – or rather made yours truly here do it, like the massive sap I am. I really didn't want to have anything to do with him after that. That's why I decided to go to the bar and forget about him for the evening. He was so needy. Always demanding this and that, always making every little thing about him. My grandmother went into hospital a few months back and I took a few days off to visit her. He acted like a total brat after that, sulky and petulant. He said I'd abandoned him during a "vulnerable time", whatever the hell that meant.'

Her voice wobbled and Phil put a hand on her back to comfort her.

'I used to give him the sleeping tablets,' Marilla said. She lifted her eyes to Phil's. 'Even when he didn't ask for them.'

It had all come out then: Oli Cromwell's creeping hands and never-ending sexual advances; Marilla's constant rebuttals; her increasing frustration at finding polite ways to fend him off; her conviction that he would never stop.

'He was always pestering for drugs, too,' she said. 'He found out I had the diet pills and the sleeping pills, so he started to treat me like a pharmacy. And, to be honest, if he'd had a sleeping tablet, it meant I wouldn't get a phone call at 3am demanding I come keep him company. I wouldn't have to go to his house in the middle of the night and fend off his relentless and pathetic sexual advances. So sometimes I slipped one into his nightcap before I left.'

'And that's what you did on the night he died?' said Phil.

'Yes,' said Marilla. 'I crushed one up and put it in his drink. I didn't think for a minute he'd take an overdose. What happens if that extra pill was the one that killed him?'

'I don't think it works that way,' said Phil and then: 'What drink did you put it in?'

'His Jack Daniels and Coke,' said Marilla.

After that, Marilla had been too distraught to speak any more and Phil had given her a banana and a croissant (pilfered from the breakfast buffet earlier) and put her to bed.

Why was Marilla claiming to have killed him? A person might feel it was their fault someone had overdosed on drugs they had supplied, but: 'I think I might have killed him.' That was a brutal way to describe an accident, wasn't it? Phil tried to take it all in. She was exhausted. She had found a dead man this morning, and it felt like a lifetime ago. The hours spent wandering the corridors today, avoiding police and Marchmont management, and trying to piece together Oli Cromwell's final moments, had given her a strange sense of time. She felt jet-lagged, dazed from the soporific hum of hotels and the sound of fire doors being opened in faraway corridors.

When she closed her eyes, she could see him there before her, lying face down, naked on the bed, laid out like a consumptive poet, beautiful and perfect. He was so young – only four years older than Phil. He had been destined to become one of those gnarly tough action movie stars with two-day stubble and too many muscles. But when he died, he had still been lean, almost willowy.

Now it was all gone.

It seemed obvious to say, but all she could think was, 'What a terrible waste.' Maybe Adam Jenkins wasn't the only journalist who thought in clichés. But it was a waste. She thought about Oli Cromwell's final meal, resting near his leg. The JD and Coke Marilla had made him on the bedside table.

Something struck her.

She grabbed her laptop and made for the alcove where Dean had questioned them. There was a moment of hesitation before she plucked up the courage to open up the pictures of Oli's hotel room for the second time today. It was a distasteful act, no doubt about it, taking pictures of a dead man. Maybe one day she would have time for a reckoning, but not today. She flicked through the photos, and there it was.

The wrong drink.

TWENTY-SEVEN

Charles Getgood's name had made Jen's ears prick up. Older cops could tell you about Getgood's early days in Aldhill – before he left to seek his fortune in the big smoke – causing trouble, getting into local crime groups, serving time for various crimes. The County Lines investigators had paid a keen interest in him, but these days, nothing seemed to stick. These days Charles Getgood was an upstanding local citizen.

Charles had rinsed his money clean – for the most part. He owned the nightclub that Dan Mehta worked in. Dan Mehta's name was on the business that had built the IT Solutions website. Dan's design agency held almost the same name as Virtua Services, one of the biggest employers in the county and currently the subject of a large enquiry. Meanwhile, Telligence Industries was the company that looked after countless customer service calls for businesses around the country. It was a seemingly endless loop that confused the hell out of Jen. A corporate ouroboros designed to bamboozle any casual enquiry. All she knew was something fishy was going on.

So why not start at the tail and try to work her way around to the head? The Telligence call centre was on the way to Jen's appointment at the clinic. She wasn't sure what she had been expecting. Perhaps some dark and shady, evil-looking headquarters? What she got was a standard low rise office block with a rickety lift, stained grey carpet, poly-styrene ceiling tiles and the sort of strip lighting that should come with a migraine warning.

To Jen's eye, the dreary cubicles seemed to have been designed by someone suffering with a terrible midwinter depression – all grey metal and melamine desks and ugly blue office chairs. It was the epitome of a faceless call centre with screened-off booths that gave each desk an element of privacy for taking calls. Not unlike the police station, she supposed, but somehow that felt more welcoming. Perhaps it was Grant's desk clutter and the constant flow of expletives coming from Lee's office that gave the Incident Room more of a lived-in feel.

Then there was the manager, Stephen Murray, whose name, for some reason, was listed as the owner of the Infer-ence Technology Solutions domain name, despite the fact he was employed by Telligence. He came darting over to her as she exited the lift. He was exactly the sort of person you'd expect to find in charge of a call centre, all bland, grey suit and spectacles. He seemed to match the building.

'Do you know anything about the CCTV footage?' Jen asked.

'I'm afraid I can't tell you anything more than you already know,' he said, eager to be rid of her.

Jen spotted a couple of women looking over, listening into the conversation.

'Who took the call?' she said.

'Liane was the one who took the call. Liane Benbow,' said a young white woman with blonde hair and bee-stung lips. She had the sort of eyebrows that Jen admired but couldn't wear herself. How would she look her colleagues in the face if she turned up one day with a set of micro-bladed brows? She'd never hear the end of it.

'Yeah,' said a young black woman in the neighbouring cubicle. 'She took the call. You remember, don't you, Stephen?'

The line manager shifted awkwardly under her gaze.

'And where is Liane?' said Jen, picking up on the unspoken exchange between the line manager and his subordinate. 'Sorry, what was your name?' said Jen.

'Faith James,' said the woman.

Jen looked at the white woman with the amazing eyebrows.

'Dashae,' the woman said. 'Dashae O'Brien.'

Jen noted down their names and then looked up at Stephen Murray.

'I'm afraid we had to let Liane go,' said Stephen.

Let go. In the lexicon of corporate euphemisms that had to be one of the worst. Presumably, companies imagined it sounded like they were releasing a captive tiger back into the wild, but to Jen's ears it sounded like they just released their grip on someone hanging over the edge of a cliff.

'Unfortunately, we can't allow for mistakes like that to happen, and that was a rather big one,' continued Stephen. 'After all, an awful lot of very important CCTV footage was lost that night. And our clients expect better from us.'

'So, hang on, why did Liane get fired?' said Jen. 'Surely she was just the person who answered the phone?'

'That's what we all wondered,' said Faith, leaning round from her cubicle. There was some soft murmuring from the other desks, but everyone kept their heads down. The manager eyeballed them.

'Could you tell me why you thought it was strange?'

'Well, for one thing, Liane's like all of us. She just answers the phone. And for another, she knows nothing about it. Like, at all. We're just there to answer basic questions off the template we get given.' Faith picked up a laminated sheet from her desk and waved it at Jen. Jen would have liked to have a better look, but Stephen swiftly reached out and snatched it away. 'Then we pass it on to the IT people.'

'And where are they?'

Faith shrugged. 'Mostly in India, I think.' Faith continued, unaware of or unfazed by Stephen's stink-eye. 'If you ask me, she handled it pretty well.'

'Yes,' said Stephen. 'She did her best. But, as I always say, the clients expect better than your best.'

'Better than your best?' said Jen. 'Is that possible?'

'Well, we like to believe so here at Telligence. We certainly offer a better than your best service,'

'So, Liane was let go for answering the call about the missing CCTV footage?' said Jen. 'But could someone please explain to me who was actually responsible for losing it? I'm assuming Liane didn't press the delete button herself? Was it someone in India? Can you give me a number to call?'

'Ah, well, I'm afraid I can't tell you that. That's above my pay grade,' said Stephen.

'Can you give me a clue?' said Jen. She noticed he had started to sweat.

'It's not entirely clear where in the chain the footage was lost,' he said. 'We're still reviewing the finer details at the moment. But one thing we know for sure, was that Liane should have alerted the team sooner than she did.'

'What, like before the phone call actually came in? How was she supposed to know that there was a problem until someone rang her and told her there was a problem?'

Jen felt like she was talking to an alien about something neither of them understood.

'Right,' said Stephen. 'I'm afraid once again, this is beyond my pay grade and I will have to ask you to leave because we are extremely busy, as you can see.'

He gestured to Faith who was staring at him. Jen perched on the edge of an adjustable office chair.

'Who do you work for, Stephen?' she said.

'What do you mean?' said Stephen impatiently. 'I work for Telligence.'

'So, not Inference Technology?'

'No. Inference is one of our clients.'

'I see. So Inference is a client, and what about Virtua Services?'

'Yes, we work for Virtua Services,' said Stephen. 'We run call centres and virtual offices for a number of clients in the local area.'

'What about Virtua Creatives?'

'Who?'

'They're a local web design agency.'

'Never heard of them.'

'I suspect they've heard of you. They did the web design for Inference Technology Solutions.'

'Is that so?' said Stephen. 'Fascinating as that is, I'm going to have to insist you leave now, please.'

'And the domain name is registered in your name.'

He looked utterly baffled. Not quite what Jen was hoping for. Why did no one in this job ever just go pale, swallow, and say, 'It's a fair cop, guv'?

'I'm afraid I have no idea what you're talking about.'

'You seem to be very afraid, Mr Murray,' said Jen.

Stephen stiffened further, scarlet marks of anger rising in his cheeks.

'I'm afraid I have... I mean, I *have* work to do. Please see yourself out.'

He strode off towards the far reaches of the office. Faith and Dashae shared a look. Jen thought Faith was about to say something helpful, but instead the woman rose to her feet, clasping her water bottle.

'I wouldn't sit there,' she said, nodding at Jen's chair. 'The last two women who sat there got knocked up.'

Jen jumped to her feet.

The trudge up the hill from the clinic to the police station felt unusually gruelling. Jen had walked down because she needed time to think, but now that was the last thing she wanted to do. She would rather be back in the office, working, burying herself in things that felt more pressing than the need to decide about whether she was going to have a baby or not.

Her appointment had gone well. Deborah Ellis, the overfamiliar email writer, had greeted her at reception and led her through to Dr Friendly's room. Jen had almost cancelled the booking when the name of the doctor came through. She wasn't sure she could spend so much time in a room with someone called Friendly. And, just her luck, it turned out Dr Friendly lived up to the moniker. She smiled up at Jen as she walked in and gestured to a seat in front of her desk.

'Hello, Jen! Do come in,' Dr Friendly said. 'Make yourself comfy.' Too friendly, Jen thought. A bit like Deborah Ellis, she was beginning to suspect everyone who worked here was sucking laughing gas in their lunch breaks. She imagined they all owned a poster that said, 'You don't have to be mad to work here but it helps' and lived their lives by it like it was some kind of creed.

'So, how are you feeling about everything?' said Dr Friendly.

Oh god, not someone who wants to talk about feelings, groaned Jen inwardly. But something about the kindness of her tone and the unexpected generosity of the question made Jen's eyes fill with tears against her will. She didn't dare answer because she knew the only sound that would come out would be a blubbering whimper. Luckily, Dr Friendly was an old hand at this.

'It's not an easy decision to make, I know. How about I talk you through the process and you can have a think about whether you want to continue?'

But really Jen already knew the answer. How could she live on this planet knowing that a piece of Nate still existed out there somewhere? She just couldn't. She had to have that piece of him. She wanted to create a person who could bring her closer to the man she had loved so much – who she missed with every fibre of her being.

He had died at precisely the wrong time. All the early problems you get in relationships had been ironed out. They had mostly had all their arguments and resolved as many of them as they possibly could before deciding that they would have to put up with the unchangeables. Jen would accept his inability to load the dishwasher properly and Nate would accept her need to interfere pointlessly in every task. It was shaping up to be a long and happy marriage. And then Nate went and spoiled it all.

Not that Jen had expected the marriage to last forever. She was a firm believer that humans weren't meant to mate for life; nature intended a period of monogamy, but only to a point. She had fully expected them to manage at least ten happy years together, however. Maybe longer if they worked hard at it and didn't let the dishwasher squabble become any more heated. As it was, they'd made it to five years before Nate had ended things in the worst way possible.

Jen had tried to persuade herself it was a good thing. This way it ended on a high note. They would never have the chance to grow bored of each other. But, for all her outspoken beliefs on the nature of humanity and the unrealistic expectations of monogamy, she knew deep down they would have easily made it past ten years. They would have sailed past twenty. They had the right constitution for a long marriage, because although she was difficult and cranky and sarcastic, those seemed to be the qualities Nate liked in her. And neither of them seemed at all fazed by the years ahead, by the sameness of every day, by the dreadful predictability of their lives together. If anything, they were glad of it.

Jen didn't need excitement. She got enough of that at work. She found just the sight of him calmly reassuring, and it was all she really wanted. She never really understood the people who found reliability a turn off. Coming home and discovering him building shelves in the alcove was enough to make her fall in love with him all over again. It was those little things she missed more than anything. How she envied her friends when they complained about the boredom of marriage, the repetitiveness of their sex life. If only they knew just how special those things were, and how much they would miss them if they were ever taken away.

Jen plucked a piece of long grass from the verge and kept on walking. She tried to focus on Telligence instead. Why had Stephen fired an innocent young woman? The thought of it made a bubble of anger rise in her throat. If Liane had been on the staff payroll, she could have sued for unfair dismissal; as it was, she was basically powerless. There was no law against being a prick. Jen stewed for a few minutes, allowing the rage to carry her up the hill and distract her from her personal life.

Faith had walked next to Jen all the way to the lift, keeping her distance, apparently on an odyssey to the water cooler with her giant water bottle. Jen wondered if she had reached the end of the woman's willingness to share.

'So, what do you think happened?' Jen asked. Faith shrugged.

'I don't want to get into trouble. I need this job.'

'Sure, I understand. Maybe if you think of anything, you could get in touch.'

Jen held out one of her cards and the young woman glanced around to check that no one was looking before she took it.

'One thing I'll say,' said Faith, 'is that it was weird that it was Liane.'

Jen waited for Faith to finish her thought.

'It was like she was targeted or something,' Faith said eventually. 'It sounds stupid, I know.'

'Not at all,' said Jen. 'Sounds anything but to me.'

Faith glanced over and saw the manager staring from across the office, upright like a meerkat on lookout. He pursed his lips.

'Anyway, have a nice day,' Faith said loudly as Jen entered the lift.

Faith stared at Jen's business card, then lifted her gaze to meet Jen.

'It felt like they picked her out for a reason,' she said.

TWENTY-EIGHT

Phil stepped out into the cool evening. It was the first time she'd left the building since she'd stood behind the fire exit door the day before. It felt weird to break the seal on her strange incarceration. Like a kind of culture shock. Everything seemed too alive and noisy. Now she would have to return to her normal life. She would no longer be surrounded by the muted hum of the hotel and its sumptuous smells. But she couldn't live in the hotel forever like one of those old ladies who gets lost in time. She had to return to her usual life and become Phil – Poodicca – once again. It had been an odd little parentheses in her existence. She got to imagine she was part of something almost glamorous, albeit, playing the role of the lowliest character slinking about the hallways, hiding from all the staff, hoping not to be discovered.

Apparently, Barry Brooker and Mike Hungerford had waited outside for an hour for Phil to open the side door. They were well known in the area, and Duncan the security guard (along with the extra security Ruby had summoned), had already shooed them away from the entrance multiple times.

'I'm sorry, I was being interviewed by the police,' said Phil in her best apologetic voice. 'And then I had coffee with the last person to see him alive.'

He had been a little mollified at that.

'Ok, Phil, you win. The story's yours. I want all the juicy details, mind you,' said Adam Grant. 'The whole kit and kaboodle.'

She was starting to suspect he spoke like that on purpose just to annoy his journalists.

'I'll set up a live blog?' she suggested.

That way, any new tidbit of information she picked up could be thrown up online (to be plagiarised by the national papers, no doubt, but that couldn't be helped). She didn't put everything on the website. She put up snippets of her interviews with Marilla, Judith and Callum, but nothing that might incriminate them – or identify them directly ('a guest who did not want to be named,' was the closest she got.) Even if she had her own theories about who the police should be talking to, she wasn't prepared to share them with the world just yet. She did not want to risk another nickname in the office. If it turned out to be just a simple suicide and she had made swivel-eyed claims about a poisoning chef or a vengeful publicist, she would never hear the end of it. And if it did turn out to be a murder, she didn't want to be the journalist who jeopardised any court case by revealing too much information. No, she would save up all the notes for one blistering tell-all piece once it was over. Maybe even a book.

God, when did she get so mercenary?

She stuffed her hands into her pockets, the cold of the air making her wish she had a coat. The Marchmont car park was speckled with candles and battery-powered fairy lights that sent a warm flickering light into the faces of the weeping attendees. At the far end, protected by some grey metal railings, surrounded by bouquets of flowers, was a giant 'O' formed from sprays of white flowers and green foliage.

The sight was unexpectedly moving. She had been prepared to feel slightly aloof and disdainful, but all those people, mostly female, holding each other and crying, hands over their mouths and noses, rubbing their eyes, gripping at the railings: it was incredibly affecting. There must have been a few hundred people, all of them united in their sadness. They stood bereft, with tear-stricken faces, glancing around as though hoping for someone to save them. They spoke softly to each other, and the air was filled with the feminine sounds of sadness.

Phil considered interviewing some of them, but her heart wasn't in it. She had been on the clock now for what felt like eternity. Let these people be alone with their grief. They didn't need a journalist, asking them for a pithy one liner. They didn't need to explain what it was they found so special about a man they didn't know. Phil didn't pull out her camera to take photos of the weeping teens, and it was good not to be the person after the money shot for a change.

She stayed for longer than she'd intended. Witnessing these people crying at the vigil so openly, so willing to share in their grief had affected her. Is that where she'd gone wrong? When Clive died, she felt the sadness travel inwards, eating away at her, leaving her hollow. At times it was as though she was filled with tiny grubs, like woodworms burrowing into her, eating everything that made her happy and cheerful. Everything that made her Phil. Eventually, she'd managed to replicate the old Phil. She did a good job for the most part. People still knew her as cheerful and happy and friendly. But really, the holes remained. She was still hollowed out.

It's why she'd become a journalist. Her father dying had started something in her, woke her up to the injustices in the world. She became fixated on finding someone to blame for what happened to him. Because it was someone's fault. Somewhere, someone had messed up royally. She had worked so hard to get that job at the local paper, had worked for months as an intern, scraping by, earning extra money at the weekends stacking shelves in Asda. For what? So that she could interview people on their opinions about a dead celebrity, or unmasking the Poo Fiend, or writing up the news in briefs about the local fête or the 'Wear a Silly Hat' parade. She had meant to become a crusader for good. Instead she was slowly turning into a hack.

Not that she hadn't done well at uncovering the truth behind her father's death, but it didn't do her any good. She knew who had killed Clive, but she was convinced it went further than that. Finding the murderer was one thing, but there was someone higher up who had orchestrated things. She was convinced there was. And once she had built up her reputation, got a reporting budget to match her ambition, she intended to find out who. In the meantime, she was the go-to person for anyone who had a grievance about dog turds, litter on the streets, or the council's lack of action regarding the pothole situation on lower Frith Street.

She looked around a little guiltily at the mourners. They had come to pay their respects, while she was feeling sorry for herself because she still hadn't been promoted. She was about to take her self-pity home when she spotted someone in the crowd she recognised.

Mr Llewellyn stood up near the front by the floral display the hotel had commissioned. Candles threw shadows and light across his grief-stricken face. No, not grief-stricken, she thought. Worried. He looked worried. Phil watched him. He seemed to be wringing his hands. She couldn't remember seeing someone actually do that. And was he talking to himself? His mouth was making words, but from this distance, she couldn't hear if he was making any sound. Reluctantly, giving in to her usual instincts, she lifted her camera and took a burst of photos. She tried to get closer, but a surge of mourners arrived quite suddenly, singing and linking arms as they weaved their way to the front. It's like they've been bussed in from somewhere, thought Phil. Maybe they had. When she looked again, Llewellyn was gone.

She spent a minute or two trying to track down the Welshman, before giving up. Perhaps he had been swept away by the wave of newcomers. Perhaps he had come to his senses and headed back to wherever he'd come from. It was time for her to do the same. She was so tired. Bone tired. She closed her eyes and opened them again immediately, her hand going to her neck, realising that she she he had forgotten to give Marilla back her necklace. Had she done it accidentally on purpose so she would have an excuse to get in touch with Marilla again? She had kept so many secrets from that woman that there was no hope of any real relationship between them.

As she turned to go, she caught another familiar face out of the corner of her eye. She turned back and there he was: Callum Geering the chef. Over to the side, near the railings, in his own clothes, crying again. He squatted down, his shoulders heaving in misery. He was gripping some garage flowers wrapped in cellophane, their sorrowful bent stems no match for the florist's professional tribute. Then, just as he had last time, he recovered abruptly and stood, wiping his nose and rubbing the remnants on his jeans. (Phil hoped his hygiene in the hotel kitchens was better.)

She lifted her camera – no regret this time – and snapped another burst of shots as he walked over to the tribute and placed his flowers on the ground over the railings, alongside all the other wilting cellophane-wrapped bouquets and miniature teddy bears. Then, stuffing his hands in his pockets, he headed off.

It was the briefest of decisions. She watched him leave and, without really thinking, followed him.

TWENTY-NINE

'You left without saying goodbye, Judy,' Charles said.

Judith detected an air of menace. After all these years, she could still tell when she was in danger from his temper. She had taken a different route home, but apparently he had figured it out. He pulled his car alongside and she turned to look at him, staring once more into those cold grey eyes.

'Well, you know me Charles,' she said. 'I need my beauty sleep.' He laughed at that.

'You're telling me! You're no spring chicken anymore, sweetheart,' said Charles.

'We've got that in common, Charles,' she replied, just to see the flash of annoyance across his face. But he masked it quickly and grinned.

'Me, darling? I'm in the prime of my life. In fact, you need to congratulate me.'

'Let me guess. You've married some young dolly bird and you're about to be a father.'

She could see from his face he was right. She knew he'd

be furious. He loved trying to surprise people with these little moments, and she loved depriving him of the pleasure.

'You always were a witch, Judy,' he said. 'I always said we should employ you as our fortune teller.'

'It's not hard when people are predictable.' Inwardly, she cursed her big mouth. Just shut up and then you can get home.

'You didn't predict that police raid, though, did you?'

Judith felt the air darken, like some portent in a fantasy movie.

'It's funny because it didn't occur to me at the time,' said Charles, his hands still on the wheel of his car. 'I knew someone on the crew must have tipped off the coppers, but I never once thought it was my Judy. But then you didn't visit me in prison and I started to wonder...'

'I just wanted to get on with my life, Charlie. I was so young.'

Charlie looked at her, the evening shadows casting strange expressions that Judith found hard to read.

'We both were,' he said. 'Still, it's all water under the bridge now, isn't it? I've moved on, you've moved on.'

'Yes,' she said.

'It's funny, you know, Judy. I thought when you left me, *let her have her life*. I didn't want you waiting around for me to get out of prison, wasting all that youth and beauty. But then, when I got out, I thought I'd look you up. It didn't take me long to find out about you. I sent one of the lads to follow you.'

'You did what?'

'Oh, it's OK, Judy, nothing came of it. The fella turned out to be a total waste of space. Kept drinking on the job.

And smoking weed. He followed you down to some squat in Brixton.'

Judith went cold all over. Colin, the beautiful man who'd shown her how to knit.

'Yeah, I had to get shot of him. He was meant to follow you, not seduce you, Judes.'

Judith tried to hide her shaking hands so Charles wouldn't see how scared she was. She wanted to walk away, could have done it easily – turned down a twitten where his car couldn't follow – but a perverse part of her wanted to hear what he was going to say next. He knew the power he had over her, even sitting in his car, staring out of the windscreen, barely glancing in her direction.

'Anyway, I was going to get back in touch, but when I heard what a washed up loser you'd become, taking drugs and having it off with anything that moved, I went off the idea. Shortly after that, I got banged up again, and I started to wonder if perhaps you were a bit of an unlucky omen...'

He said the last sentence like it was a threat, but Judith was too busy thinking about Colin. They had spent a wonderful evening together in Mary's squat, but when he didn't call her, she had assumed the feeling wasn't mutual and had, with some sadness, moved on. Colin had seen she had a child. Kenneth was there in the squat with them both on the night they slept together. He had been running around naked and causing mayhem all afternoon and then, later in the evening, tucked up in bed with all the other children in the top floor of the house while the partying continued. Anyone who knew Charles would soon guess Kenneth was his son. And yet, Colin hadn't told Charlie the truth about what he'd discovered. At least she hoped he hadn't.

Charles seemed about to go on, but then his phone

buzzed and he picked it up to glance at the message on screen.

'Saved by the bell! Afraid I'm going to love you and leave you Judy,' he said. 'Oh, and she's not a dolly bird, Judy. I grew out of that phase a long time ago.'

'OK Charles,' she said, feeling weak.

'I'll see you again soon, though, Judy. Don't go running off. We've got a lot of catching up to do.'

And with that, he revved the engine and drove off at speed, leaving Judith to walk home alone.

THIRTY

Phil reached up and touched the horseshoe around her neck. She checked her phone. A message from her mother: 'What are we having for dinner?' She put the phone back in her pocket.

Up ahead, Callum was taking long strides, gaining distance from her with every step along the promenade. Back at school, Callum had been the go-to guy for anyone who wanted drugs – weed, coke, molly, K, speed. Not the big ones, though. No crack or heroin. At least, not that Phil had heard. He knew everyone in the criminal underworld – or certainly had that's how it seemed to them as teenagers.

Phil considered catching up with him. She could ask him outright, 'Why did you say your shift hadn't started? Where had you gone when Judith came looking for you? Why did you lie about making Oli Cromwell's final meal?' If Oli had killed himself, it seemed like a series of pointless fibs. But if hadn't killed himself and something else that happened, what did that have to do with Callum? But then Dan Mehta appeared, running across the wide road and grabbing Callum from behind. He pressed down on Callum's shoulders and used him as a springboard to leap up high in the air.

'Alright chief?! How are we doing this evening?' said Dan.

God, she couldn't stand his cheeky chappie routine. Dan had been nice as pie at school, with a squeaky clean face and glossy hair and teeth. She'd fancied him in year 12. She was about to ask him out when school heartthrob Dean Martin had joined the school and swept her off her feet. She was glad it had been Dean and not Danny, because, looking back, Danny was already turning into the arsehole she could see harassing Callum right now.

You meet an arsehole every day. It occurred to Phil that maybe Judith wasn't today's arsehole after all.

'What's wrong, big fella?' said Dan. 'Having a bad day?'

They hadn't noticed Phil but it was only a matter of time. She was coming up too close behind them, trying to listen in. She hung back a little.

'Piss off,' said Callum.

But Phil couldn't hear the rest. Dan's voice came to her in tantalising snatches. Something about being a 'good boy,' and 'playing nice.' Something about a 'boss.' And Callum stopped and turned slightly, looming over Dan. Phil had to veer off towards a bench to avoid being seen. She tied her shoelace and strained her ears.

'Good, does this mean I'm free to go, or...?' Callum was being sarcastic. Disrespectful, thought Phil. This wouldn't end well.

'What do we say about keeping a civil tongue, Callum my friend? It's not difficult, is it?' Dan said. 'You hurt my feelings.'

'Sorry Dan. It's been a long day.'

'Easy there fella,' said Dan. Phil missed the rest. She could no longer continue doing up shoelaces indefinitely. She was forced to head over to the railings along the promenade and pretend to admire the flat evening sea.

Dan's voice wafted over the air toward her.

'Yes, and we're very grateful, chief, very grateful. You made the best out of a bad situation. I think it's fair to say, the boss was impressed. Boy done good.'

Phil took out her phone and, leaning casually over the railings, set the camera to selfie mode so she could see the two of them. Callum had his back to her and she couldn't hear what he was saying. His body language looked defeated.

'Almost, almost,' Dan was saying in reply. 'Just got one more thing, buddy, ok?'

Callum said something that Phil once again couldn't catch.

'Well, things change, chief, innit,' replied Dan.

Something shifted in that moment. Callum rose to his full height. He started to move towards Dan with purpose. She realised he was about to punch the smaller man.

'Get a room!' she called out.

Dan's face morphed from deadly serious to a broad grin in a split second.

'Philippa McGinty as I live and breathe,' he said in mock chimney sweep.

'What the hell are you doing here, Phil?' Callum said through gritted teeth.

'Just about to head home when I saw you two idiots,' she said, standing up from the railings. 'I thought I should come over and say "hi". It's been ages – well, not for you, Callum, but for you, Dan – how's it going, mate?'

'What's up then, Dan,' she said. 'You trying to get Callum involved in your criminal underworld again?'

'Philly, Philly, Philly. Always the joker,' he said, punching her arm playfully. 'You know me, I'm squeaky clean.'

'Of course you are, Dan,' said Phil. 'What would your poor mum say if you weren't?'

There was a palpable shift in the air around them.

'Don't go bringing my mum into this, Phil,' Dan said.

'How is Rahi anyway? I haven't seen her for a while. I used to bump into her regularly on her way to the shops.'

Talking about his mother seemed to neuter Dan. Somehow, Phil had steered them through dangerous waters and into Dan's most vulnerable harbour.

'She's... Actually, right now she's not so good,' he said. She's got problems with arthritis in her knees. Doesn't get on about as much as she used to.'

'That's a shame, Dan. I like your mum.'

'Me too, me too.' Dan put an arm around Phil's shoulder and turned her a little away from Callum, as though he was about to share a secret. 'But anyway, listen, Phil, we've got stuff to talk about here, so maybe you'd like to run along now.'

'What?' said Phil. 'Back to the kitchen?'

'If you like,' said Dan.

Yep, he's definitely today's arsehole, she thought. Callum was looking at her pleadingly, as though desperate for her to leave – or stay, she wasn't sure which.

'All right,' she said. 'I can see when I'm not wanted. I'll leave you boys to your... Whatever it is you're up to, and be on my merry way.'

And then without warning, she leaned in, held up her phone in front of them, and took a selfie.

'Oh, look at that,' she said.. 'Not as young as we were lads. Anyway, see ya! Night!'

Before either of them had time to protest, Phil stuffed her phone back in her pocket and headed off, innocent as a lamb in spring.

———————

It wasn't until Callum got home and saw the note that he checked his phone. That's when he saw all the messages from Liane, starting with the calm, quiet ones, and finishing with the desperate, *where are you?* pleading ones.

He hadn't known about the vagaries of due dates until Liane got pregnant – hadn't really given it all much thought, truth be told. Why would he? But then he discovered that a 'due date' was more 'due-ish date'. That had been a surprise.

He had been even more surprised to discover that, despite the somewhat relaxed concept of a 'due date', there appeared to be a very hard line in the sand when it came to a 'best before date'. Two weeks to the dot after the due date, the baby went off – like yoghurt or something – and had to be coaxed out urgently. Equally, there was a date earlier in proceedings that was a kind of 'fully cooked' date. Thirty-seven weeks and all was good. Before that? There was a chance the baby wouldn't be only be part-baked. Where was Liane? Thirty-six weeks, he remembered. Would the baby be ok?

He kicked himself. Normally he was glued to his phone, keeping it on him despite the threats of management and Chef (who didn't approve of modern day appliances like phones and bread machines). But today had been a series of interruptions – from Phil, to the manager asking him to stay to speak to the police, to the team pep talk they'd been made to gather for in the sweaty kitchens right when they were trying to serve up 50 breakfast covers. Not to mention the constant questions from his colleagues wanting to talk about the hot topic of the day: Oli Cromwell's last meal. Which is why he'd made sure he was long gone by the time the detective came looking for him. But then, on his walk home, he'd been caught by Dan – and Phil McGinty, for God's sake.

Would these people never leave him alone?

All he wanted was a quiet life with Liane and the baby. The encounter with Dan and Phil sent him into a deep, dark, brooding session, and he had kicked a stone ruefully along the pavement and sucked on his vape and had failed to look at his phone. So, when he finally saw the texts, he felt his body go hot and cold all over. In a panic, he grabbed his car keys and headed straight back out the door.

Of course, Phil hadn't really headed home after she said goodbye to Dan and Callum. That would have been far too sensible. Instead, she walked on ahead, turned off down an alleyway and hid, with her camera primed and pointed in their direction.

She had watched the pair of them continuing their conversation, Callum leaning in, shoulders tense, Dan more relaxed, but his face no longer in cheeky chappy mode. She managed to get a couple of shots of them before, eventually, Dan peeled off, leaving Callum to walk home along the promenade on his own. For a moment, she couldn't settle on which one to follow, but then her feet seemed to make the choice for her. She followed Dan Mehta.

Dan was blithely oblivious to her trailing him. He spent the entire time he was walking texting on his phone, the other hand stuffed into a pocket, his head swaying about as though he was listening to music. At one point, he made another call, which consisted almost exclusively of him saying things like: 'Yo, yo, yo, how's it going, bruv? Me? I'm tight bro, yeah? Listen, listen, listen, brother, come over, come over. I got something I want to show you. Yeah, yeah, yeah, yeah. All right. See ya soon. Keep it tight, yeah?'

He was like a bad pastiche of a Brixton rap act. Phil thought of Dan's older brother. He had gone off to film school and was now making documentaries that were gaining critical success. Dan's mother Rahi was a lovely woman who baked samosas for the church fête and cooked meals for the homeless with her husband and sister. She didn't deserve a son like Danny.

He made another call. This time, his tone was more polite, respectful.

'Yes, boss, on my way in now. I told him he did good with the Cromwell situation. Said you were proud.' There was a pause and Dan said, 'Boss?'

He looked at the phone, confirming something. Judging by his reaction, Phil assumed whoever he was speaking to had hung up on him without saying anything. She took a photo of him heading into The Red Room club and decided it was time to stop playing detective and go home. She called Angela.

'Hey, mum, remember me?' she said. 'I'm coming home!'

Nice as it was to eat hotel food, Phil's body was starting to crave simpler things. This evening she was planning on having cheese on toast or maybe even something with vegetables. Something blameless that wasn't covered in salad dressing, or mayonnaise.

'Ooh, lovely!' said Angela. 'What are you making us?'

Damn it. She'd forgotten it was her turn to cook.

'Fancy a Chinese takeaway?' she said.

'Your treat,' said Angela.

In a top window, Phil saw Dan Mehta greeting a tall elderly man. The man had a face like thunder, and Dan seem to shrink even smaller under his glare. The older man turned, and for a moment she thought he might be looking straight at her, but then he turned away again, and Phil felt herself exhale. In that brief moment, Phil had a taste of what it might be like to fall onto the radar of the most dangerous man in Aldhill-on-Sea.

THIRTY-ONE

Phil had spent three hours in a meeting for the recycling committee of the local council wondering whether her time would be better spent volunteering in a food shelter, or maybe just giving blood. She had begun to look back on her time at The Marchmont – five days and an eternity ago – as a highlight of her career. She called her mum and told her she thought she had already peaked.

'It's all right for you,' said Angela. 'At least you've found a peak. I've never peaked. I'd have been delighted to peak at any point in my life. It's all just flat lines as far as the eye can see.'

'Don't be silly, mum. You peaked when you gave birth to me.'

'Is that right? I think you'll find I only had you so I could use the parent-child parking spaces at Asdas.'

'In that case, Einstein, what did you have my brother for?'

'Oh, he was to keep you company so we didn't have to.'

'How did that work out for you?'

They said goodbye eventually and Phil returned to her write up. The office was empty. These days, more of the team worked from home as freelancers. Legacy media truly was dying.

Her phone rang and it took her a moment to decide whether to answer it.

'I've got a strange favour to ask you,' Marilla said when she finally did.

The strange favour turned out not to be that strange. Or, at least, Phil found it perfectly understandable. Oli Cromwell's parents had asked to meet with Marilla.

'But I'm stuck in London,' said Marilla. 'Would you be willing to go and meet them? They want to get a little more closure, I think.'

Closure was what Phil wanted, too. It made no sense, really; dead was dead, closure wouldn't bring her father or Oli back. But the brain craved it. The Cromwells' son had died; they had not been there to care for him. Phil knew her testimony might bring them some small comfort at the very least.

'I'm actually going to The Marchmont today,' she said. 'I've got an interview with Ruby Davies, the manager.'

'Thank you, thank you! I'm so glad you said that,' said Marilla, 'because I told them you would meet them there.'

Ken was strangely thankful when Phil arrived at The Marchmont. He grasped her hands in greeting and then apologising any time he asked another question about the night his son died – as though he didn't have a perfect right to know. He looked devastated, yet what struck Phil was how young he was – not much older than her mum, probably. Despite that, he seemed to be reaching towards old age.

He was handsome, but he kept it well hidden under the badly trimmed beard and the cheap barbershop haircut. In another life, twenty pounds lighter, Phil could imagine him being a rugged movie star, still at the height of his powers. Emily was a dainty little woman who looked older than her husband, but no less handsome. She reminded Phil of those older Hollywood actresses who get nominated for Oscars every year for playing 'brave' roles, which translated as 'minimal makeup'.

Phil answered all their questions, leaving out the unpleasant details. She didn't mention the pills, or the strange behaviour, or the constant requests for sexual favours. Let the police tell them the things they needed to hear. In the meantime, let them mourn their perfect son.

'He wasn't suicidal,' said Ken with such abruptness Phil didn't quite know how to respond.

'It must have been a terrible shock,' said Phil.

'No, you don't understand,' Ken said. 'He wasn't suicidal. He was afraid. I know he was.'

Emily nodded. 'We think someone was threatening him,' she said. 'Why else would he cancel all his events? He loved meeting his fans.'

'He loved attention,' added Ken, with a tinge of judgement. 'Cancelling on us was one thing. We expected that, but not cancelling on the kids; not cancelling on the press.'

'He was too scared to leave his room,' said Emily. 'He wasn't suicidal. He was petrified. We tried to tell the police, but they wouldn't listen.'

'Something happened to him when he walked through

these doors,' said Ken. 'And I'm telling you now: my boy didn't kill himself.'

THIRTY-TWO

Judith didn't know what to do. She had walked into the lobby and there he was, deep in conversation with Phil McGinty. Her baby boy. Should she hide? He hadn't seen her, so she could – could turn tail and flee from the building – but hiding was undignified. And anyway, darting off might draw his attention. Instead, she tried to continue as normal, hampered only by the constant urge she had to glance in his direction. But then he was standing and shaking the McGinty girl by the hand, his plain little wife giving the girl a hug and a shoulder squeeze. And before Judith could decide what to do, he made eye contact with her, startling a little before leaving the women and heading Judith's way.

'Hello mum,' he said.

Judith's hands began to shake. It made sense that he would turn up; he wanted to visit the place his boy was found. But seeing him in The Marchmont foyer was strange – incongruous.

'Hello Kenny,' she said.

He had put on weight and grown into a plump man with a beard. Still tall and attractive, though, like his father. Like his mother too, for that matter.

'I'm so sorry,' she said.

'I've got something to tell you,' he said.

They had spoken at the same time and now he looked at her in shock, realisation dawning. 'You knew about him? How did you know?' Tears began to stream down his face.

'He had your eyes,' she said.

'They weren't my eyes,' he said. 'They were your eyes, mum.'

His body was racked with silent sobs. Judith moved quickly around the reception desk and caught him in an emotional embrace.

'My poor, poor baby,' she said.

Kenneth cried into her shoulder and Judith shut her eyes, remembering how good it felt to hold her child, wishing it was for happier reasons.

'What on earth is going on here?'

Judith looked over to see Ruby the manager's appalled face. Standing next to her was Philippa McGinty. Judith had been aching to see Kenneth for so long, but how she wished he had turned up on any other day.

'Ken,' the journalist said when he lifted his red face from his mother's shoulder. 'Is everything okay?'

'What do you think?' said Judith, almost spitting the words at Phil.

'Judith!' said Ruby, in horror. 'Miss McGinty I am so sorry about Judith's behaviour. I'm afraid we've all had a terrible shock over the last few days, and it's not been easy, as you can imagine. And poor Judith was one of the last people to see Mr Cromwell alive.'

'Oh, that's okay! Judith and I are old friends.' said Phil. 'We've got that kind of love-hate relationship, haven't we, Judith?'

Judith should have been grateful Phil was covering for her, but really she just wanted both of them to sod off so she could take care of her son. He stood next to her still, mopping his tear-streaked face with his hands. She reached across the front desk and collected up a couple of tissues from the box next to her computer and passed them to him.

'Yes, well, it's important that we leave personal relationships behind when we're at work, isn't it Judith?' said Ruby.

'Ruby, this is Oli Cromwell's dad,' said Phil. 'Ken, this is Ruby, the manager of the hotel.'

Ruby's face turned ashen.

'Mr Cromwell, I didn't realise. I am so sorry for your loss. Let me tell you that we so devastated to have lost someone here in our hotel. It was a dreadful tragedy and an awful day for everyone here at The Marchmont.'

'I'm sorry. I was just a bit overwhelmed,' said Kenneth. He didn't seem to have registered what Ruby said.

'Yes. Well, we like to look after people here at The Marchmont and Judith is one of our very finest. Such an asset,' said Ruby.

Two-faced cow, thought Judith.

'Actually, Ruby,' said Judith, making a decision. 'I'm afraid I can't work this shift any longer. I've come down with a terrible stomach ache.' She began gathering up her handbag.

'Judith!' Ruby said. Judith really was getting tired of hearing her say her name. 'You can't leave me, not now. Philippa here has come to interview me for the paper about...' She cast sideways glance at Kenneth, clearly realising this wasn't a good moment to revel in The Marchmont's enhanced newsworthiness thanks to the death of his son.

'Mr Cromwell,' she said. 'If you'll allow me, I would love to take you on a tour of some of the tributes we have placed outside for your son?'

'No thank you,' Kenneth said. 'If you don't mind, I'd rather Judith here take me. If you're not feeling too poorly?'

'If you like,' said Ruby, disappointed. I'm sure Judith is more than well enough, aren't you Judith? Probably just one of your funny turns like the one you had when you found out Mr Cromwell had died.'

Judith could feel Philippa McGinty's bright eyes assessing her. The journalist wouldn't have missed that connection, she was sure of it. 'Yes, that's fine. Perhaps the fresh air will help make me feel better.'

'Wonderful, Judith!' said Ruby. 'You take Mr Cromwell here out to the vigil area and show him the beautiful floral display that The Marchmont has paid for. Perhaps Miss McGinty could take a photo of us outside later, if you feel up to it, Mr Cromwell?'

'You want to take a photo with Oli Cromwell's grieving father for a piece about The Marchmont?' said the journalist.

Philippa McGinty went up in Judith's estimation.

'Only if he feels up to it,' said Ruby, with a defensive simper.

'Perhaps see you in a minute then, Mr Cromwell,' Ruby called out as Judith and Kenneth began making their way to the exit. Judith held the door open for her son to leave and had a sudden premonition: she knew what was going to happen next and she wished with all her heart she could get Kenneth out of the door before it did.

'Actually, my name isn't Mr Cromwell,' Kenneth said.

'Oh I do apologise,' said Ruby.

'Let's go,' said Judith, trying to hurry him out, but Kenneth was already speaking.

'It's Jones,' he said.

THIRTY-THREE

Marilla stared at her dinner date, eyes wide with surprise

'You're kidding me? So the dragon from the front desk is Ken's mother?'

'Well, I guess she could be his aunt,' said Phil, ripping off a hunk of bread and transporting it to her plate to pick at, 'but they've got the same surname and he was crying on her shoulder.'

Marilla's face suddenly crumpled in horror. 'Oh god, does that mean I've been calling him Mr Cromwell all this time by mistake?'

'Did you think Oli's real name was Oliver Cromwell?'

Marilla saw Phil trying to suppress amusement. 'If you laugh at me, I will throw this bread roll at your head.'

Phil raised her hands in submission, her eyes twinkling. 'He used to be Tom Jones,' she said. Marilla raised the bread roll, ready to throw. 'I'm serious! Thomas Oliver Jones. That's partly why he changed it. I can't believe I didn't put two and two together when I interviewed Judith. It was staring me in the face. Judith Jones. But it's not like it's a rare surname, is it? I didn't think anything of it.'

'Why didn't she tell you? Why didn't she tell her employer? How absolutely bizarre.'

'I know, right?' said Phil. 'It does *not* make sense. Pass the oil, please.'

Marilla handed her the oil. They were in an Italian restaurant that Phil said was the best in the area. It was the sort that felt more like a café, with gingham tablecloths and candles in old straw-covered chianti bottles. Marilla watched Phil picking at her bread. She seemed to have zoned out. Was she staring out of the window over Marilla's shoulder? Marilla resisted the urge to turn to see what was so fascinating.

'Have you noticed how people give their children the same names as them?' said Phil suddenly, eyes glazed, feeding herself tiny bites of bread crust. She looked at Marilla at last and Marilla felt herself exhale in relief. She had begun to wonder if she'd stopped existing. 'My name is Philippa,' said Phil. 'My mum's called Angela. Judith called her son Kenneth. Same sounds, same syllable length.'

She pronounced the names again, exaggerating their syllables and finishing on a lispy "Kenn-eth".

'I can't say I had noticed that, no,' said Marilla. 'Are you sure this theory holds up under scrutiny?'

'What's your mum's name?' Phil asked, accepting the challenge.

'Vampira,' said Marilla, 'the dark princess, thresher of souls, gobbler of egos...' She ran out of ideas at this point. She wished, not for the first time, that she was funnier. ('It's a shame you're not in the slightest bit witty, Marilla,' her mother told her once with a mournful sigh, as though she'd contracted something incurable.)

Phil tried to give her a stern look. Marilla relented, 'Okay, okay. She's called Lucilla.'

'Ha! See!' crowed Phil. 'I told you! My theory stands. People call their kids the same name as themselves.' She fed herself a piece of celebratory bread crust.

'I think we should just go back to the old days where everyone named their children the exact same name and be done with it,' she announced.

'In the circles I frequent people still do that,' replied Marilla. 'My oldest sister's name is Lucilla.

'So there are two Lucillas and a Marilla,' said Phil. 'What are your other sisters called?'

'Julia and Mariella,' said Marilla. 'I suppose you're right. They do all end in 'a', don't they?'

Phil looked at her in astonishment. 'Mariella? But that's basically your name.'

'Yes,' said Marilla. 'It didn't go unnoticed. I think my mother was attempting to try again with a slightly upgraded model. And of course my younger sister is exactly that. Better looking, better at everything. The funny one. The thin one.'

Phil's eyes boggled.

'If she's the better looking one, well... Firstly, that's impossible. And secondly, please can I meet your sister?'

She gave an angelic smile and fluttered her eyelashes. Marilla took the only available option; she threw the bread roll at Phil's head.

In that moment, when the bread sailed past her face, Phil realised she was in very great danger with Marilla Hunter Davy. She had been mercenary in befriending her – wanting the interview with Oli – and she had been doing quite well at convincing herself that spending time with the publicist was just a pleasant way to pass the time. She had planned to use this meal as an opportunity to do a little surveillance work. The Red Room club was right opposite the Italian café and Phil had selected a seat that gave her a clear view. Not that she'd seen much: the windows were tinted downstairs, and the lights were off upstairs.

'Marilla?' Phil said. Her tone was wheedling, like a child.

'Yes?' said Marilla, like a cautious parent. They both grinned, but then Phil got serious. Time to ask the difficult question.

'You said you made Oli a Jack Daniels and Coke when you went in to check on him? Is that right?'

'That's right,' Marilla replied. 'He hasn't moved on to grown up drinks yet.' Phil watched her face fall as she realised her present tense mistake, 'and I guess he never will now,' she said.

'Are you sure it wasn't gin and tonic or vodka and soda maybe?' said Phil.

'What an odd question,' said Marilla. 'No he hated gin – couldn't stand the smell – and he wasn't keen on vodka. And he always had Coke as a mixer. I don't remember him ever having tonic or soda.'

'Or lemonade?' said Phil.

'You're being weird, Phil,' said Marilla, perplexed. 'Can we change the subject?'

'Sorry, you're right. It was a weird question, I know. It was just I was sure the drink next to him on the bed was clear,' said Phil. She didn't add, 'And I've got the photo to prove it.'

'That was probably his water, wasn't it?' said Marilla. 'The water he took the overdose with.'

'Yes,' said Phil, 'Of course. That must be it.'

But it wasn't. She knew it wasn't. He had two drinks next to him on the bedside table. And both of them were clear. So where had the second drink come from? But Marilla looked anguished and Phil felt a little guilty for bringing it up – and for bringing her here so Phil could stare over her shoulder. At least she hadn't lied about the restaurant being a good one. The pasta, when it arrived, was freshly made, and the tiramisu was lovingly prepared by the owner's 'nonna' who refused to divulge her secret recipe and only made enough of the pudding to satisfy about half of the restaurant. The fact that they got any at all was a kind of miracle.

'That'll be my influence,' said Marilla. 'The Hunter Davys are used to getting what they want.'

She was clearly joking, her tongue very much in her cheek, but Phil knew it was true. How else to explain Phil's burgeoning affection for this posh girl from the right side of the tracks? She couldn't be more of a mismatch for her, really. Perhaps it was irrelevant – Phil was assuming Marilla would want anything to do with her. Maybe she had more self-respect than to date a woman who just spent an entire evening looking past her to the building across the street. But, knowing Marilla (and Phil realised that she did know her), that was unlikely. Lucilla the elder was a gobbler of egos, alright. Phil could spot it a mile off. She'd scoffed down her daughter's entire self-worth; Vampira was the right name for her.

'Well, that was delicious,' announced Marilla, patting her

carb-loaded tummy. Phil had already surreptitiously unbuttoned her jeans before the pudding arrived. Soon she would have to attempt to reverse the process, something that would take considerable courage and a lot of breathing in. All she wanted to do now was head home to lie on the sofa in a carb coma.

'Do you fancy going to a nightclub?' she said.

THIRTY-FOUR

The verdict was in. Jen read the toxicology report: given the cocktail of drugs he had taken and the fact his fingerprints were all over the glass next to his bed, it seemed likely that Oli Cromwell had taken an overdose. So suicide, then. Jen was relieved in some ways, it meant one more case off her desk – it was now the coroner's problem – but it also meant facing a stark reality. There she was trying to bring new life into this world, while the youth of today were busy trying to snuff themselves out.

One thing that struck her as weird about this particular suicide – two things come to think of it: the glass next to his bed had a lot of the drugs in it, and the drugs he had in his system included some really bizarre things.

'Like what?' said Dean.

'GHB,' she said. 'That's a date rape drug. And Loperamide hydrochloride. That's Imodium, for diarrhoea. Do they seem like normal drugs to top yourself with?'

'Maybe he had diarrhoea?' shrugged Dean. 'Could he have taken them before the overdose?'

'It was a lot of Imodium,' said Jen. 'No one takes that much just for diarrhoea. You only need to take a couple of tablets.'

She raised her hand. 'And yes, before you say anything, I do know a lot about diarrhoea medication.'

Looking at his innocent face, she realised he hadn't been planning on making a joke. He was a nice boy, this Dean. Best one she'd had in a long time. She found the smart mouths exhausting. Being able to finish a sentence uninterrupted was an underrated experience in her view.

'What I'm saying is, it would be weird to take so many. It's hardly the normal choice for an overdose is it?'

'I suppose not. What did the SOCO say?' asked Dean.

'Nadene said an overdose of that much would usually have made him vomit, but the other drugs killed him first,' said Jen.

'Maybe he just grabbed whatever was to hand,' Dean suggested.

'But it doesn't fit with his image,' said Jen. 'Even in the depths of despair, would his vanity allow him to risk that story getting out? "Movie star took overdose of diarrhoea medication, coroner says." That would be the headline, wouldn't it?'

'What was the other odd thing?' asked Dean.

'Some of the drugs were dissolved in the glass next to his bed,' said Jen.

'So?'

'So, he'd decanted all the little plastic pills into a glass and crushed up the rest and then he'd dissolved it all into a concoction,' she said. 'Why not just swallow the tablets? Doesn't that strike you as something you do if you want to poison someone?'

'Maybe,' agreed Dean. 'But how do we know he just didn't want to take that many pills? Perhaps he can't swallow them?'

'But he had other drugs in his system. How did they get there? And also: where were all the pill cases? There weren't any at the scene.'

'Maybe he flushed them?' said Dean.

'We know he was already pretty drunk. Did he really tidy up after himself? You saw his room. He was hardly a clean freak.'

'Marilla would know if he could swallow pills. You could ask her?'

The DI walked past at that moment.

'Case closed,' he tapped the desk with satisfaction. 'Time to move on, Jen.'

He went off whistling to himself and parked his rump on his swivel chair throwing Jen a pointed look. She returned his look with the sort of hard stare that sent shivers down the spine of hardened criminals, but then she sighed and set the report to one side and opened her computer.

An email from the fertility clinic was waiting in her personal email giving her more information about the roadmap towards IVF. Dr Friendly had gone through it all with Jen at the appointment, but what with the unexpected crying, and the distraction of the Oli Cromwell case, Jen hasn't really paid attention. She still wasn't even sure it was the right thing to do. Would Nate mind? She tried to imagine explaining herself to him. 'I'm using a piece of you to try to reanimate you. Like those rich old ladies, that get their dogs cloned.'

She'd met Nate at a training day. He was leading the Digital Forensics Lab team. Like her, he had a convoluted family history. In his case it was Iranian and Tamil and Scottish, although no one seemed to be entirely clear how everything fitted together. One of those heritage websites might hold the answer, but Jen wasn't about to sacrifice the last of her beloved's DNA, currently being held by Dr Lovely in sub-zero temperatures, just to discover precisely why he had tanned so nicely.

He had insinuated his way into her heart simply by being the loveliest man she had ever met. That was partly why she had considered trying for a baby. Not passing on his genes felt wrong somehow. This child would be her gift to the world. She smiled at the ridiculousness of the thought, but she meant it really. The world needed more Nate Carvers. And thanks to the sperm he had put into cold storage before the chemo, there was a chance his DNA could rise again to charm everyone with gentle kindness. All she had to do was hope the egg she supplied was one of the good ones (did she have any of those? She hoped so) and then try not to mess the poor kid up. How hard could it be?

She stared at Oli Cromwell's toxicology report lying face down on the corner of her desk, a stark reminder of how hard it could be. She imagined her own child's suicide being pushed aside like junk mail. She thought of Marilla and the pills, of Inference Technology and the lost CCTV footage. She thought of Judith the hotel clerk and her strange collapse. The missing chef. None of it added up to anything much at all.

Over at his desk, Lee was making a call. Usually, the DI would be salivating at the chance to put his name to such a high profile murder, but despite his bovine appearance, he wasn't stupid. He knew how much the local politicians and senior police officers had been rooting for a nice blameless outcome.

'I'm very happy to tell you that our movie star definitely took his own life,' he said to someone. Presumably the mayor.

Jen could just imagine the mayor's face. The woman who volunteered for the local hospital radio station probably didn't want to hear a police officer crowing about a man's tragic ending, but no doubt she would be relieved. The local MP would be happy to get the call as well. The last thing the area needed was a celebrity murdered in their poshest hotel. As far as Aldhill's senior leaders were concerned, this was a good outcome. Jen put the tox report into Oli Cromwell's file and closed it.

'Dean,' she said. Dean turned in his chair. 'Can you track down Liane Benbow? She's the person who got fired from Telligence for finding out that the CCTV had gone missing. The whole thing just sounds off to me. Speak to her colleagues if you need to – Faith and Dashae. Faith was convinced they had picked on Liane for a reason. There might not be anything in it, but...' She shrugged.

'Sarge,' said Dean obediently, but she caught his questioning gaze.

'I know,' she sighed. 'It's probably suicide, but humour me, ok? I want to know what happened to that CCTV.' She thought for a moment. 'And I want to know if Oli Cromwell had diarrhoea.'

A simple call to Marilla was all it took to confirm that Oli Cromwell could very definitely swallow pills.

'So he didn't need to put them into his drink,' she told DC Nandini Roy when she arrived to catch up with her over lunch.

'But what does that mean, really?' said Nandini, shovelling in a stack of crisps. 'He might just not have fancied swallowing loads of tablets.'

Jen tried to organise her thoughts. So far, her mental Crazy Wall was filling up with things that seemed unconnected.

'Tell me what you've got,' said Nandini.

'Marilla his publicist was jumpy and stressed on the day Oli Cromwell died,' Jen began.

'Not in itself unusual,' said Nandini, laying some crisps in her sandwich like she was tucking them up for bed.

'No,' agreed Jen. 'But her prescription pill supply seems to have propped up Oli's recreational drug habit, and that makes it more suspicious than usual.'

'But did she give him the diarrhoea tablets?'

'She says not. I asked her and she said, "what's Imodium?"'

'Either the sign of a liar,' said Nandini, 'or the sign of a young woman with a very healthy gut biome.'

'When I told her what it was, she assured me that Oli's own guts had been in perfect working order. She said, "Trust me, he would have told me about it otherwise." Apparently, that was the sort of relationship they had – him telling her everything, her having to listen.'

'So what next?' said Nandini, taking a big bite of her crisp sarnie.

Jen admired her commitment to revolting eating habits. She shrugged.

'Dean's looking further into the missing CCTV footage. I mean, anyone could have gone in or out of Oli's room.'

Nandini swallowed her mouthful and gave Jen a look she recognised. Jen raised her hands.

'I know, it's probably nothing, but I can't help it,' she said. 'I just...'

'Do not say,' interrupted Nandini, 'that you have a funny feeling.'

Jen laughed. 'Look,' she said. 'Everyone is just being a bit... off, ok? Like, Judith from the front desk. She collapsed when she heard the news, despite years of cold water experience. That's weird, right? Then there's Callum, the AWOL chef. And, YES, perhaps that was simply a coincidence, but I would love to catch up with him to find out where he got to that evening. And maybe you're right. When I say it out loud, it does sound pretty unlikely.'

She put her head down on the table.

'Are you going through some personal stuff?' said Nandini. Jen lifted her head up briefly from the table and nodded.

Nandini reached over and patted Jen's arm. 'Please don't tell me about it,' she said.

Jen laughed, feeling the last few days of tension lifting. She roused herself as Dean Martin appeared.

'Sarge,' he said. 'I've found Liane Benbow.'

'Great,' said Jen. She could see from his expression there was something else. 'What is it?'

'She's Callum Geering's girlfriend.'

'Who's that?' said Nandini.

'It's the chef,' said Jen. 'The one who went missing on the night Oli Cromwell died.'

'I looked them both up and he's got a record,' said Dean.

'Let me guess. Drugs?'

Dean nodded. 'Possession with intent to supply.'

Callum Geering. The chef who made the final meal. Who had gone missing for more than an hour on the night

Oli Cromwell died; who had slunk off without giving a statement; who was, it turned out, in a relationship with the woman who discovered the CCTV was missing. Had Jen read this all wrong? Was Liane actually to blame for the missing footage after all? Had she made it vanish to protect her boyfriend from having his drug deal discovered? Lee was not going to be happy about all of this: as far as he was concerned, this was all done and dusted, but Jen needed to satisfy her own curiosity at the very least.

'What school did they go to?' she said.

She didn't wait for Dean to look, opening a browser herself and typing in Callum's name. Nothing came up, but she soon found Liane and showed Nandini, who was older, but an Aldhill local like Dean.

'Nope, don't know her,' said Nandini.

Neither did Dean. But then he brought up a photo of Callum from Liane's Instagram and frowned at it. It was an older shot of the chef, younger and slimmer with more hair.

'I might recognise him,' he said. 'I joined Aldhill Academy late and only went there for a year.'

'You moved mid-way through your GCSEs?' said Jen. 'That must have been hard.'

Dean didn't say anything, but Jen got the unspoken, 'Yeah it was,' from his body language alone.

'I have a vague memory of another boy starting at the same time.' He nodded towards the photo. 'It could have been him.'

'And you were at school with Dan Mehta and Philippa McGinty too, right?' said Jen. Dean looked down, clearly thrown by the mention of Phil, and Jen once again had cause to feel sorry for the poor boy. 'So, if he was a new kid, he transferred in from somewhere else.'

They started checking the most obvious places online that might reveal his school history. Callum didn't seem to have much by way of social media, but Liane shared quite a bit of personal information. There were photos of them on nights out, including a photo in a club with friends.

'There's Dan,' said Jen. She looked at the tagged location. 'They're in The Red Room.'

Dean found a mention of a Callum Geering playing for a local football team and they pursued that avenue for a while, but reached a dead end, eventually. Jen started looking up some of the other children in the team photo with him. 'They often go to the same schools if they're in a particular local team.'

Eventually she worked it out, tracking down the coach who had been the PE teacher for Parker Boys, a now defunct state secondary school.

'He was at Parker before then,' said Jen. 'You know who else was at Parker don't you?'

Nandini swallowed the last of her sandwich and stole Dean's moment.

'Oli Cromwell.'

THIRTY-FIVE

Phil rolled over in bed and stared at Marilla lying there naked, and beautiful, and fast asleep. She allowed herself a smile before she climbed out of bed and began getting ready for the day ahead. The smile was indulgent, because really she knew that it was a terrible idea to get involved with this woman. And yet, here she was preparing eggs – just regular scrambled, no Benediction this time – for a woman she shouldn't have anything to do with.

But the fact was... No. She couldn't justify it. There was no excuse. She shouldn't have done it. They had gone to the club. They'd had a lot of fun. They had danced, they had laughed, they had drunk a little too much. And Phil had invited her back. Where was her professional distance? Miles away. In the other direction.

Phil had bumped into Dan last night. She had approached him from behind as he leaned on the bar, and put her hands on his shoulders and shouted in his ears, 'Do you come here often?'

'Phil. What are you doing here?' For a moment he failed to hide his displeasure, but then readjusted his features back into his usual cheerful chappy nonsense. 'Come sit down. Haven't seen you for about five years and then I see you twice in a few days. What's all that about?' He said it innocently enough, but it was clear to Phil that he was suspicious. Phil nodded towards Marilla, who was still jiggling arhythmically on the dance floor.

'My friend wanted a night out,' lied Phil 'and I haven't been here yet, so I thought I should give it a try. I didn't know you worked here.'

'I've been here for a while now. In fact, I'm one of the partners in the business.'

'Shut up!' said Phil, elbowing him. 'That's, like, proper grown up.'

He laughed at that, disarmed.

'Get you!' she said.

And she intended to.

She was interrupted in her egg scrambling by her mother. Angela appeared at the doorway, and mouthed, 'Who's in there?' while pointing to Phil's bedroom.

'I thought you were at work?' said Phil.

'I took the day off,' said Angela. 'I've had it. There was a sex offender complaining his case worker looked at him funny. I had to escape. Have you put the kettle on?'

'Yeah, tea's in the pot,' said Phil, whisking up the eggs.

'Oh no, no. I need something stronger than that.'

She started spooning coffee granules into a mug.

'Why don't you use the machine dad got you?' said Phil.

'I don't know.'

But Phil knew it was because she couldn't face using

something that Clive had loved playing with so much. His favourite toy.

'Maybe we should give it away,' said Phil.

Angela looked shocked. 'It's barely been used!'

Phil wished she had never started on the subject. What was the point? Angela didn't want to get rid of the coffee machine, but she didn't want to use it either. She watched her mother head back to the bed with her cup of instant, her mule slippers slapping her heels with each step.

'Hope you're gonna introduce me to your friend,' Angela called loudly over her shoulder.

'Shh!' said Phil as Angela shut her bedroom door, cackling.

Next to arrive was her brother, Lucas, who sloped in and poured himself a mug of tea from the pot.

'Morning,' said Phil, hoping to rouse him from his limping zombie act.

'Alright,' he stated in a deep voice that still surprised his sister years after it broke. He grabbed a packet of biscuits from the cupboard and, like his mother before him, retreated back to his bedroom.

'Great chat,' said Phil and then cringed. God, I'm turning into an old fart already, she thought. Come to think of it, by Lucas's standards it really was a great chat. 'Alright' was more than he'd said to her in days. If there was some sort of East Asian art form for saying the fewest words possible in any given situation, Lucas would be one of its grand masters.

Marilla arrived next, staggering sleepily into the kitchen looking pale and dishevelled.

'I think someone might have poisoned me,' she said, before heading to the kitchen table and slumping down dramatically, her head resting on the melamine surface.

'I'm making eggs,' Phil said.

'No. Don't talk about food. I'll be sick.'

Phil set a glass of orange juice down and Marilla raised her head, drank it in a couple of gulps like it was an elixir, and slumped back onto the table. Phil fetched her a cup of tea, which Marilla nursed whilst taking deep breaths, as though hoping to exhale the hangover out of her body.

'What are your plans for the day, then?' said Phil.

'Ugh,' said Marilla. 'I probably should have gone back to London yesterday, not that anyone will have noticed.'

'Oh really? I thought they were all hands on deck panicking about the Oli situation?'

'Amazing how quickly something becomes yesterday's news, isn't it? He's not top priority anymore now he's dead. They've got living stars to suck money out of.'

'Ouch, and people say my industry is scummy.'

'It seems like everyone's moved on without me,' said Marilla, indulging in a little self-pity. Phil didn't blame her. If you couldn't feel sorry for yourself with a hangover, when could you?

'There's a zoo nearby. You can always see if they've got any job openings.'

'Don't be silly,' said Marilla. 'I already have my mother's dream job, why would I want my own?'

'Job satisfaction?' said Phil.

'Listen, of the two jobs – publicist or zookeeper – one pays for my very lavish lifestyle, and the other one involves caring for giraffes.'

'Lose an extravagant lifestyle, gain a giraffe. Where's the hardship?'

'That's true, I do really like giraffes,' said Marilla. Phil turned her attention to the toast so Marilla wouldn't notice the flash of shame. Breaking into Marilla's laptop was not her finest hour, and every time she heard the word 'giraffe' she would feel a pang of guilt.

'Now,' said Marilla, 'where are my eggs?'

THIRTY-SIX

The man in the beige trousers had stuck to his plan. He had destroyed most of his paperwork, tossing identifying documents, his passport, his driving licence, into public bins around the town. His intention had been to leave as little evidence of himself on the planet as he could, and he was nearly there. He would disintegrate all evidence of his life, then he would dispose of himself just as tidily. Today was the day.

But when it came time to throw away his diaries, he had paused. Why? It was all just pages and pages and pages of nothing. Nothing worth reading. He had no idea what had prompted him to begin a diary in the first place. The man with the most boring life in existence has no business recording the beigeness of his days for posterity. Who could possibly care? He could barely look at them himself. It was like reading a VAT return. He could have boiled the whole set down to one page: got up, ate breakfast, did nothing, had lunch, gave the same lessons, went for the same walk, nodded politely at the same people, read the same terrible news, watched the same programs, ate dinner, went to bed. The sum total of his life.

So why the reluctance to throw them away? He imagined people finding his diaries after he had killed himself. They would marvel at a life half lived. Or would some historian excavate them in years to come and use them as evidence that the planet had once been an exceedingly boring place populated by unimaginative, anti-social celibates who lived with their mothers and recorded purchasing a pork pie from the butcher's as a highlight of their week?

Probably the most notable thing that ever happened in the man's life (aside from the incidents with the boy) was the day his mother died in the freak accident on their shared driveway. Every other day had been a bland nothingness of ham sandwiches and homework marking. When his father had passed away fifteen years ago, the old man had gone off with very little fanfare, driving himself to the hospital with a sore arm and dying that afternoon of heart failure. Doing it there in the hospital meant the man and his mother didn't even have to deal with calling an ambulance. The biggest drama had been locating his dad's car in the car park and paying the parking fine.

But his mother's death had been a public catastrophe. People on the estate had gathered around her like antelope watching one of the herd get eaten by lions. And, of course, in all the kerfuffle of his mother's accident, he had failed to write an entry for his diary that evening, and despite his intention to fill it in later, he didn't ever go back to it. It never felt like the right time to write up an entry about the grisly demise of his only friend (even though she hadn't been a very good one). It was the first page ever left blank.

Then there was the day the boy came to his classroom.

On that day, he had manufactured something appropriately bland to fill the white space in his journal since realised that not writing anything would look suspicious (if the boy ever did report him). He talked at length about the pudding he had made, ('Didn't think much of that, you needn't make it again, I prefer a tin of treacle sponge,' his mother had told him), and wrote in his *Countdown* score (which he watched on catch up after school every day). He discussed the weather (cold, blowy). It wasn't much different to his usual entries.

So, he had missed the opportunity to write two interesting entries and now, he realised with a jolt, he had missed a third. Since he planned on ending things, he hadn't written anything since he arrived in Aldhill-on-Sea. What would be the point? But a thought struck him. Perhaps before he destroyed the last trace of himself, he could fill in the blanks. Why shouldn't he have the satisfaction of recording three interesting things that happened to him? Three times that his life was real with full-colour, panoramic, dolby surround-sound experiences that showed he had some impact in the world after all.

He sat on the edge of his bed and looked out at the line where the grey sky met the grey sea. The new hotel was further along the coast. It was less pleasant than The Marchmont, but it was less expensive – and he did have a sea view. Yes, he would do it, he decided. He took out a pen and found a pad of hotel paper and moved to the small desk to write his entries, dating each carefully. He didn't write up his time with the florist, however. That was for him alone. Then he put the diary into his rucksack, secreted the new entries into an inner pocket, put on his anorak, and headed off to the cliffs.

THIRTY-SEVEN

Charles had walked in today, taking the coastal path along the cliff tops and then down the stone steps into town. The exercise felt good.

He wasn't sure why he had lied to Judith about Nancy. He hadn't married her; he didn't have a baby on the way. She had left him a few weeks ago and this one had been a hard loss. Nancy was an intelligent woman in her early forties who had felt the last minute rallying call of her fading fertility and headed off to find a viable partner. 'I love you dearly, Charlie, but I want my child to have a dad who will be there at her graduation.' She had placed a gentle hand on his cheek and given him a farewell kiss before driving off into the sunset alone. Perhaps he was dramatising that memory a little. Perhaps she had given him a good few weeks' warning and had taken a while to extricate her affairs from his. Perhaps she had been as gentle and generous as she could be. But either way, he was still reeling from the dust cloud she left behind.

She was by far the most intelligent woman he had dated

– probably since Judith. All the partners he had selected in between had been thin on intellect. Not that he went for the thick ones, far from it. They all had something about them – cunning, native wisdom, guile – but Nancy had been educated, refined. In the old days, he would have called her 'classy.' Even after all these years, he had the sense that she was slightly out of his league. He was sorry to see her go.

Perhaps the loss of Nancy was another reason he had returned to his old stomping ground. And he didn't admit it to himself, but seeing Judith had shocked him in more ways than one. She had looked so old. Ridiculous in all that makeup. Slightly deranged, even. And yet, he could still see his Judy through the rouge and the wrinkles. It wasn't what he'd expected – to be so moved at the sight of her after all these years. Not that he was under any illusions. A man like him couldn't be seen with a woman like Judith: she was far too old; it would look plain odd. He sipped his coffee and silently acknowledged the stupidity of that thought. She was, after all, six years younger than him. But there it was. That was just the way the world worked. If they'd married when they were younger, they could still be a couple of oldies together, probably with a clutch of grandkids. But he couldn't be seen dating a woman like that now. What would his boys think? Face cream was one thing, old biddies quite another.

When Nancy had got into her car he had wanted to say, 'Don't go, I love you.' But he didn't. More than that, he wanted to say, 'I want babies too.'

He hadn't admitted it to himself, so he couldn't say it out loud to Nancy. His mother always asked where her grand-kids were. She was ninety-five with so much love to give still. He had let down both his parents. But where his dad had made it plain ('What a bitter disappointment you've been Charlie'), his mum had hidden her sadness behind stoic smiles and undying loyalty. She had visited him every week in prison (unlike his dad, who came only occasionally and didn't stay long). He would have told her not to come, the sadness in her heavy eyelids almost too much to bear, but he was lonely. If she didn't come to see him, who would? Judith had vanished without a trace. He owed his mum the grand-kids, even if she only lived for a few more years.

In the office Lesley, his executive assistant (what happened to secretaries?), brought Charles a cafetière of strong black coffee. Not as good as the stuff he made himself with his coffee machine, but it would do. He sipped it while he looked through his post and avoided the inevitable for a while longer.

'You wanted to see me?' said a voice.

Dan Mehta knocked and poked his head through the door without an invitation. He was a little prick, but a good boy really, deep down. In the absence of a son, Charles had pinned a lot of hope on the young lad. What was he? Twenty-five? Something like that. Older than Charles had been when he started working for his uncle. People were older back then. He was serving his first sentence by Dan's age. Saying goodbye to Judith, expecting her to visit, holding out hope for longer than he should have.

'I asked you to do one thing.' Charles sat back in his chair and regarded him. 'One, I believe, very simple thing.' Charles could see Dan's face freeze, could see him regretting poking his head round the boss's door. 'Get the boy in a compro-mising position, I said, gain some leverage. And what did you do? Create a huge bloody mess for me to clear up.'

'Naw, naw, boss,' said Dan, putting his hands out in

supplication. 'I did what you asked. Wasn't my fault the dumb bitch didn't show.'

Charles tensed at the coarse language. He didn't like the way men spoke about women these days. Granted, in the past he had occasionally been forced to show one or two of his girls the back of his hand, but not very often and only under duress, when there had been no other option. He certainly wouldn't refer to women as 'bitches'. For one thing, it lacked class.

'Really?' he said. 'Because that's not what I heard. I heard that Agata was waiting for her cab like a good girl and some idiot forgot to send one for her.'

'I asked Lesley to book it!' said Dan, his voice reaching a shrill note.

'Lesley has worked for me for thirty-five years,' Charles replied. 'And in all that time, she has never forgotten to do anything.'

'Well, I'm telling you, boss, she's getting cracked. Her mind is going.' He tapped his head.

Charles looked at Dan until the boy began to visibly shrink, all the puff and bluster disintegrating under his master's gaze.

'We have been over this already, Dan, and the conclusion we already came to is that you failed to get the girl to the hotel, then your man on the inside killed our film star—'

'Yeah, and then I sorted it, boss. I got rid of the evidence like you said. No harm, no foul.'

'And now,' continued Charles, as though the interruption hadn't happened, 'we've got the police sniffing round our business practices and some journalist paying you a bit too much interest. It's not been the best few days for you, has it, Danny boy?'

Dan's top lip grew moist. Fear sparkled in his round brown eyes. He didn't have the face of a criminal, he had the face of an innocent. Charles imagined Dan's mother was probably as heart-broken as his own.

'It's not like that, boss. Callum says he dosed him the right amount, just enough to make him relaxed for when the girl arrived. Swears he didn't kill him. The copper's only suspicious because the CCTV footage went MIA, innit. She'll calm down.'

'And Liane?' said Charles. 'Why did that bloody idiot fire her? She's meant to be your leverage.'

'That was a mistake, chief, I'm not gonna lie to you. Stephen will be spoken to.'

'And the journalist?'

'You leave her to me, she's not going to be any trouble. We went to school together. She's sound. No trouble with her.'

Charles gazed up at the office ceiling a moment, hoping for deliverance. It was a crummy room, not a patch on the oak panelled Victorian space he had worked from in London. This was more like the offices he had in the old days – a back room in some scruffy nightclub with flickering strip lights and rickety partition walls. It was strangely comforting.

'Is she still hanging around outside?' said Charles.

Dan's face registered surprise. Charles was disappointed: the boy had no idea she had been there, watching from the street. Was this the man he was pinning all his hopes on? This flighty boy who couldn't see what was right under his nose.

'First she loiters outside,' said Charles, 'and then she comes in for a night out with the film star's assistant.'

Charles could see Dan trying to work out what to say

next, weighing up how to play it. Charles didn't give him the chance.

'I'm told she was the person who found his body,' said Charles. 'But did she speak to him beforehand? That's what I need to know.'

'I'll find out,' said Dan. 'Like I said, leave her to me.'

'No,' said Charles. 'I'll deal with her.'

THIRTY-EIGHT

Phil found a picnic bench along the promenade and sat
down to take in the view. The sea was dark today. Phil
zipped up her coat and watched as a tattooed middle-aged
woman tried to coax her miniature schnauzer to walk on the
pebbles, eventually persuading it to tiptoe across the shingle.
Then she took out her phone and called Adam Jenkins,
editor.

'Adam,' she said, 'got a story.'

'Oh God. Here we go again,' Adam said. 'What is it this
time? Old lady's been putting her recycling in the wrong bin?
Or did you find another dead celebrity? It's the sublime to
the ridiculous with you, isn't it?'

'Liane Benbow,' she said.

'What about her?' he said. 'Never heard of her.'

'She went into labour in the middle of the Telligence call
centre the other day,'

'Okay,' said Adam, considering. 'Could be a news-in-
brief in that.'

'She'd just been fired,' said Phil.

'Interesting.' Phil could almost hear him stroking his chin. 'What for, though? It's no good if it turns out she'd been thieving.'

'She was fired because she told The Marchmont Hotel that their IT company had lost all the CCTV footage from the night that Oli Cromwell died.'

'Bloody hell. You're gonna have to go through all that again.'

And so she had told the story in more detail, with Adam interrupting to ask her who her sources were, and how she could possibly know all of this. She was about to explain the whole rigmarole – how she had heard about it from her friend, who was flatmates with Faith, who had come home complaining about Liane's dreadful mistreatment – but instead she decided to pretend to be Kirsty Mathieson, who worked for *The* (actual) *Observer* and was far more senior and important than Phil, and so she simply said, 'I've got my sources.'

Adam snorted at that.

'Sources? Wasn't the same source that tipped you off about the dog poo bag dude was it?'

That was how Phil eventually found herself knocking on the door of Liane and Callum's little ground-floor flat.

'Find out if she is dodgy first, yeah?' Adam Jenkins had instructed. 'Don't want to write a sob story about a shoplifter.' But Phil had already asked around. The consensus was Liane Benbow was sound. She had a reputation for being kind and helpful and a good friend and daughter. Liane and her mother were there when Phil appeared at the door. Callum was at work.

'We need all the money we can get,' explained Liane. 'But he will be taking some time off soon I hope.'

Diane, gave a look that said: 'He had better take some bloody time off.'

Liane looked shattered, pale and shaky. But the house itself was tidy and orderly. Phil assumed that was down to her mother, Diane, who was even now rushing around, wiping surfaces and carrying items from place to place.

'How's everything going?' said Phil

'Oh, you know,' said Liane, giving a tearful shrug that somehow conjured up the rest of her sentence. She puffed out a big breath of air and leaned forward to take a biscuit from the plate in front of them. Phil did the same.

'I heard Callum only just made it to the hospital?' said Phil. The story of Liane's labour – which had nearly ended abruptly in the carpark, before happily reaching its conclusion in the labour ward – had been the talk of the Courts. Everyone knew the story by now.

'He got there just in time to see her arrive,' said Liane. 'She came out like a ball down a bowling alley. Nearly sent everyone flying.'

Phil made a resolution never to have a baby.

'So why are you here?' said Liane, crunching on her biscuit, eyes still a little tearful.

'The paper thought it be interesting to write a piece on you,' said Phil. 'It's a good story: "Local woman goes into labour in Telligence's offices." And then there's the other angle.'

Phil wondered how Liane might take this. 'I heard – and maybe I got this wrong – That you were fired just before it happened.'

Phil could see the questions forming on Liane's lips: who told you that? What did they say exactly? Why do you want to know? But instead Liane just shrugged and said:

'Yep.'

'Want to tell me about it?' said Phil.

And so she did.'

So, Stephen Murray fired her for losing the CCTV footage? Presumably, he was attempting to pass the buck onto a subordinate – or he was using her as his unfortunate punching bag. Either way, Phil was glad Liane's body unleashed a personal tsunami all over the company carpet.

'If you like I can ask our editor if we can start a campaign to get your job reinstated,' offered Phil. 'I'm sure there will be a big response to your story'

'I'd have to think. It's not like I'm going back to work anytime soon, is it?' Liane nodded down at her baby, who was sleeping peacefully in her arms.

Phil smiled. 'I didn't ask her name.'

'Olivia,' said Liane dreamily. 'Callum wanted to name her after Oli Cromwell.'

'Did you know him?' Phil asked.

'No, he went to my school for a bit, but I didn't know him really.'

'What about Callum?' said Phil, wondering if Liane would give her a different answer than Callum had.

'I don't think so,' said Liane, staring at her baby.

'So were you big fans, then?' said Phil.

'Not particularly. He just felt so devastated about what happened.'

One of Angela's sayings – handed down to her from Gran – came back to Phil: 'Never let a pregnant woman pick out curtains.'

When Phil was born, Angela had stared down at the fuzzy head of her new baby and insisted she wanted to call her 'Bobina'. 'Because you looked so like my dad,' she explained.

'Why not Roberta or Bobby?' said Phil.

'And that is why,' said Gran, butting in, 'you don't let someone filled with love drugs and pain relief make decisions you'll have to live with. You've got me to thank for the fact you're not called Bobina. Never heard anything like it.'

Not that Philippa was much better. Such a *jolly hockey sticks* name. Roosevelt Court had never housed a Philippa and probably never would again. Gran had saved her from Bobina only to leave her wide open to Philippa.

'Thanks Gran,' Phil said.

Phil wondered if, after the hormone haze has worn off, Liane would one day turn to Callum and say, 'Tell me again why you wanted to name our baby after a dead celebrity you didn't know at school and weren't a fan of?'

And if she did turn to Callum and say that, Phil wondered what Callum would say in reply.

THIRTY-NINE

Liane had enjoyed telling the journalist about her weird experience in the Telligence offices. Phil was friendly and funny and adamant that Liane shouldn't take her redundancy lying down.

'Stride in there like you own the place and ask him when he wants you back after your maternity leave,' Phil McGinty told her. 'That's what I would do. Just act like the whole thing never happened.'

Thing is, Liane *did* want to pretend the whole thing had never happened. She wanted to pretend she never had a job in the first place – or any responsibilities at all, for that matter. She wanted to take it lying down. Lying down seemed like the most intoxicating thing in the world. Given the choice, she would just snuggle up into bed with Olivia – Liv, she had already started calling her – and never see the rest of the world.

'I'm serious,' said Phil. 'Front it out. See what this Stephen guy says. I bet he backs down. Feign total amnesia. What's he going to do while you're in there and everyone's cooing over Olivia? Ask him in front of people and I bet you he backs down.'

They had fun discussing what his reactions might be.

'I think he would probably start crying if I challenged him,' said Liane.

And she realised that probably wasn't far from the mark. He had been very shaken when her waters had broken. She could actually imagine him pretending none of that day had happened. Maybe Phil was right. And yet, she wasn't sure she had the guts to do it. Her confidence, already pretty easy to knock, was rock bottom since Liv arrived. Still, she smiled at the thought of unnerving her boss. Maybe she would do it.

'Hey, I saw Callum with Dan the other night,' Phil said. 'I didn't know they were still friends.'

The atmosphere changed in an instant. Liane would have fallen for the casual tone if she hadn't noticed Phil studying her so intently. She tried to understand what Phil was telling her, but her brain was all fizzy, love bubbling through her synapses and sleep deprivation making it hard to get her thoughts straight. *Callum talking to Dan?* She couldn't for the life of her fathom why Callum would be doing that. He had sworn off that world permanently and she had never doubted him for a minute; he had promised.

She wanted the journalist to go. She couldn't concentrate on the conversation: she needed to sit quietly and try to work out when Callum had started seeing Dan again. It felt like a betrayal, like discovering an affair. The last thing she wanted right now was a nosey audience.

'I need to put the baby down for a nap,' she lied.

The baby was never put down. The baby had been permanently attached to someone's chest since she was born, only being inserted into her crib when Liane wanted to sleep and there was no one else who wanted a turn at inhaling the perfume of her warm head. Her mum, Diane, took control of the situation, ushering Phil out and depositing her onto the street before she had time to finish her cup of tea.

'I'll be in touch,' Phil had called out cheerfully. 'Congratulations again on little Olivia.'

But Liane was already lost in her thoughts, kissing the baby's head and trying to get her thoughts in order. Later, when Callum came home, she managed to keep her tone light.

'What's this I hear about you and Dan hanging out together?'

'Who's told you that?' said Callum and Liane couldn't believe the cheek of it. He was actually indignant! Caught in the act, but more interested in rooting out the grass than falling to his knees to ask for mercy. The calm demeanour she had settled on fell away like cream pie from a clown's face.

'What the hell are you playing at?' she said.

He flushed pink. 'It's not what you think. I bumped into him when I was walking home. He was just being friendly.'

'Dan is never just friendly.'

'I'm telling you, he just wanted to congratulate us on the baby.

Liane felt a pain in her head. She was clenching her teeth so hard she could imagine them ground to dust.

'I don't want him talking about our baby,' she said. 'Not ever. You promised you'd stay away from all that.'

She didn't need to say the rest: You promised on your baby's life.

Then, something happened she didn't expect. His eyes began to fill up. Big giant wells of saltwater that bulged from his lids until, eventually, a pair of matching teardrops sprang from his lashes and landed on his cheeks.

'I think I might have killed Oli Cromwell,' he said.

Callum told her everything, although afterwards she would only recall parts of it. There was a lot of crying. She found it hard to concentrate over the fog of baby hormones, sleep deprivation and sheer disbelief. She felt raw, fleshless, like an anatomical model covered in exposed blood vessels.

'You drugged Oli Cromwell's food?' she said for the second time.

'They made me,' he said. His voice was pinched, anguished.

'Who did?' she said. 'The bigger boys?'

'You don't understand.'

She wanted to shake him. Her headache pierced her temple. He waffled on for a bit longer. Excuses came thick and fast. Something about a 'call girl' who didn't show up and Callum being forced to improvise. Liane wondered if maybe the pethidine hadn't worn off yet. Maybe that was it: she was still high. It was all too awful to contemplate. She found herself zoning out – her mind trying to protect itself – when he started explaining how he had gone to Oli Cromwell's room and found him there naked and unconscious. He'd taken photos of him, naked and passed out, hoping that would be enough leverage to stop him spilling any potential secrets about Charles Getgood's enterprise. Was the poor bloke even alive when Callum got to him, she wondered.

'Of course he was alive,' said Callum. 'Jesus. What do you take me for?'

She had to ask, though she didn't really want the answer. 'And was he alive when you *left*?'

A few hours later, fresh from a blazing row, a painful nursing session, deliverance from parental responsibility in the form of Diane, and a half-hearted effort at making herself look presentable, Liane found herself entering the Telligence offices, attempting to save her family – attempting to clean up Callum's mess.

The missing CCTV footage hadn't been deleted, Callum told her.

'Dan's got a copy as insurance to stop me telling anyone about it all,' he said. 'And they made sure you took the call so you'd be dragged into it too.'

'But Stephen wasn't meant to fire you,' said Callum.

What had Phil said?

Stride in there like you own the place.

Liane stepped gingerly out of the lift and shuffled towards Stephen Murray's office, not making eye contact with anyone. She had that disorientated feeling – like she had just stepped out of a dark cinema to discover it was daylight outside. OK, she had flunked the bold entrance, but she had every intention of getting the next bit right. She steeled herself, trying not to think about how much her body didn't want to be out in the world.

Stephen looked up as she tapped lightly on his door frame and stepped inside. Firing her had been his own act of pettiness, and now he was staring up at her, his face opening and closing like a pedal bin.

'Just wanted to check in and say, "Hi" and find out when you want me back,' she said.

It wasn't really an office, just a sad little cupboard at the end of the call centre. The window looked out onto the concrete render of the neighbouring building.

'Obviously, it won't be for at least twelve weeks,' she continued. 'After I've had my maternity leave.'

She had been shaking when she arrived, but Stephen's face gave her confidence; he looked more terrified than she felt. She carried on before he found his way back to coherent thoughts.

'I had a very interesting chat with the local paper. They want to do a piece about me going into labour in the Telligence office. And all the other drama.'

She watched with satisfaction as the colour drained from his face.

'I told them I could prove that you deleted the footage and saved it to your own work hard drive. I've got the activity logs on the account,' she said.

He looked at her.

Jackpot. It had been a massive gamble, a shot in the dark, but the truth was right there on his face: he had the footage.

'How did you...?'

'I've been working for IT Solutions for a while now,' she said. 'It's a pretty clever set up – taking over old ladies' computers, messing around with their settings and charging them for security software they don't need every month just to make it stop.' Liane prayed to god she'd got this right. 'It didn't take much for me to do the same to your computer. I've seen everything.'

'Oh god,' said Stephen. He was panicking. 'They made me do it. I have child support to pay. It's not easy.'

Liane rolled her eyes. 'My heart bleeds for you, Stephen, it really does.'

'What do you want?' said Stephen.

'I want you to put the CCTV footage onto this USB

stick,' she said, sliding a tiny green flash drive his way, 'and then I want you to delete every single existing copy.'

Stephen took the stick and did as he was told. He laboured over it all, taking an age to locate the files. She had to show him how to copy them across to the USB. Until this moment she had thought she was useless with technology, but watching him slowly deleting the files one by one was pure agony. In the end, she moved him aside and checked his computer for copies before deleting all the files from his Trash.

'Does anyone else have a copy?' she said.

'No,' he said. 'I was told to look after it in case it was needed.'

'And have you watched it?' she said.

'When would I have had the time?' he said. She raised an eyebrow. He sighed and sat back in his chair. 'No I haven't watched it. I find it's better to know as little as possible in these situations.'

Liane couldn't imagine having so little curiosity. Still, she had no choice but to believe him. Her fingers wrapped around the USB key and she ejected it from his PC.

'Thank you,' she said. 'I guess I'll see you back at work in a few months.'

Liane could see a thought forming.

'If you had control of my computer, why did you need to come in to do that?'

'I had to be sure no one else had it.' She was just pulling lies from the air now. God help her if he asked a technical question. She leaned forward across his desk. 'But if you retrieve another copy from anywhere, I'll know.'

· · ·

At home Liane fed the baby with relief. Her breasts were like cannonballs and the baby had been giving her mother grief for the past half an hour ('She's her father's daughter – always starving'). Liane put her feet up on the coffee table and retrieved her laptop, perching it on the nursing pillow next to the baby's head. An hour later Liv was asleep on her shoulder and Liane was still staring at the footage. She had nearly seen it all now, the last hours of Oli Cromwell's life. She watched a young woman leaving Oli's room in the early evening, tapping at her phone, running her fingers through her hair. She watched as a tall, elderly woman in Marchmont staff uniform carried the room service – the meal Callum had laced with GHB – into Oli Cromwell's room. She watched as Callum appeared, walking the corridors of The Marchmont, his body language screaming *furtive* as he used the room key he had been given to let himself in.

She waited for what felt like forever, staring at the empty corridor on screen, waiting for Callum to reappear. He must have been in there for an hour. What the hell was he doing? Eventually, he emerged. His body language now screamed *defeated*. She could almost feel sorry for him. *What a mess.* She watched as he hurried off, not even taking the time to close the door after him. She felt tears prick her eyes and drop onto her cheeks. She sat there for a while, allowing the sadness to wash over her.

Through blurred vision something on the screen caught her eye. She wiped away the tears and took a closer look. She watched for a moment and rewound the footage, jumping back to the first moment the figure had appeared. Someone else had just gone into Oli Cromwell's room. Liane stared into space for a few moments.

When she was little she had run straight into the door

between the kitchen and the hallway. Pieces of safety glass rained down onto her head, leaving little cuts all over her tiny body. The glass broke into a million pieces, creating piles of shining crystal. She remembered looking at them and thinking they were so beautiful, but they were trapping her. She couldn't move without risking more pain. When she closed her eyes she was back in that moment, surrounded by glass. She felt shattered and broken, bleeding and trapped. She wanted to run away, to play, to forget about picking up all the pieces. But what choice did she have? She had to find a way out of this.

Her finger hovered over the delete button. She looked down at her sleeping baby, a tiny version of Callum, named after a dead man. Time to make a decision.

FORTY

The man on the edge of the cliff was going to jump. Phil was sure of it. She raised her hand to her brow to block the sun and squinted over at the mass of brush and wildflowers that clung to the furthest corners of the precipice. Perhaps, after all, she had been mistaken. Doubt began to creep in. Surely it couldn't be a jumper? Maybe it was just a tree with a jaunty humanlike stance, or a flasher waiting to waggle his cock in her direction (this being a popular hotspot for local perverts). She hoped so. Even a sex pest would be a relief next someone about to end it all.

She had gone up to the cliff on a whim. After her promenade, she had allowed her long legs to carry her, two steps at a time, up the large staircase built into the cliff face. There she stood, staring out to sea, sucking in the swirling wind as it whipped her hair in all directions, feeling truly alive. She enjoyed indulging in a little poetic fantasy; in these moments she was Cathy on the moors, or maybe Emily Brontë herself, composing stanzas and couplets, a world away from the local under-twelves hockey results and photographing dead celebrities. She hadn't expected to be brought back to reality with such a resounding thud.

There he was, leaning over the edge, his body tense. He was holding a rucksack over his right shoulder as though he might just step off the edge like a traveller heading off on a hike. She stopped squinting and started walking. It didn't matter if the man was real or imagined, her legs didn't give her logical brain long enough to get a definitive answer. Before she had made any conscious choice, her feet began carrying her to a trot, and within half a heartbeat she was running, pounding towards the edge as fast as she could go. Phil was a quick runner, but the field was longer than it looked. By the time she reached the place he had been standing on the cliff, he was gone.

The sun had been in her eyes the entire time and so she couldn't be sure where he had vanished to. She rushed over to the cliff edge as though she could still save him. Peering over the side, she fully expected to see his body smashed on the rocks below, but there was no sign of anyone. He must have found a path lower down, that was all. This seemed like a better option than the alternative: that his body was currently floating out to sea. She moved back from the edge swiftly and rushed around to the side, hoping to spot him walking back towards the stone steps along a hidden animal track. But if he had gone down that way, he must have been going at a fair pace to get away from her so quickly. She took a few moments to catch her breath, still looking for evidence of him, before slowly making her way down to the promenade and back towards the office.

In retrospect, she felt a little foolish. Maybe he had just been in quiet contemplation and had been spooked to see a woman thundering towards him shouting. From that distance, it had seemed like a suicide attempt – that's what her gut had told her – but maybe he was just enjoying the view. Maybe he didn't exist at all. Had she conjured him up in her imagination, like Cathy on the moor?

Perhaps she just had suicidal men on her mind after Oli Cromwell. The thing was, in that moment when her animal brain had been making all the choices for her, she knew three things right away: that there was definitely a man; that the man had been planning to jump; that the man was Llewellyn, the eye witness from The Marchmont Hotel. And if it was him, then someone needed to find him before he tried to kill himself again. She took out her phone and made a call.

'Dean,' she said, 'I need to talk to someone about the death of Oli Cromwell.'

FORTY-ONE

'Phil McGinty just called me,' Dean said.

'Oh god.'

Jen had been at the Virtua Creatives registered office when Dean called her. The building was down an alley, behind a nondescript door with no identifying features, not even a nameplate. To Jen's mind, it wasn't the kind of office you would expect from a design agency and she was unsurprised to receive no answer when she rang the buzzer. It was clearly just an empty registered address. The real office would be somewhere else – if it existed at all.

After Jen had pressed the bell five times, an elderly man appeared at the window next door and tried to shoo her away. She waved her warrant card and smiled. He let the net curtain fall back over the window and disappeared. She had expected him to appear at the door (presumably after he had tackled the inevitable buffet of door locks), ready and willing to gossip about his missing neighbours, but he never materialised. She tried knocking on his door, but the neighbour remained silent, and the curtain no longer rippled.

That was when when Dean's cherubic face appeared on screen.

'She wants to speak to you,' he said. 'She's heading to Beachy Shed now.'

'Tell her I'll meet her there in five,' said Jen.

Fifteen minutes later, Jen was in the café still waiting for her order to arrive. The day was cold, clouds of vapour pluming from the dogs and walkers on the beach. The café was a little chilly, too. Jen kept her coat on. It was a hipster joint – had to be with a name like 'Beachy Shed' – and though Jen wouldn't want to admit to it, their pour-over filter coffee was out of this world, even if it did take the sleepy young bearded bloke behind the counter an age to prepare. The area was most definitely gentrifying – almost against its own wishes, Jen always thought. It was a town slouching towards Boden, but it wouldn't give up without a fight... Probably down by the candy stand on a Saturday night.

Jen looked up as Philippa McGinty swung the door open. She was a local journalist with a gift for finding trouble, and Jen knew that if Phil wanted to speak to her, it was probably worth hearing – even if Jen would rather not. Because she had a horrible feeling Phil was about to confirm her worst suspicions.

They knew each other of old and, Jen liked to think, both had a respect for the other. She certainly knew not to underestimate the daughter of Clive McGinty, who just last year had almost single-handedly solved her own father's murder, even if Phil hadn't received the outcome she'd been hoping for.

'I didn't know what to order you,' said Jen, after they had made the usual polite hellos.

'It's okay, I'll sort it,' said the journalist.

'Better do it fast if you want service before the end of this week,' said Jen. 'I'll be retired by the time my coffee arrives.'

Phil turned to the man at the counter.

'Oi, Dom, pot of tea please, flower.' She gave Dom an endearing smile and he grinned at her.

'Anything for you, Philbo,' he said in his Australian accent.

'And get this lady her coffee while she's young, please,' said Phil, still with the winning smile. 'She is extremely busy and important.'

Jen grunted. Dom saluted and started moving a little faster.

'Coming right up,' he said.

Jen had seen Phil's charm in action before and it never ceased to impress her. Here was a woman who knew how to get what she wanted. Jen wondered if police interviews would be easier if she had a little more bright-toothed good humour about her. Sarcastic eye rolls tended to have their limitations.

'Dean said you wanted to talk,' she said, keen to get the conversation going.

She was expecting an awful lot of journalistic equivocating – lots of, 'I can't reveal my sources,' and some, 'you scratch my back and I'll scratch yours' bargaining, but either Phil McGinty was young and inexperienced (which she was, but only to a point), or she was stupid (which she definitely wasn't), or something else was going on because the journalist simply poured herself a cup of tea and began.

'I don't think Oli Cromwell killed himself,' she said.

Jen said nothing. She was hardly about to clasp the woman's hand across the table and declare they were of one mind. The journalist might not know how to play her part (cynical journalist), but she certainly did (tight-lipped copper).

'When we found him he had a clear drink next to his bed, next to the glass of water. I'm assuming it was gin and tonic – maybe vodka' said Phil. 'Either way, it doesn't matter. He only ever drank spirits with Diet Coke. And that's what Marilla made him – a JD and Coke.'

'Right,' said Jen, slowly. 'It's hardly a smoking gun is it? Hold the front page: "Man decides to have different drink on the night he dies." People make strange choices when they're having a mental health crisis.'

'Sure, but don't you think it's a bit odd – to make yourself something you don't even like as your final drink?

'So what are you saying?' said Jen. But she already knew where this was going.

'I'm saying that I think there was someone else in the room with him that night,' said Phil. 'Someone who drinks gin and tonics.'

Jen had meant what she said – 'It's hardly a smoking gun, is it?' – and yet it did give her something else to think about. A mystery gin and tonic drinker who laces a glass with painkillers and – for reasons unfathomable – anti-diarrhoea medication. Marilla drank gin and tonics. Jen had seen her downing one after the other on the only existing CCTV footage from the night Oli Cromwell died. Was she drowning her sorrows like she said, distraught at the poor disappointed school children, or was she actually drowning her guilt, waiting for him to swallow down the lethal cocktail she had prepared from him?

Perhaps. It was feasible.

Marilla was clearly fed up with the guy – demanding drugs and behaving like a baby – who's to say he wasn't up to worse? It would not have surprised Jen to discover Oli was more than a little handsy. Perhaps Marilla had finally had enough. But why go to the trouble of adding such a random assortment of drugs? Especially when she appeared to have her own pharmacy that she already made available to her boss. And why mix a gin and tonic when he was unlikely to drink it?. If she had wanted to see him off she could have slipped all of her tablets into his bedtime JD and Coke.

'Someone else was in the room with him,' Phil said. 'Mr Llewellyn heard a second woman's voice.'

'Who?' The cafe seemed to fall to silence as Jen digested this news.

'Llewellyn,' said Phil again, trying to jog Jen's memory. 'The guy in room 302 down the hall? Very beige. Anxiety issues. Unhappy about the noise? Didn't you speak to him?'

'He checked out before anyone could speak to him,' Jen replied.

'Well, I spoke to him and he promised me he would ring you to report that he'd heard two women in the room – one at a time – through the evening. Presumably the first was Marilla, but I think the second one was Judith.'

'Right,' said Jen, her mind still processing the news about Mr Llewellyn, let alone the fact the journalist somehow knew about Judith and the room service. 'You think one of them killed Oli Cromwell? I can't see it.'

'Neither can I,' said Phil. 'Especially given Judith's relationship with him.'

'How do you mean?' said Jen.

'Judith's Oli Cromwell's grandmother,' said Phil. 'Didn't she tell you?'

'Judith Jones from the front desk?'

'You didn't know? I assumed she was keeping it from me because I'm a journalist.'

Jen really didn't want to admit she didn't know, even if it was obvious from her response. Luckily, Phil was still talking.

'But the way she behaved when I spoke to her was weird, you know? She said she had "only just met him". To me that suggests she spoke to him. But she denied it. She said she just meant that she'd seen him in the flesh. I dunno. That just seemed a bit strange to me. She took up his room service, but she didn't stop to say hello to her grandson?'

Jen tried to process all the new information. There appeared to be two missed leads in the case so far. A case for which she was the most senior officer at the scene. The journalist, not content with flooring her, decided to keep kicking her when she was down.

'There's something dodgy going on with Callum, too,' said Phil, and then mistook Jen's confused look and explained who she meant. 'Callum Geering. The sous-chef at The Marchmont Hotel.'

After the double bombshells of the missed eyewitness (Llewellyn) and the missed grandmother (Judith Jones), Jen had been bracing herself for Philippa McGinty's finale. But when the journalist told her a story – how she had seen Callum crying on the afternoon before Oli Cromwell was found dead and the day after as well; how he had been on a call talking about entering a guest's room, and how she had later followed the chef and watched him meet up with Dan Mehta – Jen had felt laughter bubbling in her throat. It was simply too ridiculous. There was no way they could have missed all of that. Was there?

'And then there's what happened with his girlfriend Liane,' said Phil. 'And the missing CCTV.'

This was the icing on the cake. No. This was the cherry on top of the icing on the cake. It was the final kick in the teeth.

'How do you know about that?' said Jen. She felt indignant. They had only just found out themselves thanks to some, she felt, pretty nice police work. And here was Philippa McGinty sipping her tea and casually sharing information like it was nothing. The journalist shrugged.

'One of my mates lives with someone who works at Telligence,' she said.

'So what are you trying to tell me, Philippa?' said Jen, feeling a sudden irritation with this young woman who seemed to be constantly underfoot.

'I don't know,' said Phil with an honesty that disarmed Jen. 'I just think something's a bit weird about it all, you know?'

Funnily enough, thought Jen, I do know. But she wasn't about to let Phil in on that secret.

'Well, thanks for all this,' she said. 'I'll pay for the drinks.'

She had risen to go, suddenly, desperate to be out of there, but she forced herself to ask a final question. 'This Llewellyn person,' she said. 'Do you have his details?'

'Sorry, no,' said Phil. 'I'm not even sure that was his real name. But,' she added. 'I do know that he was a teacher. And there's something else...'

Jen waited.

'I think I just saw him up on the cliff about to chuck himself off.'

FORTY-TWO

'Dean, Grant' said Jen, 'I need a word.'

Jen's mind was still whirring from her meeting with Phil. Now she was back at the office and keen to find answers.

They went to an empty interview room. Not the ideal place for a meeting about who had or hadn't shat the bed in a high-profile enquiry that the press were watching like hawks, but it would have to do.

Jen looked at Dean. 'Did anything about Judith Jones strike you as strange?'

'Well,' said Dean, slowly. 'Just that she collapsed when she found out Mr Cromwell had died. But that was just a reaction to the cold water swimming, I believe.'

Jen turned back to Grant. 'And what about you? Anything odd about her?'

'Yeah, she was one of them mad bags who goes in the sea when it's brass monkeys. Prickly old bat and all – didn't want to answer my questions and tottered off back to work as soon as she could get away.'

Dean thought for a moment. 'But that made it weird,

didn't it? The fact she needed medical assistance? You think she'd be used to cold water.'

'Let's say for a minute,' said Jen, 'that it wasn't the cold water that gave her the funny turn.'

She looked at them both. 'There's a chance Judith is Cromwell's grandmother'

'What?' replied Grant. 'Seriously?'

Jen shrugged. 'Could be.'

Dean blinked. 'But Ken never mentioned it. Neither did Judith.'

'Yep, that's pretty odd, don't you think?'

Even Grant paused for some unsanctioned speculation. 'Yeah,' he agreed at last. 'It's strange.'

'There's someone else we need to find, too,' said Jen. 'We need to find the man in room 302.'

FORTY-THREE

The car pulled up alongside Phil.

'Phil, my buddy! Need a lift?' said the grinning face of Dan Mehta.

'No thanks,'

'But we got this posh car and everything!' said Dan. 'Come for a ride.'

She peered a little closer. There was a man behind Dan in the back seat.

Charles Getgood.

Brilliant. Just what she needed. Aldhill's most notorious criminal overlord was offering her a lift. Now she had a decision to make: get in the car with them and put herself at risk, or run for her life and miss out on what would almost certainly be a great story, even if that story turned out to be, 'Local journalist found dead in boating lake.'

Dan leaned out the window a little. 'We've got a story for you.'

Phil sighed and got into the car.

'It's a pleasure to meet you at last, Philippa,' Charles said.

He was a charmer, getting in there early with his winning smile and his firm handshake. Phil didn't trust him.

'You said you had a story for me,' she said.

'Straight down to business, I see,' he said smiling, 'I like it. First off I should say this is strictly off the record.'

He put his hand out to stop her as Phil took out her phone. She hesitated, but then she switched the phone off, placing it on her leg so he could see it, feeling like she had been stripped of her armour.

'Okay,' she said. 'What have you got for me?'

'Our Oli Cromwell wasn't the nice local lad he seemed to be.' said Charles.

Phil didn't let her gaze waver.

'And? Is that the story? "Hollywood star a bit of a knob" isn't quite the scoop I was expecting.'

'Oh ye of little faith, Ms McGinty,' said Charles flashing his veneers. 'The story I've got for you is a lot better than that.'

'Go on,' she said.

'I have it on good authority that Oli Cromwell has paid off a young woman,' and here he left a dramatic pause, 'who he sexually assaulted.'

It was Phil's turn to pause. She studied his face, trying to work out why he was telling her this.

'Told you we had a story for you, chief,' crowed Dan from the front.

'And how do you know this?' said Phil.

'Ah,' said Charles, sitting back and raising his hands helplessly, 'I'm afraid your source declined to comment at this stage.'

Phil smiled.

'I can't just go on hearsay. Have you got any evidence for me at all? If I write it without anything concrete, the paper will be public enemy number one for speaking ill of the dead.'

'Well, then I suggest you find someone willing to go on the record, Philippa,' said Charles.

'Right. So, what you're telling me is, you know Oli Cromwell has committed sex offences, but you won't tell me how or why you know, and you're not prepared to go on the record?'

'Quite the investigative journalist,' said Charles, leaning back in his chair.

'Not even as an "anonymous source"?'

'Oh, I expect you can do better than that. I expect you can find a "source close to the actor" to give you something juicy.'

Phil looked confused.

'The one you brought to my nightclub the other day.'

Phil felt her heart quail. Of course he knew she had been into his club. He was the friendly neighbourhood drug lord – he knew everything.

'Why are you telling me this?' she heard herself say. Amazing how she could keep her head while her guts were turning to liquid.

'Oh, let's just say I believe it's a story that should be more widely known.'

She realised she could study his face all day and she would never capture anything like the truth in his expression.

'Did you know him?' she said.

'I never met him,' replied Charles.

'Let me guess. He worked for you, didn't he?'

She saw a flicker of annoyance and ploughed on, despite a flush of adrenaline.

'Is that what this is? Has someone got something on you that you're trying to bury? A sex scandal is a good way to go about it, but why give it to me? This is a national story.'

He adopted a weary tone, as though he were disappointed in the youth of today. 'Philippa, if you don't want this story, that's entirely up to you. I'm just trying to get the truth out there, and I thought you could use the break. All that time you're spending sniffing around my club when you could be tracking down the real villains. But if you don't think you're ready...'

'Callum worked for you too, didn't he? Funny he was in the hotel that night. The night Cromwell died.'

'A lot of people have worked for me over the years, Philippa. You should know. Your mother... Angela isn't it? She works for me now. Did you know that? You'd think it was the council employing her, wouldn't you? But one of my companies took over the contract a couple of years ago.' He gazed out the window as a few spots of rain landed on the glass. 'The sad truth is, we are struggling to maintain all those employee contracts. We may have to let a few people go.'

He leaned slightly towards her and Phil resisted the urge to flinch backwards. He was threatening her mother's job, but in that moment she could only feel fear.

'Now then, where can we drop you?'

She met his gaze and mustered a breezy smile.

'Oh, anywhere around here is fine.'

'Actually,' he said, evidently unsatisfied by her response. 'I've just got a couple of errands to run. You don't mind, do you?'

'You know what?' She tried to keep her voice light. 'I've got an appointment, so I'll just jump out here.'

'Oh, cancel it,' said Charles. 'I'm sure they'll understand. You can keep me company a little longer.'

After what felt like an eternity, Dan pulled up in the furthest reaches of the town. They were in the middle of a half-built, half-abandoned industrial estate of a spur road. Charles reached over and opened her door.

'You take care getting home, Philippa. Wouldn't want Angela and Lucas worrying about you.'

Phil got out as quickly as she could, before he could change his mind, and watched the car pull away. She took a breath. What started as fear was being winnowed into anger.

'Watch the ones with the big smiles and the sharp suits,' she heard Angela say. 'They've got big teeth and sharp bites.'

She took out her phone and dialled.

'Did Oli Cromwell rape someone?' said Phil.

'How did you find out?' Marilla said.

'An anonymous source tipped me off.'

'Who? No one knew about it apart from me and the lawyers,' said Marilla. 'I didn't tell anyone, and she certainly wasn't allowed to – the girl – she signed an NDA. It wasn't the lawyers was it?'

'I don't know,' said Phil.

'I didn't tell anyone about what Oli had done,' Marilla said.

'You said that already,' Phil replied.

She started walking.

'Well,' said Marilla, eventually. 'Maybe I did tell one person.'

FORTY-FOUR

'This is Aldhill,' said DI Lee Hudson. 'You can't chuck a rock on the promenade without hitting someone who went to school with Oli Cromwell. My nephew went to school with him. Are you going to question him too?'

'Depends,' said Jen. 'Does he have a conviction for intent to supply, a couple of hours missing on the night Oli Cromwell died and a witness who says he was distraught on the phone and talking about going into a guest's room?'

Lee gave her a withering smile and then got suddenly serious. 'It was a suicide, Jen. We've got the tox report.'

Lee had appeared, as if by magic, as soon as Jen set Dean and Grant to work on finding Llewellyn and Callum, presumably drawn by the scent of rebellion.

'And what about Judith Jones? *His grandmother,* Lee. Why didn't she mention that little detail? And what happened when she took up the room service? And did Callum's girlfriend really take the call about the lost CCTV or did she just tell everyone that? Because Dean hasn't managed to track down anyone from the actual IT company we can speak to.'

'The last thing we need is the press finding out you're off interviewing everyone who ever farted in Cromwell's vicinity.'

'Lee, I'm not even close to suggesting that,' said Jen, exasperated. 'But we should at the very least speak to Callum to find–'

Lee interrupted her. 'The kid killed himself. He'd had a bad day, we've got a witness who told us as much. We've got a star sulking in his room and refusing to come out. We've got every indication that this is exactly what it looks like.'

Jen would have argued normally. She would have tried to win him over, tried to convince him to let her just confirm Callum's whereabouts for the sake of putting a neat bow on the case, but she was so, so tired. She just wanted to go home and open a bottle of wine and fall asleep in front of a prestige drama.

'OK, boss,' she said.

Lee hesitated, giving her a second look. 'Good,' he said.

He walked out with evident suspicion, as though he was expecting her to shout, 'Ha! Psych!' and start arguing with him all over again.

Dean and Grant looked at her, evidently waiting for her to tell them to ignore Lee and get to work. But before she could shrug and say, 'Let's drop it,' Lee walked back in.

'Jesus Christ, Jen. I suppose if you must interview them, I won't stop you,' he said.

'Right,' said Jen, wrong-footed.

'But I'm not sure we really need to re-open a neatly closed file.'

And then it made sense. Lee had tried to stop Jen from

opening a closed file before and it hadn't gone well for him. The last thing he needed was another botched murder enquiry.

'Just don't make too much noise about it, will you?' he added.

'I'll cancel the press release,' she said.

While Dean and Grant went to pick up Callum Geering, and Nandini, skiving from her work with DCI Petra Gull, had a go at finding Llewellyn, Jen went to speak to Judith Jones.

'Just a few follow up questions,' she said.

Judith reluctantly let her in. Her small flat – part of a converted Victorian town house – gave off a bohemian vibe that Jen felt didn't quite match the receptionist's uptight manner. There were scarves wrapped around lamp stands and gold framed paintings collected in clusters and leaned against walls (presumably waiting for someone to hang them one day), not to mention some truly impressive houseplants that made Jen feel like a failure for somehow murdering hers with the ruthless efficiency of a serial killer. The walls were painted bright colours, deep pinks and rich greens, giving a sumptuous air despite the general shabbiness of both walls and furniture.

Jen perched on the firmest-looking seat while the hotel receptionist sank into a deep, aged sofa and crossed her legs. She was an impressive woman, Jen thought. The sort of woman who could leave your ego in tatters from behind the makeup counter of a department store. Jen could imagine her painting her toenails in the bath.

'What do you want?' said Judith.

'What's your relationship with Oli Cromwell,' Jen asked.

Judith's expression shifted slightly, her lips pursing in displeasure.

'I have no relationship with him,' she said and then corrected herself. 'Had.'

'And are you related to him in any way?'

Judith picked imaginary lint off her skirt and paused.

'He was my grandson,' she said.

'And did you not think that was worth mentioning to the police?'

'Not really.'

'Why not?'

'I wasn't meant to know about him. I was estranged from my son. And anyway, I only worked it out recently.' She began fiddling with the edge of the sofa, prodding her nail into the grooves of the warp and weft. 'And because it didn't feel important. We never even spoke.'

'See, that's interesting because we've got an eyewitness who claims they heard Oli Cromwell speaking to a woman the night he died.'

'The man in room 302, I presume? I wouldn't take anything he said too seriously. Giant mummy's boy. Probably imagines there are monsters under the bed.'

'Are you saying you didn't speak to Oli Cromwell?'

'I went up there to deliver his room service because we were understaffed,' she said. Then, catching Jen's palpable cynicism, seemed to give in. 'OK, I admit I wanted to see him. But I knocked on the door, carried the food inside, and left. It was hardly the time for a big family reunion.' Tears glinted suddenly in her eyes. 'I didn't know it would be the only time.'

'You didn't say anything to him?'

'Not beyond the usual "hello" and "where would you like this" – that sort of thing.'

'Nothing else?'

'No,' said Judith,

'And how did he seem to you? What was his demeanour?'

'He seemed a bit glassy eyed. One too many bourbons I should think.'

'Was he drinking a bourbon when you saw him?'

'He was holding one when I came in,' she said, tracking the weave back up the arm of the sofa, leaving a dent where her nail had been.

'You're sure it was a Jack Daniels and Coke?' said Jen.

'Something with Diet Coke. I assumed bourbon. Rum maybe,' replied Judith. 'I remember thinking it was a young person's drink.'

'But you didn't speak to him?'

'I told you. No. I think we're done now.'

'I'll need you to come down the station to give a formal statement.'

Judith pursed her lips but didn't disagree.

'We're looking to recover the CCTV footage,' said Jen.

Judith looked up sharply. 'I heard it had been lost.'

'There might still be a backup.'

'I see.'

'Which would be good, because then we can find out if there was anyone in his room that evening.'

Jen could see Judith mulling this over.

'Do you think someone... Did this to him?'

'The CCTV footage going missing bothers me,' said Jen by way of a reply. She didn't want to go making bold claims to a family member. Lee would be furious if he found out.

But Judith was one of the last people to see Oli Cromwell alive, and while she couldn't imagine Judith wanting to dose her only grandchild, she couldn't rule it out either.

'That'll be the Inference Tech,' said Judith. 'I had to ring them recently when the hotel computer system went down. Absolutely hopeless, took me days to get through to anyone.'

'Well, they have lost vital evidence. We believe someone else went to his room after you left.' A thought came to her. 'Have you lived here all your life, Judith?'

'I moved away for a long time. But, yes, I was born and raised here.'

'You must have known a lot of people back then?' Jen said.

'That was why I left.'

'In that case, you might know someone we think is involved with Inference somehow. He went away for a while too, but now he's back. His name's Charles Getgood.'

Jen watched as Judith's lips pursed even tighter.

'Never heard of him,' she said.

FORTY-FIVE

Charles sat in the darkness. He was freezing. He should move really, but he stayed where he was on the bench, staring at the moonlight reflecting on the sea. The waves were crashing gently onto the shingle, sending out a clatter and hiss as the pebbles rolled forwards and sucked backwards with the water. He was unsure what to do for the first time in his life.

Just an hour before he had been his usual self, dreaming his big dreams, scheming and plotting. He had taken matters into his own hands with Phil McGinty, the annoyingly ambitious local hack who thought she was the next big deal in investigative journalism. It hadn't taken much to send her off on the hunt for a better story. Sex sells. No one cares about boring little corruption and shell company shenanigans; it was all too dry and confusing. The Oli Cromwell scandal would give the upstart journalist something to sink her teeth into. She had Charles's ambition. He could smell it on her. At the time he had been satisfied, confident she would forget all about snooping around his business, confident all was right with the world again. Confident he was one more step towards the establishment elite. The thought of it bored him to tears.

But then a bomb exploded his entire life.

'I've got something to tell you,' Judith said. She had called him at his nightclub, which had surprised him. He hadn't realised she knew about his club. 'Meet me at the pier in twenty minutes. The bench by the telescope.'

He wasn't used to being told what to do, and he was going to put the phone down without replying, but she beat him to it, and he found himself listening to silence for a long second before he realised she wasn't there anymore. He knew he would go. It wasn't just the tone of her voice; it was the meeting spot she had chosen. Their bench.

He arrived before her, which was a surprise: she was always the first to get anywhere. He felt like an old man, sitting on a bench with nothing to do but stare at the waves. He rose to greet her when she arrived, but she put out a hand, asking him to listen, refusing any greetings, and again he found himself obeying. When she spoke, the news seemed to hit him squarely in the chest. He felt himself staggering back just a little, grasping the bench for support.

'I have a son,' she said. 'He's yours.'

He had a son.

A son!

Hurt pierced his heart. They sat down, Charles, bewildered beyond all comparison.

'You kept him from me.'

Judith just nodded, her face implacable.

'You kept my boy from me.'

'Yes,' she said.

So many questions, but where to start?

'When did you know?' he asked.

'Before you went to prison,' she replied, eventually.

Again, it hit him physically in the chest. 'You knew before I went to prison and you didn't tell me?'

'I wanted to have a normal life. I didn't want to be some gangster's bird anymore. And I didn't want my son growing up the son of a crook.'

'I could have changed,' said Charles. 'I could have turned it around, could have become a decent dad.'

'No,' she said.

Charles desperately wanted to tell her she was wrong; he didn't want to admit that she had made the right decision. Her face was as hard as stone. Remorseless.

'He would have disappointed you,' she said. 'He's not like you. He's soft and kind and sensitive. You would have despised him.'

He was angry now. The pain washed through him and made him clench his fists. 'You had no right.'

'I had every right,' said Judith. 'I had every right to do what was best for him and best for me. I couldn't live like that anymore. I don't know why anyone would.'

'I need to see him.' Charles heard his voice grow threatening. He wasn't used to being in someone else's power. He saw Judith tense and it occurred to him for the first time that she was still beautiful, those eyes penetrating anyone in her way.

She shrugged. 'Maybe,' she said. 'Now's probably not the best time.'

'What do you mean not the best time?'

'He's had a bereavement.' She looked down at her feet. There was something else she hadn't told him. 'His son died.'

'Son?' said Charles. How could his boy have a son? He couldn't be old enough to have a son, surely? He was confused. He had imagined a young man, but of course he wouldn't be that young now. It had been fifty-odd years since he'd last seen Judith. 'I'm a grandad?'

'I never met him,' said Judith and he remembered what she had said – his son's son had died. 'He was famous. You might have heard of him.'

'Who?' Charles managed and something in his gut suddenly told him the answer. 'Oli Cromwell.'

She nodded, not meeting his gaze.

Oli Cromwell. He had worked for Charles as a teenager, right there under his nose all that time. And now he was gone. His grandson, the global star. It was impossible.

'I only met him once,' she said. Now it was her turn to look anguished. But then, just like that, she returned to frosted stone. 'But that's what I needed to see you for. I was with him the night he died and I know he was alive when I left,' she said. 'And who knows what happened afterwards. Maybe he really did go on to kill himself, but without the CCTV footage, we can't be sure if someone didn't go in there.'

A horrible thought began to form in Charles's mind and his eyes began darting about as though he could find the answer on the wooden slats of the pier floor. Had he killed his own grandson? Was he responsible for the young man's death?

'I don't know why your company lost it, Charles, and I don't want to know, but I know that people like you don't tend to simply mislay things like that,' she said. 'You need to find that CCTV.'

That was it. That was all she said. He watched helplessly as she got up and walked away. For the first time in many years. Charles felt truly powerless. All the things he had missed, all of the moments he had lost, all for what? For money, notoriety, power? He sat on the bench until he couldn't feel his fingers.

FORTY-SIX

Judith ran herself a cold bath. She hadn't had time for a swim today and she missed the feeling of the cool water on her skin. Had she made the right choice telling Charles about Kenneth and the boy? She didn't know. Seeing him again had shaken her once more. Her body seemed to react to him in ways she couldn't understand – hadn't experienced for a long time.

She had told him the truth and in some ways she felt lighter for it: a secret lifted. But she had risked everything to do it. And what about Kenneth? He would be exposed to the truth about his father. A criminal and a thug, a charmer and a bully; she couldn't even begin to imagine how things would go from here. But she had to do it: she had to find out the truth about Oli Cromwell, even if it meant finding out the worst.

She thought of him now: the local superstar Oli Cromwell. Thomas Jones. The day he walked into The Marchmont the staff had come out to greet him in the entrance like fans lining the red carpet. Judith had intended to stay in her place at the front desk, avoiding the whole fiasco, but when the car pulled up, she felt her body moving from behind the counter, over the Persian rug and over to the lobby staircase. When the door opened she thought her heart had stopped, but then the blood began thumping loudly in her brain and it was all she could do to stay upright.

In the flesh he was less handsome, more normal looking, more like a boy who could be her grandson. He looked tired, thinner than she expected, with a small cut on his chin – presumably from shaving. Still beautiful of course, but no longer glowing under movie lighting and airbrushed to perfection. She felt the love welling in her heart for him. She had seen all his films but it was nothing to seeing him here – her own flesh and blood.

To begin with the boy had seemed both charmed and charming, but as he walked along the line he faltered a little. She recognised that tightening around the lips and eyes. It was the same face Kenneth pulled as a child just before he burst into tears. By the time he reached the lift, he looked like a lost lamb and Judith wanted to run over and give him a cuddle. The last thing she saw before the elevator doors pressed together was his anguished face staring at someone in the crowd.

She thought that would be an end to it. After all, what choice did she have? She couldn't exactly rush over to him and shout, 'I'm your granny.' People already thought she was a mad old bat. But then Callum went missing that night and all hell broke loose. Despite the staffing issue, plenty of people had offered to take up the room service, all of them keen to get a glimpse of the star, but somehow Judith elbowed her way to the fore and insisted that she was the correct person since she was not central to the team. She made it sound like she was doing them all a favour.

'It's okay I'll take it up,' she said, grasping the tray and heading for the door.

He was drunk when he opened the door. Drunk or high – or both – she wasn't sure, but she could see it in the glassy gaze and the swagger. She set the food down and felt his eyes on her. She turned and spotted his disappointment at her age.

'Aren't you a bit old to be working here?' he said.

She managed to stay polite.

'Got to keep myself busy,' she said.

He was rude. Worse than that he was lecherous.

'Do you feel like giving me a blowjob?' he said.

'Does anyone ever feel like giving a blowjob?' she heard herself reply.

'Suit yourself,' he shrugged. 'It's just I've never been sucked off by an old lady. Are those teeth removable?'

He grinned at her then. His whole face lit up, his head swaying a little like a shaken ragdoll.

'I'm only kidding. Your face is a picture. Sorry, but I really had you there, didn't I?'

He was lying. Covering for his embarrassment. She wanted to slap him around the face and tell him to behave himself. She wondered how Kenneth could have raised such an awful child. She was ashamed on his behalf. He's just like his grandad, she thought. Is this what happens? We keep creating these monsters and sending them out into the world? If she had known would she have had her tubes tied to prevent the handing on of obnoxiousness from one generation to the next. This boy was testament to the awfulness of Charles's genes. Hers too probably. Her auntie and her father had been very far from saints. Her grandfather had scurried off without a trace at the first sound of a baby's cries. So here was this boy, the product of his forebears, a handsome disappointment, fit for nothing. But still she loved him so much her heart felt painful.

'Can I get you anything else, sir?' she said.

'JD and Diet Coke,' he said, throwing himself onto the bed in a self-pitying slump. A muffled voice emanated from the pillow. 'And a blow job.'

'Let me get you a glass of water,' she said. 'Then you can eat and maybe get to sleep. I expect it's been a long day.'

She brought his food over and put it down on the side next to him. In the kitchenette, she found a glass and filled it with water, which she drank down in one gulp. It was as she was grasping the edge of the kitchen counter, wondering how she had got things so wrong that she saw the makeup bag and the pills. She considered dissolving a few into the glass, removing her descendants from the gene pool. But she couldn't hurt him, even though she wanted to. She loved him as much as she disliked him.

When she emerged with his water, he had eaten all the chicken from his salad and a handful of chips and was struggling to take off his shirt. 'Let me help you,' she said, unbuttoning his shirt sleeve.

She fetched a white robe from the cupboard and brought it over.

'Let's get you tucked up.'

He looked so sad and sleepy. He's not well, she told herself. He's probably having a breakdown. Isn't that what happens to all Hollywood stars? Her heart went out to him and she sat down next to him on the bed, ready to comfort him. But he unbuttoned his trousers and pointed at his penis like he was directing someone to a landmark.

'Want to get stuck in?' he said.

Cold fury turned her to ice. She slapped him.

'You're a disgrace,' she said. 'I'm ashamed of you.'

She got up to go, but she turned back at the sound of his crying. She looked at his watery eyes staring up to her. Her son's eyes – her eyes, according to Kenneth. The eyes of a stupid little boy who thought he was a man. The eyes of someone old enough to know better.

'I hate myself,' he said. He was dazed, sharing it like a child admitting a secret.

'I'm not surprised,' she said. 'I don't like you very much either.'

And that was the last thing she said to him. She would never tell another soul what he had done that day, nor that she had left him with such a stark message that there was every chance he had finished his evening by swallowing all those pills, sure that even an old lady thought he wasn't worth knowing. Had she done it? Had she been the straw that broke the camel's back? Was he now lying in an under-taker's fridge because she hadn't given him a bit of basic human kindness? He had cried for help, and she had left him there to take his own life. Or so she had believed.

She hoped with every fibre of her being that the CCTV would show another person going into the room after her, because if she truly had been the last person to see him alive, if it turned out he really had ended his own life, then she wasn't sure how she would live with that.

Electric jolts of guilt and remorse sent her gasping into the cold water. She plunged her head under and stayed there staring up at the ceiling for a long time.

FORTY-SEVEN

'I didn't tell anyone about what Oli had done.'

That's what Marilla had said to Phil, but she was lying. She *had* told someone, of course. Marilla had told her father. After all, stories were currency to her family, and he was so sweet to her in the evenings when she caught him on his second brandy. She could get him to tell her all kinds of tales. Like the one about the dreadful businessman, a borderline crook who spoke like a barrow boy and was forever trying to get accepted into polite society. Or the family lawyer, who they couldn't seem to get rid of despite his inadequacies. She would sit there delighted, happy in the warmth of his amusement.

But he would tire easily if she didn't keep him laughing, and so she would try to entertain him too, telling him the gossip from the office, forming her stories into perfect little after dinner anecdotes. It was vital she stopped him from sending her out of his study and back to her cold bedroom or (worse) the drawing room where her mother sat, glassy-eyed and bitter. Marilla was a grown woman now, but she still craved these moments of happiness with daddy.

So she told him the story about Oli Cromwell and the young girl called Cora. She wanted to tell it with spit and venom. She wanted to tell her father all about how Cora had cried and cried, about how ashamed she was of her own part in it, how she had stood to one side as the lawyer insisted Cora hand over her mobile phone and any media she had taken of Oli.

But Marilla didn't. Instead, she told him as if it were a funny story of the silly Hollywood boy who blubbed on the sofa like a baby and ruined her afternoon. And she told him how she still had her own copies of Cora's recordings, because the lawyers didn't think to check if Marilla had them. And her father was delighted to hear how stupid this Hollywood star was and how clever his daughter was.

But her father wouldn't tell anyone, surely? She had stewed on it all night, and now she sat at her desk worrying, biting her cuticles. With a sudden fluid motion, she lifted her phone and called him, rising from her chair and making for one of the agency's glass-fronted phone booths, gaining a fraction more privacy in return for far more visibility. He didn't answer right away and Marilla steeled herself for the inevitable voicemail, but then, at the last moment, his voice filled her head with his clipped efficiency.

'Dad,' she said, after the briefest of hellos. 'You didn't tell anyone about Oli Cromwell and that girl, did you?'

Her voice sounded childish, she realised.

'Darling,' he said, and she could hear him shuffling impatiently in his leather seat. 'You might want to be a little more discreet in future. I can't be expected to remember what is a secret and what isn't. If you're going to tell tales, you had better make damn sure they can't be traced back to you.'

She laughed and told him she supposed he was right, but felt anger rising in her.

'And I hope none of this can be traced back to you, daddy,' she said, 'because it's about to get rather a lot of attention, I should imagine,' and then she told him she had a meeting about to start and, without waiting for his response, she hung up.

In for a penny, in for a pound, she decided. It was time to tell the truth about who Oli Cromwell was. Yes, he was dead, and yes, he could be a nice person when he wanted to be, but she had a duty to Cora – and who knows how many other Coras out there, who all suffered at Oli's hand because she didn't have the balls to tell anyone about it.

She texted Phil: 'I'm going to send you an audio file.'

Really, she should share it with someone more high profile. The publicist in her knew that telling a local journalist about it was almost like telling no one at all. But she had faith that Phil could get the story seen, and she felt she owed it to her for some reason.

She opened up her laptop and logged in. It took her a moment to realise, but soon she was panicking: all her files were gone.

All of them.

Not just the odd ones here and there. Her entire hard drive had been wiped. She checked her phone. All her emails were gone. Her cloud storage was empty. She had lost everything.

FORTY-EIGHT

'Danny, I've got two jobs for you,' Charles said. 'Destroy the Oli Cromwell sexual assault confession and give me the CCTV footage from The Marchmont.'

Charles had warmed up now. He'd pulled himself together and gone to work. Dan grinned at him, delighted that some hijinks were afoot. Charles supposed these were the moments the kid lived for, but they felt like irritating distractions to him. The last thing Charles wanted was for Inference to start getting attention, but he had no choice. Thankfully, it didn't take Dan long to get rid of the confession. In just a few moments he had accessed the girl's computer and reformatted her hard drive. Charles once again had reason to be glad that he had set up Inference Technology Solutions. They had won nearly all the local government contracts for providing tech support. They had Trojan Horse access to nearly every council, school and local services computer – not to mention a lucrative sideline selling overpriced assistance to the credulous. And, thanks to his business partner, they had recently been given the accounts for some extremely prestigious companies, including the publicity firm employed by Oli Cromwell.

'I'm afraid your hard drive has corrupted, so we will need to provide you with a new machine,' Dan told the girl when she rang, needing IT support. Charles could hear her voice, shrill and panicked, piping out from Dan's phone. After a few more minutes of Dan calmly explaining that her computer was at fault (Charles was impressed by how nicely the boy spoke when he wanted to), the girl hung up. And just like that, he had destroyed the sex scandal evidence. It meant he no longer had a story to distract the journalist with, but what choice did he have? The last thing he wanted was for the memory of his grandson to be tarnished by a sordid little story about a sordid little girl who couldn't keep her knickers on.

When it came to the CCTV footage, however, things didn't go as smoothly.

'Stephen's lost it,' said Dan.

Charles had wanted to reach up and wring the skinny little idiot's head.

'Thing is, boss, I didn't want it to be on our property.' Dan buzzed around Charles's office like a coked up mosquito. Charles's patience was already spent when Dan continued his litany of excuses. 'I told Stephen to take care of it. Then, if the police found it there, at least there was a legit reason for it being on his computer. I thought it was safer to keep us away from it all, chief. Plausible deniability and all that.'

What the hell was he on about? In Charles's day, people just learned to keep their traps shut. They didn't need to be protected from the truth, like little babies who couldn't stop their tongues flapping.

'What's the problem, boss?' said Dan, apparently confused. 'I only kept the footage for insurance – to stop Callum misbehaving, you know what I mean?'

Charles closed his eyes. He should have retired. That's what he should have done. He could be on a motorised scooter right now, eating an ice cream at the seafront. He was too tired and old for all this nonsense. All through life he had to contend with idiots like Dan. People you employ thinking they're bright only to discover they're dim as a pauper's candle – or, at least, lacking in basic common sense.

'You've lost vital evidence,' he said.

This meant Charles couldn't identify who had killed his grandson. He felt the anger rising in him and took a breath, allowing the fury to slowly engulf him. He started thinking about how he'd have handled this in days gone by. How he would have thought nothing of making Dan pay in the most final way possible. But now he was a respectable – or almost respectable – member of society. He couldn't have someone fitted with concrete shoes and tipped into the ocean. What would HR say?

Still, he was giving full vent to his fantasies when a young woman came hobbling into view, appearing in his office like the crippled cavalry. He could have kissed her.

'I've got the CCTV footage,' she said.

It was Liane Benbow, girlfriend of Callum Geering and mother of his new baby daughter, Olivia.

'Bullshit,' said Dan, but Charles nodded towards the door.

'Dan, go and make our guest here a cup of tea,' he said. 'And I'll have one too.'

Dan looked ready to argue, but then slunk off with a sullen air.

'I've got all of the information I need to prove that you ordered the CCTV to be deleted,' Liane said. She was ready for a fight, her whole body leaning forward. Charles had no idea if she was telling the truth, but he admired her spirit.

'Right,' he said, carefully, calmly, slowing the conversation down, making it harder for Liane to maintain her righteous fury. He was used to dealing with emotional people. 'But you do realise your boyfriend's all over that footage?'

Charles smiled when she replied. 'Not anymore he isn't.'

'I see,' he said. 'What do you want, Liane?'

'I want my job back. And I want you to leave Callum alone – you and Dan and all your cronies – and never interfere with our lives again.'

'Is that all?' He knew better than to laugh at a young woman on the warpath, but he could see her lose a little confidence. She hadn't thought it all through.

'And I want maternity pay.' She fidgeted slightly, but held her nerve. Charles liked this kid. He could see her thinking fast. 'I want six months paid maternity leave in the highest band.'

She was gabbling a little now. 'And if I have even a sniff that you've tried to bring Callum back into the business again, I will release all of the files I have proving that Inference Technology ordered the CCTV footage to be withheld from the police.'

'I'm not sure I believe you have that evidence,' he said to her.

'Well, I guess you'll just have to find out, won't you?'

He stared at her a moment longer and then smiled. 'I tell you what, as a gesture of goodwill, I'll give you nine months maternity pay at a higher band rate, and there will be a job waiting for you when you're ready to return. What's more, I promise that none of us will ever darken your doorstep again. You have my word.' He could see her deflate a little, as though she wasn't sure her luck would hold out. She was waiting for the 'but'.

'But you have to do me a favour,' he said, reaching into a drawer and pulling out an envelope. 'You have to put that CCTV footage of yours into this envelope and you have to deliver it to this address.'

He wrote a name and address on the envelope and slid it across the table to Liane who stared at it a moment. 'I'm sure I could manage that,' she said. She reached forward and grasped the envelope. 'I hope to never see you again.'

'Likewise,' said Charles. And he watched as Liane walked carefully out of the room.

'Didn't you want to see it for yourself first, boss,' said Dan when he returned, too late, with the tea

'No,' said Charles without elaborating.

The truth was, he couldn't trust himself. He was trying to avoid trouble, but if he watched that footage and saw the person who had killed his grandson, he would hunt that person down and kill him with his bare hands. He couldn't take that risk. He didn't want to go back to prison: he finally had something to lose.

No, he would let the police work out who killed his grandson. And, once the murderer was in prison, he'd organise for one of his old acquaintances to deal with them.

FORTY-NINE

Callum jumped out of the car and ran to open Liane's door as she approached. She glanced up at him, her skin pallid, sweat on her top lip. Last night, she had woken up drenched in sweat, the bedsheets wet. Liane thought she might have a fever. Hormones, Diane said. The day before, Liane had called him to come and see something harrowing in the toilet bowl. It looked like a kidney, he thought, and he was ready to call her an ambulance, but Diane appeared, still holding a laundry basket.

'It's just a blood clot. You'll live,' she told her daughter.

Why did no one warn you, he wondered? All that time spent explaining how to give birth, and none of the antenatal classes covered the basics like, how was Liane meant to go to the toilet with stitches holding her flesh together? Callum felt there should be a leaflet or something. What to expect when you're no longer expecting. Perhaps the author could include an explanation of how to deal with a girlfriend who recently discovered you were back working for a local crime lord.

Liane got into the car without a word, hefting herself gingerly into her seat with the aid of the passenger side roof handle.

'Ok?' said Callum. He was sweating too, he realised, despite the cold air.

'I sorted it,' was all she said.

They were silent the whole journey home, Liane staring out the windscreen with an unreadable expression. Callum glanced over a few times, but he didn't have the courage to ask her what had happened. He pulled up in a space near their flat and turned off the engine, hanging his head slightly as he reached for the door handle. Diane would be inside, keeping the house together, caring for the baby. He should be grateful – he *was* grateful – she had brought sanity and calm to their lives, not to mention a freezer full of cooked meals, but he really wished she wasn't there right now. He needed to talk to Liane.

'Thank you,' he said.

'You didn't kill him,' she said. He felt a jolt of shock. 'If that's what you're worried about?' He was too ashamed to speak. 'You drugged an innocent man and you did something, god knows what – please don't tell me – to his unconscious body and took photos or whatever... But he wasn't dead when you left.'

'How,' Callum began. He wanted to know how she knew because knowing the truth felt suddenly vital, knowing he wasn't to blame was the most important thing in the world, but he couldn't bring himself to finish the sentence. She answered it anyway.

'Someone else went in after you,' she said.

FIFTY

Phil stopped writing. She had been trying to write a piece about Oli Cromwell's final hours. She had tracked down some quotes from her new friends at The Marchmont – Anya the maître d' providing information about Llewellyn's evening meal and Judith reluctantly supplying details about the noise complaint, which came in just before her shift finished and which Judith therefore decided wasn't her problem – but she was still missing a lot of detail. In fact, she realised with a sigh, she was, as Angela would say, 'Putting the arse before the horse.'

After her encounter with Charles, Phil didn't want to admit she was shaken. Why had he told her about Oli Cromwell's sex scandal? Why had Marilla's computer been wiped? The company that looked after Marilla's IT support was Inference Technology Solutions. It was like there was a giant red arrow pointing down from the sky with a sign saying, 'Big story here,' with a klaxon bleating out an alarm. And yet, in the face of a proper investigation, Phil had changed tack. She had pitched Adam Jenkins, editor, a piece about the strange man in room 302. A man who could well have some important questions to answer about what happened the night Oli Cromwell died. Why? She couldn't honestly say, beyond the fact that she had seen him – she was sure she had – on the cliff, contemplating suicide.

Yes, there was a story there about Oli Cromwell. She knew there was. And it would go global if she wrote it. It could make her career. If she got it right, sold it to a reputable outlet, it could see her waving goodbye to Aldhill and heading for London – or America. But this story, about the missing man in room 302, somehow felt more pressing. She wasn't ready to drop the ball on this. Or, to mix metaphors, she couldn't let go of this yarn thread to try to untangle another. Because a man had died in a hotel that, so far as she could tell, had been something of a hub of strange activity. A weeping chef making promises on the phone about entering a guest's room. A woman taking up room service to a long-lost grandson. A publicist acting like a pharmacist. And an eyewitness who had vanished without speaking to the police.

Still, she didn't really have enough to go on. What she needed was some actual solid facts about Llewellyn. Judith and Anya hadn't been able to tell her much at all. Anya could barely remember him beyond the fact that he didn't have much to say and dined alone. She looked up his meal – chicken salad – which was notable only in that it was the same meal Oli ordered. Phil wondered if she should include that detail in the piece. At this stage, anything could be useful. Judith had made it clear she considered Llewellyn almost beneath contempt for his 'weasly little frog face' and his obsession with the trouser press. Beyond the slight details around how he paid and what name he gave, she didn't have much more to say.

Phil pulled up the photo she had taken of the man at the vigil on Saturday night. There was Llewellyn, incongruous in his beige trousers and equally bland anorak. He seemed to be staring not at the candles and offerings, but exclusively at the large wreath, the giant floral 'O' that sat in the centre of the makeshift shrine created by the many weeping visitors who had come to pay their respects to someone they didn't know.

She checked editorial image sites first, but the vigil shots the press photographers had taken were all of beautiful young girls crying in candlelight, their faces haunted and arresting in the warm yellow glow. The photographers hadn't focused any attention on a solitary middle-aged male standing awkwardly to one side, staring at a wreath. Next, she turned to social media. The vigil had been wall-to-wall cameras, phones being waved around, their little LED lights adding to the starry glow of the candles. She scrolled through the quagmire of the various algorithms, trying not to get distracted by the pull of cute animal clips, eventually focusing on a few people who had documented their visit to The Marchmont car park on both TikTok and Instagram. One person seemed to have been there since before the ambulances arrived, presumably drawn to the hotel via the same rumours that had induced Phil to take a punt as Kirsty Mathieson from *The* (actual) *Observer* to see if she could blag an interview.

The person – MoronicaMars2528 – had done a series of live videos throughout the day, many of them shaky and badly framed, some more focused on capturing the girl in a flattering winter light than in documenting the day. She had made an effort with a couple to edit them to songs, but she wasn't the most accomplished user. So much for the younger generation being digital natives, thought Phil.

Not that she could judge. She herself was surprisingly inept at creating compelling content, having always preferred tales from the golden age of journalism to Instagram Stories. For a year at school, when she was deep into nineties shoegaze and hanging out with the arty kids, she had made a point of not even having a smartphone. But her skills would need to improve, she knew. Large Language Models were already stealing jobs in her industry, and if she was going to find work in the future, she would almost certainly be expected to know how to put together a viral TikTok. Already, even at her tender age, she could feel the younger generation coming for her.

She watched as MoronicaMars2528 (could there really be 2527 Moronica Marses before her?) discovered the news of Oli's death. Her tears were strangely performative, as though she were watching herself cry (which she certainly was) and trying to do it as attractively as possible. No snotty mess for Moronica. No blotchy patches and spit bridges. Just two black, romantic tracks where two pretty tears had chased mascara down her cheeks.

After that, her videos became more slick, as though the sudden increase in her viewer counts had kick-started her professionalism. Clearly, Moronica had discovered her calling. While Phil had been inside talking to police and capturing eyewitness accounts, Moronica was outside reporting live as events unfolded. Phil watched as Judith arrived and had to be supported as she collapsed before being ushered towards an ambulance. Moronica mistook her for a fan, and zoomed in on Judith's face until the shot became grainy and low resolution.

The next video was slightly later. By now, The Marchmont staff had moved the assembling crowd to the other side of the carpark and Moronica was capturing the moment the florist put the finishing touches on the large wreath. Phil found herself wishing Moronica would get out of the way, but the girl was front and centre of every shot, perhaps imagining it would be her big chance at fame. The video approached its end and Phil was about to swipe up for the next when she spotted something. She tapped the screen, pausing the frame right at the moment the florist began talking to a man.

A man in beige trousers.

After that, Phil spent a frantic quarter of an hour trying to track down any video she could find of the wreath being made. So many of them came tantalisingly close to what she wanted to see, but only Moronica seemed to have captured the moment when Llewellyn began talking to the florist.

She headed over to Moronica's Instagram and found a post about the wreath, flicking through the still images until she came to the right one. There he was, five photos into the gallery.

The man in room 302.

The florist proved easy to track down. Her van, with its green Flora & Moss logo, was visible in many of the videos and images, and although her Instagram was quite neglected, there was a link to a website, which had a phone number, contact form and company address. She had a little shop on one of the side streets in the hipster side of town. Phil dialled the number and waited, pinching her bottom lip in suppressed anticipation. When the call connected, the voice that came through was bright and cheerful.

'Oh hello there,' said Phil in her nicest voice. 'I wonder if you could help me?'

Phil had taken a bus to the shop, deciding it would be easier to ask everything she needed – and show the photo of Llewellyn – in person. The florist was called Flora Wright, an excellent example of nominative determinism, in Phil's view.

'My mother likes to claim she's psychic,' said Flora.

Once Phil had explained that Flora may have been one of the last people to speak to a missing person, she was keen to offer up any information she had. Phil didn't mention that the man was only missing in the sense that she hadn't the faintest clue where to find him. She showed Flora her photo of Llewellyn, and Flora nodded immediately.

'Nice man. Extremely helpful. Perhaps a little...' it was clear she didn't like to speak ill of anyone and here she changed tack. 'I got the feeling he was lonely. He seemed to want to chat, but it was like he didn't quite know how, you know?'

Phil couldn't quite square it with the man who had been so eager to shut the door on her a few days ago.

'What did you talk about?'

'Oh, this and that. I do like to natter.'

Flora was doing herself a disservice. She was evidently as good at social engineering as Phil – if not better. During their short time together, Flora had managed to extract details that Phil imagined the man in 302, given his secrecy so far, hadn't intended to share with anyone.

'He told me his name was Owen, and he was a teacher –

or had been until his mother died.' She returned to her work, putting together a spray of flowers in muted pinks and yellows. Phil watched her deft hands moving as she spoke, her voice echoing in the high ceilings of her shop. 'He taught geography. He said he'd lived down here for a while, but he'd ended up going home to care for his parents. I asked him if he'd seen any of his students and he mentioned that he'd bumped into a couple.' She cut the stem of a rose and inserted it into the display. 'He clammed up a bit after that, and I got the sense he didn't have a good time here. I changed the subject. I can't remember what to. Probably something to do with flowers. He helped me with the display, bless him...' She paused. 'I hope he's alright. I really did think he seemed lonely.'

'Thanks Flora,' said Phil, before taking a seat in the cafe next door.

Phil googled Owen Llewellyn. As expected, it brought up too many search results – even when she tried to add in additional cues like '+teacher.' Tracking him down online was going to be impossible without more information. The same was true for Llewellyn Owen. She tried looking for school websites with his name listed, but that was fruitless. Flora had mentioned he had worked as a teacher down in Aldhill and had bumped into some students.

Some students... He can't have meant her. She was excellent at faces and there was no way she'd have forgotten his. Who else might he have taught? She thought of the people she had seen in the hotel. Callum Geering. Callum had been to Parker school before he joined them at Aldhill Academy. More importantly, he had been there with Oli Cromwell.

Surely not. She picked up her phone and texted Liane,

who informed Phil that her privates hurt and, yes, Callum was at home.

'Ok if I pop over?' said Phil. 'I've got a weird question for him.'

FIFTY-ONE

Nearly twenty-four hours after Jen met Phil in Beachy Shed café, the team's attempts at tracking down the man in room 302 had moved slightly further forward, with a fairly established timeline courtesy of The Marchmont staff.

He dined alone. He asked for a trouser press at the front desk. He used the stairs. Later in the evening, around midnight, he complained about the noise coming from Oli Cromwell's suite. Nothing was done because the noise stopped shortly after that and the staff shift changed. He checked out the next morning, simply leaving his key on the desk without speaking to anyone. There was CCTV from reception which gave checkout time as 9am.

Public CCTV showed him leaving the hotel and making his way down the seafront. From there, he vanished into a CCTV black spot, before reappearing further down the promenade.

'But now he no longer has his rucksack,' said Jen, pointing at the slim figure on her screen.

They were in the Incident Room and she was updating Lee on their latest findings.

'But he does have a plastic bag,' added Dean.

'Which looked like it possibly contained clothes,' said Jen.

'Huh,' said Lee, folding his arms. 'You're thinking he disposed of his bag?'

'Dropped it off,' said Jen. 'Grant checked the area around the CCTV black spot and it's right by Smuggler's Rest B&B.'

'The owner recognised his description,' said Grant, joining the conversation by spinning his chair ninety degrees and leaning back. 'He paid cash and gave his name as Llewellyn again. He had a Welsh accent, she said, and wasn't interested in chatting. Not that she was the sort of woman you want to chat to, if you know what I mean.'

Jen chose not to pursue that comment, intuiting it would only end in fury on her part.

'We know he's still at the hotel,' said Jen. 'And the owner has very *kindly*,' she gave Grant a meaningful look, which he ignored, 'given us the CCTV from the front desk. I went down there this morning to speak to Llewellyn, but he had already gone out. I've asked her to let us know when he returns, but she said he's usually out all day.'

'I checked CCTV near the hotel and he's either very good at avoiding cameras or he has stayed within a few metres of the hotel blind spot all day,' said Dean. 'So I haven't been able to trace his movements yet.'

'Well, when he's back, get down there and have a word with him,' said Lee.

He obviously hadn't fully resigned himself to the additional investigating they were doing on what had been, until yesterday, a nice and neat case of suicide. But even DCI Petra Gull, a woman renowned for keeping the team running as leanly as possible, had agreed this needed to be looked at. In fact, she was on her way over as they spoke, which was why Lee was keen to have something to tell her when she arrived.

'There was something else, boss,' said Jen.

He raised his eyebrows wearily and waited for her to continue. She nodded to Dean, who turned to his computer and showed Lee the footage.

'Just something I noticed on the lobby CCTV.' He pointed to the screen as Llewellyn appeared, heading towards the guesthouse exit. 'Remember he had that plastic bag? Well, later he comes back without it. And the next day, the same: he leaves with a full bag and comes home with an empty one.'

Lee leaned forward over Dean's chair and squinted at the screen. Jen found herself scrutinising his face for a reaction as Dean spoke.

'Right,' said Lee, clearly unsure where this was heading.

'Day two, same thing. Here he is leaving, here he is coming back in. Each time, he just has his rucksack when he gets back.'

Dean showed him more examples. It seemed as though Llewellyn was heading in and out just to ferry things out of the building.

'What's he got in there, you reckon?' Lee glanced up at them.

Jen shrugged. 'We're not sure, but sometimes it seems like clothes and other times it seems like maybe books or paperwork?'

She was about to push her luck by asking if they could send someone out to check nearby public bins when Lee's phone buzzed. Jen couldn't quite read his face. Was he nervous? Agitated? He stepped away to answer.

'Right, ok,' he said to the caller. 'That's great news. Send it through.'

He hung up and looked at their expectant faces. Petra Gull and Nandini Roy chose that moment to walk into the Incident Room.

'What's up?' said Nandini.

'That was Inference Technology Solutions,' said Lee. 'They've managed to salvage some of the footage from the night Oli Cromwell died.'

FIFTY-TWO

Phil knew not to come empty-handed. She had brought a cake from the Co-op and Liane was now sitting on the sofa, breastfeeding and eating a huge slab of Victoria sponge.

Through a mouthful of cake, Liane made the order and, eventually, reluctantly, Callum poked his head around the door.

'What?' he said.

'I never knew it was possible to feel this hungry,' Liane said to Phil, her mouth full. 'Callum, answer Phil's questions about Oli Cromwell. You owe her.'

'Does he?' said Phil.

'You helped me get my job back,' said Liane. 'I went in there like you said and demanded my job back and they gave it to me. And a pay rise too!'

Phil grinned and Liane smiled back.

'Wow! That's amazing. I'll have to hear the full story.' Phil turned to Callum, still lingering by the doorjamb. 'But first, I really need to ask you about a teacher.'

To begin with, he didn't recall a geography teacher named Owen Llewellyn, but then Phil pulled out her phone and showed him a photo.

'That's Mr Evans,' he said. 'Not Mr Llewellyn.'

'Right,' said Phil, trying to keep calm. She had found him. 'Mr Evans.'

'Maybe he was Owen?' said Callum. 'Yeah, come to think of it, that rings a bell.'

'Would he have taught Oli?' said Phil.

'Maybe,' said Callum. 'Probably. We only had one geography teacher, so he would have had him at some point, even if he gave it up at GCSE. Tom would have given him hell, I'm sure.'

'In what way?' said Phil, sensing a story forming.

'He was so mean to the teachers. Used to try to get them in trouble for being pervs.'

Phil's eyes widened. 'What? How?'

'I never saw it, but apparently he'd flirt with them and if any of them responded, he'd blackmail them so he could get good marks.'

'But you didn't hear about him doing that to Mr Evans.'

'No, but Mr Evans was a really shit teacher. Like *really* shit. He had no control over the class at all. We used to just turn our chairs round while he droned on.' Callum paused. 'You know, it's funny you ask about him.'

'Yeah? Why's that?'

'I couldn't place him at the time, but now you've reminded me, I'm sure it was him I saw the other day – going up the stairs when I was going out the fire exit for a vape.'

Liane shook her head very slightly, trying to send Callum a warning that he failed to notice.

'So you didn't see him when you went up to Oli's room?' Phil asked.

'How did you know about that?' said Callum.

'I didn't,' said Phil. 'You just confirmed a hunch, that's all.'

He seemed to deflate slightly.

'What were you doing there?' she asked.

'I just wanted his autograph.'

'Is that right? For your special autograph book? Are you sure it wasn't something to do with Dan Mehta and Charles Getgood and the phone call I overheard you having that afternoon?'

'No,' said Callum, giving her a look seasoned with anger and fear. 'I just wanted to meet him, but he didn't answer.'

'OK, Cal,' said Phil. 'I believe you, thousands wouldn't.'

Liane had finished feeding Olivia now. 'Let me see the photo,' she said.

The change of subject probably saved Phil from whatever showdown was coming, and she decided to go with it. She unlocked her phone.

'Just tell me this, Callum,' she said. 'Was he still alive when you left him?'

'Of course he was,' Callum hissed.

She nodded, deciding not to push, not wanting to start throwing out accusations in front of Liane based on nothing more than a couple of overheard conversations. But she couldn't help offering a final warning.

'Whatever else Dan is asking you to do, I would stay well away.'

'Oh, would you?' he said. 'Thanks, I hadn't thought of that.'

'It's OK,' Liane said. She flicked her nails out like she was despatching some dirt. 'You don't need to worry about that.'

She looked down at the photo on Phil's phone and Phil watched as her face turned white.

'What is it?'

'That's the man who walked into Oli Cromwell's room on the night he died.'

FIFTY-THREE

It hadn't even been good music, not in his opinion, anyway. But when it had begun pounding through the wall and disturbing his final hours, the man in beige had become disorientated. He had a plan, but he'd been knocked off kilter. He had been through it a hundred times. He had the tablets ready to go, collected from the family medicine box in the top cupboard in the kitchen. (His mother used to use the tongs to reach it.) But already things had gone wrong.

The plan had been to spend the week here, but the noise coming from room 301 was making this untenable. And when he had tried to dispose of the first batch of his possessions, he had been unable to get out because there was a broad man in dirty chef's whites lingering near the stairwell. Then he hadn't been able to press his trousers because the rude receptionist had failed to send one up. He decided to abandon the plan and just end it all now. Why wait?

He wasn't very good at taking tablets, a hangup, presumably, from years of his mother fretting about him choking on grapes or fish bones, or her preference for soluble painkillers.

No matter, he was going to just dissolve the whole lot into a drink and then he could guzzle it down in one go. But by the time he had finished this fiddly task, the music was driving him to distraction.How could he end his life with that atrocious noise thumping the wall next to his head?

Almost in a daze, he had walked from his room, still carrying his loaded gin and tonic, and headed to the room next door. The door was open, which he hadn't expected. He walked in and there, standing before him, looking at him in surprise, was the boy who had tormented him all those years ago.

'It's you, he said.'

The boy – a man now, he realised with surprise – stared at him for a few moments, his eyelids drooping.

Then he began to laugh.

'Mr...' he clicked his fingers a few times, trying to remember.

He felt a stab of hurt. Of *course* the boy didn't remember his name. He could remember him, however. Thomas Jones. The boy who had ruined his life and sent him back to his parents with his tail between his legs. The boy pointed at him triumphantly, '...Evans! What the fuck are you doing here?' And then he laughed.

The man hesitated. The shock of seeing him was extreme. It hadn't occurred to him that the boy might still be in this town.

He felt like a fool.

He felt confused. The same confusion that had crippled all those years ago. The lad who had ruined his life. The lad who had given him something to write about in his diary. He seemed woozy – drunk and unstable on his legs.

'Come and have a drink,' the boy said.

And so he did.

FIFTY-FOUR

Jen's heart was racing. Was it wrong to admit to enjoying this a little? These moments when they were in pursuit and could feel they might be getting somewhere?

They had watched the CCTV footage in silence.

There he was: Llewellyn, walking from his room – a minute after midnight, a minute or two after he had complained to Judith on the front desk about the noise next door, right after Judith had decided it wasn't her problem and finished her shift – heading to the door of the suite in 301.

At the door he paused.

Although his hand was raised to knock, in that eerie silence that comes with grainy CCTV footage, Llewellyn could be seen pushing the door and walking straight into the room. Thirty minutes later, the door opened again and he emerged, walking hastily towards his own room.

When he walked in, he was holding a tumbler filled with a clear liquid. When he exited, he had a brown drink.

In the minutes after they watched and then rewatched the footage, the Incident Room went from silent to buzzing with action. Petra Gull had taken the lead, sending Lee and Grant out to surveil the hotel, dispatching some constables to search the bins around the Smugglers' Rest B&B in the hope of finding the contents of Llewellyn's plastic bags and directing Jen, Dean and Nandini to speak to anyone and everyone who knew Oli Cromwell to find out if he had mentioned a man of this description.

'Marm?' Jen had said when Petra had finished.

Petra shot her a surprised look and Jen approached her next sentence with caution.

'Nandini and Dean both went to local schools. I wondered if...'

Petra, with her usual cyborg-like efficiency, picked up Jen's intimation immediately.

'Nandini and Dean, connect with any teachers or students who knew Cromwell. Find out if they recognise this man. Jen, speak to Cromwell's family and colleagues.'

Ten minutes later, Nandini had a name.

'Owen, Ian or Brian Evans,' she said. 'He taught at Parker Boys school. Apparently he was dull as f... fudge,' she finished, spotting Petra's disapproval.

'Owen seems the most likely,' said Jen.

Another ten minutes after that, Jen had tracked down a teacher from Parker Boys – Ms Sarah Davies, who once sat opposite Mr Evans at a staff night out and regretted it.

'I ended up leaving early,' she said. 'I said I had to look after my dog. I couldn't keep up the small talk any longer. It was like talking to an ironing board.'

'Did he teach Oli Cromwell?' said Jen.

'Funny you ask,' said Sarah. 'We never really knew the full story, but Mr Evans definitely left under a bit of a cloud. And you know how these rumours can get carried away, but there was always a suggestion that something had gone on with him and Thomas Jones.'

'In what way?'

'I'm not sure, to be honest, it was all just hearsay and rumours, you know? Nothing ever got reported, no complaint was ever made, but you just pick up on these things in schools, you know?'

'Do you think something inappropriate happened?'

'Owen was a funny fish. A loner, you know? But I never got the impression he was... I can't imagine him touching a child.' There was a pause on the line as though Ms Davies was carefully considering her next words. 'If anything, I'd say Owen was scared of Thomas.'

She had continued to furnish Jen with details: how Oli Cromwell had been a difficult kid, treating teachers with disrespect, getting them into trouble with false accusations. How he had often seemed to have a strange power over certain teachers, his charm sometimes curdling into something more sinister that Sarah Davies couldn't quite put her finger on.

'He had that type of charisma, you know?' she said. 'The sort I imagine a lot of powerful people have. He could make you feel like you were the centre of the world. Or like nothing at all.'

Jen would have liked to point out that he was just a boy, but Sarah hadn't finished. 'When I heard he'd killed himself I have to say I wasn't surprised. People like that... I've seen it before. The self-loathing. They believe they're the best thing since sliced bread, but they hate themselves too, you know?'

And what about Mr Owen Evans?

'Oh, he was hard to read. But I always felt as though he was the loneliest person I'd ever known.'

Sarah Davies gave Jen a clue to where Mr Owen Evans had fled to.

'He went back to his mother somewhere in south Wales. I think near Swansea. Began with an A.'

The nearest town beginning with A on the map was Ammanford. Ammanford only had one secondary school. Jen gave them a call and soon established that Mr Owen Davies had been with them for the past twelve years but had resigned suddenly towards the end of the school year. Shortly after his mother died.

'Terrible it was,' said Mrs Powell. 'She was run over by her own car. Awful. It was in the paper and everything.'

Jen read the article. Mrs Gwen Davies had been walking on the pavement outside her house when her car, which was parked on the steep drive of her bungalow, rolled over her. Her son, Owen, had just finished cleaning the car and had been heading back inside when the incident occurred. There were quotes from neighbours, all very much of the, 'She was a very quiet, very polite woman, I didn't really speak to her,' variety. 'She kept herself to herself,' said one. 'They both did, really.' There was no quote from Mr Owen Evans.

She set Nandini in pursuit of more details from the police just as Dean appeared at her shoulder.

'We've had a sighting,' he said.

FIFTY-FIVE

The man in the beige anorak sat in the cafe and stared into the middle distance. He had, for reasons unknown, opted for an all day breakfast and a mocha. He had never ordered a mocha in his life, and the all day breakfast was sure to interfere with his innards. He suspected the mocha had something in it – was it chocolate? A child's drink. What could have possessed him? The young Australian man with the green-framed glasses came over to ask what he could get him and he had panicked.

He thought of the florist. Flora. He was willing to bet she never panicked. She had such an aura of calm and good nature. He imagined her sailing through life, unbuffeted by any storms. Still, when the drink and the food arrived, he would dutifully consume them all. It was just fuel, after all.

His heart was still racing a little from escaping the police. He had spotted them at the B&B. Two men parked up on the opposite side of the street, staring at the hotel. They was obviously not tourists: they were staring in the wrong direction. The sea was to their left and yet they were both peering out at the scruffy hotel exterior. Not that he imagined they were anything to do with him. God knew the hotel was the sort of place that attracted police stakeouts. He expected they were waiting for a drug deal or a fugitive or something.

Still, seeing them had given him a fright, and he'd had enough frights lately. Seeing the journalist careering towards him on the cliff the other day was more than enough for a lifetime.

He just wanted to look over the edge, he told himself, to see if he would ever have it in him to take that kind of exit. Now he had no pills left, he needed to find a similar neat exit, and this option appealed to him: he could vanish without a trace if he picked the right spot.

He had assumed he wouldn't have it in him, but standing over the vast expanse of sea, staring at the dark ripples, he suspected that perhaps he could do it after all. The ocean seemed to call to him, inviting him down into its shining waters. He realised the notion made him sound like a teenage girl reading too much Tennyson, but the impulse had been genuine and that's all there was to it. And anyway, he was growing tired of trying to police his own thoughts all the time. He didn't imagine Flora expended so much energy on self-flagellation for every incorrect notion. She was far too calm and happy. She probably meditated, he decided. Or maybe she did yoga or cold water swimming – something wholesome and healthy. The sort of nonsense he normally would have sniffed at.

If only he had met her sooner. He might have found a reason to live. Maybe he would even have given yoga a go. But now he had gone and messed everything up. Was there a moment when his life had taken an unplanned turn? He didn't need to think about it. It had been the day the boy had come into his classroom.

After, he moved back home to Wales to live with his mother. He spent every night staring at the small television in the corner of the room or reading a book. He got a job in a nearby school where he stopped trying to make his classes interesting, simply reading the information from notes he had written over the years, his monotone sending the classes into a torpor after a carb-loaded lunch.

He couldn't talk to his mother about what he had done. She would change the subject at the merest hint there might be something salacious in his story. She simply wouldn't hear it. She'd turn on the TV, switch the volume up and claim that it was 'her programme' that she'd been looking forward to. Then she'd settle down into her fat armchair, stuffed with pillows, and suggest he might like to get them both a bit of cake or a biccie. Or else she'd fight gravity and the mountains of plumped cushions and rise from her armchair to start clearing away tea cups, before venturing into the kitchen to commence the clattering of dishes. No, there would be no use trying to confide in his mother. She may have been his only friend in the world, but she wasn't a very good friend.

She had been coming out of the front door just as he was vacuuming the footwell of the car. The handbrake had been unreliable for a while, but perhaps he had adjusted it just a little before he shut the car door.

He couldn't say for sure.

The car had begun to roll down towards her as he finished waxing the bonnet – giving it some elbow grease, pressing hard on the front of the bonnet. In retrospect, he supposed he should have said something. Instead, he found himself walking into the house to ring for an ambulance just as the vehicle slowly reversed off the drive.

Perhaps he should have done more.

His drink still hadn't arrived. No matter. He paid the bill and walked out into the daylight, following his preferred route avoiding as many CCTV cameras as he could. It would take him twice as long to get there because of it, but his destination was already in sight. He turned away from it as he took a detour via an alleyway between houses, but it was still there when he emerged and reconnected with the path. The journey continued like this, with diversions via twittens and side streets that sometimes took him north, and sometimes south, but still his destination remained in view. The cliff loomed up out of the edge of town, growing closer with every step.

It was time to do what he had come here to do.

FIFTY-SIX

Beachy Shed was closer than the office. After she left Liane and Callum's, Phil ducked in there and threw herself onto a seat, grabbing her laptop and phone out of her bag. For a moment she cast about slightly drunkenly, unsure where to begin. She wanted more than anything to tell someone. This was the moment, she supposed, she should be sharing her discoveries with her colleagues, but something held her back. She didn't trust them, for starters. Adam Jenkins, editor, was too keen to take stories off her and hand them to Barry or Mike. And anyway, she still didn't have any cast iron evidence.

But she had an eyewitness who had seen the CCTV footage of Mr Owen Evans walking into Oli Cromwell's room. Mr Owen Evans was the last person to see Oli Cromwell alive. She held a pen and flicked it, tip to end on the paper, her finger acting as a fulcrum, the action providing her body with something to do while her mind raced.

She should tell the police. That was the right thing to do, wasn't it?

She pulled up MoronicaMars's photo of the man she still thought of as Llewellyn. She tried to remember that day she saw him possibly contemplating suicide on the edge of a cliff. He had been carrying a bag, hadn't he? He definitely had. She remembered him leaning over the edge and peering down, the weight of his right arm heavier from the black rucksack hanging down. But when she tried to picture him running away, she couldn't see the rucksack any more.

Dom appeared at her shoulder.

'You ready to order, Philbo?'

He looked at her screen and pointed amiably.

'I know that fella.'

'What?' said Phil.

'In here just a minute ago. He left a tenner for a drink I hadn't made him yet. Mocha. Scurried out the door like his arse was on fire.'

'Did you see where he went?' said Phil.

'Turned left out the door, but I couldn't say after that.'

She got up and grabbed her things and with a quick smile and a, 'Thanks Dom,' headed out the door.

Dom's sighting of Owen Evans suggested he'd headed in the direction of the East Hill, but there were a hundred-and-one other places he could have gone on this route. Still, she raced along the promenade and made her way towards the cliffs. She wasn't looking for Evans – though bumping into him would be nice – she was looking for the bag. The bag she had seen him carrying in one hand by the edge of the cliff.

She took the steps up the cliff face as quickly as she could, her legs burning as she reached the summit. First, she walked up the field to look back down the slope in a bid to orientate herself and discovered he had been much further along than she imagined. She kept her eye fixed on the spot as she walked back, eventually locating a slim track etched into the earth by countless small mammals.

The scrub was overgrown, and it took some time for Phil to pick her way through the brambles and gorse. She had to stop twice to disengage her trouser legs from a sharp thorn before eventually she made it to the path. To her left was what felt like a sheer drop, and she approached the edge of the cliff cautiously. Landslides were not uncommon. It was as she inched closer that she saw it: a black backpack hanging from a sapling on a tiny ledge just a metre below where she stood.

Of course it had to be a black bag hanging from a tree.

Poodicca rides again.

Evans had presumably thrown the bag in a panic when he saw her thundering towards him, or perhaps he had simply dropped it in a bid to get away. Maybe he had intended to throw it into the sea, but the cliff curves more than you might realise, which was why it ended up snagged on a branch.

Getting hold of the bag would not be easy, but now she had found it she couldn't bear to leave it. She had to get it down. Hunting around her, she eventually located a stick that was long enough to hook onto a strap. It took her a few attempts, but she managed to catch it and began drawing it towards her, praying it wouldn't slip off the stick and fall into the water. Eventually she managed to grasp one of the straps by hand and lifted the bag above the brambles and onto the path.

Phil opened the zip cautiously. She had no idea what to expect. A severed head? A bomb?

What she found made her eyes bulge.

FIFTY-SEVEN

The man in the beige tie had stayed in the classroom marking papers, avoiding the eye rolling and dark humour of the staff room where all the teachers went to decompress and tell bleak stories of their morning so far.

'Benny tried to bite Sally. The boy's 14 for gawd's sake.'

'Tracy Marks copied her entire essay from Wikipedia, complete with "citation needed" in the text. Does she think I was born yesterday?'

'Monty Jackson's dad's been battering him again. I saw the bruises when he scratched his stomach. Social services are fucking useless, just because he's a big lad...'

And so on all morning long until the man felt desperate to get away.

He preferred to stay in his classroom, quietly marking, or maybe staring out of one of the wide windows on his terrapin block. His classroom was in one of those temporary structures the school had chucked up forty years ago and never got round to replacing. He was convinced it would be condemned for asbestos if anyone thought to check it. The maths block had been replaced a while ago, the builders installing a light and airy space that looked fantastic inside but loomed with grim, plastic-clad ugliness over the prim Victorian buildings nearby.

He had been marking homework when the boy appeared at the door. He was not equipped to deal with a boy like Thomas. Thomas and his kind were the kids that terrorised him at school. They were the kids who smelled a victim and didn't mind exploiting his weaknesses: namely, the man's complete inability to control a classroom. Thomas and his gang terrorised him from the start of every class until the end.

But something was different today. Thomas had appeared and knocked on the door, walking straight in before he was invited. He sat down on one of the desks and tried to chat.

'I'm busy with my marking, if you wouldn't mind,' the man said peevishly. He didn't have the right tone for a teacher. His voice had the timbre and pitch of an adenoidal rodent.

'Come on, sir, don't you want a bit of company. You're always shut up here on your own. It ain't normal.' The boy was chewing gum. He smirked at him and the man felt a warning shot of adrenaline through his body. He stood up, suddenly. So did the boy.

'I assure you I'm quite alright,' said the man. He wanted the boy to leave more than anything, and yet he could feel something beside panic in his body. A strange fascination was there too. A part of him wanted to know what would happen next. He didn't have to wait for long.

'Thing is, sir, I've seen the way you look at me.' The boy approached him and the man began backing up towards the board behind. The previous lesson was still up detailing the different types of rock and their influence on coastal forms. The students had talked all the way through his lecture on the local geological structure.

'What if I did you a little favour?' the boy said. He could smell the boy's gum, his spearmint breath scenting the air between them as the boy grew closer.

That's when, with his back against the wall, Thomas had reached out to him and begun unbuckling his trousers. The man had hesitated, staring at the boy with confusion. He was paralysed with horror, but – there it was again – he was fascinated too.

Abruptly Thomas stopped. 'You dirty nonce,' he said, taking a step back, leaving the man standing there, his belt and top trouser button undone. 'You were going to actually let me do it. I'm just a kid. You know it's illegal, right? What an old perv.'

He'd been even more confused then. He wasn't a pervert... was he? He'd barely had a sexual thought in his life. He had never had any interest in that sort of thing, finding the thought of it distasteful. The mess and the indignity. All those bodily fluids, the unsanitary nature of it. No thank you.

But then Thomas stepped in close and he felt the pull of the boy's charisma and the spark of his sexual energy. It seemed to create a strange kind of gravity all of its own. That must be why he was so popular with boys and girls. Everyone felt the pull of his orbit. To this day, the man couldn't tell you what he would have done if the boy had continued to undo his trousers. It alarmed him even now, to think how powerless he had been in that moment. Anyone else – boy or girl – and he would have pulled away well before he had found himself in that predicament.

His stuttered reply to the boy was half apology, half denial.

'It's a bit late now. You've scarred me for life, you old perv,' the boy responded. He was laughing at him, the man could tell. 'What would happen if I went out there right now and told everyone you'd asked me to suck you off.'

Then the boy suddenly grinned at him and winked.

'It's alright, sir, your dirty little secret is safe with me. I won't tell a soul,' he said. 'Cross my heart and hope to die.'

Then he pointed over at the desk where the man had been marking homework. 'I hope mine's done ok. I worked really hard on it.' He sauntered to the door, took his gum from his mouth and, with a cheerful smile, squashed it into the doorframe before walking out. The man, still pressed up against the wall, stared after him in horror.

The event had shaken the man. The boy was sixteen, but that was no excuse in the man's eyes. He was still an inno-cent – not even fully grown – and the man was entirely to blame for the situation. He should have found a way to extri-cate himself; he shouldn't have hesitated when the boy unbuckled his belt (why did he hesitate?); he should have never given anyone a moment's doubt.

As it was, the boy didn't seem to have told anyone about the encounter. He made threatening noises, though, taunting the man with it constantly.

'I'm just off to dob you in to the head teacher,' he said once as he passed him in the corridor.

'Alright sexy,' he said another time as the man was heading into the toilet. 'Need me to hold your knob?'

The man had never felt more afraid.

———

He had buried the story for so long he could almost pretend it didn't happen. But then the boy came back to ruin his life again. Afterwards, he found it hard to recall precisely what had happened. The man in the beige had drunk a lot of gin before he went in. The night had become smudged around the edges, fuzzy at the peripheries. He remembered still clutching his glass filled with pills, the ice cubes long melted and the liquid growing warmer in his hand. At one point, the man was perched on the edge of the bed as the boy, wrapped only in a dressing gown, lay against the pillows and told him how he had become a famous film star. The man had not seen any of his movies and did not recognise him.

'You obviously exist in more elevated circles, sir,' laughed the boy, putting on a hoity-toity accent. He still had the same cheeky expression and the same innocent-seeming face. He was like Oliver Twist and the Artful Dodger rolled into one.

'You should watch some of my films,' he said. 'You never know, you might like them.'

The man wanted to ask him about the day that he had come to see him after class, but he didn't know where to begin. In any case, the boy appeared to have no intention of asking him any questions about *his* life, he simply wanted to talk about himself. Initially, the man found it easy to sit there silently listening, but after a while, he became bored and awkward, his glass heavy in his hand, reminding him of his purpose.

'I should probably get back,' he said, standing 'I'm sure you've got better things to do than talk to me.'

'No, no! Sit,' the boy instructed.

The man sensed the boy was panicking, as though he was afraid to be left, and the man found himself hesitating before once again perching back on the end of the bed.

It was clear that the boy was on something. He was slurring his words, his eyes and head occasionally rolling around like a marble in a jar. He had been cheerful when the man entered, but at some point his mood shifted, and the man felt the boy's gaze harden. He wanted to leave now more than anything. Again, he rose to go, but this time the boy leaned forward and grabbed his glass.

'What are you drinking there?' he said, eyeballing the cloudy liquid in the glass.

'Nothing. It's just my special drink.'

He tried to get the glass back, but of course, by now it had become a game. The boy held the drink away from him. The man lunged forward to try and take it back. The boy staggered to his feet and held it high in the air. He was tall and he had Hollywood muscles. The boy put out his hand and pressed into the man's forehead, preventing him from reaching it. The man felt himself grow emotional, his frustration making him feel like a bullied child in the playground. He made one last snatch for it and then... felt something in him shift.

What if he didn't take it back? What if he decided to live, after all? The man watched as the boy grinned triumphantly.

'Cheers!' the boy said and began drinking it down in one. But he stopped before the final gulp. 'Yuck! That tastes revolting.'

The boy stared at the glass accusingly and then looked up at the man as though expecting an explanation. The man should have said something. He knew he should have said something. But – and here he felt a moral certainty harden his heart – why should he? It seemed a kind of justice. Here was a boy who wouldn't take no for an answer, who felt no compunction in tormenting someone.

Instead, the man picked up the boy's glass of warm Jack Daniels from the bedside table. He attempted to gulp it down in one, but the liquid spilled onto his cheeks and snuck into his shirt collar.

'Goodnight,' he said, carrying the glass out with him.

FIFTY-EIGHT

Phil couldn't believe it: Llewellyn's diaries. His own words. She took out the most recent one, using her sleeves to protect what was probably vital evidence and almost certainly something she should have handed straight to police, and sat down on the dirt path, legs crossed, to read it. But a few pages in she was disappointed: it was just a mundane account of the man's life. He talked about watching a game show with his mother and going to bed early because he had stayed up a little late the night before, seeing in the new year with a gin and tonic on his own. She flicked through the next few pages, but it was all the same, just a series of dreary accounts of day to day living. A week into the new year, the man spoke of his dread of returning to school.

She was used to reading boring documents. She had to read court records about the dullest crimes – all those white collar offences that never get punished because the lawyers put the judges into comas – but, my god, she thought, this diary puts them all to shame. In fact, she was increasingly offended at how uninteresting the man's life was.

And it wasn't as though interesting things weren't happening around him. One entry detailed how Mrs Pritchard had come rushing into the staff room to share some gossip. But what was the gossip?! They would never know because Evans left before she could finish her sentence, annoyed at the intrusion. Not knowing was going to haunt her, Phil realised.

He would detail what he had for dinner, or what TV shows he watched, but then glossed over anything even mildly interesting.

Had been enjoying a quiet cup of tea and biscuit when Mr Godley walked in and started talking about a boy who threw up in another boy's sweater hood. I left.

There was no getting around it: he was a prig and a bore. He sniffed at a teacher's gossip and then described packet mash potato. He didn't add any colour. No opinions were offered about the TV shows he watched beyond 'quite interesting.' He taught teenagers all day, but only ever recorded the details of his lesson ('covered the Abyssinia crisis today'), without mentioning what the students thought. He appeared to have no interest in them at all.

He talked about his mother a lot.

Inwardly, Phil rolled her eyes. He had the creepy mummy complex thing going on, and yet there was no love there. At one point, he wrote that his mother had been scared when he returned home a little later than planned due to an unexpected item in his bagging area that led to him having his entire Tesco shop re-scanned. He did not seem to be particularly sorry that she was scared. If anything, his tone was of mild annoyance. Not Phil could really blame him. She sounded like a nightmare. Phil got the sense she was both uninterested in her son and yet strangely controlling.

Worried about the smallest things, but not concerned if he was happy.

After reading the whole of January, Phil began flicking through the pages. God save me from a life this ordinary, she thought. It wasn't just that it was a small life, it was that it was a mean life too. Nothing moved him or made him truly passionate. His tone was that of a man who tutted regularly and laughed rarely. In fact, she could find no evidence he found anything funny at all. As she flicked through she tried not to be disappointed. She didn't want to admit the truth to herself: that she had hoped for something scandalous. It was a shameful hope. What would have made her happy? If he turned out to be a serial killer? If he gobbled up babies in the school canteen?

She flicked through more of the diary and came to a sudden stop.

A blank page.

The only blank page, yet somehow – because of it – the most interesting one.

Phil shut the book and returned to the rucksack.

'There must be something else in here,' she muttered.

Even if it was a complimentary pen that might give her a new clue to investigate. She felt around inside. There were countless little pouches and compartments for stationery and other bits and bobs. It was a good bag. She slid her hand into a narrow card pocket and pulled out two pieces of tightly folded paper. She opened the first one and began to read, expecting more of the same dull drudgery. After she had read the first one twice she opened the second. She read that one twice too.

She took out her phone to call the police, but the sound of moving undergrowth made her look up. She tried to stay calm, using her well-honed skills from years of texting under school desks to compose a message and hit send almost entirely without looking down. Because there, staring out at sea, standing just a few metres away, was Mr Owen Evans, the man in room 302.

FIFTY-NINE

Jen parked the car and headed east. Owen Evans could be hiding anywhere among the cobbled alleys and twittens separating the mediaeval cottages that were tucked into the cliff edges rising up on either side, but some eyewitnesses had suggested he might be over this side of town.

Although Dean and Nandini had made their enquiries as casually as they could, word had already spread that the police were looking for an ex-Parker Boys teacher. The old boys' network (namely, a couple of WhatsApp groups previously reserved for stupid memes, videos and the occasional conversation about football or which pub they were going to), had kicked into gear, and now it seemed like everyone was on the hunt for the missing geography teacher.

'Who needs CCTV when you've got a load of lads out on the streets?' said Jen. 'Don't any of your schoolmates have jobs, Dean?'

'Yes,' said Dean, looking a little offended on their behalf. 'Digby's a scaffolder.'

'Makes sense.'

Digby Bianco spotted Evans on the narrow path on West Street when he was putting up a three-storey tower.

'Reece delivers parcels.'

Reece Fielding had seen him on Winding street down an alleyway between two blocks of flats.

'What about Harley?'

'He's unemployed,' conceded Dean.

Harley Dugdale was sitting on a bench outside a pub when he thought he saw Evans heading towards him on All Saints Street. At that point, he'd been distracted by a dog and when he looked up from petting her, Evans had vanished.

Petra had decided it was time to go public with a, 'Police are seeking this man in connection with the recent death of the film star Oli Cromwell' statement. It was a tough call. They didn't want to alarm Evans, especially since Philippa McGinty had seen him up on the cliff a few days ago, possibly contemplating suicide, but given Owen was adept at evading CCTV cameras, it made sense to appeal to the public for sightings. What concerned them most, however, was generating wild speculation, which would almost certainly lead to conspiracy theories and madcap finger pointing from a fleet of keyboard warriors, not to mention the press hysteria that would begin forming like froth on whisked milk. But at this stage, Petra felt they had no choice.

'It's time to bring him in,' she said. 'Before the press catches up to the rumours.'

It was probably too late for that. The town was already alive with gossip, no doubt helped by the old boys' network, not to mention the employees at The Marchmont and Smugglers' Rest, who had answered detailed questions about their missing guest. In fact, Petra's police appeal hadn't even been issued when yet another sighting from the public came in.

This time, he was on Crown Lane, heading towards the Tackleway.

This was where Jen was currently making a beeline for, because she had already guessed where he was going. Tackleway took you to the steps, and the steps took you to the exact spot Phil McGinty had seen the elusive 'Llewellyn,' aka Owen Evans, contemplating his own mortality.

Jen just hoped it wasn't too late.

That was when she got a call.

'Phil McGinty's just texted,' said Dean down the phone.

'Oh god,' said Jen. 'What now?'

SIXTY

Phil sat like a prey animal, still and silent, hoping that Mr Owen Evans wouldn't spot her – nor the paper in her hand, or the black bag behind her. *His* black bag. His confessions – of sorts.

She had probably only been there for a minute – if that – but it felt like an age. The wind was cool on her face, and she wanted more than anything to move the strands of hair that were flicking her cheeks. But she stayed stock still, somehow convinced that if she didn't breathe or blink, he wouldn't know she was there.

He turned, apparently drawn by some primeval sixth sense, and looked directly at her. He seemed as surprised as she was. He was right by the edge of the cliff, and now she had been spotted, Phil felt it was somehow rude not to stand. She had intended to do so slowly, like a fugitive handing herself in, but something clicked into gear in her brain, and she jumped up cheerfully as though she hadn't been hiding at all, just relaxing in the winter sunshine. In a fluid motion, she picked up the bag like it was her own and put it on, folding the papers while calling over cheerfully like a magician attempting to distract from a clumsy sleight of hand.

'Hey there! It's Llewellyn, isn't it?' She put a hand on her chest while the other stuffed the papers in her back pocket. 'Philippa McGinty. We met in the hotel a few days ago. How's it going?' She stepped forward. 'Did you come up for the view? Isn't it gorgeous?'

He leaned back a little away from her and she turned to look out to sea as though she hadn't noticed any awkwardness.

'Bit chilly out here today, though,' she said. 'I think winter is finally here to stay. We've been so lucky with the weather, haven't we? But I guess that's global warming for you.'

She gifted him with one of her broad, friendly smiles and continued, well aware that she was prattling, but unable to stop.

'How has the rest of your holiday been? A bit less stressful, I hope?'

She thought he wasn't going to reply. He looked ready to turn tail and run, just as he had the last time she saw him up here, but then he straightened stiffly and replied, 'Fine, thank you.'

'Oh, that's good to hear! It must have been a pretty horrible surprise to wake up to?'

She wasn't sure where she was going with this. She just wanted to keep him talking – keep him away from the edge, keep him from noticing the bag on her shoulder. Masking her movements by casually reaching for a stem of dead grass, she got closer, though still not near enough to stop him from jumping.

He stepped sideways, putting the same distance between them once again.

'Have you been following me?' he said peevishly.

She grinned as though it were a perfectly normal question. Her teeth forming a row of gleaming tombstones as she tilted her head and squinted.

'No. Why? Should I have been? Have you been doing something exciting?'

The question ruffled him. He turned away again slightly and turned back again as though unsure how to respond to this cheerful young woman on the cliff top.

'I come out here a lot,' she said. 'It's a good place to think.' She looked down at the shoreline. Far below on the beach, a handful of scattered people were walking their dogs or collecting sea glass or entertaining toddlers in welly boots as they dabbled near the edges of the shore.

'It never gets old,' she said.

She glanced over at Owen. He was also staring out to sea.

'Sometimes,' she said. 'I am convinced that if I leapt from the edge, I would be able to fly out over the sea.' She stopped and laughed. 'What do you think? I know. I know what you're going to say. It's a stupid idea, right? But I can't help it. Call me crazy.' She held up her hands. Being chatty like this was second nature, but still.... She wondered if he could hear a faint tone of panic in her voice, or if she really was that good at faking it. 'I reckon flying would have to be my superpower if I were a superhero. How about you?'

He looked startled at the question and Phil took a moment to guess how many conversations he had on an average day. Fewer now, she imagined – now he had pushed a car into his mother. He should be a threat to her, this dangerous man who had killed two people, and yet, despite the chill the thought gave her, she couldn't help a little swell of pity grow at the same time. He's lonely, she realised. All those diary entries, all those sniffy comments, all that running away from other people and new experiences, avoiding the staff room, avoiding gossip and debate. Really, it was just covering up how truly solitary this man was. His interaction with a young Oli Cromwell – Tom Jones, as was – may have been inexcusable, but it was more easily understood when you realised he didn't know how to speak to people. Still, she thought, it didn't excuse the murdering.

It was probably unwise of her to underestimate him. He may have rationalised both his crimes, may have convinced himself they were accidental, but Phil didn't buy it. How *fortunate* that the brake was dodgy on his mother's car, how *handy* that he couldn't recall precisely if he'd pressed it slightly in as he cleaned around it just moments before. How lucky that he'd been heading into the house and was too far away from the car to prevent it rolling downwards. Even then, his own account didn't add up. He described seeing his mother's body vanish under the wheels as he looked through the windscreen, which meant he was right there the moment it happened, very likely, in Phil's opinion, with his hands on the bonnet, pushing as hard as he could.

And what about Oli Cromwell? She might be willing to put his stay in the same hotel down to pure fluke, but Owen's sudden muteness when Oli took the glass filled with pills out of his hands and swallowed it down was a stretch. And anyway, it didn't explain why he left without alerting Oli to the danger, why he wandered out of the room and headed off to sleep off the effects of what he thought was a strong Jack

Daniels and Coke and what Phil knew was Marilla's sleeping tablet dissolved into Oli's nightcap. It didn't explain, either, why he didn't call an ambulance, or call for help. He simply went to his room and then wrote about it later as though none of it was his business – how it was inconvenient he no longer had his cache of tablets that had taken so many weeks for him to collect up and horde, first from his mother and later from the local pharmacy who were scrupulous about how many blister packets they would sell at a time. He mourned the loss of his stomach medicine more than the loss of a young man whose life he had at best done nothing to save and at worst had been responsible for taking.

'Invisibility,' said the man and Phil startled a little. She had almost forgotten she had asked him a question. And *of course* invisibility. How on brand.

'Invisibility. That's a good one!' she said. She was flirting with him a little, patronising him a little – how younger women could with older men they didn't really consider to be sexual beings. 'And what would you do with your powers?'

It was the wrong question. He wasn't interested in the slightest in answering hypothetical questions that took you to the realms of fantasy.

'I really don't know,' he said. 'Would you mind? I'm actually trying to have a moment of peace before I leave.'

She hesitated, unsure how to play it next. Did she really want to save him before he jumped? Perhaps it would be best for everyone if he did just see himself off. She wouldn't put it past him to kill again and write another 'Oops, I accidentally stood by while someone's life ended' diary entry. She could see it now. 'Today a woman tried to save me from falling down the cliff, lost her balance and fell off, dashing her brains out on the rocks below.'

Still, she didn't want him to die. Aside from her very real human emotions about not wanting another life to be lost in all this, and aside from her belief that justice should be done, she also had a very self-preserving desire not to see a man fling himself off a cliff. She'd never sleep properly again. But what should she do? She wasn't about to rugby tackle him to the ground, and she wasn't sure her current attempts to talk him round were getting very far (what with the very obvious request that she shut up and go away). So what next? She decided the best thing to do was to try and get away with the bag of evidence before he noticed and tried to add her to his collection of unfortunate events.

'Fair enough,' she said cheerfully. 'I should get back, anyway. They'll be wondering where I got to.'

She didn't say who, she just wanted to let him know people were expecting her. On this narrow path through the brush and scrub, she was going to have to walk right by him – unless she wanted to be ripped to shreds by shards of bramble, blackthorn, and gorse. She felt her heart thump suddenly, as though it had only just realised what a terrible idea this was.

'Right then,' she said, walking closer and getting ready to pass. 'Cheerio.'

Cheerio?

She had never said that in her life. She wasn't sure she had ever heard *anyone* say it. She felt her face fix into an increasingly manic rictus and began edging past, very aware that she was on the outer edge closest to the sea. Evans had shifted backwards, his calves pressed into the scrub. Phil was extremely aware of how near they were, their bodies almost grazing as she stepped around him.

'Ooh, look at that!' she said, pointing to something over his shoulder up the cliff side.

He turned to look and she trotted a little to gain some distance. By the time he turned back, she was already a few metres from him.

'What?' he said.

'My mistake. Thought I saw a hare. Must have imagined it.'

She was walking backwards the whole time, hoping he wouldn't notice the backpack, but then his eyes narrowed.

'Is that my bag?'

'Err, no?' she laughed. 'That would be weird. Why would I have your bag?'

'It is my bag,' he said. 'It's got a blue carabiner on it in the same place.'

She was opening her mouth to say, 'Lots of people have blue carabiners,' when he was right there.

'Wow, you're fast,' she said, and turned to run, but she lurched backwards as he grabbed the top handle on the rucksack. 'Lemme go,' she heard herself say, like a child being caught stealing sweets in some ancient comic book.

'Give it back!' he said, tugging at the bag.

She nearly fell, but she managed to twist away enough to keep her balance. Unfortunately, that gave him the opportunity to get one strap off her shoulder. He yanked it sideways, sending her veering out into the scrub below. Despite his slight frame and her relative fitness, he was stronger by quite some way, his hand grip like iron as she tried to pull back against him. As she pulled, her shoulders already beginning to burn as he yanked her off balance, she heard the main zip make an ominous noise. He had reached over and grabbed at the front fabric with his free hand, and now the zipper was giving under the tug-of-war. She threw her body backwards, hoping the scrub would prevent her from rolling down the cliff face and onto the rocks below. The gamble paid off and, as she fell into the brambles, she was rewarded with the sight of Evans stumbling towards her. Unfortunately, the zipper had come fully undone, and she watched in horror as a diary fell out over her head towards the water below.

The sight of it made her come to her senses. She didn't really need the diaries: she had the confessions. Why was she even doing this? She needed to get away. She let go and Evans fell backwards, landing hard on the rocky path, the journals spilling out as Phil struggled from the grip of the brambles. As soon as she was free, she planned to run. She was fast, too. She was sure she could get away from him, given enough of a head start.

She was wrong.

As soon as she broke out, she scrambled upright and began to run, but she could feel him coming after her – felt that he was close behind and getting closer. The path at this point narrowed to an even smaller track cut hard into the edge of the cliff, the drop below more sheer without the reassuring mattress of brush to break any fall. She put her head down and made another drive towards freedom, her thighs burning with the effort. But then, she was falling. He had grabbed her around the legs and Phil hit the ground hard. She reached out desperately for something in front that might help in her fight to escape his grip. Nothing. She flipped onto her back and tried to free one leg so she could kick him in the face. Her boot scuffed in the dirt and sent up a cloud of dead grass and dirt. Evans, blinded by the dust, let go of her legs and began wiping at his eyes. Phil snatched her chance to escape, scrabbling backwards away from him before twisting upwards to standing. It was then that she realised she was right on the edge of the cliff, the animal track having given way to rocks, the outcrop ending in front of her and a thicket of gorse blocking her way back to the footpath above.

She looked around desperately for the animal track that had ended so abruptly and realised it was back towards Evans, a thin line of sandstone and dirt cutting through the shrubs upwards towards the cliff top. She was about to run for it, but she heard a sudden yell and Evans was barrelling towards her blindly. She watched in horror as he flew towards her; she tried to step aside, but there was barely any space. He was going to carry her over the edge.

She heard a roaring sound and realised it was coming from her own mouth.

'Stop, police!' yelled a voice, but Phil didn't really register it. She was still making her own guttural cry as she moved towards him, dropping down to a crouch and pushing her body weight forwards, shoulder jutted outwards ready for impact. He hit her hard, and she felt his middle crumple as her shoulder caught him. He pitched forward, crushing her as he fell and she made herself as small as she could as his weight carried him over her towards the rocky edge. As their bodies tangled, his head caught on a lump of sandstone – a sharp rock emerging from the dirt like a bandit from a pit trap – and Owen Evans lay motionless.

Phil had barely begun to process what had happened when a sound made her look up. Detective Sergeant Jen Collet was scrambling down from above her. Another movement. She saw Detective Constable Dean Martin racing her way along the animal track. Evans's body was pressing her into the earth and she reached up and felt for a pulse.

'Alive,' she said.

Jen and Dean pulled Evans off her and helped her up. Dean asking her if she was alright, Phil not quite ready to make a joke about how she'd been better.

'Bloody hell, McGinty,' said Jen. 'You do know that chasing a lead is figurative, right?'

SIXTY-ONE

'Penny for them?' said Angela, sticking her head round the door to Phil's bedroom. Phil knew it was unlikely Angela would pay that much. She had a saying about it. 'Thoughts are worthless. Actions are what add value – or cost you dearly.' Not her strongest epigram, in Phil's view, and one that Angela often couldn't get to the end of without losing her place.

Phil had been staring over the top of her laptop at the wall behind, but now she shook herself and smiled at her mother.

'I was just thinking it was your turn to make a cuppa,' she replied.

'Well, that was an expensive question,' said Angela, rolling her eyes and heading off to boil the kettle. When she began whistling tunelessly in their little kitchen, Phil returned to staring. She had things on her mind. A week had passed since she captured a killer by essentially using her entire body as a crash mat. Owen Evans was remanded in custody, and Phil was still finding bramble thorns on random parts of her anatomy.

Callum had been questioned and let go. There was no way to prove he had been in Oli Cromwell's room thanks to Liane's editing skills. She had confessed the truth to Phil, and Phil had decided not to separate a baby from her father.

'But if you screw this up,' she told him. 'I will dob you straight in.'

'Some things never change,' said Callum.

Judith refused to tell Phil what had happened in the room, but the police appeared to be satisfied that she was nothing to do with it. Her son Kenneth seemed to be supporting her. Phil was glad to see the two of them together one day on the beach, Judith plunging into the cold water while Ken stood on the shore laughing at her insanity.

So that just left Marilla. Where was the closure with Marilla Hunter Davy?

Well, it turned out there wasn't any. Phil hadn't felt able to confess that she had a copy of Marilla's hard drive, which meant that she had a copy of Cora's recording of the Oli Cromwell assault. And perhaps that was just as well. Because, shortly after Owen Evans was charged with the murder of Oli Cromwell, Barry Brooker had appeared at Phil's desk.

'Follow the money,' he once told her after she failed to get the justice she wanted for Clive's death.

And Phil had tried to, she really had. Someone involved with Virtua Services had caused the death of her dad, but she couldn't even find out who owned the business. But eventually she had to admit it: she wasn't good enough.

'Yet,' she told Barry. 'Not good enough, yet.'

So, with only a small amount of crowing, Barry Brooker had agreed to help her on her quest for truth.

He started by helping her to trace as many of the companies associated with Virtua Services as he could, travelling on a virtual journey around the Cayman Islands and various offshore trusts to land on some surprising conclusions.

Charles Getgood was associated with all of them. It seemed as though his money had been injected at some point, making him a stakeholder in practically all of the biggest companies in East Sussex. Virtua Services, Telligence Industries, Inference Technology Solutions, the list of bland company names went on and on. But when Barry turned up by her desk, he had another bombshell for her.

'I think I've found out who Charles's business partner is,' he said. 'You might want to sit down.'

'I am sitting down,' she said.

'Max Hunter Davy,' said Grant, chucking a photo of a distinguished man in a three-piece suit on the table. 'Your friend's dad.'

Suddenly, owning a copy of Marilla's hard drive seemed less like a moral failure on her part and more like an inspired decision.

Back in her room, while Angela filled the kettle, Phil opened the hard drive disk and clicked on a file marked 'Virtua Press Releases'. She opened the first document. It was a basic release about the new Virtua Services CEO's plan to embark on a listening exercise within her company, 'From bottom to top.' There was a lot of talk about how she wanted to get to know the people on the ground. Phil had first-hand experience with Virtua Services and she wasn't convinced this new CEO would ever make it off the fourth floor. The previous CEO – Gloria Reynolds MBE – certainly hadn't been keen to meet her subjects.

The press releases didn't hold her attention long. After all, they were freely available on the Virtua website. Instead, it was time to look at Marilla's emails. This was a whole new level of betrayal. Phil opted to – once again – park any doubts she was having and just carry on. Time to go in, she thought.

The phone rang, saving her from herself for a few more minutes. Phil stared at the screen, wondering if it was somehow more than a coincidence, and then answered.

'Hello, you,' she said.

'Oh hello. Is that Aldhill-on-Sea's foremost investigative journalist?' said Marilla.

'Just call me Poodicca Thornbum,' said Phil.

'Well, Poodicca Thornbum, I'm ringing to see if you'd like to come to my parents' house next month.'

Phil could hear Marilla's voice getting shriller and tighter as she continued. She was nervous.

'They're having a big party for their fortieth wedding anniversary and, well, it's going to be full of posh nobs and other dreadful people and I just thought, maybe if you were there, it wouldn't be quite so vile.'

Phil laughed. 'Wow, you're really selling it to me.'

'I know, I know. It will be awful. But it will also be hilarious. Some of daddy's friends are genuinely funny, and the rest are funny by accident because they're so appalling. I think you'd enjoy it. There will be plenty of booze and food, my mother will happily bankrupt the family for good catering. Plus, you never know, you might meet some useful contacts for your career. Daddy knows a lot of people.'

'Well, in that case,' said Phil, smiling into the mouth-
piece, 'I'd love to come.'

ACKNOWLEDGMENTS

Emily-Jane, Kat, Kirsty, Lorna and Lucy get the first thank you, because I forgot to thank them last time. A shocking oversight. Knowing you has been one of the great privileges of my life.

My eternal gratitude once again to my first readers, Darika Ahrens, Caroline Battersby, and my editor Sophie Lazar. You got me over the finishing line, so thank you.

Chris Everest and Graham Bartlett: every bit of advice you gave made this a better story.

Thank you to my lovely newsletter subscribers. If you're not one of them, come and join us!

My husband, Alex Milway, thank you for the copyediting, cover design and, more importantly, the endless love. Thanks also to our girls, Cecily and Arrietty, who kept coming up to check how the final edits were going and to tell me they believed in me.

And thank you to Jo in Wales for inspiring me to create Phil McGinty in the first place.

JOIN ME FOR MORE

ALDHILL MYSTERIES

There's a lot of fun to be had over on www.kjlyttleton.com, so come join the Lyttle League and get all the news, stories and exclusive content.

Jen and Phil will return soon!

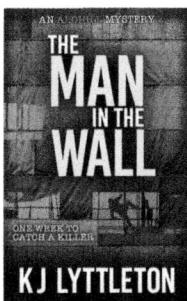

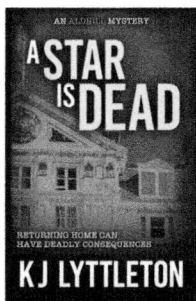

Printed in Dunstable, United Kingdom